MAY

EX LIBRIS

VINTAGE CLASSICS

THE CRANFORD CHRONICLES

Elizabeth Gaskell was born on 29 September 1810 in London. She was brought up in Knutsford, Cheshire by her aunt after her mother died when she was two years old. In 1832 she married William Gaskell, who was a Unitarian minister like her father. After their marriage they lived in Manchester with their children. Elizabeth Gaskell published her first novel, *Mary Barton*, in 1848 to great success. She went on to publish much of her work in Charles Dickens's magazines, *Household Words* and *All the Year Round*. Along with short stories and a biography of Charlotte Brontë, she published five more novels including *North and South* (1855) and *Wives and Daughters* (1866). *Wives and Daughters* is unfinished as Elizabeth Gaskell died suddenly of heart failure on 12 November 1865.

OTHER WORKS BY ELIZABETH GASKELL

Novels

Mary Barton

Ruth

Cranford

North and South

Sylvia's Lovers

Wives and Daughters

Collected Short Stories

The Moorland Cottage

Lizzie Leigh and Other Tales

Round the Sofa

Right at Last and Other Tales

A Dark Night's Work

Cousin Phillis and Other Tales

The Grey Woman and Other Tales

Non-Fiction

The Life of Charlotte Brontë

ELIZABETH GASKELL

The Cranford Chronicles

VINTAGE BOOKS
London

Published by Vintage 2007

14 16 18 20 19 17 15 13

Mr Harrison's Confessions first published in the *Ladies Companion and
Monthly Magazine* 1851
This revised edition published in *Lizzie Leigh and Other Tales* in 1855
Cranford first published in *Household Words* in 1851
This revised edition published in 1853
My Lady Ludlow first published in *Household Words* in 1858
This revised edition published in *Round the Sofa* in 1859

Vintage
Random House, 20 Vauxhall Bridge Road,
London SW1V 2SA

www.vintage-classics.info

Addresses for companies within The Random House Group Limited
can be found at: www.randomhouse.co.uk/offices.htm

The Random House Group Limited Reg. No. 954009

A CIP catalogue record for this book
is available from the British Library

ISBN 9780099518457

The Random House Group Limited supports The Forest
Stewardship Council (FSC), the leading international forest
certification organisation. All our titles that are printed on
Greenpeace approved FSC certified paper carry the FSC logo.
Our paper procurement policy can be found at:
www.rbooks.co.uk/environment

Typeset by SX Composing DTP, Rayleigh, Essex

Printed and bound in Great Britain by
CPI Bookmarque, Croydon, CR0 4TD

Contents

Mr Harrison's Confessions

Chapter I

The fire was burning gaily. My wife had just gone upstairs to put baby to bed. Charles sat opposite to me, looking very brown and handsome. It was pleasant enough that we should feel sure of spending some weeks under the same roof, a thing which we had never done since we were mere boys. I felt too lazy to talk, so I ate walnuts and looked into the fire. But Charles grew restless.

'Now that your wife is gone upstairs, Will, you must tell me what I've wanted to ask you ever since I saw her this morning. Tell me all about the wooing and winning. I want to have the receipt for getting such a spicy little wife of my own. Your letters only gave the barest details. So set to, man, and tell me every particular.'

'If I tell you all, it will be a long story.'

'Never fear. If I get tired, I can go to sleep, and dream that I am back again, a lonely bachelor, in Ceylon; and I can waken up when you have done, to know that I am under your roof. Dash away, man! "Once upon a time, a gallant young bachelor – " There's a beginning for you!'

'Well, then, "Once upon a time, a gallant young bachelor" was sorely puzzled where to settle, when he had completed his education as a surgeon – I must speak in the first person; I cannot go on as a gallant young bachelor. I had just finished walking the hospitals when you went to Ceylon, and, if you remember, I wanted to go abroad like you, and thought of offering myself as a ship-surgeon; but I found I should rather lose caste in my profession; so I hesitated, and while I was hesitating, I received a letter from my father's cousin, Mr Morgan – that old gentleman who used to write such long letters of good advice to my mother, and who tipped me a five-pound note when I agreed to be bound apprentice to Mr Howard, instead of going to sea. Well, it seems the old gentleman had all along thought of taking me as his partner, if I turned out pretty well; and as he heard a good account of me from an old friend of his, who was a surgeon at Guy's, he wrote to propose this arrangement: I was to have a third of the profits for five years; after that, half; and eventually I was to succeed to the whole. It was no bad offer for a penniless man like me, as Mr Morgan had a capital country practice, and, though I did not know him personally, I had formed a pretty good idea of him, as an honourable, kind-hearted fidgety, meddlesome old bachelor; and a very correct notion it was, as I found out in the very first half-hour of seeing him. I had had some idea that I was to live in his house, as he was a bachelor and a kind of family friend; and I think he was afraid that I should expect this arrangement, for when I walked up to his door, with the porter carrying my portmanteau, he met me on the steps, and while he held my hand and shook it, he said to the porter, "Jerry, if you'll wait a moment, Mr Harrison will be ready to go with you to his lodgings, at Jocelyn's, you know;" and then turning to me, he addressed his first words of welcome. I was a little inclined to think him inhospitable, but I got to understand him better afterwards. "Jocelyn's," said he, "is the best place I have been able to hit upon in a hurry, and there is a good deal of fever about, which made me desirous that you should come this month – a low kind of typhoid, in the oldest part of the town. I think you'll be comfortable there for a week or two. I have taken the liberty of desiring my housekeeper to send down one or two things which give the place a little more of a home aspect – an easy-chair, a beautiful case of preparations, and one or two little matters in the way of eatables; but if you'll take my advice, I've a plan in my head which we will talk about to-morrow morning. At present, I don't like to keep you standing out on the steps here, so I'll not detain you from your lodgings, where I rather think my housekeeper is gone to get tea ready for you."

'I thought I understood the old gentleman's anxiety for his own health, which he put upon care for mine, for he had on a kind of loose grey coat, and no hat on his head. But I wondered that he did not ask me indoors, instead of keeping me on the steps. I believe, after all, I made a mistake in supposing he was afraid of taking cold; he was only afraid of being seen in dishabille. And for his apparent inhospitality, I had not been long in Duncombe before I understood the comfort of having one's house considered as a castle into which no one might intrude, and saw good reason for the practice Mr Morgan had established of coming to his door to speak to every one. It was only the effect of habit that made him receive me so. Before long, I had the free run of his house.

'There was every sign of kind attention and forethought on the part of some one, whom I could not doubt to be Mr Morgan, in my lodgings. I was too lazy to do much that evening, and sat in the little bow-window which projected over Jocelyn's shop, looking up and down the street. Duncombe calls itself a town, but I should call it a village. Really, looking from Jocelyn's, it is a very picturesque place. The houses are anything but regular; they may be mean in their details; but altogether they look well; they have not that flat unrelieved front, which many towns of far more pretensions present. Here and there a bow-window – every now and then a gable, cutting up against the sky – occasionally a projecting upper story – throws good effect of light and shadow along the street; and they have a queer fashion of their own of colouring the whitewash of some of the houses with a sort of pink blotting-paper tinge, more like the stone of which Mayence is built than anything else. It may be very bad taste, but to my mind it gives a rich warmth to the colouring. Then, here and there a dwelling-house has a court in front, with a grass-plot on each side of the flagged walk, and a large tree or two – limes or horse-chestnuts – which send their great projecting upper branches over into the street, making round dry places of shelter on the pavement in the times of summer shows.

'While I was sitting in the bow-window, thinking of the contrast between this place and the lodgings in the heart of London, which I had left only twelve hours before – the window opens here, and, although in the centre of the town, admitting only scents from the mignonette boxes on the sill, instead of the dust and smoke of — Street – the only sound heard in this, the principal street, being the voices of mothers calling their playing children home to bed, and the eight o'clock bell of the old parish church bimbomming in remembrance of the curfew; while I was sitting thus idly, the door opened, and the little maid-servant, dropping a courtesy, said –

"'Please, sir, Mrs Munton's compliments, and she would be glad to know how you are after your journey."

'There! was not that hearty and kind? Would even the dearest chum I had at Guy's have thought of doing such a thing? while Mrs Munton, whose name I had never heard of before, was doubtless suffering anxiety till I could relieve her mind by sending back word that I was pretty well.

"'My compliments to Mrs Munton, and I am pretty well: much obliged to her." It was as well to say only "pretty well," for "very well" would have destroyed the interest Mrs Munton evidently felt in me. Good Mrs Munton! Kind Mrs Munton! Perhaps, also young – handsome – rich – widowed Mrs Munton! I rubbed my hands with delight and amusement, and, resuming my post of observation, began to wonder at which house Mrs Munton lived.

'Again the little tap, and the little maid-servant:

"'Please, sir, Miss Tomkinsons' compliments, and they would be glad to know how you feel yourself after your journey."

'I don't know why, but Miss Tomkinsons' name had not such a halo about it as Mrs Munton's. Still it was very pretty in Miss Tomkinsons to send and inquire. I only wished I did not feel so perfectly robust. I was almost ashamed that I could not send word I was quite exhausted by fatigue, and had fainted twice since my arrival. If I had but had a headache, at least! I heaved a deep breath: my chest was in perfect order; I had caught no cold; so I answered again –

'"Much obliged to the Miss Tomkinsons; I am not much fatigued; tolerably well; my compliments."

'Little Sally could hardly have got downstairs, before she returned, bright and breathless:

'"Mr and Mrs Bullock's compliments, sir, and they hope you are pretty well after your journey."

'Who would have expected such kindness from such an unpromising name? Mr and Mrs Bullock were less interesting, it is true, than their predecessors; but I graciously replied –

'"My compliments; a night's rest will perfectly recruit me."

'The same message was presently brought up from one or two more unknown kind hearts. I really wished I were not so ruddy-looking. I was afraid I should disappoint the tender-hearted town when they saw what a hale young fellow I was. And I was almost ashamed of confessing to a great appetite for supper when Sally came up to inquire what I would have. Beef-steaks were so tempting; but perhaps I ought rather to have water-gruel, and go to bed. The beef-steak carried the day, however. I need not have felt such a gentle elation of spirits, as this mark of the town's attention is paid to every one when they arrive after a journey. Many of the same people have sent to inquire after you – great, hulking, brown fellow as you are – only Sally spared you the infliction of devising interesting answers.

Chapter II

'The next morning Mr Morgan came before I had finished breakfast. He was the most dapper little man I ever met. I see the affection with which people cling to the style of dress that was in vogue when they were beaux and belles, and received the most admiration. They are unwilling to believe that their youth and beauty are gone, and think that the prevailing mode is unbecoming.

Mr Morgan will inveigh by the hour together against frock-coats, for instance, and whiskers. He keeps his chin close shaven, wears a black dress-coat, and dark-grey pantaloons; and in his morning round to his town patients, he invariably wears the brightest and blackest of Hessian boots, with dangling silk tassels on each side. When he goes home, about ten o'clock, to prepare for his ride to see his country patients, he puts on the most dandy top-boots I ever saw, which he gets from some wonderful boot-maker a hundred miles off. His appearance is what one calls "jemmy:" there is no other word that will do for it. He was evidently a little discomfited when he saw me in my breakfast costume, with the habits which I brought with me from the fellows at Guy's; my feet against the fire-place, my chair balanced on its hind legs (a habit of sitting which I afterwards discovered he particularly abhorred); slippers on my feet (which, also, he considered a most ungentlemanly piece of untidiness "out of the bedroom"); in short, from what I afterwards learned, every prejudice he had was outraged by my appearance on this first visit of his. I put my book down, and sprang up to receive him. He stood, hat and cane in hand.

'"I came to inquire if it would be convenient for you to accompany me on my morning's round, and to be introduced to a few of our friends." I quite detected the little tone of coldness, induced by his disappointment at my appearance, though he never imagined that it was in any way perceptible. "I will be ready directly, sir," said I; and bolted into my bedroom, only too happy to escape his scrutinising eye.

'When I returned, I was made aware, by sundry indescribable little coughs and hesitating noises, that my dress did not satisfy him. I stood ready, hat and gloves in hand; but still he did not offer to set off on our round. I grew very red and hot. At length he said –

'"Excuse me, my dear young friend, but may I ask if you have no other coat besides that – 'cut-away,' I believe you call them? We are rather sticklers for propriety, I believe, in Duncombe; and much depends on a first impression. Let it be professional, my dear sir. Black is the garb of our profession. Forgive my speaking so plainly, but I consider myself *in loco parentis*."

'He was so kind, so bland, and, in truth, so friendly, that I felt it would be most childish to take offence; but I had a little resentment in my heart at this way of being treated. However, I mumbled, "Oh, certainly, sir, if you wish it;" and returned once more to change my coat – my poor cut-away.

'"Those coats, sir, give a man rather too much of a sporting appearance, not quite befitting the learned professions; more as if you came down here to hunt than to be the Galen or Hippocrates of the neighbourhood." He smiled graciously, so I smothered a sigh; for, to tell you the truth, I had rather anticipated – and, in fact, had boasted at Guy's of the runs I hoped to have with the hounds; for Duncombe was in a famous hunting district. But all these ideas were quite dispersed when Mr Morgan led me to the inn-yard, where there was a horse-dealer on his way to a neighbouring fair, and "strongly advised me" – which in our relative circumstances was equivalent to an injunction – to purchase a little, useful, fast-trotting, brown cob, instead of a fine showy horse, "who would take any fence I put him to," as the horse-dealer assured me. Mr Morgan was evidently pleased when I bowed to his decision, and gave up all hopes of an occasional hunt.

'He opened out a great deal more after this purchase. He told me his plan of establishing me in a house of my own, which looked more respectable, not to say professional, than being in lodgings; and then he went on to say that he had lately lost a friend, a brother surgeon in a neighbouring town, who had left a widow with a small income, who would be very glad to live with me, and act as mistress to my establishment; thus lessening the expense.

'"She is a lady-like woman," said Mr Morgan, "to judge from the little I have seen of her; about forty-five or so; and may really be of some help to you in the little etiquettes of our profession; the slight delicate attentions which every man has to learn, if he wishes to get on in life. This is Mrs Munton's, sir," said he, stopping short at a very unromantic-looking green door, with a brass knocker.

'I had no time to say, "Who is Mrs Munton?" before we had heard Mrs Munton was at home, and were following the tidy elderly servant up the narrow carpeted stairs into the drawing-room. Mrs Munton was the widow of a former vicar, upwards of sixty, rather deaf; but like all the deaf people I have ever seen, very fond of talking; perhaps because she then knew the subject, which passed out of her grasp when another began to speak. She was ill of a chronic complaint, which often incapacitated her from going out; and the kind people of the town were in the habit of coming to see her and sit with her, and of bringing her the newest, freshest, tid-bits of news; so that her room was the centre of the gossip of Duncombe — not of scandal, mind; for I make a distinction between gossip and scandal. Now you can fancy the discrepancy between the ideal and the real Mrs Munton. Instead of any foolish notion of a beautiful blooming widow, tenderly anxious about the health of the stranger, I saw a homely, talkative, elderly person, with a keen observant eye, and marks of suffering on her face; plain in manner and dress, but still unmistakably a lady. She talked to Mr Morgan, but she looked at me; and I saw that nothing I did escaped her notice. Mr Morgan annoyed me by his anxiety to show me off; but he was kindly anxious to bring out every circumstance to my credit in Mrs Munton's hearing, knowing well that the town-crier had not more opportunities to publish all about me than she had.

'"What was that remark you repeated to me of Sir Astley Cooper's?" asked he. It had been the most trivial speech in the world that I had named as we walked along, and I felt ashamed of having to repeat it: but it answered Mr Morgan's purpose, and before night all the town had heard that I was a favourite pupil of Sir Astley's (I had never seen him but twice in my life); and Mr Morgan was afraid that as soon as he knew my full value I should be retained by Sir Astley to assist him in his duties as surgeon to the Royal Family. Every little circumstance was pressed into the conversation which could add to my importance.

'"As I once heard Sir Robert Peel remark to Mr Harrison, the father of our young friend here – The moons in August are remarkably full and bright." – If you remember, Charles, my father was always proud of having sold a pair of gloves to Sir Robert, when he was staying at the Grange, near Biddicombe, and I suppose good Mr Morgan had paid his only visit to my father at the time; but Mrs Munton evidently looked at me with double respect after this incidental remark, which I was amused to meet with, a few months afterwards, disguised in the statement that my father was an intimate friend of the Premier's, and had, in fact, been the adviser of most of the measures taken by him in public life. I sat by, half indignant and half amused. Mr Morgan looked so complacently pleased at the whole effect of the conversation, that I did not care to mar it by explanations; and, indeed, I had little idea at the time how small sayings were the seeds of great events in the town of Duncombe. When we left Mrs Munton's, he was in a blandly communicative mood.

'"You will find it a curious statistical fact, but five-sixths of our householders of a certain rank in Duncombe are women. We have widows and old maids in rich abundance. In fact, my dear sir, I believe that you and I are almost the only gentlemen in the place – Mr Bullock, of course, excepted. By gentlemen, I mean professional men. It behoves us to remember, sir, that so many of the female sex rely upon us for the kindness and protection which every man who is worthy of the name is always so happy to render."

'Miss Tomkinson, on whom we next called, did not strike me as remarkably requiring protection from any man. She was a tall, gaunt, masculine-looking woman, with an air of defiance about her, naturally; this, however, she softened and mitigated, as far as she was able, in favour of Mr Morgan. He, it seemed to me, stood a little in awe of the lady, who was very *brusque* and plain-spoken, and evidently piqued herself on her decision of character and sincerity of speech.

11

"'So, this is the Mr Harrison we have heard so much of from you, Mr Morgan? I must say from what I had heard, that I had expected something a little more – hum – hum! But he's young yet; he's young. We have been all anticipating an Apollo, Mr Harrison, from Mr Morgan's description, and an Æsculapius combined in one; or, perhaps I might confine myself to saying Apollo, as he, I believe, was the god of medicine!"

'How could Mr Morgan have described me without seeing me? I asked myself.

'Miss Tomkinson put on her spectacles, and adjusted them on her Roman nose. Suddenly relaxing from her severity of inspection, she said to Mr Morgan – "But you must see Caroline. I had nearly forgotten it; she is busy with the girls, but I will send for her. She had a bad headache yesterday, and looked very pale; it made me very uncomfortable."

'She rang the bell, and desired the servant to fetch Miss Caroline.

'Miss Caroline was the younger sister – younger by twenty years; and so considered as a child by Miss Tomkinson, who was fifty-five, at the very least. If she was considered as a child, she was also petted and caressed, and cared for as a child; for she had been left as a baby to the charge of her elder sister; and when the father died, and they had to set up a school, Miss Tomkinson took upon herself every difficult arrangement, and denied herself every pleasure, and made every sacrifice in order that "Carry" might not feel the change in their circumstances. My wife tells me she once knew the sisters purchase a piece of silk, enough, with management, to have made two gowns; but Carry wished for flounces, or some such fal-lals; and, without a word, Miss Tomkinson gave up her gown to have the whole made up as Carry wished, into one handsome one; and wore an old shabby affair herself as cheerfully as if it were Genoa velvet. That tells the sort of relationship between the sisters as well as anything, and I consider myself very good to name it thus early, for it was long before I found out Miss Tomkinson's real goodness; and we had a great quarrel first. Miss Caroline looked very delicate and die-away when she came in; she was as soft and sentimental as Miss Tomkinson was hard and masculine; and had a way of saying, "Oh, sister, how can you?" at Miss Tomkinson's startling speeches, which I never liked – especially as it was accompanied by a sort of protesting look at the company present, as if she wished to have it understood that she was shocked at her sister's *outré* manners. Now, that was not faithful between sisters. A remonstrance in private might have done good – though, for my own part, I have grown to like Miss Tomkinson's speeches and ways; but I don't like the way some people have of separating themselves from what may be unpopular in their relations. I know I spoke rather shortly to Miss Caroline when she asked me whether I could bear the change from "the great metropolis" to a little country village. In the first place, why could not she call it "London," or "town," and have done with it? And in the next place, why should she not love the place that was her home well enough to fancy that every one would like it when they came to know it as well as she did?

'I was conscious I was rather abrupt in my conversation with her, and I saw that Mr Morgan was watching me, though he pretended to be listening to Miss Tomkinson's whispered account of her sister's symptoms. But when we were once more in the street, he began, "My dear young friend" –

'I winced; for all the morning I had noticed that when he was going to give a little unpalatable advice, he always began with "My dear young friend." He had done so about the horse.

'"My dear young friend, there are one or two hints I should like to give you about your manner. The great Sir Everard Home used to say, 'a general practitioner should either have a very good manner, or a very bad one.' Now, in the latter case, he must be possessed of talents and acquirements sufficient to insure his being sought after, whatever his manner might be. But the rudeness will give notoriety to these qualifications. Abernethy is a case in point. I rather, myself, question the taste of bad manners. I, therefore, have studied to acquire an attentive, anxious politeness, which combines ease and grace with a tender regard and interest. I am not aware whether I have succeeded (few men do) in coming up to my ideal; but I recommend you to strive after this manner, peculiarly befitting our profession. Identify yourself with your patients, my dear sir. You have sympathy in your good heart, I am sure, to really feel pain when listening to their account of their sufferings, and it soothes them to see the expression of this feeling in your manner. It is, in fact, sir, manners that make the man in our profession. I don't set myself up as an example – far from it; but – This is Mr Hutton's, our vicar; one of the servants is indisposed, and I shall be glad of the opportunity of introducing you. We can resume our conversation at another time."

'I had not been aware that we had been holding a conversation, in which, I believe, the assistance of two persons is required. Why had not Mr Hutton sent to ask after my health the evening before, according to the custom of the place? I felt rather offended.

Chapter III

'The vicarage was on the north side of the street, at the end opening towards the hills. It was a long low house, receding behind its neighbours; a court was between the door and the street, with a flag-walk and an old stone cistern on the right-hand side of the door; Solomon's seal growing under the windows. Some one was watching from behind the window-curtain; for the door opened, as if by magic, as soon as we reached it; and we entered a low room, which served as hall, and was matted all over, with deep, old-fashioned window-seats, and Dutch tiles in the fire-place; altogether it was very cool and refreshing, after the hot sun in the white and red street.

'"Bessy is not so well, Mr Morgan," said the sweet little girl of eleven or so, who had opened the door. "Sophy wanted to send for you; but papa said he was sure you would come soon this morning, and we were to remember that there were other sick people wanting you."

'"Here's Mr Morgan, Sophy," said she, opening the door into an inner room, to which we descended a step, as I remember well; for I was nearly falling down it, I was so caught by the picture within. It was like a picture – at least, seen through the door-frame. A sort of mixture of crimson and sea-green in the room, and a sunny garden beyond; a very low casement window, open to the amber air; clusters of white roses peeping in, and Sophy sitting on a cushion on the ground, the light coming from above on her head, and a little sturdy round-eyed brother kneeling by her, to whom she was teaching the alphabet. It was a mighty relief to him when we came in, as I could see; and I am much mistaken if he was easily caught again to say his lesson, when he was once sent off to find papa. Sophy rose quietly, and of course we were just introduced, and that was all, before she took Mr Morgan upstairs to see her sick servant. I was left to myself in the room. It looked so like a home, that it at once made me know the full charm of the word. There were books and work about, and tokens of employment; there was a child's plaything on the floor; and against the sea-green walls there hung a likeness or two, done in water-colours; one, I was sure, was that of Sophy's mother. The chairs and sofa were covered with chintz, the same as the curtains – a little pretty red rose on a white ground. I don't know where the crimson came from, but I am sure there was crimson somewhere; perhaps in the carpet. There was a glass door besides the window, and you went up a step into the garden. This was, first, a grass plot, just under the windows, and beyond that, straight gravel walks, with box-borders and narrow flower-beds on each side, most brilliant and gay at the end of August, as it was then; and behind the flower-borders were fruit-trees trained over woodwork, so as to shut out the beds of kitchen-garden within.

'While I was looking round, a gentleman came in, who, I was sure, was the Vicar. It was rather awkward, for I had to account for my presence there.

'"I came with Mr Morgan; my name is Harrison," said I, bowing. I could see he was not much enlightened by this explanation, but we sat down and talked about the time of year, or some such matter, till Sophy and Mr Morgan came back. Then I saw Mr Morgan to advantage. With a man whom he respected, as he did the Vicar, he lost the prim artificial manner he had in general, and was calm and dignified; but not so dignified as the Vicar. I never saw any one like him. He was very quiet and reserved, almost absent at times; his personal appearance was not striking; but he was altogether a man you would talk to with your hat off whenever you met him. It was his character that produced this effect − character that he never thought about, but that appeared in every word, and look, and motion.

'"Sophy," said he, "Mr Morgan looks warm; could you not gather a few jargonelle pears off the south wall? I fancy there are some ripe there. Our jargonelle pears are remarkably early this year."

'Sophy went into the sunny garden, and I saw her take a rake and tilt at the pears, which were above her reach, apparently. The parlour had become chilly (I found out afterwards it had a flag floor, which accounts for its coldness), and I thought I should like to go into the warm sun. I said I would go and help the young lady; and without waiting for an answer, I went into the warm, scented garden, where the bees were rifling the flowers, and making a continual busy sound. I think Sophy had begun to despair of getting the fruit, and was glad of my assistance. I thought I was very senseless to have knocked them down so soon, when I found we were to go in as soon as they were gathered. I should have liked to have walked round the garden, but Sophy walked straight off with the pears, and I could do nothing but follow her. She took up her needlework while we ate them: they were very soon finished, and when the Vicar had ended his conversation with Mr Morgan about some poor people, we rose up to come away. I was thankful that Mr Morgan had said so little about me. I could not have endured that he should have introduced Sir Astley Cooper or Sir Robert Peel at the vicarage; not yet could I have brooked much mention of my "great opportunities for acquiring a thorough knowledge of my profession," which I had heard him describe to Miss Tomkinson, while her sister was talking to me. Luckily, however, he spared me all this at the Vicar's. When we left, it was time to mount our horses and go the country rounds, and I was glad of it.

Chapter IV

'By-and-by the inhabitants of Duncombe began to have parties in my honour. Mr Morgan told me it was on my account, or I don't think I should have found it out. But he was pleased at every fresh invitation, and rubbed his hands, and chuckled, as if it was a compliment to himself, as in truth it was.

'Meanwhile, the arrangement with Mrs Rose had been brought to a conclusion. She was to bring her furniture, and place it in a house, of which I was to pay the rent. She was to be the mistress, and, in return, she was not to pay anything for her board. Mr Morgan took the house, and delighted in advising and settling all my affairs. I was partly indolent, and partly amused, and was altogether passive. The house he took for me was near his own: it had two sitting-rooms downstairs, opening into each other by folding-doors, which were, however, kept shut in general. The back room was my consulting-room ("the library," he advised me to call it), and gave me a skull to put on the top of my bookcase, in which the medical books were all ranged on the conspicuous shelves; while Miss Austen, Dickens, and Thackeray were, by Mr

Morgan himself, skilfully placed in a careless way, upside down or with their backs turned to the wall. The front parlour was to be the dining-room, and the room above was furnished with Mrs Rose's drawing-room chairs and table, though I found she preferred sitting downstairs in the dining-room close to the window, where, between every stitch, she could look up and see what was going on in the street. I felt rather queer to be the master of this house, filled with another person's furniture, before I had even seen the lady whose property it was.

'Presently she arrived. Mr Morgan met her at the inn where the coach stopped, and accompanied her to my house. I could see them out of the dining-room window, the little gentleman stepping daintily along, flourishing his cane, and evidently talking away. She was a little taller than he was, and in deep widow's mourning; such veils and falls, and capes and cloaks, that she looked like a black crape haycock. When we were introduced, she put up her thick veil, and looked around and sighed.

'"Your appearance and circumstances, Mr Harrison, remind me forcibly of the time when I was married to my dear husband, now at rest. He was then, like you, commencing practice as a surgeon. For twenty years I sympathised with him, and assisted him by every means in my power, even to making up pills when the young man was out. May we live together in like harmony for an equal length of time! May the regard between us be equally sincere, although, instead of being conjugal, it is to be maternal and filial!"

'I am sure she had been concocting this speech in the coach, for she afterwards told me she was the only passenger. When she had ended, I felt as if I ought to have had a glass of wine in my hand, to drink, after the manner of toasts. And yet I doubt if I should have done it heartily, for I did not hope to live with her for twenty years; it had rather a dreary sound. However, I only bowed and kept my thoughts to myself. I asked Mr Morgan, while Mrs Rose was upstairs taking off her things, to stay to tea; to which he agreed, and kept rubbing his hands with satisfaction, saying –

'"Very fine woman, sir; very fine woman! And what a manner! How she will receive patients, who may wish to leave a message during your absence. Such a flow of words to be sure!"

'Mr Morgan could not stay long after tea, as there were one or two cases to be seen. I would willingly have gone, and had my hat on, indeed, for the purpose, when he said it would not be respectful, "not the thing," to leave Mrs Rose the first evening of her arrival.

'"Tender deference to the sex – to a widow in the first months of her loneliness – requires a little consideration, my dear sir. I will leave that case at Miss Tomkinson's for you; you will perhaps call early to-morrow morning. Miss Tomkinson is rather particular, and is apt to speak plainly if she does not think herself properly attended to."

'I had often noticed that he shuffled off the visits to Miss Tomkinson's on me, and I suspect he was a little afraid of the lady.

'It was rather a long evening with Mrs Rose. She had nothing to do, thinking it civil, I suppose, to stop in the parlour, and not go upstairs and unpack. I begged I might be no restraint upon her if she wished to do so; but (rather to my disappointment) she smiled in a measured, subdued way, and said it would be a pleasure to her to become better acquainted with me. She went upstairs once, and my heart misgave me when I saw her come down with a clean folded pockethandkerchief. Oh, my prophetic soul! – she was no sooner seated, than she began to give me an account of her late husband's illness, and symptoms, and death. It was a very common case, but she evidently seemed to think it had been peculiar. She had just a smattering of medical knowledge, and used the technical terms so very *mal à propos* that I could hardly keep from smiling; but I would not have done it for the world, she was evidently in such deep and sincere distress. At last she said –

'"I have the 'dognoses' of my dear husband's complaint in my desk, Mr Harrison, if you would like to draw up the case for the *Lancet*. I think he would have felt gratified, poor fellow, if he had been told such a compliment would be paid to his remains, and that his case should appear in those distinguished columns."

'It was rather awkward; for the case was of the very commonest, as I said before. However, I had not been even this short time in practice without having learnt a few of those noises which do not compromise one, and yet may bear a very significant construction if the listener chooses to exert a little imagination.

'Before the end of the evening, we were such friends that she brought me down the late Mr Rose's picture to look at. She told me she could not bear herself to gaze upon the beloved features; but that if I would look upon the miniature, she would avert her face. I offered to take it into my own hands, but she seemed wounded at the proposal, and said she never, never could trust such a treasure out of her own possession; so she turned her head very much over her left shoulder, while I examined the likeness held by her extended right arm.

'The late Mr Rose must have been rather a good-looking jolly man; and the artist had given him such a broad smile, and such a twinkle about the eyes, that it really was hard to help smiling back at him. However, I restrained myself.

'At first Mrs Rose objected to accepting any of the invitations which were sent her to accompany me to the tea-parties in the town. She was so good and simple, that I was sure she had no other reason than the one which she alleged – the short time that had elapsed since her husband's death; or else, now that I had had some experience of the entertainments which she declined so pertinaciously, I might have suspected that she was glad of the excuse. I used sometimes to wish that I was a widow. I came home tired from a hard day's riding, and if I had but felt sure that Mr Morgan would not come in, I should certainly have put on my slippers and my loose morning coat, and have indulged in a cigar in the garden. It seemed a cruel sacrifice to society to dress myself in tight boots, and a stiff coat, and go to a five-o'clock tea. But Mr Morgan read me such lectures upon the necessity of cultivating the of their young ladies – one of them belonged to a "county family," Mrs Bullock told me in a whisper; then came Mr and Mrs and Miss Bullock, and a tribe of little children, the offspring of the present wife. Miss Bullock was only a step-daughter. Mrs Munton had accepted the invitation to join our party, which was rather unexpected by the host and hostess, I imagine, from little remarks that I overheard; but they made her very welcome. Miss Horsman (a maiden lady who had been on a visit from home till last week) was another. And last, there were the Vicar and his children. These, with Mr Morgan and myself, made up the party. I was very much pleased to see something more of the Vicar's family. He had come in occasionally to the evening parties, it is true; and spoken kindly to us all; but it was not his habit to stay very long at them. And his daughter was, he said, too young to visit. She had had the charge of her little sisters and brother since her mother's death, which took up a good deal of her time, and she was glad of the evenings to pursue her own studies. But to-day the case was different; and Sophy and Helen, and Lizzie, and even little Walter, were all there, standing at Mrs Bullock's door; for we none of us could be patient enough to sit still in the parlour with Mrs Munton and the elder ones, quietly waiting for the two chaises and the spring-cart, which were to have been there by two o'clock, and now it was nearly a quarter past. "Shameful! the brightness of the day would be gone." The sympathetic shopkeepers, standing at their respective doors with their hands in their pockets, had, one and all, their heads turned in the direction from which the carriages (as Mrs Bullock called them) were to come. There was a rumble along the paved street; and the shopkeepers turned and smiled, and bowed their heads congratulatingly to us; all the mothers and all the little children of the place stood clustering round the door to see us set off. I had my horse waiting; and, meanwhile, I assisted people into their vehicles. One sees a good deal of management on such occasions. Mrs Munton was handed first into one of the chaises; then there was a little hanging back, for most of the young people wished to go in the cart – I don't know why. Miss Horsman, however, came forward, and as she was known to be the intimate friend of Mrs Munton, so far was satisfactory. But who was to be third – bodkin with two old ladies, who liked the windows shut? I saw Sophy speaking to Helen; and then she came forward and offered to be the third. The two old ladies looked pleased and glad (as every one did near Sophy); so that chaise-full was arranged. Just as it was going off, however, the servant from the vicarage came running with a note for her master. When he had read it, he went to the chaise-door, and I suppose told Sophy, what I afterwards heard him say to Mrs Bullock, that the clergyman of a neighbouring parish was ill, and unable to read the funeral service for one of his parishioners, who was to be buried that afternoon. The Vicar was, of course, obliged to go, and said he should not return home that night. It seemed a relief to some, I perceived, to be without the little restraint of his dignified presence. Mr Morgan came up just at the moment, having ridden hard all the morning to be in time to join our party; so we were resigned, on the whole, to the Vicar's absence. His own family regretted him the most, I noticed, and I liked them all the better for it. I believe that I came next in being sorry for his departure; but I respected and admired him, and felt always the better for having been in his company. Miss Tomkinson, Mrs Bullock, and the "county" young lady, were in the next chaise. I think the last would rather have been in the cart with the younger and merrier set, but I imagine that was considered *infra dig*. The remainder of the party were to ride and tie; and a most riotous laughing set they were. Mr Morgan and I were on horseback; at least I led my horse, with little Walter riding on him; his fat, sturdy legs standing stiff out on each side of my cob's broad back. He was a little darling, and chattered all the way, his sister Sophy being the heroine of all his stories. I found he owed this day's excursion entirely to her begging papa to let him come; nurse was strongly against it – "cross old nurse!" he called her once, and then said, "No, not cross; kind nurse; Sophy tells Walter not the hall, where it had been arranged that we were to dine. I saw Miss Carry take Miss Tomkinson aside, and whisper to her; and presently the elder sister came up to me, where I was busy, rather apart, making a seat of hay, which I had fetched from the farmer's loft for my little friend Walter, who, I had noticed, was rather hoarse, and for whom I was afraid of a seat on the grass, dry as it appeared to be.

'"Mr Harrison, Caroline tells me she has been feeling very faint, and she is afraid of a return of one of her attacks. She says she has more confidence in your medical powers than in Mr Morgan's. I should not be sincere if I did not say that I differ from her; but as it is so, may I beg you to keep an eye upon her? I tell her she had better not have come if she did not feel well; but, poor girl, she had set her heart upon this day's pleasure. I have offered to go home with her; but she says, if she can only feel sure you are at hand, she would rather stay."

'Of course I bowed, and promised all due attendance on Miss Caroline; and in the meantime, until she did require my services, I thought I might as well go and help the Vicar's daughter, who looked so fresh and pretty in her white muslin dress, here, there, and everywhere, now in the sunshine, now in the green shade, helping every one to be comfortable, and thinking of every one but herself.

'Presently, Mr Morgan came up.

'"Miss Caroline does not feel quite well. I have promised your services to her sister."

'"So have I, sir. But Miss Sophy cannot carry this heavy basket."

'I did not mean her to have heard this excuse; but she caught it up and said –

'"Oh, yes, I can! I can take the things out one by one. Go to poor Miss Caroline, pray, Mr Harrison."

'I went; but very unwillingly, I must say. When I had once seated myself by her, I think she must have felt better. It was, probably, only a nervous fear, which was relieved when she knew she had assistance near at hand; for she made a capital dinner. I thought she would never end her modest requests for "just a little more pigeon-pie, or a merry-thought of chicken." Such a hearty meal would, I hope, effectually revive her; and so it did; for she told me she thought she could manage to walk round the garden, and see the old peacock yews, if I would kindly give her my arm. It was very provoking; I had so set my heart upon being with the Vicar's children. I advised Miss Caroline strongly to lie down a little, and rest before tea, on the sofa in the farmer's kitchen; you cannot think how persuasively I begged her to take care of herself. At last she consented, thanking me for my tender interest; she should never forget my kind attention to her. She little knew what was in my mind at the time. However, she was safely consigned to the farmer's wife, and I was rushing out in search of a white gown and a waving figure, when I encountered Mrs Bullock at the door of the hall. She was a fine, fierce-looking woman. I thought she had appeared a little displeased at my (unwilling) attentions to Miss Caroline at dinner-time; but now, seeing me alone, she was all smiles.

'"Oh, Mr Harrison, all alone! How is that? What are the young ladies about to allow such churlishness? And, by the way, I have left a young lady who will be very glad of your assistance, I am sure – my daughter, Jemima (her step-daughter, she meant). Mr Bullock is so particular, and so tender a father, that he would be frightened to death at the idea of her going into the boat on the moat unless she was with some one who could swim. He is gone to discuss the new wheel-plough with the farmer (you know agriculture is his hobby, although law, horrid law, is his business). But the poor girl is pining on the bank, longing for my permission to join the others, which I dare not give unless you will kindly accompany her, and promise, if any accident happens, to preserve her safe."

'Oh, Sophy, why was no one anxious about you?

26

Chapter VI

'Miss Bullock was standing by the water-side, looking wistfully, as I thought, at the water party; the sound of whose merry laughter came pleasantly enough from the boat, which lay off (for, indeed, no one knew how to row, and she was of a clumsy flat-bottomed build) about a hundred yards, "weather-bound," as they shouted out, among the long stalks of the water-lilies.

'Miss Bullock did not look up till I came close to her; and then, when I told her my errand, she lifted up her great heavy, sad eyes, and looked at me for a moment. It struck me, at the time, that she expected to find some expression on my face which was not there, and that its absence was a relief to her. She was a very pale, unhappy-looking girl, but very quiet, and, if not agreeable in manner, at any rate not forward or offensive. I called to the party in the boat, and they came slowly enough through the large, cool, green lily leaves towards us. When they got near, we saw there was no room for us, and Miss Bullock said she would rather stay in the meadow and saunter about, if I would go into the boat; and I am certain from the look on her countenance that she spoke the truth; but Miss Horsman called out, in a sharp voice, while she smiled in a very disagreeable knowing way –

'"Oh, mamma will be displeased if you don't come in, Miss Bullock, after all her trouble in making such a nice arrangement."

'At this speech the poor girl hesitated, and at last, in an undecided way, as if she was not sure whether she was doing right, she took Sophy's place in the boat. Helen and Lizzie landed with their sister, so that there was plenty of room for Miss Tomkinson, Miss Horsman, and all the little Bullocks; and the three vicarage girls went off strolling along the meadow side, and playing with Walter, who was in a high state of excitement. The sun was getting low, but the declining light was beautiful upon the water; and, to add to the charm of the time, Sophy and her sisters, standing on the

27

green lawn, in front of the hall, struck up the little German canon, which I had never heard before –

'"Oh wie wohl ist mir am abend," &c.

At last we were summoned to tug the boat to the landing-steps on the lawn, tea and a blazing wood fire being ready for us in the hall. I was offering my arm to Miss Horsman, as she was a little lame, when she said again, in her peculiar disagreeable way, "Had you not better take Miss Bullock, Mr Harrison? It will be more satisfactory."

'I helped Miss Horsman up the steps, however, and then she repeated her advice; so, remembering that Miss Bullock was in fact the daughter of my entertainers, I went to her; but though she accepted my arm, I could perceive she was sorry that I had offered it.

'The hall was lighted by the glorious wood fire in the wide old grate; the daylight was dying away in the west; and the large windows admitted but little of what was left, through their small leaded frames, with coats of arms emblazoned upon them. The farmer's wife had set out a great long table, which was piled with good things; and a huge black kettle sang on the glowing fire, which sent a cheerful warmth through the room as it crackled and blazed. Mr Morgan (who I found had been taking a little round in the neighbourhood among his patients) was there, smiling and rubbing his hands as usual. Mr Bullock was holding a conversation with the farmer at the garden-door on the nature of different manures, in which it struck me that if Mr Bullock had the fine names and the theories on his side, the farmer had all the practical knowledge and the experience, and I know which I would have trusted. I think Mr Bullock rather liked to talk about Liebig in my hearing; it sounded well, and was knowing. Mrs Bullock was not particularly placid in her mood. In the first place, I wanted to sit by the Vicar's daughter, and Miss Caroline as decidedly wanted to sit on my other side, being afraid of her fainting fits, I imagine. But Mrs Bullock called me to a place near her daughter. Now I thought I had done enough civility to a girl who was evidently annoyed rather than pleased by my attentions, and I pretended to be busy stooping under the table for Miss Caroline's gloves, which were missing; but it was of no avail; Mrs Bullock's fine severe eyes were awaiting my reappearance, and she summoned me again.

'"I am keeping this place on my right hand for you, Mr Harrison. Jemima; sit still!"

'I went up to the post of honour and tried to busy myself with pouring out coffee to hide my chagrin; but after forgetting to empty the water put in ("to warm the cups," Mrs Bullock said), and omitting to add any sugar, the lady told me she would dispense with my services, and turn me over to my neighbour on the other side.

'"Talking to the younger lady was, no doubt, more Mr Harrison's vocation than assisting the elder one." I dare say it was only the manner that made the words seem offensive. Miss Horsman sat opposite me, smiling away. Miss Bullock did not speak, but seemed more depressed than ever. At length, Miss Horsman and Mrs Bullock got to a war of innuendoes, which were completely unintelligible to me; and I was very much displeased with my situation. While, at the bottom of the table, Mr Morgan and Mr Bullock were making the young ones laugh most heartily. Part of the joke was Mr Morgan insisting upon making tea at that end; and Sophy and Helen were busy contriving every possible mistake for him. I thought honour was a very good thing, but merriment a better. Here was I in the place of distinction, hearing nothing but cross words. At last the time came for us to go home. As the evening was damp, the seats in the chaises were the best and most to be desired. And now Sophy offered to go in the cart; only she seemed anxious, and so was I, that Walter should be secured from the effects of the white wreaths of fog rolling up from the valley; but the little violent affectionate fellow would not be separated from Sophy. She made a nest for him on her knee in one corner of the cart, and covered him with her own shawl; and I hoped that he would take no harm. Miss Tomkinson, Mr Bullock, and some of the young ones walked; but I seemed chained to the windows of the chaise, for Miss Caroline begged me not to leave her, as she was dreadfully afraid of robbers; and Mrs Bullock implored me to see that the man did not overturn them in the bad roads, as he had certainly had too much to drink.

'I became so irritable before I reached home, that I thought it was the most disagreeable day of pleasure I had ever had, and could hardly bear to answer Mrs Rose's never-ending questions. She told me, however, that from my account the day was so charming that she thought she should relax in the rigour of her seclusion, and mingle a little more in the society of which I gave so tempting a description. She really thought her dear Mr Rose would have wished it; and his will should be law to her after his death, as it had ever been during his life. In compliance, therefore, with his wishes, she would even do a little violence to her own feelings.

'She was very good and kind; not merely attentive to everything which she thought could conduce to my comfort, but willing to take any trouble in providing the broths and nourishing food which I often found it convenient to order, under the name of kitchen-physic, for my poorer patients; and I really did not see the use of her shutting herself up, in mere compliance with an etiquette, when she began to wish to mix in the little quiet society of Duncombe. Accordingly I urged her to begin to visit, and even when applied to as to what I imagined the late Mr Rose's wishes on that subject would have been, answered for that worthy gentleman, and assured his widow that I was convinced he would have regretted deeply her giving way to immoderate grief, and would have been rather grateful than otherwise at seeing her endeavour to divert her thoughts by a few quiet visits. She cheered up, and said, "as I really thought so, she would sacrifice her own inclinations, and accept the very next invitation that came."

Chapter VII

'I was roused from my sleep in the middle of the night by a messenger from the vicarage. Little Walter had got the croup, and Mr Morgan had been sent for into the country. I dressed myself hastily, and went through the quiet little street. There was a light burning upstairs at the vicarage. It was in the nursery. The servant, who opened the door the instant I knocked, was crying sadly, and could hardly answer my inquiries as I went upstairs, two steps at a time, to see my little favourite.

'The nursery was a great large room. At the farther end it was lighted by a common candle, which left the other end, where the door was, in shade, so I suppose the nurse did not see me come in, for she was speaking very crossly.

'"Miss Sophy!" said she, "I told you over and over again it was not fit for him to go, with the hoarseness that he had, and you would take him. It will break your papa's heart, I know; but it's none of my doing."

'Whatever Sophy felt, she did not speak in answer to this. She was on her knees by the warm bath, in which the little fellow was struggling to get his breath, with a look of terror on his face that I have often noticed in young children when smitten by a sudden and violent illness. It seems as if they recognised something infinite and invisible, at whose bidding the pain and the anguish come, from which no love can shield them. It is a very heart-rending look to observe, because it comes on the faces of those who are too young to receive comfort from the words of faith, or the promises of religion. Walter had his arms tight round Sophy's neck, as if she, hitherto his paradise-angel, could save him from the dread shadow of Death. Yes! of Death! I knelt down by him on the other side, and examined him. The very robustness of his little frame gave violence to the disease, which is always one of the most fearful by which children of his age can be attacked.

'"Don't tremble, Watty," said Sophy, in a soothing tone; "it's Mr Harrison, darling, who let you ride on his horse." I could detect the quivering in the voice, which she tried to make so calm and soft to quiet the little fellow's fears. We took him out of the bath, and I went for the leeches. While I was away, Mr Morgan came. He loved the vicarage children as if he were their uncle; but he stood still and aghast at the sight of Walter – so lately bright and strong – and now hurrying along to the awful change – to the silent mysterious land, where, tended and cared for as he had been on earth, he must go – alone. The little fellow! the darling!

'We applied the leeches to his throat. He resisted at first; but Sophy, God bless her! put the agony of her grief on one side, and thought only of him, and began to sing the little songs he loved. We were all still. The gardener had gone to fetch the Vicar; but he was twelve miles off, and we doubted if he would come in time. I don't know if they had any hope; but the first moment Mr Morgan's eyes met mine, I saw that he, like me, had none. The ticking of the house-clock sounded through the dark quiet house. Walter was sleeping now, with the black leeches yet hanging to his fair, white throat. Still Sophy went on singing little lullabies, which she had sung under far different and happier circumstances. I remember one verse, because it struck me at the time as strangely applicable.

> '"Sleep, baby, sleep!
> Thy rest shall angels keep;
> While on the grass the lamb shall feed,
> And never suffer want or need.
> Sleep, baby, sleep."

The tears were in Mr Morgan's eyes. I do not think either he or I could have spoken in our natural tones; but the brave girl went on clear though low. She stopped at last, and looked up.

'"He is better, is he not, Mr Morgan?"

'"No, my dear. He is – ahem" – he could not speak all at once. Then he said – "My dear! he will be better soon. Think of your mamma, my dear Miss Sophy. She will be very thankful to have one of her darlings safe with her, where she is."

'Still she did not cry. But she bent her head down on the little face, and kissed it long and tenderly.

'"I will go for Helen and Lizzie. They will be sorry not to see him again." She rose up and went for them. Poor girls, they came in, in their dressing-gowns, with eyes dilated with sudden emotion, pale with terror, stealing softly along, as if sound could disturb him. Sophy comforted them by gentle caresses. It was over soon.

'Mr Morgan was fairly crying like a child. But he thought it necessary to apologize to me, for what I honoured him for. "I am a little overdone by yesterday's work, sir. I have had one or two bad nights, and they rather upset me. When I was your age I was as strong and manly as any one, and would have scorned to shed tears."

'Sophy came up to where we stood.

'"Mr Morgan! I am so sorry for papa. How shall I tell him?" She was struggling against her own grief for her father's sake. Mr Morgan offered to await his coming home; and she seemed thankful for the proposal. I, new friend, almost stranger, might stay no longer. The street was as quiet as ever; not a shadow was changed; for it was not yet four o'clock. But during the night a soul had departed.

'From all I could see, and all I could learn, the Vicar and his daughter strove which should comfort the other the most. Each thought of the other's grief – each prayed for the other rather than for themselves. We saw them walking out, countrywards; and we heard of them in the cottages of the poor. But it was some time before I happened to meet either of them again. And then I felt, from something indescribable in their manner towards me, that I was one of the

'"Peculiar people, whom Death had made dear."

That one day at the old hall had done this. I was, perhaps, the last person who had given the little fellow any unusual pleasure. Poor Walter! I wish I could have done more to make his short life happy!

Chapter VIII

'There was a little lull, out of respect to the Vicar's grief, in the visiting. It gave time to Mrs Rose to soften down the anguish of her weeds.

'At Christmas, Miss Tomkinson sent out invitations for a party. Miss Caroline had once or twice apologized to me because such an event had not taken place before; but, as she said, "the avocations of their daily life prevented their having such little *réunions* except in the vacations." And, sure enough, as soon as the holidays began, came the civil little note:

'"The Misses Tomkinsons request the pleasure of Mrs Rose's and Mr Harrison's company at tea, on the evening of Monday, the 23rd inst. Tea at five o'clock."

'Mrs Rose's spirit roused, like a war-horse at the sound of the trumpet, at this. She was not of a repining disposition, but I do think she believed the party-giving population of Duncombe had given up inviting her, as soon as she had determined to relent, and accept the invitations, in compliance with the late Mr Rose's wishes.

'Such snippings of white love-ribbon as I found everywhere, making the carpet untidy! One day, too, unluckily, a small box was brought to me by mistake. I did not look at the direction, for I never doubted it was some hyoscyamus which I was expecting from London; so I tore it open, and saw inside a piece of paper, with "No more grey hair," in large letters, upon it. I folded it up in a hurry, and sealed it afresh, and gave it to Mrs Rose; but I could not refrain from asking her, soon after, if she could recommend me anything to keep my hair from turning grey, adding that I thought prevention was better than cure. I think she made out the impression of my seal on the paper after that; for I learned that she had been crying, and that she talked about there being no sympathy left in the world for her since Mr Rose's death; and that she counted the days until she could rejoin him in the better world. I think she counted the days to Miss Tomkinson's party, too; she talked so much about it.

'The covers were taken off Miss Tomkinson's chairs, and curtains, and sofas; and a great jar full of artificial flowers was placed in the centre of the table, which, as Miss Caroline told me, was all her doing, as she doated on the beautiful and artistic in life. Miss Tomkinson stood, erect as a grenadier, close to the door, receiving her friends, and heartily shaking them by the hand as they entered: she said she was truly glad to see them. And so she really was.

'We had just finished tea, and Miss Caroline had brought out a little pack of conversation cards – sheaves of slips of cardboard, with intellectual or sentimental questions on one set; and equally intellectual and sentimental answers on the other; and as the answers were fit to any and all the questions, you may think they were a characterless and "wersh" set of things. I had just been asked by Miss Caroline –

'"*Can you tell what those dearest to you think of you at this present time?*" and had answered –

'"*How can you expect me to reveal such a secret to the present company!*" when the servant announced that a gentleman, a friend of mine, wished to speak to me downstairs.

'"Oh, show him up, Martha; show him up!" said Miss Tomkinson, in her hospitality.

'"Any friend of our friend is welcome," said Miss Caroline, in an insinuating tone.

'I jumped up, however, thinking it might be some one on business; but I was so penned in by the spider-legged tables, stuck out on every side, that I could not make the haste I wished; and before I could prevent it, Martha had shown up Jack

Marshland, who was on his road home for a day or two at Christmas.

'He came up in a hearty way, bowing to Miss Tomkinson, and explaining that he had found himself in my neighbourhood, and had come over to pass a night with me, and that my servant had directed him where I was.

'His voice, loud at all times, sounded like Stentor's, in that little room, where we all spoke in a kind of purring way. He had no swell in his tones; they were *forte* from the beginning. At first it seemed like the days of my youth come back again, to hear full manly speaking; I felt proud of my friend, as he thanked Miss Tomkinson for her kindness in asking him to stay the evening. By-and-by he came up to me, and I dare say he thought he had lowered his voice, for he looked as if speaking confidentially, while in fact the whole room might have heard him.

'"Frank, my boy, when shall we have dinner at this good old lady's? I'm deuced hungry."

'"Dinner! Why, we had had tea an hour ago." While he yet spoke, Martha came in with a little tray, on which was a single cup of coffee and three slices of wafer bread-and-butter. His dismay, and his evident submission to the decrees of Fate, tickled me so much, that I thought he should have a further taste of the life I led from month's end to month's end, and I gave up my plan of taking him home at once, and enjoyed the anticipation of the hearty laugh we should have together at the end of the evening. I was famously punished for my determination.

'"Shall we continue our game?" asked Miss Caroline, who had never relinquished her sheaf of questions.

'We went on questioning and answering, with little gain of information to either party.

'"No such thing as heavy betting in this game, eh Frank?" asked Jack, who had been watching us. "You don't lose ten pounds at a sitting, I guess, as you used to do at Short's. Playing for love, I suppose you call it?"

'Miss Caroline simpered, and looked down. Jack was not thinking of her. He was thinking of the days we had had at the "Mermaid." Suddenly he said, "Where were you this day last year, Frank?"

'"I don't remember!" said I.

'"Then I'll tell you. It's the 23rd – the day you were taken up for knocking down the fellow in Long Acre, and that I had to bail you out ready for Christmas-day. You are in more agreeable quarters to-night."

'He did not intend this reminiscence to be heard, but was not in the least put out when Miss Tomkinson, with a face of dire surprise, asked –

'"Mr Harrison taken up, sir?"

'"Oh, yes, ma'am; and you see it was so common an affair with him to be locked up that he can't remember the dates of his different imprisonments."

'He laughed heartily; and so should I, but that I saw the impression it made. The thing was, in fact, simple enough, and capable of easy explanation. I had been made angry by seeing a great hulking fellow, out of mere wantonness, break the crutch from under a cripple; and I struck the man more violently than I intended, and down he went, yelling out for the police, and I had to go before the magistrate to be released. I disdained giving this explanation at the time. It was no business of theirs what I had been doing over a year ago; but still Jack might have held his tongue. However, that unruly member of his was set a-going, and he told me afterwards he was resolved to let the old ladies into a little of life; and accordingly he remembered every practical joke we had ever had, and talked and laughed, and roared again. I tried to converse with Miss Caroline – Mrs Munton – any one; but Jack was the hero of the evening, and every one was listening to him.

'"Then he has never sent any hoaxing letters since he came here, has he? Good boy! He has turned over a new leaf. He was the deepest dog at that I ever met with. Such anonymous letters as he used to send! Do you remember that to Mrs Walbrook, eh, Frank? That was too bad!" (the wretch was laughing all the time). "No; I won't tell about it – don't be afraid. Such a shameful hoax!" (laughing again).

'"Pray do tell," I called out; for he made it seem far worse than it was.

'"Oh no, no; you've established a better character – I would not for the world nip your budding efforts. We'll bury the past in oblivion."

'I tried to tell my neighbours the story to which he alluded; but they were attracted by the merriment of Jack's manner, and did not care to hear the plain matter of fact.

'Then came a pause; Jack was talking almost quietly to Miss Horsman. Suddenly he called across the room – "How many times have you been out with the hounds? The hedges were blind very late this year, but you must have had some good mild days since."

'"I have never been out," said I, shortly.

'"Never! – whew – ! Why, I thought that was the great attraction to Duncombe."

'Now was not he provoking? He would condole with me, and fix the subject in the minds of every one present.

'The supper trays were brought in, and there was a shuffling of situations. He and I were close together again.

'"I say, Frank, what will you lay me that I don't clear that tray before people are ready for their second helping? I'm as hungry as a hound."

'"You shall have a round of beef and a raw leg of mutton when you get home. Only do behave yourself here."

'"Well, for your sake; but keep me away from those trays, or I'll not answer for myself. 'Hould me, or I'll fight,' as the Irishman said. I'll go and talk to that little old lady in blue, and sit with my back to those ghosts of eatables."

'He sat down by Miss Caroline, who would not have liked his description of her; and began an earnest, tolerably quiet conversation. I tried to be as agreeable as I could, to do away with the impression he had given of me; but I found that every one drew up a little stiffly at my approach, and did not encourage me to make any remarks.

'In the middle of my attempts, I heard Miss Caroline beg Jack to take a glass of wine, and I saw him help himself to what appeared to be port; but in an instant he set it down from his lips, exclaiming, "Vinegar, by Jove!" He made the most horribly wry face; and Miss Tomkinson came up in a severe hurry to investigate the affair. It turned out it was some black-currant wine, on which she particularly piqued herself; I drank two glasses of it to ingratiate myself with her, and can testify to its sourness. I don't think she noticed my exertions, she was so much engrossed in listening to Jack's excuses for his *mal-à-propos* observation. He told her, with the gravest face, that he had been a teetotaller so long that he had but a confused recollection of the distinction between wine and vinegar, particularly eschewing the latter, because it had been twice fermented; and that he had imagined Miss Caroline had asked him to take toast-and-water, or he should never have touched the decanter.

Chapter IX

'As we were walking home, Jack said, "Lord, Frank! I've had such fun with the little lady in blue. I told her you wrote to me every Saturday, telling me the events of the week. She took all in." He stopped to laugh; for he bubbled and chuckled so that he could not laugh and walk. "And I told her you were deeply in love" (another laugh); "and that I could not get you to tell me the name of the lady, but that she had light brown hair – in short, I drew from life, and gave her an exact description of herself; and that I was most anxious to see her, and implore her to be merciful to you, for that you were a most timid, faint-hearted fellow with women." He laughed till I thought he would have fallen down. "I begged her, if she could guess who it was from my description – I'll answer for it she did – I took care of that; for I said you described a mole on the left cheek, in the most poetical way, saying Venus had pinched it out of envy at seeing any one more lovely – oh, hold me up, or I shall fall – laughing and hunger make me so weak; – well, I say, I begged her, if she knew who your fair one could be, to implore her to save you. I said I knew one of your lungs had gone after a former unfortunate love-affair, and that I could not answer for the other if the lady here were cruel. She spoke of a respirator; but I told her that might do very well for the odd lung; but would it minister to a heart diseased? I really did talk fine. I have found out the secret of eloquence – it's believing what you've got to say; and I worked myself well up with fancying you married to the little lady in blue."

'I got to laughing at last, angry as I had been; his impudence was irresistible. Mrs Rose had come home in the sedan, and gone to bed; and he and I sat up over the round of beef and brandy-and-water till two o'clock in the morning.

'He told me I had got quite into the professional way of mousing about a room, and mewing and purring according as my patients were ill or well. He mimicked me, and made me laugh at myself. He left early the next morning.

'Mr Morgan came at his usual hour; he and Marshland would never have agreed, and I should have been uncomfortable to see two friends of mine disliking and despising each other.

'Mr Morgan was ruffled; but with his deferential manner to women, he smoothed himself down before Mrs Rose – regretted that he had not been able to come to Miss Tomkinson's the evening before, and consequently had not seen her in the society she was so well calculated to adorn. But when we were by ourselves, he said –

'"I was sent for to Mrs Munton's this morning – the old spasms. May I ask what is this story she tells me about – about prison, in fact? I trust, sir, she has made some little mistake, and that you never were − ; that it is an unfounded report." He could not get it out − "that you were in Newgate for three months!" I burst out laughing; the story had grown like a mushroom indeed. Mr Morgan looked grave. I told him the truth. Still he looked grave. "I've no doubt, sir, that you acted rightly; but it has an awkward sound. I imagined from your hilarity just now that there was no foundation whatever for the story. Unfortunately, there is."

"'I was only a night at the police-station. I would go there again for the same cause, sir."

"'Very fine spirit, sir − quite like Don Quixote; but don't you see you might as well have been to the hulks at once?"

"'No, sir; I don't."

"'Take my word, before long, the story will have grown to that. However, we won't anticipate evil. *Mens conscia recti*, you remember, is the great thing. The part I regret is, that it may require some short time to overcome a little prejudice which the story may excite against you. However, we won't dwell on it. *Mens conscia recti!* Don't think about it, sir."

'It was clear he was thinking a good deal about it.

Chapter X

'Two or three days before this time, I had had an invitation from the Bullocks to dine with them on Christmas-day. Mrs Rose was going to spend the week with friends in the town where she formerly lived; and I had been pleased at the notion of being received into a family, and of being a little with Mr Bullock, who struck me as a bluff good-hearted fellow.

'But this Tuesday before Christmas-day, there came an invitation from the Vicar to dine there; there were to be only their own family and Mr Morgan. "Only their own family." It was

41

getting to be all the world to me. I was in a passion with myself for having been so ready to accept Mr Bullock's invitation – coarse and ungentlemanly as he was; with his wife's airs of pretension and Miss Bullock's stupidity. I turned it over in my mind. No! I could not have a bad headache, which should prevent me going to the place I did not care for, and yet leave me at liberty to go where I wished. All I could do was to join the vicarage girls after church, and walk by their side in a long country ramble. They were quiet; not sad, exactly; but it was evident that the thought of Walter was in their minds on this day. We went through a copse where there were a good number of evergreens planted as covers for game. The snow was on the ground; but the sky was clear and bright, and the sun glittered on the smooth holly-leaves. Lizzie asked me to gather her some of the very bright red berries, and she was beginning a sentence with –

'"Do you remember – " when Ellen said "*Hush*," and looked towards Sophy, who was walking a little apart, and crying softly to herself. There was evidently some connection between Walter and the holly-berries, for Lizzie threw them away at once when she saw Sophy's tears. Soon we came to a stile which led to an open breezy common, half-covered with gorse. I helped the little girls over it, and set them to run down the slope; but I took Sophy's arm in mine, and though I could not speak, I think she knew how I was feeling for her. I could hardly bear to bid her good-by at the vicarage-gate; it seemed as if I ought to go in and spend the day with her.

Chapter XI

'I vented my ill-humour in being late for the Bullocks' dinner. There were one or two clerks, towards whom Mr Bullock was patronising and pressing. Mrs Bullock was decked out in extraordinary finery. Miss Bullock looked plainer than ever; but she had on some old gown or other, I think, for I heard Mrs Bullock tell her she was always making a figure of herself. I began to-day to suspect that the mother would not be sorry if I took a fancy to the step-daughter. I was again placed near her at dinner, and when the little ones came in to dessert, I was made to notice how fond of children she was, and indeed when one of them nestled to her, her face did brighten; but the moment she caught this loud-whispered remark, the gloom came back again, with something even of anger in her look; and she was quite sullen and obstinate when urged to sing in the drawing-room. Mrs Bullock turned to me –

'"Some young ladies won't sing unless they are asked by gentlemen." She spoke very crossly. "If you ask Jemima, she will probably sing. To oblige me, it is evident she will not."

'I thought the singing, when we got it, would probably be a great bore; however I did as I was bid, and went with my request to the young lady, who was sitting a little apart. She looked up at me with eyes full of tears, and said, in a decided tone (which, if I had not seen her eyes, I should have said was as cross as her mamma's), "No, sir, I will not." She got up, and left the room. I expected to hear Mrs Bullock abuse her for her obstinacy. Instead of that, she began to tell me of the money that had been spent on her education; of what each separate accomplishment had cost. "She was timid," she said, "but very musical. Wherever her future home might be, there would be no want of music." She went on praising her till I hated her. If they thought I was going to marry that great lubberly girl, they were mistaken. Mr Bullock and the clerks came up. He brought out Liebig, and called to me.

'"I can understand a good deal of this agricultural chemistry," said he, "and have put it in practice – without much success, hitherto, I confess. But these unconnected letters puzzle me a little. I suppose they have some meaning, or else I should say it was mere book-making to put them in."

'"I think they give the page a very ragged appearance," said Mrs Bullock, who had joined us. "I inherit a little of my late father's taste for books, and must say I like to see a good type, a broad margin, and an elegant binding. My father despised variety; how he would have held up his hands aghast at the cheap literature of these times! He did not require many books, but he would have twenty editions of those that he had; and he paid more for binding than he did for the books themselves. But elegance was everything with him. He would not have admitted your Liebig, Mr Bullock; neither the nature of the subject, nor the common type, nor the common way in which your book is got up, would have suited him."

'"Go and make tea, my dear, and leave Mr Harrison and me to talk over a few of these manures."

'We settled to it; I explained the meaning of the symbols, and the doctrine of chemical equivalents. At last he said, "Doctor! you're giving me too strong a dose of it at one time. Let's have a small quantity taken 'hodie;' that's professional, as Mr Morgan would call it. Come in and call when you have leisure, and give me a lesson in my alphabet. Of all you've been telling me I can only remember that C means carbon and O oxygen; and I see one must know the meaning of all these confounded letters before one can do much good with Liebig."

'"We dine at three," said Mrs Bullock. "There will always be a knife and fork for Mr Harrison. Bullock! don't confine your invitation to the evening!"

'"Why, you see, I've a nap always after dinner, so I could not be learning chemistry then."

'"Don't be so selfish, Mr B. Think of the pleasure Jemima and I shall have in Mr Harrison's society."

'I put a stop to the discussion by saying I would come in in the evenings occasionally, and give Mr Bullock a lesson, but that my professional duties occupied me invariably until that time.

'I liked Mr Bullock. He was simple, and shrewd; and to be with a man was a relief, after all the feminine society I went through every day.

Chapter XII

'The next morning I met Miss Horsman.

'"So you dined at Mr Bullock's yesterday, Mr Harrison? Quite a family party, I hear. They are quite charmed with you, and your knowledge of chemistry. Mr Bullock told me so, in Hodgson's shop, just now. Miss Bullock is a nice girl, eh, Mr Harrison?" She looked sharply at me. Of course, whatever I thought, I could do nothing but assent. "A nice little fortune, too – three thousand pounds, Consols, from her own mother."

'What did I care? She might have three millions for me. I had begun to think a good deal about money, though, but not in connection with her. I had been doing up our books ready to send out our Christmas bills, and had been wondering how far the Vicar would consider three hundred a year, with a prospect of increase, would justify me in thinking of Sophy. Think of her I could not help; and the more I thought of how good, and sweet, and pretty she was, the more I felt that she ought to have far more than I could offer. Besides, my father was a shopkeeper, and I saw the Vicar had a sort of respect for family. I determined to try and be very attentive to my profession. I was as civil as could be to every one; and wore the nap off the brim of my hat by taking it off so often.

'I had my eyes open to every glimpse of Sophy. I am over-stocked with gloves now that I bought at that time, by way of making errands into the shops where I saw her black gown. I bought pounds upon pounds of arrowroot, till I was tired of the eternal arrowroot-puddings Mrs Rose gave me. I asked her if she could not make bread of it, but she seemed to think that would be expensive; so I took to soap as a safe purchase. I believe soap improves by keeping.

Chapter XIII

'The more I knew of Mrs Rose, the better I liked her. She was sweet, and kind, and motherly, and we never had any rubs. I hurt her once or twice, I think, by cutting her short in her long stories about Mr Rose. But I found out that when she had plenty to do she did not think of him quite so much; so I expressed a wish for Corazza shirts, and in the puzzle of devising how they were to be cut out, she forgot Mr Rose for some time. I was still more pleased by her way about some legacy her elder brother left her. I don't know the amount, but it was something handsome, and she might have set up housekeeping for herself: but, instead, she told Mr Morgan (who repeated it to me), that she should continue with me, as she had quite an elder sister's interest in me.

'The "county young lady," Miss Tyrrell, returned to Miss Tomkinson's after the holidays. She had an enlargement of the tonsils, which required to be frequently touched with caustic, so I often called to see her. Miss Caroline always received me, and kept me talking in her washed-out style, after I had seen my patient. One day she told me she thought she had a weakness about the heart, and would be glad if I would bring my stethoscope the next time, which I accordingly did; and while I was on my knees listening to the pulsations, one of the young ladies came in. She said:

'"Oh dear! I never! I beg your pardon, ma'am," and scuttled out. There was not much the matter with Miss Caroline's heart; a little feeble in action or so, a mere matter of weakness and general languor. When I went down I saw two or three of the girls peeping out of the half-closed schoolroom door, but they shut it immediately, and I heard them laughing. The next time I called, Miss Tomkinson was sitting in state to receive me.

'"Miss Tyrrell's throat does not seem to make much progress. Do you understand the case, Mr Harrison, or should we have further advice? I think Mr Morgan would probably know more about it."

'I assured her it was the simplest thing in the world; that it always implied a little torpor in the constitution, and that we preferred working through the system, which of course was a slow process, and that the medicine the young lady was taking (iodide of iron) was sure to be successful, although the progress would not be rapid. She bent her head, and said, "It might be so; but she confessed she had more confidence in medicines which had some effect."

'She seemed to expect me to tell her something; but I had nothing to say, and accordingly I bade good-by. Somehow, Miss Tomkinson always managed to make me feel very small, by a succession of snubbings; and whenever I left her I had always to comfort myself under her contradictions by saying to myself, "Her saying it is so, does not make it so." Or I invented good retorts which I might have made to her brusque speeches if I had but thought of them at the right time. But it was provoking that I had not had the presence of mind to recollect them just when they were wanted.

Chapter XIV

'On the whole, things went on smoothly. Mr Holden's legacy came in just about this time; and I felt quite rich. Five hundred pounds would furnish the house, I thought, when Mrs Rose left and Sophy came. I was delighted, too, to imagine that Sophy perceived the difference of my manner to her from what it was to any one else, and that she was embarrassed and shy in consequence, but not displeased with me for it. All was so flourishing that I went about on wings instead of feet. We were very busy, without having anxious cares. My legacy was paid into Mr Bullock's hands, who united a little banking business to his profession of law. In return for his advice about investments (which I never meant to take, having a more charming, if less profitable, mode in my head), I went pretty frequently to teach him his agricultural chemistry. I was so happy in Sophy's blushes that I was universally benevolent, and desirous of giving pleasure to every one. I went, at Mrs Bullock's general invitation, to dinner there one day unexpectedly; but there was such a fuss of ill-concealed preparation consequent upon my coming, that I never went again. Her little boy came in, with an audibly given message from the cook, to ask –

'"If this was the gentleman as she was to send in the best dinner-service and dessert for?"

'I looked deaf, but determined never to go again.

'Miss Bullock and I, meanwhile, became rather friendly. We found out that we mutually disliked each other; and were contented with the discovery. If people are worth anything, this sort of non-liking is a very good beginning of friendship. Every good quality is revealed naturally and slowly, and is a pleasant surprise. I found out that Miss Bullock was sensible, and even sweet-tempered, when not irritated by her step-mother's endeavours to show her off. But she would sulk for hours after Mrs Bullock's offensive praise of her good points. And I never saw such a black passion as she went into when she suddenly came into the room when Mrs Bullock was telling me of all the offers she had had.

'My legacy made me feel up to extravagance. I scoured the country for a glorious nosegay of camellias, which I sent to Sophy on Valentine's-day. I durst not add a line, but I wished the flowers could speak, and tell her how I loved her.

'I called on Miss Tyrrell that day. Miss Caroline was more simpering and affected than ever; and full of allusions to the day.

' "Do you affix much sincerity of meaning to the little gallantries of this day, Mr Harrison?" asked she, in a languishing tone. I thought of my camellias, and how my heart had gone with them into Sophy's keeping; and I told her I thought one might often take advantage of such a time to hint at feelings one dared not fully express.

'I remembered afterwards the forced display she made, after Miss Tyrrell left the room, of a valentine. But I took no notice at the time; my head was full of Sophy.

'It was on that very day that John Brouncker, the gardener to all of us who had small gardens to keep in order, fell down and injured his wrist severely (I don't give you the details of the case, because they would not interest you, being too technical; if you've any curiosity, you will find them in the *Lancet* of August in that year). We all liked John, and this accident was felt like a town's misfortune. The gardens, too, just wanted doing up. Both Mr Morgan and I went directly to him. It was a very awkward case, and his wife and children were crying sadly. He himself was in great distress at being thrown out of work. He begged us to do something that would cure him speedily, as he could not afford to be laid up, with six children depending on him for bread. We did not say much before him, but we both thought the arm would have to come off, and it was his right arm. We talked it over when we came out of the cottage. Mr Morgan had no doubt of the necessity. I went back at dinner-time to see the poor fellow. He was feverish and anxious. He had caught up some expression of Mr Morgan's in the morning, and had guessed the measure we had in contemplation. He bade his wife leave the room, and spoke to me by myself.

' "If you please, sir, I'd rather be done for at once than have my arm taken off, and be a burden to my family. I'm not afraid of dying, but I could not stand being a cripple for life, eating bread, and not able to earn it."

'The tears were in his eyes with earnestness. I had all along been more doubtful about the necessity of the amputation than Mr Morgan. I knew the improved treatment in such cases. In his days there was much more of the rough and ready in surgical practice; so I gave the poor fellow some hope.

'In the afternoon I met Mr Bullock.

'"So you're to try your hand at an amputation to-morrow, I hear. Poor John Brouncker! I used to tell him he was not careful enough about his ladders. Mr Morgan is quite excited about it. He asked me to be present, and see how well a man from Guy's could operate; he says he is sure you'll do it beautifully. Pah! no such sights for me, thank you."

'Ruddy Mr Bullock went a shade or two paler at the thought.

'"Curious! how professionally a man views these things. Here's Mr Morgan, who has been all along as proud of you as if you were his own son, absolutely rubbing his hands at the idea of this crowning glory, this feather in your cap! He told me just now he knew he had always been too nervous to be a good operator; and had therefore preferred sending for White from Chesterton. But now any one might have a serious accident who liked, for you would be always at hand."

'I told Mr Bullock, I really thought we might avoid the amputation; but his mind was preoccupied with the idea of it, and he did not care to listen to me. The whole town was full of it. That is a charm in a little town, everybody is so sympathetically full of the same events. Even Miss Horsman stopped me to ask after John Brouncker with interest; but she threw cold water upon my intention of saving the arm.

'"As for the wife and family, we'll take care of them. Think what a fine opportunity you have of showing off, Mr Harrison!"

'That was just like her. Always ready with her suggestions of ill-natured or interested motives.

'Mr Morgan heard my proposal of a mode of treatment by which I thought it possible that the arm might be saved.

'"I differ from you, Mr Harrison," said he. "I regret it, but I differ *in toto* from you. Your kind heart deceives you in this instance. There is no doubt that amputation must take place – not later than to-morrow morning, I should say. I have made myself at liberty to attend upon you, sir; I shall be happy to officiate as your assistant. Time was when I should have been proud to be principal, but a little trembling in my arm incapacitates me."

'I urged my reasons upon him again; but he was obstinate. He had, in fact, boasted so much of my acquirements as an operator, that he was unwilling I should lose this opportunity of displaying my skill. He could not see that there would be greater skill evinced in saving the arm; nor did I think of this at the time. I grew angry at his old-fashioned narrow-mindedness, as I thought it; and I became dogged in my resolution to adhere to my own course. We parted very coolly; and I went straight off to John Brouncker to tell him I believed that I could save the arm, if he would refuse to have it amputated. When I calmed myself a little, before going in and speaking to him, I could not help acknowledging that we should run some risk of locked jaw; but, on the whole, and after giving most earnest conscientious thought to the case, I was sure that my mode of treatment would be best.

'He was a sensible man. I told him the difference of opinion that existed between Mr Morgan and myself. I said that there might be some little risk attending the non-amputation; but that I should guard against it, and I trusted that I should be able to preserve his arm.

'"Under God's blessing," said he, reverently. I bowed my head. I don't like to talk too frequently of the dependence which I always felt on that holy blessing, as to the result of my efforts; but I was glad to hear that speech of John's, because it showed a calm and faithful heart; and I had almost certain hopes of him from that time.

'We agreed that he should tell Mr Morgan the reason of his objections to the amputation, and his reliance on my opinion. I determined to recur to every book I had relating to such cases, and to convince Mr Morgan, if I could, of my wisdom. Unluckily, I found out afterwards that he had met Miss Horsman in the time that intervened before I saw him again at his own house that evening; and she had more than hinted that I shrunk from performing the operation, "for very good reasons, no doubt. She had heard that the medical students in London were a bad set, and were not remarkable for regular attendance in the hospitals. She might be mistaken; but she thought it was, perhaps, quite as well poor John Brouncker had not his arm cut off by —. Was there not such a thing as mortification coming on after a clumsy operation? It was, perhaps, only a choice of deaths!"

'Mr Morgan had been stung at all this. Perhaps I did not speak quite respectfully enough; I was a good deal excited. We only got more and more angry with each other; though he, to do him justice, was as civil as could be all the time, thinking that thereby he concealed his vexation and disappointment. He did not try to conceal his anxiety about poor John. I went home weary and dispirited. I made up and took the necessary applications to John; and, promising to return with the dawn of day (I would fain have stayed, but I did not wish him to be alarmed about himself), I went home, and resolved to sit up and study the treatment of similar cases.

'Mrs Rose knocked at the door.

'"Come in!" said I, sharply.

'She said she had seen I had something on my mind all day, and she could not go to bed without asking if there was nothing she could do. She was good and kind; and I could not help telling her a little of the truth. She listened pleasantly; and I shook her warmly by the hand, thinking that though she might not be very wise, her good heart made her worth a dozen keen, sharp, hard people, like Miss Horsman.

'When I went at daybreak, I saw John's wife for a few minutes outside of the door. She seemed to wish her husband had been in Mr Morgan's hands rather than mine; but she gave me as good an account as I dared to hope for of the manner in which her husband had passed the night. This was confirmed by my own examination.

'When Mr Morgan and I visited him together later on in the day, John said what we had agreed upon the day before; and I told Mr Morgan openly that it was by my advice that amputation was declined. He did not speak to me till we had left the house. Then he said – "Now, sir, from this time, I consider the case entirely in your hands. Only remember the poor fellow has a wife and six children. In case you come round to my opinion, remember that Mr White could come over, as he has done before, for the operation."

'So! Mr Morgan believed I declined operating because I felt myself incapable. Very well! I was much mortified.

'An hour after we parted, I received a note to this effect –

'"Dear Sir – I will take the long round to-day, to leave you at liberty to attend to Brouncker's case, which I feel to be a very responsible one.

'"J. MORGAN."

'This was kindly done. I went back, as soon as I could, to John's cottage. While I was in the inner room with him, I heard the Miss Tomkinsons' voices outside. They had called to inquire. Miss Tomkinson came in, and evidently was poking and snuffing about. (Mrs Brouncker told her that I was within; and within I resolved to be till they had gone.)

'"What is this close smell?" asked she. "I am afraid you are not cleanly. Cheese! – cheese in this cupboard! No wonder there is an unpleasant smell. Don't you know how particular you should be about being clean when there is illness about?"

'Mrs Brouncker was exquisitely clean in general, and was piqued at these remarks.

'"If you please, ma'am, I could not leave John yesterday to do any house-work, and Jenny put the dinner-things away. She is but eight years old."

'But this did not satisfy Miss Tomkinson, who was evidently pursuing the course of her observations.

'"Fresh butter, I declare! Well now, Mrs Brouncker, do you know I don't allow myself fresh butter at this time of the year? How can you save, indeed, with such extravagances!"

'"Please, ma'am," answered Mrs Brouncker, "you'd think it strange, if I was to take such liberties in your house as you're taking here."

'I expected to hear a sharp answer. No! Miss Tomkinson liked true plain-speaking. The only person in whom she would tolerate round-about ways of talking was her sister.

'"Well, that's true," she said. "Still, you must not be above taking advice. Fresh butter is extravagant at this time of the year. However, you're a good kind woman, and I've a great respect for John. Send Jenny for some broth as soon as he can take it. Come, Caroline, we have got to go on to Williams's."

'But Miss Caroline said that she was tired, and would rest where she was till Miss Tomkinson came back. I was a prisoner for some time, I found. When she was alone with Mrs Brouncker, she said –

'"You must not be hurt by my sister's abrupt manner. She means well. She has not much imagination or sympathy, and cannot understand the distraction of mind produced by the illness of a worshipped husband." I could hear the loud sigh of commiseration which followed this speech. Mrs Brouncker said –

'"Please, ma'am, I don't worship my husband. I would not be so wicked."

'"Goodness! You don't think it wicked, do you? For my part, if . . . I should worship, I should adore him." I thought she need not imagine such improbable cases. But sturdy Mrs Brouncker said again –

'"I hope I know my duty better. I've not learned my Commandments for nothing. I know whom I ought to worship."

'Just then the children came in, dirty and unwashed, I have no doubt. And now Miss Caroline's real nature peeped out. She spoke sharply to them, and asked them if they had no manners, little pigs as they were, to come brushing against her silk gown in that way? She sweetened herself again, and was as sugary as love when Miss Tomkinson returned for her, accompanied by one whose voice, "like winds in summer sighing," I knew to be my dear Sophy's.

'She did not say much; but what she did say and the manner in which she spoke, was tender and compassionate in the highest degree; and she came to take the four little ones back with her to the vicarage, in order that they might be out of their mother's way; the older two might help at home. She offered to wash their hands and faces; and when I emerged from my inner chamber, after the Miss Tomkinsons had left, I found her with a chubby child on her knees, bubbling and spluttering against her white wet hand, with a face bright, rosy, and merry under the operation. Just as I came in, she said to him, "There, Jemmy, now I can kiss you with this nice clean face."

'She coloured when she saw me. I liked her speaking, and I liked her silence. She was silent now, and I "lo'ed a' the better." I gave my directions to Mrs Brouncker, and hastened to overtake Sophy and the children; but they had gone round by the lanes, I suppose, for I saw nothing of them.

'I was very anxious about the case. At night I went again. Miss Horsman had been there; I believe she was really kind among the poor, but she could not help leaving a sting behind her everywhere. She had been frightening Mrs Brouncker about her husband; and been, I have no doubt, expressing her doubts of my skill; for Mrs Brouncker began:

'"Oh, please, sir, if you'll only let Mr Morgan take off his arm, I will never think the worse of you for not being able to do it."

'I told her it was from no doubt of my own competency to perform the operation that I wished to save the arm; but that he himself was anxious to have it spared.

'"Ay, bless him! he frets about not earning enough to keep us, if he's crippled; but, sir, I don't care about that. I would work my fingers to the bone, and so would the children; I'm sure we'd be proud to do for him, and keep him; God bless him! it would be far better to have him only with one arm, than to have him in the churchyard, Miss Horsman says – '

'"Confound Miss Horsman!" said I.

'"Thank you, Mr Harrison," was her well-known voice behind me. She had come out, dark as it was, to bring some old linen to Mrs Brouncker; for, as I said before, she was very kind to all the poor people of Duncombe.

'"I beg your pardon;" for I really was sorry for my speech, or rather, that she had heard it.

'"There is no occasion for any apology," she replied, drawing herself up, and pinching her lips into a very venomous shape.

'John was doing pretty well: but of course the danger of locked jaw was not over. Before I left, his wife entreated me to take off the arm; she wrung her hands in her passionate entreaty. "Spare him to me, Mr Harrison," she implored. Miss Horsman stood by. It was mortifying enough; but I thought of the power which was in my hands, as I firmly believed, of saving the limb; and I was inflexible.

'You cannot think how pleasantly Mrs Rose's sympathy came in on my return. To be sure she did not understand one word of the case, which I detailed to her; but she listened with interest, and, as long as she held her tongue, I thought she was really taking it in; but her first remark was as *mal à propos* as could be.

'"You are anxious to save the tibia – I see completely how difficult that will be. My late husband had a case exactly similar, and I remember his anxiety; but you must not distress yourself too much, my dear Mr Harrison; I have no doubt it will end well."

'I knew she had no grounds for this assurance, and yet it comforted me.

'However, as it happened, John did fully as well as I could have hoped for; of course, he was long in rallying his strength; and, indeed, sea-air was evidently so necessary for his complete restoration, that I accepted with gratitude Mrs Rose's proposal of sending him to Highport for a fortnight or three weeks. Her kind generosity in this matter made me more desirous than ever of paying her every mark of respect and attention.

Chapter XV

'About this time there was a sale at Ashmeadow, a pretty house in the neighbourhood of Duncombe. It was likewise an easy walk, and the spring days tempted many people thither, who had no intention of buying anything, but who liked the idea of rambling through the woods, gay with early primroses and wild daffodils, and of seeing the gardens and house, which till now had been shut up from the ingress of the townspeople. Mrs Rose had planned to go, but an unlucky cold prevented her. She begged me to bring her a very particular account, saying she delighted in details, and always questioned the late Mr Rose as to the side dishes of the dinners to which he went. The late Mr Rose's conduct was always held up as a model to me, by the way. I walked to Ashmeadow, pausing or loitering with different parties of townspeople, all bound in the same direction. At last I found the Vicar and Sophy, and with them I stayed. I sat by Sophy, and talked and listened. A sale is a very pleasant gathering after all. The auctioneer, in a country place, is privileged to joke from his rostrum; and having a personal knowledge of most of the people, can sometimes make a very keen hit at their circumstances, and turn the laugh against them. For instance, on the present occasion, there was a farmer present, with his wife, who was notoriously the grey mare. The auctioneer was selling some horse-cloths, and called out to recommend the article to her, telling her, with a knowing look at the company, that they would make her a dashing pair of trousers, if she was in want of such an article. She drew herself up with dignity, and said, "Come, John, we've had enough of these." Whereupon there was a burst of laughter, and in the midst of it John meekly followed his wife out of the place. The furniture in the sitting-rooms was, I believe, very beautiful, but I did not notice it much. Suddenly I heard the auctioneer speaking to me, "Mr Harrison, won't you give me a bid for this table?"

'It was a very pretty little table of walnut-wood. I thought it would go into my study very well, so I gave him a bid. I saw Miss Horsman bidding against me, so I went off with full force, and at last it was knocked down to me. The auctioneer smiled, and congratulated me.

'"A useful present for Mrs Harrison, when that lady comes."

'Everybody laughed. They like a joke about marriage; it is so easy of comprehension. But the table which I had thought was for writing, turned out to be a work-table, scissors and thimble complete. No wonder I looked foolish. Sophy was not looking at me, that was one comfort. She was busy arranging a nosegay of wood-anemone and wild sorrel.

'Miss Horsman came up, with her curious eyes.

'"I had no idea things were far enough advanced for you to be purchasing a work-table, Mr Harrison."

'I laughed off my awkwardness.

'"Did not you, Miss Horsman? You are very much behindhand. You have not heard of my piano, then?"

'"No, indeed," she said, half uncertain whether I was serious or not. "Then it seems there is nothing wanting but the lady."

'"Perhaps she may not be wanting either," said I, for I wished to perplex her keen curiosity.

Chapter XVI

'When I got home from my round, I found Mrs Rose in some sorrow.

'"Miss Horsman called after you left," said she. "Have you heard how John Brouncker is at Highport?"

'"Very well," replied I. "I called on his wife just now, and she had just got a letter from him. She had been anxious about him, for she had not heard for a week. However, all's right now; and she has pretty well of work at Mrs Munton's, as her servant is ill. Oh, they'll do, never fear."

'"At Mrs Munton's? Oh, that accounts for it, then. She is so deaf, and makes such blunders."

'"Accounts for what?" asked I.

'"Oh, perhaps I had better not tell you," hesitated Mrs Rose.

'"Yes, tell me at once. I beg your pardon, but I hate mysteries."

'"You are so like my poor dear Mr Rose. He used to speak to me just in that sharp, cross way. It is only that Miss Horsman called. She had been making a collection for John Brouncker's widow, and – '

'"But the man's alive!" said I.

'"So it seems. But Mrs Munton had told her that he was dead. And she has got Mr Morgan's name down at the head of the list, and Mr Bullock's."

'Mr Morgan and I had got into a short, cool way of speaking to each other ever since we had differed so much about the treatment of Brouncker's arm; and I had heard once or twice of his shakes of the head over John's case. He would not have spoken against my method for the world, and fancied that he concealed his fears.

'"Miss Horsman is very ill-natured, I think," sighed forth Mrs Rose.

'I saw that something had been said of which I had not heard, for the mere fact of collecting money for the widow was good-natured, whoever did it; so I asked, quietly, what she had said.

'"Oh, I don't know if I should tell you. I only know she made me cry; for I'm not well, and I can't bear to hear any one that I live with abused."

'Come! this was pretty plain.

'"What did Miss Horsman say of me?" asked I, half laughing, for I knew there was no love lost between us.

'"Oh, she only said she wondered you could go to sales, and spend your money there, when your ignorance had made Jane Brouncker a widow, and her children fatherless."

'"Pooh! pooh! John's alive, and likely to live as long as you or I, thanks to you, Mrs Rose."

'When my work-table came home, Mrs Rose was so struck with its beauty and completeness, and I was so much obliged to her for her identification of my interests with hers, and the kindness of her whole conduct about John, that I begged her to accept of it. She seemed very much pleased; and, after a few apologies, she consented to take it, and placed it in the most conspicuous part of the front parlour, where she usually sat. There was a good deal of morning calling in Duncombe after the sale, and during this time the fact of John being alive was established to the conviction of all except Miss Horsman, who, I believe, still doubted. I myself told Mr Morgan, who immediately went to reclaim his money; saying to me, that he was thankful of the information; he was truly glad to hear it; and he shook me warmly by the hand for the first time for a month.

Chapter XVII

'A few days after the sale, I was in the consulting-room. The servant must have left the folding-doors a little ajar, I think. Mrs Munton came to call on Mrs Rose; and the former being deaf, I heard all the speeches of the latter lady, as she was obliged to speak very loud in order to be heard. She began:

'"This is a great pleasure, Mrs Munton, so seldom as you are well enough to go out."

'Mumble, mumble, mumble, through the door.

'"Oh, very well, thank you. Take this seat, and then you can admire my new work-table, ma'am; a present from Mr Harrison."

'Mumble, mumble.

'"Who could have told you, ma'am? Miss Horsman? Oh, yes, I showed it Miss Horsman."

'Mumble, mumble.

'"I don't quite understand you, ma'am."

'Mumble, mumble.

'"I am not blushing, I believe. I really am quite in the dark as to what you mean."

'Mumble, mumble.

'"Oh, yes, Mr Harrison and I are most comfortable together. He reminds me so of my dear Mr Rose – just as fidgety and anxious in his profession."

'Mumble, mumble.

'"I'm sure you are joking now, ma'am." Then I heard a pretty loud –

'"Oh, no;" mumble, mumble, mumble, for a long time.

'"Did he really? Well, I'm sure I don't know. I should be sorry to think he was doomed to be unfortunate in so serious an affair; but you know my undying regard for the late Mr Rose."

'Another long mumble.

'"You're very kind, I'm sure. Mr Rose always thought more of my happiness than his own" – a little crying – "but the turtle-dove has always been my ideal, ma'am."

'Mumble, mumble.

'"No one could have been happier than I. As you say, it is a compliment to matrimony."

'Mumble.

'"Oh, but you must not repeat such a thing. Mr Harrison would not like it. He can't bear to have his affairs spoken about."

'Then there was a change of subject; an inquiry after some poor person, I imagine. I heard Mrs Rose say –

'"She has got a mucous membrane, I'm afraid, ma'am."

'A commiserating mumble.

'"Not always fatal. I believe Mr Rose knew some cases that lived for years after it was discovered that they had a mucous membrane." A pause. Then Mrs Rose spoke in a different tone.

'"Are you sure, ma'am, there is no mistake about what he said?" 'Mumble.

'"Pray don't be so observant, Mrs Munton; you find out too much. One can have no little secrets."

'The call broke up; and I heard Mrs Munton say in the passage, "I wish you joy, ma'am, with all my heart. There's no use denying it; for I've seen all along what would happen."

'When I went in to dinner, I said to Mrs Rose –

'"You've had Mrs Munton here, I think. Did she bring any news?" To my surprise, she bridled and simpered, and replied, "Oh, you must not ask, Mr Harrison: such foolish reports."

'I did not ask, as she seemed to wish me not, and I knew there were silly reports always about. Then I think she was vexed that I did not ask. Altogether she went on so strangely that I could not help looking at her; and then she took up a hand-screen, and held it between me and her. I really felt rather anxious.

'"Are you not feeling well?" said I, innocently.

'"Oh, thank you, I believe I'm quite well; only the room is rather warm, is it not?"

'"Let me put the blinds down for you? the sun begins to have a good deal of power." I drew down the blinds.

'"You are so attentive, Mr Harrison. Mr Rose himself never did more for my little wishes than you do."

'"I wish I could do more – I wish I could show you how much I feel – " her kindness to John Brouncker, I was going to say; but I was just then called out to a patient. Before I went I turned back, and said –

'"Take care of yourself, my dear Mrs Rose; you had better rest a little."

'"For your sake, I will," said she, tenderly.

'I did not care for whose sake she did it. Only I really thought she was not quite well, and required rest. I thought she was more affected than usual at tea-time; and could have been angry with her nonsensical ways once or twice, but that I knew the real goodness of her heart. She said she wished she had the power to sweeten my life as she could my tea. I told her what a comfort she had been during my late time of anxiety, and then I stole out to try if I could hear the evening singing at the vicarage, by standing close to the garden-wall.

Chapter XVIII

'The next morning I met Mr Bullock by appointment, to talk a little about the legacy which was paid into his hands. As I was leaving his office, feeling full of my riches, I met Miss Horsman. She smiled rather grimly, and said:

'"Oh! Mr Harrison, I must congratulate you, I believe. I don't know whether I ought to have known, but as I do, I must wish you joy. A very nice little sum, too. I always said you would have money."

'So she had found out my legacy, had she? Well, it was no secret, and one likes the reputation of being a person of property. Accordingly I smiled, and said I was much obliged to her, and if I could alter the figures to my liking, she might congratulate me still more.

'She said, "Oh, Mr Harrison, you can't have everything. It would be better the other way, certainly. Money is the great thing, as you've found out. The relation died most opportunely, I must say."

'"He was no relative," said I; "only an intimate friend."

'"Dear-ah-me! I thought it had been a brother! Well, at any rate, the legacy is safe."

'I wished her good morning, and passed on. Before long I was sent for to Miss Tomkinson's.

'Miss Tomkinson sat in severe state to receive me. I went in with an air of ease, because I always felt so uncomfortable.

'"Is this true that I hear?" asked she, in an inquisitorial manner.

'I thought she alluded to my five hundred pounds; so I smiled, and said that I believed it was.

'"Can money be so great an object with you, Mr Harrison?" she asked again.

'I said I had never cared much for money, except as an assistance to any plan of settling in life; and then, as I did not like her severe way of treating the subject, I said that I hoped every one was well; though of course I expected some one was ill, or I should not have been sent for.

'Miss Tomkinson looked very grave and sad. Then she answered: "Caroline is very poorly – the old palpitations at the heart; but of course that is nothing to you."

'I said I was very sorry. She had a weakness there, I knew. Could I see her? I might be able to order something for her.

'I thought I heard Miss Tomkinson say something in a low voice about my being a heartless deceiver. Then she spoke up. "I was always distrustful of you, Mr Harrison. I never liked your looks. I begged Caroline again and again not to confide in you. I foresaw how it would end. And now I fear her precious life will be a sacrifice."

'I begged her not to distress herself, for in all probability there was very little the matter with her sister. Might I see her?

'"No!" she said, shortly, standing up as if to dismiss me. "There has been too much of this seeing and calling. By my consent, you shall never see her again."

'I bowed. I was annoyed, of course. Such a dismissal might injure my practice just when I was most anxious to increase it.

'"Have you no apology, no excuse to offer?"

'I said I had done my best; I did not feel that there was any reason to offer an apology. I wished her good morning. Suddenly she came forwards.

'"Oh, Mr Harrison," said she, "if you have really loved Caroline, do not let a little paltry money make you desert her for another."

'I was struck dumb. Loved Miss Caroline! I loved Miss Tomkinson a great deal better, and yet I disliked her. She went on:

'"I have saved nearly three thousand pounds. If you think you are too poor to marry without money, I will give it all to Caroline. I am strong, and can go on working: but she is weak, and this disappointment will kill her." She sat down suddenly, and covered her face with her hands. Then she looked up.

'"You are unwilling, I see. Don't suppose I would have urged you if it had been for myself; but she has had so much sorrow." And now she fairly cried aloud. I tried to explain; but she would not listen, but kept saying, "Leave the house, sir! leave the house!" But I would be heard.

'"I have never had any feeling warmer than respect for Miss Caroline, and I have never shown any different feeling. I never for an instant thought of making her my wife, and she has had no cause in my behaviour to imagine I entertained any such intention."

'"This is adding insult to injury," said she. "Leave the house, sir, this instant!"'

Chapter XIX

'I went, and sadly enough. In a small town such an occurrence is sure to be talked about, and to make a great deal of mischief. When I went home to dinner I was so full of it, and foresaw so clearly that I should need some advocate soon to set the case in its right light, that I determined on making a confidante of good Mrs Rose. I could not eat. She watched me tenderly, and sighed when she saw my want of appetite.

'"I am sure you have something on your mind, Mr Harrison. Would it be – would it not be – a relief to impart it to some sympathising friend?"

'It was just what I wanted to do.

'"My dear kind Mrs Rose," said I, "I must tell you, if you will listen."

'She took up the fire-screen, and held it, as yesterday, between me and her.

'"The most unfortunate misunderstanding has taken place. Miss Tomkinson thinks that I have been paying attentions to Miss Caroline; when, in fact – may I tell you, Mrs Rose? – my affections are placed elsewhere. Perhaps you have found it out already?" for indeed I thought I had been too much in love to conceal my attachment to Sophy from any one who knew my movements as well as Mrs Rose.

'She hung down her head, and said she believed she had found out my secret.

'"Then only think how miserably I am situated. If I have any hope – oh, Mrs Rose, do you think I have any hope? – "

'She put the hand-screen still more before her face, and after some hesitation she said she thought "If I persevered – in time – I might have hope." And then she suddenly got up, and left the room.

Chapter XX

'That afternoon I met Mr Bullock in the street. My mind was so full of the affair with Miss Tomkinson that I should have passed him without notice, if he had not stopped me short, and said that he must speak to me; about my wonderful five hundred pounds, I supposed. But I did not care for that now.

'"What's this I hear," said he, severely, "about your engagement with Mrs Rose?"

'"With Mrs Rose!" said I, almost laughing, although my heart was heavy enough.

'"Yes! with Mrs Rose!" said he, sternly.

'"I am not engaged to Mrs Rose," I replied. "There is some mistake."

'"I'm glad to hear it, sir," he answered, "very glad. It requires some explanation, however. Mrs Rose has been congratulated, and has acknowledged the truth of the report. It is confirmed by many facts. The work-table you bought, confessing your intention of giving it to your future wife, is given to her. How do you account for these things, sir?"

'I said I did not pretend to account for them. At present, a good deal was inexplicable; and when I could give an explanation, I did not think that I should feel myself called upon to give it to him.

'"Very well, sir; very well," replied he, growing very red. "I shall take care, and let Mr Morgan know the opinion I entertain of you. What do you think that man deserves to be called who enters a family under the plea of friendship, and takes advantage of his intimacy to win the affections of the daughter, and then engages himself to another woman?"

'I thought he referred to Miss Caroline. I simply said I could only say that I was not engaged; and that Miss Tomkinson had been quite mistaken in supposing I had been paying any attentions to her sister beyond those dictated by mere civility.

'"Miss Tomkinson! Miss Caroline! I don't understand to what you refer. Is there another victim to your perfidy? What I allude to are the attentions you have paid to my daughter, Miss Bullock."

'Another! I could but disclaim, as I had done in the case of Miss Caroline; but I began to be in despair. Would Miss Horsman, too, come forward as a victim to my tender affections? It was all Mr Morgan's doing, who had lectured me into this tenderly deferential manner. But on the score of Miss Bullock, I was brave in my innocence. I had positively disliked her; and so I told her father, though in more civil and measured terms, adding that I was sure the feeling was reciprocal.

'He looked as if he would like to horsewhip me. I longed to call him out.

67

'"I hope my daughter has had sense enough to despise you; I hope she has, that's all. I trust my wife may be mistaken as to her feelings."

'So, he had heard all through the medium of his wife. That explained something, and rather calmed me. I begged he would ask Miss Bullock if she had ever thought I had any ulterior object in my intercourse with her, beyond mere friendliness (and not so much of that, I might have added). I would refer it to her.

'"Girls," said Mr Bullock, a little more quietly, "do not like to acknowledge that they have been deceived and disappointed. I consider my wife's testimony as likely to be nearer the truth than my daughter's, for that reason. And she tells me she never doubted but that, if not absolutely engaged, you understood each other perfectly. She is sure Jemima is deeply wounded by your engagement to Mrs Rose."

'"Once for all, I am not engaged to anybody. Till you have seen your daughter, and learnt the truth from her, I will wish you farewell."

'I bowed in a stiff, haughty manner, and walked off homewards. But when I got to my own door, I remembered Mrs Rose, and all that Mr Bullock had said about her acknowledging the truth of the report of my engagement to her. Where could I go to be safe? Mrs Rose, Miss Bullock, Miss Caroline – they lived as it were at the three points of an equilateral triangle; here was I in the centre. I would go to Mr Morgan's, and drink tea with him. There, at any rate, I was secure from any one wanting to marry me; and I might be as professionally bland as I liked, without being misunderstood. But there, too, a *contretemps* awaited me.

Chapter XXI

'Mr Morgan was looking grave. After a minute or two of humming and hawing, he said –

'"I have been sent for to Miss Caroline Tomkinson, Mr Harrison. I am sorry to hear of this. I am grieved to find that there seems to have been some trifling with the affections of a very worthy lady. Miss Tomkinson, who is in sad distress, tells me that they had every reason to believe that you were attached to her sister. May I ask if you do not intend to marry her?"

'I said, nothing was farther from my thoughts.

'"My dear sir," said Mr Morgan, rather agitated, "do not express yourself so strongly and vehemently. It is derogatory to the sex to speak so. It is more respectful to say, in these cases, that you do not venture to entertain a hope; such a manner is generally understood, and does not sound like such positive objection."

'"I cannot help it, sir; I must talk in my own natural manner. I would not speak disrespectfully of any woman; but nothing should induce me to marry Miss Caroline Tomkinson; not if she were Venus herself, and Queen of England into the bargain. I cannot understand what has given rise to the idea."

'"Indeed, sir; I think that is very plain. You have a trifling case to attend to in the house, and you invariably make it a pretext for seeing and conversing with the lady."

'"That was her doing, not mine!" said I, vehemently.

'"Allow me to go on. You are discovered on your knees before her – a positive injury to the establishment, as Miss Tomkinson observes; a most passionate valentine is sent; and when questioned, you acknowledge the sincerity of meaning which you affix to such things." He stopped, for in his earnestness he had been talking more quickly than usual, and was out of breath. I burst in with my explanations –

'"The valentine I knew nothing about."

'"It is in your handwriting," said he, coldly. "I should be most deeply grieved to – in fact, I will not think it possible of your father's son. But I must say, it is in your handwriting."

'I tried again, and at last succeeded in convincing him that I had been only unfortunate, not intentionally guilty of winning Miss

Caroline's affections. I said that I had been endeavouring, it was true, to practise the manner he had recommended, of universal sympathy, and recalled to his mind some of the advice he had given me. He was a good deal hurried.

'"But, my dear sir, I had no idea that you would carry it out to such consequences. 'Philandering,' Miss Tomkinson called it. That is a hard word, sir. My manner has been always tender and sympathetic; but I am not aware that I ever excited any hopes; there never was any report about me. I believe no lady was ever attached to me. You must strive after this happy medium, sir."

'I was still distressed. Mr Morgan had only heard of one, but there were three ladies (including Miss Bullock) hoping to marry me. He saw my annoyance.

'"Don't be too much distressed about it, my dear sir; I was sure you were too honourable a man, from the first. With a conscience like yours, I would defy the world."

'He became anxious to console me, and I was hesitating whether I would not tell him all my three dilemmas, when a note was brought in to him. It was from Mrs Munton. He threw it to me, with a face of dismay.

'"My dear Mr Morgan – I most sincerely congratulate you on the happy matrimonial engagement I hear you have formed with Miss Tomkinson. All previous circumstances, as I have just been remarking to Miss Horsman, combine to promise you felicity. And I wish that every blessing may attend your married life.

'"Most sincerely yours,
'"JANE MUNTON."

'I could not help laughing, he had been so lately congratulating himself that no report of the kind had ever been circulated about himself. He said –

'"Sir! this is no laughing matter; I assure you it is not."

'I could not resist asking, if I was to conclude that there was no truth in the report.

' "Truth, sir! it's a lie from beginning to end. I don't like to speak too decidedly about any lady; and I've a great respect for Miss Tomkinson; but I do assure you, sir, I'd as soon marry one of her Majesty's Life Guards. I would rather; it would be more suitable. Miss Tomkinson is a very worthy lady; but she's a perfect grenadier."

'He grew very nervous. He was evidently insecure. He thought it not impossible that Miss Tomkinson might come and marry him, *vi et armis*. I am sure he had some dim idea of abduction in his mind. Still, he was better off than I was; for he was in his own house, and report had only engaged him to one lady; while I stood, like Paris, among three contending beauties. Truly, an apple of discord had been thrown into our little town. I suspected, at the time, what I know now, that it was Miss Horsman's doing; not intentionally, I will do her the justice to say. But she had shouted out the story of my behaviour to Miss Caroline up Mrs Munton's trumpet; and that lady, possessed with the idea that I was engaged to Mrs Rose, had imagined the masculine pronoun to relate to Mr Morgan, whom she had seen only that afternoon *tête-à-tête* with Miss Tomkinson, condoling with her in some tender deferential manner. I'll be bound.

Chapter XXII

'I was very cowardly. I positively dared not go home; but at length I was obliged to. I had done all I could to console Mr Morgan, but he refused to be comforted. I went at last. I rang at the bell. I don't know who opened the door, but I think it was Mrs Rose. I kept a handkerchief to my face, and muttering something about having a dreadful toothache, I flew up to my room, and bolted the door. I had no candle; but what did that signify. I was safe. I could not sleep; and when I did fall into a sort of doze, it was ten times worse wakening up. I could not remember whether I was engaged or not. If I was engaged, who was the lady? I had always considered myself as rather plain than otherwise; but surely I had made a mistake. Fascinating I certainly must be; but perhaps I was handsome. As soon as day dawned, I got up to ascertain the fact at the looking-glass. Even with the best disposition to be convinced, I could not see any striking beauty in my round face, with an unshaven beard and a nightcap like a fool's cap at the top. No! I must be content to be plain, but agreeable. All this I tell you in confidence. I would not have my little bit of vanity known for the world. I fell asleep towards morning. I was awakened by a tap at my door. It was Peggy: she put in a hand with a note. I took it.

'"It is not from Miss Horsman?" said I, half in joke, half in very earnest fright.

'"No, sir; Mr Morgan's man brought it."

'I opened it. It ran thus:

'"My dear Sir – It is now nearly twenty years since I have had a little relaxation, and I find that my health requires it. I have also the utmost confidence in you, and I am sure this feeling is shared by our patients. I have, therefore, no scruple in putting in execution a hastily formed plan, and going to Chesterton to catch the early train on my way to Paris. If your accounts are good, I shall remain away probably a fortnight. Direct to Meurice's.

'"Yours, most truly,

'"J. MORGAN.

'"P.S. – Perhaps it may be as well not to name where I am gone, especially to Miss Tomkinson."

'He had deserted me. He – with only one report – had left me to stand my ground with three.

'"Mrs Rose's kind regards, sir, and it's nearly nine o'clock. Breakfast has been ready this hour, sir."

'"Tell Mrs Rose I don't want any breakfast. Or stay" (for I was very hungry), "I will take a cup of tea and some toast up here."

'Peggy brought the tray to the door.

'"I hope you're not ill, sir?" said she, kindly.

'"Not very. I shall be better when I get into the air."

'"Mrs Rose seems sadly put about," said she; "she seems so grieved like."

'I watched my opportunity, and went out by the side door in the garden.

Chapter XXIII

'I had intended to ask Mr Morgan to call at the vicarage, and give his parting explanation before they could hear the report. Now, I thought that if I could see Sophy, I would speak to her myself; but I did not wish to encounter the Vicar. I went along the lane at the back of the vicarage, and came suddenly upon Miss Bullock. She coloured, and asked me if I would allow her to speak to me. I could only be resigned; but I thought I could probably set one report at rest by this conversation.

'She was almost crying.

'"I must tell you, Mr Harrison, I have watched you here in order to speak to you. I heard with the greatest regret of papa's conversation with you yesterday." She was fairly crying. "I believe Mrs Bullock finds me in her way, and wants to have me married. It is the only way in which I can account for such a complete misrepresentation as she had told papa. I don't care for you, in the least, sir. You never paid me any attentions. You've been almost rude to me; and I have liked you the better. That's to say, I never have liked you."

'"I am truly glad to hear what you say," answered I. "Don't distress yourself. I was sure there was some mistake."

'But she cried bitterly.

'"It is so hard to feel that my marriage – my absence – is desired so earnestly at home. I dread every new acquaintance we form with any gentleman. It is sure to be the beginning of a series of attacks on him, of which everybody must be aware, and to which they may think I am a willing party. But I should not much mind if it were not for the conviction that she wishes me so earnestly away. Oh, my own dear mamma, you would never – "

'She cried more than ever. I was truly sorry for her, and had just taken her hand, and began – "My dear Miss Bullock – " when the door in the wall of the vicarage-garden opened. It was the Vicar letting out Miss Tomkinson, whose face was all swelled with crying. He saw me; but he did not bow, or make any sign. On the contrary, he looked down as from a severe eminence, and shut the door hastily. I turned to Miss Bullock.

'"I am afraid the Vicar has been hearing something to my disadvantage from Miss Tomkinson, and it is very awkward – " She finished my sentence – "To have found us here together. Yes, but as long as we understand that we do not care for each other, it does not signify what people say."

'"Oh, but to me it does," said I. "I may, perhaps, tell you – but do not mention it to a creature – I am attached to Miss Hutton."

'"To Sophy! Oh, Mr Harrison, I am so glad; she is such a sweet creature. Oh, I wish you joy."

'"Not yet; I have never spoken about it."

'"Oh, but it is certain to happen." She jumped with a woman's rapidity to a conclusion. And then she began to praise Sophy. Never was a man yet who did not like to hear the praises of his mistress. I walked by her side; we came past the front of the vicarage together. I looked up, and saw Sophy there, and she saw me.

'That afternoon she was sent away; sent to visit her aunt

ostensibly; in reality, because of the reports of my conduct, which were showered down upon the Vicar, and one of which he saw confirmed by his own eyes.

Chapter XXIV

'I heard of Sophy's departure as one heard of everything, soon after it had taken place. I did not care for the awkwardness of my situation, which had so perplexed and amused me in the morning. I felt that something was wrong; that Sophy was taken away from me. I sank into despair. If anybody liked to marry me they might. I was willing to be sacrificed. I did not speak to Mrs Rose. She wondered at me, and grieved over my coldness, I saw; but I had left off feeling anything. Miss Tomkinson cut me in the street; and it did not break my heart. Sophy was gone away; that was all I cared for. Where had they sent her to? Who was her aunt, that she should go and visit her? One day I met Lizzie, who looked as though she had been told not to speak to me, but could not help doing so.

'"Have you heard from your sister?" said I.

'"Yes."

'"Where is she? I hope she is well."

'"She is at the Leoms" – I was not much wiser. "Oh yes, she is very well. Fanny says she was at the Assembly last Wednesday, and danced all night with the officers."

'I thought I would enter myself a member of the Peace Society at once. She was a little flirt, and a hard-hearted creature. I don't think I wished Lizzie good-by.

Chapter XXV

'What most people would have considered a more serious evil than Sophy's absence, befell me. I found that my practice was falling off. The prejudice of the town ran strongly against me. Mrs Munton told me all that was said. She heard it through Miss Horsman. It was said – cruel little town – that my negligence or ignorance had been the cause of Walter's death; that Miss Tyrrell had become worse under my treatment; and that John Brouncker was all but dead, if he was not quite, from my mismanagement. All Jack Marshland's jokes and revelations, which had, I thought, gone to oblivion, were raked up to my discredit. He himself, formerly, to my astonishment, rather a favourite with the good people of Duncombe, was spoken of as one of my disreputable friends.

'In short, so prejudiced were the good people of Duncombe that I believe a very little would have made them suspect me of a brutal highway robbery, which took place in the neighbourhood about this time. Mrs Munton told me, *à propos* of the robbery that she had never yet understood the cause of my year's imprisonment in Newgate; she had no doubt, from what Mr Morgan had told her, there was some good reason for it; but if I would tell her the particulars, she should like to know them.

'Miss Tomkinson sent for Mr White, from Chesterton, to see Miss Caroline; and, as he was coming over, all our old patients seemed to take advantage of it, and send for him too.

'But the worst of all was the Vicar's manner to me. If he had cut me, I could have asked him why he did so. But the freezing change in his behaviour was indescribable, though bitterly felt. I heard of Sophy's gaiety from Lizzie. I thought of writing to her. Just then Mr Morgan's fortnight of absence expired. I was wearied out by Mrs Rose's tender vagaries, and took no comfort from her sympathy, which indeed I rather avoided. Her tears irritated, instead of grieving me. I wished I could tell her at once that I had no intention of marrying her.

Chapter XXVI

'Mr Morgan had not been at home above two hours before he was sent for to the vicarage. Sophy had come back, and I had never heard of it. She had come home ill and weary, and longing for rest: and the *rest* seemed approaching with awful strides. Mr Morgan forgot all his Parisian adventures, and all his terror of Miss Tomkinson, when he was sent for to see her. She was ill of a fever, which made fearful progress. When he told me, I wished to force the vicarage door, if I might but see her. But I controlled myself; and only cursed my weak indecision, which had prevented my writing to her. It was well I had no patients; they would have had but a poor chance of attention. I hung about Mr Morgan, who might see her, and did see her. But from what he told me, I perceived that the measures he was adopting were powerless to check so sudden and violent an illness. Oh! if they would but let me see her. But that was out of the question. It was not merely that the Vicar had heard of my character as a gay Lothario, but that doubts had been thrown out of my medical skill. The accounts grew worse. Suddenly, my resolution was taken. Mr Morgan's very regard for Sophy made him more than usually timid in his practice. I had my horse saddled, and galloped to Chesterton. I took the express train to town. I went to Dr —. I told him every particular of the case. He listened; but shook his head. He wrote down a prescription; and recommended a new preparation, not yet in full use; a preparation of a poison, in fact.

'"It may save her," said he. "It is a chance, in such a state of things as you describe. It must be given on the fifth day, if the pulse will bear it. Crabbe makes up the preparation most skilfully. Let me hear from you, I beg."

'I went to Crabbe's; I begged to make it up myself; but my hands trembled, so that I could not weigh the quantities. I asked the young man to do it for me. I went, without touching food, to the station, with my medicine and my prescription in my pocket. Back we flew through the country. I sprang on Bay Maldon, which my groom had in waiting, and galloped across the country to Duncombe.

'But I drew bridle when I came to the top of the hill – the hill above the old hall, from which we catch the first glimpse of the town, for I thought within myself that she might be dead; and I dreaded to come near certainty. The hawthorns were out in the woods, the young lambs were in the meadows, the song of the thrushes filled the air; but it only made the thought the more terrible.

'"What, if in this world of hope and life she lies dead!" I heard the church bells soft and clear. I sickened to listen. Was it the passing bell? No! it was ringing eight o'clock. I put spurs to my horse, down hill as it was. We dashed into the town. I turned him, saddle and bridle, into the stable-yard, and went off to Mr Morgan's.

'"Is she – ?" said I. "How is she?"

'"Very ill. My poor fellow, I see how it is with you. She may live – but I fear. My dear sir, I am very much afraid."

'I told him of my journey and consultation with Dr —, and showed him the prescription. His hands trembled as he put on his spectacles to read it.

'"This is a very dangerous medicine, sir," said he, with his finger under the name of the poison.

'"It is a new preparation," said I. "Dr — relies much upon it."

'"I dare not administer it," he replied. "I have never tried it. It must be very powerful. I dare not play tricks in this case."

'I believe I stamped with impatience; but it was all of no use. My journey had been in vain. The more I urged the imminent danger of the case requiring some powerful remedy, the more nervous he became.

'I told him I would throw up the partnership. I threatened him with that, though, in fact, it was only what I felt I ought to do, and had resolved upon before Sophy's illness, as I had lost the confidence of his patients. He only said –

'"I cannot help it, sir. I shall regret it for your father's sake; but I must do my duty. I dare not run the risk of giving Miss Sophy this violent medicine – a preparation of a deadly poison."

'I left him without a word. He was quite right in adhering to his own views, as I can see now; but at the time I thought him brutal and obstinate.

Chapter XXVII

'I went home. I spoke rudely to Mrs Rose, who awaited my return at the door. I rushed past, and locked myself in my room. I could not go to bed.

'The morning sun came pouring in, and enraged me, as everything did since Mr Morgan refused. I pulled the blind down so violently that the string broke. What did it signify? The light might come in. What was the sun to me? And then I remembered that that sun might be shining on her – dead.

'I sat down and covered my face. Mrs Rose knocked at the door. I opened it. She had never been in bed, and had been crying too.

'"Mr Morgan wants to speak to you, sir!"

'I rushed back for my medicine, and went to him. He stood at the door, pale and anxious.

'"She's alive, sir," said he, "but that's all. We have sent for Dr Hamilton. I'm afraid he will not come in time. Do you know, sir,

I think we should venture – with Dr —'s sanction – to give her that medicine. It is but a chance; but it is the only one, I'm afraid." He fairly cried before he had ended.

'"I've got it here," said I, setting off to walk; but he could not go so fast.

'"I beg your pardon, sir," said he, "for my abrupt refusal last night."

'"Indeed, sir," said I; "I ought much rather to beg your pardon. I was very violent."

'"Oh! never mind! never mind! Will you repeat what Dr — said?"

'I did so; and then I asked, with a meekness that astonished myself, if I might not go in and administer it.

'"No, sir," said he, "I'm afraid not. I am sure your good heart would not wish to give pain. Besides, it might agitate her, if she has any consciousness before death. In her delirium she has often mentioned your name; and, sir, I'm sure you won't name it again, as it may, in fact, be considered a professional secret; but I did hear our good Vicar speak a little strongly about you; in fact, sir, I did hear him curse you. You see the mischief it might make in the parish, I'm sure, if this were known."

'I gave him the medicine, and watched him in, and saw the door shut. I hung about the place all day. Poor and rich all came to inquire. The county people drove up in their carriages – the halt and the lame came on their crutches. Their anxiety did my heart good. Mr Morgan told me that she slept, and I watched Dr Hamilton into the house. The night came on. She slept. I watched round the house. I saw the light high up, burning still and steady. Then I saw it moved. It was the crisis, in one way or other.

Chapter XXVIII

'Mr Morgan came out. Good old man! The tears were running down his cheeks: he could not speak; but kept shaking my hands. I did not want words. I understood that she was better.

'"Dr Hamilton says, it was the only medicine that could have saved her. I was an old fool, sir. I beg your pardon. The Vicar shall know all. I beg your pardon, sir, if I was abrupt."

'Everything went on brilliantly from this time.

'Mr Bullock called to apologise for his mistake, and consequent upbraiding. John Brouncker came home, brave and well.

'There was still Miss Tomkinson in the ranks of the enemy; and Mrs Rose too much, I feared, in the ranks of the friends.

Chapter XXIX

'One night she had gone to bed, and I was thinking of going. I had been studying in the back room, where I went for refuge from her in the present position of affairs – (I read a good number of surgical books about this time, and also *Vanity Fair*) – when I heard a loud, long-continued knocking at the door, enough to waken the whole street. Before I could get to open it, I heard that well-known bass of Jack Marshland's, once heard never to be forgotten, pipe up the negro song –

'"Who's dat knocking at de door?"

'Though it was raining hard at the time, and I stood waiting to let him in, he would finish his melody in the open air; loud and clear along the street it sounded. I saw Miss Tomkinson's night-capped head emerge from a window. She called out "Police! police!"

'Now there were no police, only a rheumatic constable in the town; but it was the custom of the ladies, when alarmed at night, to call an imaginary police, which had, they thought, an intimidating effect; but as every one knew the real state of the unwatched town, we did not much mind it in general. Just now, however, I wanted to regain my character. So I pulled Jack in, quavering as he entered.

'"You've spoilt a good shake," said he, "that's what you have. I'm nearly up to Jenny Lind; and you see I'm a nightingale, like her."

'We sat up late; and I don't know how it was, but I told him all my matrimonial and misadventures.

'"I thought I could imitate your hand pretty well," said he. "My word! it was a flaming valentine! No wonder she thought you loved her!"

'"So that was your doing, was it? Now I'll tell you what you shall do to make up for it. You shall write me a letter confessing your hoax − a letter that I can show."

'"Give me pen and paper, my boy! you shall dictate. 'With a deeply penitent heart − ' Will that do for a beginning?"

'I told him what to write; a simple, straightforward confession of his practical joke. I enclosed it in a few lines of regret that, unknown to me, any of my friends should have so acted.

Chapter XXX

'All this time I knew that Sophy was slowly recovering. One day I met Miss Bullock, who had seen her.

'"We have been talking about you," said she, with a bright smile; for since she knew I disliked her, she felt quite at her ease, and could smile very pleasantly. I understood that she had been explaining the misunderstanding about herself to Sophy; so that when Jack Marshland's note had been sent to Miss Tomkinson's, I thought myself in a fair way to have my character established in two quarters. But the third was my dilemma. Mrs Rose had really so much of my true regard for her good qualities, that I disliked the idea of a formal explanation, in which a good deal must be said on my side to wound her. We had become very much estranged ever since I had heard of this report of my engagement to her. I saw that she grieved over it. While Jack Marshland stayed with us, I felt at my ease in the presence of a third person. But he told me confidentially he durst not stay long, for fear some of the ladies should snap him up, and marry him. Indeed I myself did not think it unlikely that he would snap one of them up if he could. For when we met Miss Bullock one day, and heard her hopeful, joyous account of Sophy's progress (to whom she was a daily visitor), he asked me who that bright-looking girl was? And when I told him she was the Miss Bullock of whom I had spoken to him, he was pleased to observe that he thought I had been a great fool, and asked me if Sophy had anything like such splendid eyes. He made me repeat about Miss Bullock's unhappy circumstances at home, and then became very thoughtful – a most unusual and morbid symptom in his case.

'Soon after he went, by Mr Morgan's kind offices and explanations, I was permitted to see Sophy. I might not speak much; it was prohibited, for fear of agitating her. We talked of the weather and the flowers; and we were silent. But her little white thin hand lay in mine; and we understood each other without words. I had a long interview with the Vicar afterwards; and came away glad and satisfied.

'Mr Morgan called in the afternoon, evidently anxious, though he made no direct inquiries (he was too polite for that), to hear the result of my visit at the vicarage. I told him to give me joy. He shook me warmly by the hand; and then rubbed his own together. I thought I would consult him about my dilemma with Mrs Rose who, I was afraid, would be deeply affected by my engagement.

'"There is only one awkward circumstance," said I – "about Mrs Rose." I hesitated how to word the fact of her having received congratulations on her supposed engagement with me, and her manifest attachment; but, before I could speak, he broke in –

'"My dear sir, you need not trouble yourself about that; she will have a home. In fact, sir," said he, reddening a little, "I thought it would, perhaps, put a stop to those reports connecting my name with Miss Tomkinson's, if I married some one else. I hoped it might prove an efficacious contradiction. And I was struck with admiration for Mrs Rose's undying memory of her late husband. Not to be prolix, I have this morning obtained Mrs Rose's consent to – to marry her, in fact, sir!" said he, jerking out the climax.

'Here was an event! Then Mr Morgan had never heard the report about Mrs Rose and me. (To this day, I think she would have taken me, if I had proposed.) So much the better.

'Marriages were in the fashion that year. Mr Bullock met me one morning, as I was going to ride with Sophy. He and I had quite got over our misunderstanding, thanks to Jemima, and were as friendly as ever. This morning he was chuckling aloud as he walked.

'"Stop, Mr Harrison!" he said, as I went quickly past. "Have you heard the news? Miss Horsman has just told me Miss Caroline has eloped with young Hoggins! She is ten years older than he is! How can her gentility like being married to a tallow-chandler? It is a very good thing for her, though," he added, in a more serious manner; "Old Hoggins is very rich; and though he's angry just now, he will soon be reconciled."

'Any vanity I might have entertained on the score of the three ladies who were, at one time, said to be captivated by my charms, was being rapidly dispersed. Soon after Mr Hoggins' marriage, I met Miss Tomkinson face to face, for the first time since our memorable conversation. She stopped me, and said –

'"Don't refuse to receive my congratulations, Mr Harrison, on your most happy engagement to Miss Hutton. I owe you an apology, too, for my behaviour when I last saw you at our house. I really did think Caroline was attached to you then; and it irritated me, I confess, in a very wrong and unjustifiable way. But I heard her telling Mr Hoggins only yesterday that she had been attached to him for years; ever since he was in pinafores, she dated it from; and when I asked her afterwards how she could say so, after her distress on hearing that false report about you and Mrs Rose, she cried, and said I never had understood her; and that the hysterics which alarmed me so much were simply caused by eating pickled cucumber. I am very sorry for my stupidity, and improper way of speaking; but I hope we are friends now, Mr Harrison, for I should wish to be liked by Sophy's husband."

'Good Miss Tomkinson! to believe the substitution of indigestion for disappointed affection. I shook her warmly by the hand; and we have been all right ever since. I think I told you she is the baby's godmother.

Chapter XXXI

'I had some difficulty in persuading Jack Marshland to be groomsman; but when he heard all the arrangements, he came. Miss Bullock was bridesmaid. He liked us all so well, that he came again at Christmas, and was far better behaved than he had been the year before. He won golden opinions indeed. Miss Tomkinson said he was a reformed young man. We dined all together at Mr Morgan's (the Vicar wanted us to go there; but, from what Sophy told me, Helen was not confident of the mincemeat, and rather dreaded so large a party). We had a jolly day of it. Mrs Morgan was as kind and motherly as ever. Miss Horsman certainly did set out a story that the Vicar was thinking of Miss Tomkinson for his second; or else, I think, we had no other report circulated in consequence of our

Cranford

Chapter I

In the first place, Cranford is in possession of the Amazons; all the holders of houses, above a certain rent, are women. If a married couple come to settle in the town, somehow the gentleman disappears; he is either fairly frightened to death by being the only man in the Cranford evening parties, or he is accounted for by being with his regiment, his ship, or closely engaged in business all the week in the great neighbouring commercial town of Drumble, distant only twenty miles on a railroad. In short, whatever does become of the gentlemen, they are not at Cranford. What could they do if they were there? The surgeon has his round of thirty miles, and sleeps at Cranford; but every man cannot be a surgeon. For keeping the trim gardens full of choice flowers without a weed to speck them; for frightening away little boys, who look wistfully at the said flowers through the railings; for rushing out at the geese that occasionally venture into the gardens if the gates are left open; for deciding all questions of literature and politics without troubling themselves with unnecessary reasons or arguments; for obtaining clear and correct knowledge of everybody's affairs in the parish; for keeping their neat maid-servants in admirable order; for kindness (somewhat dictatorial) to the poor, and real tender good offices to each other whenever they are in distress, the ladies of Cranford are quite sufficient. 'A man,' as one of them observed to me once, 'is *so* in the way in the house!' Although the ladies of Cranford know all each other's proceedings, they are exceedingly indifferent to each other's opinions. Indeed, as each has her own individuality, not to say eccentricity, pretty strongly developed, nothing is so easy as verbal retaliation; but somehow goodwill reigns among them to a considerable degree.

The Cranford ladies have only an occasional little quarrel, spirted out in a few peppery words and angry jerks of the head; just enough to prevent the even tenor of their lives from becoming too flat. Their dress is very independent of fashion; as they observe, 'What does it signify how we dress here at Cranford, where everybody knows us?' And if they go from home, their reason is equally cogent: 'What does it signify how we dress here, where nobody knows us?' The materials of their clothes are, in general, good and plain, and most of them are nearly as scrupulous as Miss Tyler, of cleanly memory; but I will answer for it, the last gigot, the last tight and scanty petticoat in wear in England, was seen in Cranford – and seen without a smile.

I can testify to a magnificent family red silk umbrella, under which a gentle little spinster, left alone of many brothers and sisters, used to patter to church on rainy days. Have you any red silk umbrellas in London? We had a tradition of the first that had ever been seen in Cranford; and the little boys mobbed it, and called it 'a stick in petticoats.' It might have been the very red silk one I have described, held by a strong father over a troop of little ones; the poor little lady – the survivor of all – could scarcely carry it.

Then there were rules and regulations for visiting and calls; and they were announced to any young people, who might be staying in the town, with all the solemnity with which the old Manx laws were read once a year on the Tinwald Mount.

'Our friends have sent to inquire how you are after your journey to-night, my dear' (fifteen miles, in a gentleman's carriage); 'they will give you some rest to-morrow, but the next day, I have no doubt, they will call; so be at liberty after twelve; – from twelve to three are our calling-hours.'

Then, after they had called,

'It is the third day; I dare say your mamma has told you, my dear, never to let more than three days elapse between receiving a call and returning it; and also, that you are never to stay longer than a quarter of an hour.'

'But am I to look at my watch? How am I to find out when a quarter of an hour has passed?'

'You must keep thinking about the time, my dear, and not allow yourself to forget it in conversation.'

As everybody had this rule in their minds, whether they received or paid a call, of course no absorbing subject was ever spoken about. We kept ourselves to short sentences of small talk, and were punctual to our time.

I imagine that a few of the gentlefolks of Cranford were poor, and had some difficulty in making both ends meet; but they were like the Spartans, and concealed their smart under a smiling face. We none of us spoke of money, because that subject savoured of commerce and trade, and though some might be poor, we were all aristocratic. The Cranfordians had that kindly *esprit de corps* which made them overlook all deficiencies in success when some among them tried to conceal their poverty. When Mrs Forrester, for instance, gave a party in her baby-house of a dwelling, and the little maiden disturbed the ladies on the sofa by a request that she might get the tea-tray out from underneath, every one took this novel proceeding as the most natural thing in the world; and talked on about household forms and ceremonies, as if we all believed that our hostess had a regular servants' hall, second table, with housekeeper and steward, instead of the one little charity-school maiden, whose short ruddy arms could never have been strong enough to carry the tray upstairs, if she had not been assisted in private by her mistress, who now sat in state, pretending not to know what cakes were sent up, though she knew, and we knew, and she knew that we knew, and we knew that she knew that we knew, she had been busy all the morning making tea-bread and sponge-cakes.

There were one or two consequences arising from this general but unacknowledged poverty, and this very much acknowledged gentility, which were not amiss, and which might be introduced into many circles of society to their great improvement. For instance, the inhabitants of Cranford kept early hours, and clattered home in their pattens, under the guidance of a lantern-bearer, about nine o'clock at night; and the whole town was abed and asleep by half-past ten. Moreover, it was considered 'vulgar' (a tremendous word in Cranford) to give anything expensive, in the way of eatable or drinkable, at the evening entertainments. Wafer bread-and-butter and sponge-biscuits were all that the Honourable Mrs Jamieson gave; and she was sister-in-law to the late Earl of Glenmire, although she did practise such 'elegant economy.'

'Elegant economy!' How naturally one falls back into the phraseology of Cranford! There, economy was always 'elegant,' and money-spending always 'vulgar and ostentatious;' a sort of sour-grapeism, which made us very peaceful and satisfied. I never shall forget the dismay felt when a certain Captain Brown came to live at Cranford, and openly spoke about his being poor – not in a whisper to an intimate friend, the doors and windows being previously closed; but, in the public street! in a loud military voice! alleging his poverty as a reason for not taking a particular house. The ladies of Cranford were already rather moaning over the invasion of their territories by a man and a gentleman. He was a half-pay Captain, and had obtained some situation on a neighbouring railroad, which had been vehemently petitioned against by the little town; and if, in addition to his masculine gender, and his connection with the obnoxious railroad, he was so brazen as to talk of being poor – why! then, indeed, he must be sent to Coventry. Death was as true and as common as poverty; yet people never spoke about that, loud out in the streets. It was a word not to be mentioned to ears polite. We had tacitly agreed to ignore that any with whom we associated on terms of visiting equality could ever be prevented by poverty from doing anything that they wished. If we walked to or from a party, it was because the night was *so* fine, or the air *so* refreshing; not because sedan-chairs were expensive. If we wore prints, instead of summer silks, it was because we preferred a washing material; and so on, till we blinded ourselves to the vulgar fact, that we were, all of us, people of very moderate means. Of course, then, we did not know what to make of a man who could speak of poverty as if it was not a disgrace. Yet, somehow, Captain Brown made himself respected in Cranford, and was called upon, in spite of all resolutions to the contrary. I was surprised to hear his opinions quoted as authority, at a visit which I paid to Cranford, about a year after he had settled in the town. My own friends had been among the bitterest opponents of any proposal to visit the Captain and his daughters, only twelve months before; and now he was even admitted in the tabooed hours before twelve. True, it was to discover the cause of a smoking chimney, before the fire was lighted; but still Captain Brown walked up-stairs, nothing daunted, spoke in a voice too large for the room, and joked quite in the way of a tame man, about the house. He had been blind to all the small slights, and omissions of trivial ceremonies, with which he had been received. He had been friendly, though the Cranford ladies had been cool; he had answered small sarcastic compliments in good faith; and with his manly frankness had overpowered all the shrinking which met him as a man who was not ashamed to be poor. And, at last, his excellent masculine common sense, and his facility in devising expedients to overcome domestic dilemmas, had gained him an extraordinary place as authority among the Cranford ladies. He, himself, went on in his course, as unaware of his popularity, as he had been of the reverse; and I am sure he was startled one day, when he found his advice so highly esteemed, as to make some counsel which he had given in jest, be taken in sober, serious earnest.

It was on this subject; – an old lady had an Alderney cow, which she looked upon as a daughter. You could not pay the short quarter of an hour call, without being told of the wonderful milk or wonderful intelligence of this animal. The whole town knew and kindly regarded Miss Betsy Barker's Alderney; therefore great was the sympathy and regret when, in an unguarded moment, the poor cow tumbled into a lime-pit. She moaned so loudly that she was soon heard, and rescued; but meanwhile the poor beast had lost most of her hair, and came out looking naked, cold, and miserable, in a bare skin. Everybody pitied the animal, though a few could not restrain their smiles at her droll appearance. Miss Betsy Barker absolutely cried with sorrow and dismay; and it was said she thought of trying a bath of oil. This remedy, perhaps, was recommended by some one of the number whose advice she asked; but the proposal, if ever it was made, was knocked on the head by Captain Brown's decided 'Get her a flannel waistcoat and flannel drawers, ma'am, if you wish to keep her alive. But my advice is, kill the poor creature at once.'

Miss Betsy Barker dried her eyes, and thanked the Captain heartily; she set to work, and by-and-by all the town turned out to see the Alderney meekly going to her pasture, clad in dark grey flannel. I have watched her myself many a time. Do you ever see cows dressed in grey flannel in London?

Captain Brown had taken a small house on the outskirts of the town, where he lived with his two daughters. He must have been upwards of sixty at the time of the first visit I paid to Cranford, after I had left it as a residence. But he had a wiry, well-trained, elastic figure; a stiff military throw-back of his head, and a springing step, which made him appear much younger than he was. His eldest daughter looked almost as old as himself, and betrayed the fact that his real, was more than his apparent, age. Miss Brown must have been forty; she had a sickly, pained, careworn expression on her face, and looked as if the gaiety of youth had long faded out of sight. Even when young she must have been plain and hard-featured. Miss Jessie Brown was ten years younger than her sister, and twenty shades prettier. Her face

I wondered what the Cranford ladies did with Captain Brown at their parties. We had often rejoiced, in former days, that there was no gentleman to be attended to, and to find conversation for, at the card-parties. We had congratulated ourselves upon the snugness of the evenings; and, in our love for gentility, and distaste of mankind, we had almost persuaded ourselves that to be a man was to be 'vulgar;' so that when I found my friend and hostess, Miss Jenkyns, was going to have a party in my honour, and that Captain and the Miss Browns were invited, I wondered much what would be the course of the evening. Card-tables, with green-baize tops, were set out by daylight, just as usual; it was the third week in November, so the evenings closed in about four. Candles, and clean packs of cards were arranged on each table. The fire was made up; the neat maid-servant had received her last directions; and there we stood dressed in our best, each with a candle-lighter in our hands, ready to dart at the candles as soon as the first knock came. Parties in Cranford were solemn festivities, making the ladies feel gravely elated, as they sat together in their best dresses. As soon as three had arrived, we sat down to 'Preference,' I being the unlucky fourth. The next four comers were set down immediately to another table; and presently the tea-trays, which I had seen set out in the store-room as I passed in the morning, were placed each on the middle of a card-table. The china was delicate egg-shell; the old-fashioned silver glittered with polishing; but the eatables were of the slightest description. While the trays were yet on the table, Captain and the Miss Browns came in; and I could see, that somehow or other the Captain was a favourite with all the ladies present. Ruffled brows were smoothed, sharp voices lowered at his approach. Miss Brown looked ill, and depressed almost to gloom. Miss Jessie smiled as usual, and seemed nearly as popular as her father. He immediately and quietly assumed the man's place in the room; attended to every one's wants, lessened the pretty maid-servant's labour by waiting on empty cups, and bread-and-butterless ladies; and yet did it all in so easy and dignified a manner, and so much as if it were a matter of course for the strong to attend to the weak, that he was a true man throughout. He played for three-penny points with as grave an interest as if they had been pounds; and yet, in all his attention to strangers, he had an eye on his suffering daughter; for suffering I was sure she was, though to many eyes she might only appear to be irritable. Miss Jessie could not play cards; but she talked to the sitters-out, who, before her coming, had been rather inclined to be cross. She sang, too, to an old cracked piano, which I think had been a spinet in its youth. Miss Jessie sang 'Jock of Hazeldean' a little out of tune; but we were none of us musical, though Miss Jenkyns beat time, out of time, by way of appearing to be so.

It was very good of Miss Jenkyns to do this; for I had seen that, a little before, she had been a good deal annoyed by Miss Jessie Brown's unguarded admission (*à propos* of Shetland wool) that she had an uncle, her mother's brother, who was a shopkeeper in Edinburgh. Miss Jenkyns tried to drown this confession by a terrible cough – for the Honourable Mrs Jamieson was sitting at the card-table nearest Miss Jessie, and what would she say or think, if she found out she was in the same room with a shopkeeper's niece! But Miss Jessie Brown (who had no tact, as we all agreed the next morning) *would* repeat the information, and assure Miss Pole she could easily get her the identical Shetland wool required, 'through my uncle, who has the best assortment of Shetland goods of any one in Edinbro'.' It was to take the taste of this out of our mouths, and the sound of this out of our ears, that Miss Jenkyns proposed music; so I say again, it was very good of her to beat time to the song.

When the trays reappeared with biscuits and wine, punctually at a quarter to nine, there was conversation; comparing of cards, and talking over tricks; but, by-and-by, Captain Brown sported a bit of literature.

'Have you seen any numbers of "The Pickwick Papers"?' said he. (They were then publishing in parts.) 'Capital thing!'

Now, Miss Jenkyns was daughter of a deceased rector of Cranford; and, on the strength of a number of manuscript sermons, and a pretty good library of divinity, considered herself literary, and looked upon any conversation about books as a challenge to her. So she answered and said, 'Yes, she had seen them; indeed, she might say she had read them.'

'And what do you think of them?' exclaimed Captain Brown. 'Aren't they famously good?'

So urged, Miss Jenkyns could not but speak.

'I must say, I don't think they are by any means equal to Dr Johnson. Still, perhaps, the author is young. Let him persevere, and who knows what he may become if he will take the great Doctor for his model.' This was evidently too much for Captain Brown to take placidly; and I saw the words on the tip of his tongue before Miss Jenkyns had finished her sentence.

'It is quite a different sort of thing, my dear madam,' he began.

'I am quite aware of that,' returned she. 'And I make allowances, Captain Brown.'

'Just allow me to read you a scene out of this month's number,' pleaded he. 'I had it only this morning, and I don't think the company can have read it yet.'

'As you please,' said she, settling herself with an air of resignation. He read the account of the 'swarry' which Sam Weller gave at Bath. Some of us laughed heartily. *I* did not dare, because I was staying in the house. Miss Jenkyns sat in patient gravity. When it was ended, she turned to me, and said with mild dignity:

'Fetch me "Rasselas," my dear, out of the book-room.'

When I brought it to her, she turned to Captain Brown:

'Now allow *me* to read you a scene, and then the present company can judge between your favourite, Mr Boz, and Dr Johnson.'

She read one of the conversations between Rasselas and Imlac, in a high-pitched majestic voice; and when she had ended, she said, 'I imagine I am now justified in my preference of Dr

Johnson, as a writer of fiction.' The Captain screwed his lips up, and drummed on the table, but he did not speak. She thought she would give a finishing blow or two.

'I consider it vulgar, and below the dignity of literature, to publish in numbers.'

'How was the "Rambler" published, ma'am?' asked Captain Brown, in a low voice; which I think Miss Jenkyns could not have heard.

'Dr Johnson's style is a model for young beginners. My father recommended it to me when I began to write letters. – I have formed my own style upon it; I recommend it to your favourite.'

'I should be very sorry for him to exchange his style for any such pompous writing,' said Captain Brown.

Miss Jenkyns felt this as a personal affront, in a way of which the Captain had not dreamed. Epistolary writing, she and her friends considered as her *forte*. Many a copy of many a letter have I seen written and corrected on the slate, before she 'seized the half-hour just previous to post-time to assure' her friends of this or of that; and Dr Johnson was, as she said, her model in these compositions. She drew herself up with dignity, and only replied to Captain Brown's last remark by saying, with marked emphasis on every syllable, 'I prefer Dr Johnson to Mr Boz.'

It is said – I won't vouch for the fact – that Captain Brown was heard to say, *sotto voce,* 'D—n Dr Johnson!' If he did, he was penitent afterwards, as he showed by going to stand near Miss Jenkyns's arm-chair, and endeavouring to beguile her into conversation on some more pleasing subject. But she was inexorable. The next day, she made the remark I have mentioned, about Miss Jessie's dimples.

Chapter II

THE CAPTAIN

It was impossible to live a month at Cranford, and not know the daily habits of each resident; and long before my visit was ended, I knew much concerning the whole Brown trio. There was nothing new to be discovered respecting their poverty; for they had spoken simply and openly about that from the very first. They made no mystery of the necessity for their being economical. All that remained to be discovered was the Captain's infinite kindness of heart, and the various modes in which, unconsciously to himself, he manifested it. Some little anecdotes were talked about for some time after they occurred. As we did not read much, and as all the ladies were pretty well suited with servants, there was a dearth of subjects for conversation. We therefore discussed the circumstance of the Captain taking a poor old woman's dinner out of her hands, one very slippery Sunday. He had met her returning from the bakehouse as he came from church, and noticed her precarious footing; and, with the grave dignity with which he did everything, he relieved her of her burden, and steered along the street by her side, carrying her baked mutton and potatoes safely home. This was thought very eccentric; and it was rather expected that he would pay a round of calls, on the Monday morning, to explain and apologize to the Cranford sense of propriety: but he did no such thing; and then it was decided that he was ashamed, and was keeping out of sight. In a kindly pity for him, we began to say – 'After all, the Sunday morning's occurrence showed great goodness of heart;' and it was resolved that he should be comforted on his next appearance amongst us; but, lo! he came down upon us, untouched by any sense of shame, speaking loud and bass as ever, his head thrown back, his wig as jaunty and well-curled as usual, and we were obliged to conclude he had forgotten all about Sunday.

Miss Pole and Miss Jessie Brown had set up a kind of intimacy, on the strength of the Shetland wool and the new knitting stitches; so it happened that when I went to visit Miss Pole, I saw more of the Browns than I had done while staying with Miss Jenkyns; who had never got over what she called Captain Brown's disparaging remarks upon Dr Johnson, as a writer of light and agreeable fiction. I found that Miss Brown was seriously ill of some lingering, incurable complaint, the pain occasioned by which gave the uneasy expression to her face that I had taken for unmitigated crossness. Cross, too, she was at times, when the nervous irritability occasioned by her disease became past endurance. Miss Jessie bore with her at these times even more patiently than she did with the bitter self-upbraidings by which they were invariably succeeded. Miss Brown used to accuse herself, not merely of hasty and irritable temper; but also of being the cause why her father and sister were obliged to pinch, in order to allow her the small luxuries which were necessaries in her condition. She would so fain have made sacrifices for them and have lightened their cares, that the original generosity of her disposition added acerbity to her temper. All this was borne by Miss Jessie and her father with more than placidity – with absolute tenderness. I forgave Miss Jessie her singing out of tune, and her juvenility of dress, when I saw her at home. I came to perceive that Captain Brown's dark Brutus wig and padded coat (alas! too often threadbare) were remnants of the military smartness of his youth, which he now wore unconsciously. He was a man of infinite resources, gained in his barrack experience. As he confessed, no one could black his boots to please him, except himself; but, indeed, he was not above saving the little maid-servant's labours in every way – knowing, most likely, that his daughter's illness made the place a hard one.

He endeavoured to make peace with Miss Jenkyns soon after the memorable dispute I have named, by a present of a wooden fire-shovel (his own making), having heard her say how much the grating of an iron one annoyed her. She received the present with cool gratitude, and thanked him formally. When he was gone, she bade me put it away in the lumber-room; feeling, probably, that no present from a man who preferred Mr Boz to Dr Johnson could be less jarring than an iron fire-shovel.

Such was the state of things when I left Cranford and went to Drumble. I had, however, several correspondents who kept me *au fait* as to the proceedings of the dear little town. There was Miss Pole, who was becoming as much absorbed in crochet as she had been once in knitting; and the burden of whose letter was something like, 'But don't you forget the white worsted at Flint's,' of the old song; for, at the end of every sentence of news, came a fresh direction as to some crochet commission which I was to execute for her. Miss Matilda Jenkyns (who did not mind being called Miss Matty, when Miss Jenkyns was not by) wrote nice, kind, rambling letters; now and then venturing into an opinion of her own; but suddenly pulling herself up, and either begging me not to name what she had said, as Deborah thought differently, and *she* knew; or else putting in a postscript to the effect that, since writing the above, she had been talking over the subject with Deborah, and was quite convinced that, &c. – (here, probably, followed a recantation of every opinion she had given in the letter). Then came Miss Jenkyns – Deborah, as she liked Miss Matty to call her; her father having once said that the Hebrew name ought to be so pronounced. I secretly think she took the Hebrew prophetess for a model in character; and, indeed, she was not unlike the stern prophetess in some ways; making allowance, of course, for modern customs and difference in dress. Miss Jenkyns wore a cravat, and a little bonnet like a jockey-cap, and altogether had the appearance of a strong-minded woman; although she would have despised the modern idea of women being equal to men. Equal, indeed! she knew they were superior. – But to return to her letters. Everything in them was stately and grand, like herself. I have been looking them over (dear Miss Jenkyns, how I honoured her!), and I will give an extract, more especially because it relates to our friend Captain Brown:

'The Honourable Mrs Jamieson has only just quitted me; and, in the course of conversation, she communicated to me the intelligence, that she had yesterday received a call from her revered husband's quondam friend, Lord Mauleverer. You will not easily conjecture what brought his lordship within the precincts of our little town. It was to see Captain Brown, with whom, it appears, his lordship was acquainted in the "plumed wars," and who had the privilege of averting destruction from his lordship's head, when some great peril was impending over it, off the misnomered Cape of Good Hope. You know our friend the Honourable Mrs Jamieson's deficiency in the spirit of innocent curiosity; and you will therefore not be so much surprised when I tell you she was quite unable to disclose to me the exact nature of the peril in question. I was anxious, I confess, to ascertain in what manner Captain Brown, with his limited establishment, could receive so distinguished a guest; and I discovered that his lordship retired to rest, and, let us hope, to refreshing slumbers, at the Angel Hotel; but shared the Brunonian meals during the two days that he honoured Cranford with his august presence. Mrs Johnson, our civil butcher's wife, informs me that Miss Jessie purchased a leg of lamb; but, besides this, I can hear of no preparation whatever to give a suitable reception to so distinguished a visitor. Perhaps they entertained him with "the feast of reason and the flow of soul;" and to us, who are acquainted with Captain Brown's sad want of relish for "the pure wells of English undefiled," it may be matter for congratulation, that he has had the opportunity of improving his taste by holding converse with an elegant and refined member of the British aristocracy. But from some mundane failings who is altogether free?'

Miss Pole and Miss Matty wrote to me by the same post. Such a piece of news as Lord Mauleverer's visit was not to be lost on the Cranford letter-writers: they made the most of it. Miss Matty humbly apologized for writing at the same time as her sister, who was so much more capable than she to describe the honour done to Cranford; but, in spite of a little bad spelling, Miss Matty's account gave me the best idea of the commotion occasioned by his lordship's visit, after it had occurred; for, except the people at the Angel, the Browns, Mrs Jamieson, and a little lad his lordship had sworn at for driving a dirty hoop against the aristocratic legs, I could not hear of any one with whom his lordship had held conversation.

My next visit to Cranford was in the summer. There had been neither births, deaths, nor marriages since I was there last. Everybody lived in the same house, and wore pretty nearly the same well-preserved, old-fashioned clothes. The greatest event was, that the Miss Jenkynses had purchased a new carpet for the drawing-room. Oh the busy work Miss Matty and I had in chasing the sunbeams, as they fell in an afternoon right down on this carpet through the blindless window! We spread newspapers over the places, and sat down to our book or our work; and, lo! in a quarter of an hour the sun had moved, and was blazing away on a fresh spot; and down again we went on our knees to alter the position of the newspapers. We were very busy, too, one whole morning, before Miss Jenkyns gave her party, in following her directions, and in cutting out and stitching together pieces of newspaper, so as to form little paths to every chair, set for the expected visitors, lest their shoes might dirty or defile the purity of the carpet. Do you make paper paths for every guest to walk upon in London?

Captain Brown and Miss Jenkyns were not very cordial to each other. The literary dispute, of which I had seen the beginning, was a 'raw,' the slightest touch on which made them wince. It was the only difference of opinion they had ever had; but that difference was enough. Miss Jenkyns could not refrain from talking *at* Captain Brown; and though he did not reply, he drummed with his fingers; which action she felt and resented as very disparaging to Dr Johnson. He was rather ostentatious in his preference of the writings of Mr Boz; would walk through the street so absorbed in them, that he all but ran against Miss Jenkyns; and though his apologies were earnest and sincere, and though he did not, in fact, do more than startle her and himself, she owned to me she had rather he had knocked her down, if he had only been reading a higher style of literature. The poor, brave Captain! he looked older, and more worn, and his clothes were very threadbare. But he seemed as bright and cheerful as ever, unless he was asked about his daughter's health.

'She suffers a great deal, and she must suffer more; we do what we can to alleviate her pain – God's will be done!' He took off his hat at these last words. I found, from Miss Matty, that everything had been done, in fact. A medical man, of high repute in that country neighbourhood, had been sent for, and every injunction he had given was attended to, regardless of expense. Miss Matty was sure they denied themselves many things in order to make the invalid comfortable; but they never spoke about it; and as for Miss Jessie! 'I really think she's an angel,' said poor Miss Matty, quite overcome. 'To see her way of bearing with Miss Brown's crossness, and the bright face she puts on after she's been sitting up a whole night and scolded above half of it, is quite beautiful. Yet she looks as neat and as ready to welcome the Captain at breakfast-time, as if she had been asleep in the Queen's bed all night. My dear! you could never laugh at her prim little curls or her pink bows again, if you saw her as I have done.' I could only feel very penitent, and greet Miss Jessie with double respect when I met her next. She looked faded and pinched; and her lips began to quiver, as if she was very weak, when she spoke of her sister. But she brightened, and sent back the tears that were glittering in her pretty eyes, as she said:

'But, to be sure, what a town Cranford is for kindness! I don't suppose any one has a better dinner than usual cooked, but the best part of all comes in a little covered basin for my sister. The poor people will leave their earliest vegetables at our door for her.

They speak short and gruff, as if they were ashamed of it; but I am sure it often goes to my heart to see their thoughtfulness.' The tears now came back and overflowed; but after a minute or two, she began to scold herself, and ended by going away, the same cheerful Miss Jessie as ever.

'But why does not this Lord Mauleverer do something for the man who saved his life?' said I.

'Why, you see, unless Captain Brown has some reason for it, he never speaks about being poor; and he walked along by his lordship, looking as happy and cheerful as a prince; and as they never called attention to their dinner by apologies, and as Miss Brown was better that day, and all seemed bright, I dare say his lordship never knew how much care there was in the background. He did send game in the winter pretty often, but now he is gone abroad.'

I had often occasion to notice the use that was made of fragments and small opportunities in Cranford; the rose-leaves that were gathered ere they fell, to make into a pot-pourri for some one who had no garden; the little bundles of lavender-flowers sent to strew the drawers of some town-dweller, or to burn in the chamber of some invalid. Things that many would despise, and actions which it seemed scarcely worth while to perform, were all attended to in Cranford. Miss Jenkyns stuck an apple full of cloves, to be heated and smell pleasantly in Miss Brown's room; and as she put in each clove, she uttered a Johnsonian sentence. Indeed, she never could think of the Browns without talking Johnson; and, as they were seldom absent from her thoughts just then, I heard many a rolling three-piled sentence.

Captain Brown called one day to thank Miss Jenkyns for many little kindnesses, which I did not know until then that she had rendered. He had suddenly become like an old man; his deep bass voice had a quavering in it; his eyes looked dim, and the lines on his face were deep. He did not – could not – speak cheerfully of his daughter's state, but he talked with manly pious resignation, and not much. Twice over he said, 'What Jessie has been to us, God only knows!' and after the second time, he got up hastily, shook hands all round without speaking, and left the room.

That afternoon we perceived little groups in the street, all listening with faces aghast to some tale or other. Miss Jenkyns wondered what could be the matter, for some time before she took the undignified step of sending Jenny out to inquire.

Jenny came back with a white face of terror. 'Oh, ma'am! oh, Miss Jenkyns, ma'am! Captain Brown is killed by them nasty cruel railroads!' and she burst into tears. She, along with many others, had experienced the poor Captain's kindness.

'How? – where – where? Good God! Jenny, don't waste time in crying, but tell us something.' Miss Matty rushed out into the street at once, and collared the man who was telling the tale.

'Come in – come to my sister at once – Miss Jenkyns, the rector's daughter. Oh, man, man! say it is not true,' – she cried, as she brought the affrighted carter, sleeking down his hair, into the drawing-room, where he stood with his wet boots on the new carpet, and no one regarded it.

'Please, mum, it is true. I seed it myself,' and he shuddered at the recollection. 'The Captain was a-reading some new book as he was deep in, a-waiting for the down train; and there was a little lass as wanted to come to its mammy, and gave its sister the slip, and came toddling across the line. And he looked up sudden, at the sound of the train coming, and seed the child, and he darted on the line and cotched it up, and his foot slipped, and the train came over him in no time. Oh Lord, Lord! Mum, it's quite true – and they've come over to tell his daughters. The child's safe, though, with only a bang on its shoulder, as he threw it to its mammy. Poor Captain would be glad of that, mum, wouldn't he? God bless him!' The great rough carter puckered up his manly face, and turned away to hide his tears. I turned to Miss Jenkyns. She looked very ill, as if she were going to faint, and signed to me to open the window.

'Matilda, bring me my bonnet. I must go to those girls. God pardon me, if ever I have spoken contemptuously to the Captain!'

Miss Jenkyns arrayed herself to go out, telling Miss Matilda to give the man a glass of wine. While she was away, Miss Matty and I huddled over the fire, talking in a low and awestruck voice. I know we cried quietly all the time.

Miss Jenkyns came home in a silent mood, and we durst not ask her many questions. She told us that Miss Jessie had fainted, and that she and Miss Pole had had some difficulty in bringing her round: but that, as soon as she recovered, she begged one of them to go and sit with her sister.

'Mr Hoggins says she cannot live many days, and she shall be spared this shock,' said Miss Jessie, shivering with feelings to which she dared not give way.

'But how can you manage, my dear?' asked Miss Jenkyns; 'you cannot bear up, she must see your tears.'

'God will help me – I will not give way – she was asleep when the news came; she may be asleep yet. She would be so utterly miserable, not merely at my father's death, but to think of what would become of me; she is so good to me.' She looked up earnestly in their faces with her soft true eyes, and Miss Pole told Miss Jenkyns afterwards she could hardly bear it, knowing, as she did, how Miss Brown treated her sister.

However, it was settled according to Miss Jessie's wish. Miss Brown was to be told her father had been summoned to take a short journey on railway business. They had managed it in some way – Miss Jenkyns could not exactly say how. Miss Pole was to stop with Miss Jessie. Mrs Jamieson had sent to inquire. And this was all we heard that night; and a sorrowful night it was. The next day a full account of the fatal accident was in the county paper, which Miss Jenkyns took in. Her eyes were very weak, she said, and she asked me to read it. When I came to the 'gallant gentleman was deeply engaged in the perusal of a number of "Pickwick," which he had just received,' Miss Jenkyns shook her head long and solemnly, and then sighed out, 'Poor, dear, infatuated man!'

The corpse was to be taken from the station to the parish church, there to be interred. Miss Jessie had set her heart on following it to the grave; and no dissuasives could alter her resolve. Her restraint upon herself made her almost obstinate; she resisted all Miss Pole's entreaties, and Miss Jenkyns's advice. At last Miss Jenkyns gave up the point; and after a silence, which I feared portended some deep displeasure against Miss Jessie, Miss Jenkyns said she should accompany the latter to the funeral.

'It is not fit for you to go alone. It would be against both propriety and humanity were I to allow it.'

Miss Jessie seemed as if she did not half like this arrangement; but her obstinacy, if she had any, had been exhausted in her determination to go to the interment. She longed, poor thing! I have no doubt, to cry alone over the grave of the dear father to whom she had been all in all; and to give way, for one little half-hour, uninterrupted by sympathy, and unobserved by friendship. But it was not to be. That afternoon Miss Jenkyns sent out for a yard of black crape, and employed herself busily in trimming the little black silk bonnet I have spoken about. When it was finished she put it on, and looked at us for approbation – admiration she despised. I was full of sorrow, but, by one of those whimsical thoughts which come unbidden into our heads, in times of deepest grief, I no sooner saw the bonnet than I was reminded of a helmet; and in that hybrid bonnet, half-helmet, half-jockey cap, did Miss Jenkyns attend Captain Brown's funeral; and, I believe, supported Miss Jessie with a tender indulgent firmness which was invaluable, allowing her to weep her passionate fill before they left.

Miss Pole, Miss Matty, and I, meanwhile, attended to Miss Brown: and hard work we found it to relieve her querulous and never-ending complaints. But if we were so weary and dispirited, what must Miss Jessie have been! Yet she came back almost calm, as if she had gained a new strength. She put off her mourning dress, and came in, looking pale and gentle; thanking us each with a soft long pressure of the hand. She could even smile – a faint, sweet, wintry smile – as if to reassure us of her power to endure; but her look made our eyes fill suddenly with tears, more than if she had cried outright.

It was settled that Miss Pole was to remain with her all the watching livelong night; and that Miss Matty and I were to return in the morning to relieve them, and give Miss Jessie the opportunity for a few hours of sleep. But when the morning came, Miss Jenkyns appeared at the breakfast table, equipped in her helmet bonnet, and ordered Miss Matty to stay at home, as she meant to go and help to nurse. She was evidently in a state of great friendly excitement, which she showed by eating her breakfast standing, and scolding the household all round.

No nursing – no energetic, strong-minded woman could help Miss Brown now. There was that in the room as we entered, which was stronger than us all, and made us shrink into solemn awestruck helplessness. Miss Brown was dying. We hardly knew her voice, it was so devoid of the complaining tone we had always associated with it. Miss Jessie told me afterwards that it, and her face too, were just what they had been formerly, when her mother's death left her the young anxious head of the family, of whom only Miss Jessie survived.

She was conscious of her sister's presence, though not, I think, of ours. We stood a little behind the curtain: Miss Jessie knelt with her face near her sister's, in order to catch the last soft awful whispers.

'Oh, Jessie! Jessie! How selfish I have been! God forgive me for letting you sacrifice yourself for me as you did. I have so loved you – and yet I have thought only of myself. God forgive me!'

'Hush, love! hush!' said Miss Jessie, sobbing.

'And my father! my dear, dear father! I will not complain now, if God will give me strength to be patient. But, oh, Jessie! tell my father how I longed and yearned to see him at last, and to ask his forgiveness. He can never know now how I loved him – oh! if I might but tell him, before I die! What a life of sorrow his has been, and I have done so little to cheer him!'

A light came into Miss Jessie's face. 'Would it comfort you, dearest, to think that he does know – would it comfort you, love, to know that his cares, his sorrows – ' Her voice quivered, but she steadied it into calmness – 'Mary! he has gone before you to the place where the weary are at rest. He knows now how you loved him.'

A strange look, which was not distress, came over Miss Brown's face. She did not speak for some time, but then we saw her lips form the words, rather than heard the sound – 'Father, mother, Harry, Archy!' – then, as if it was a new idea throwing a filmy shadow over her darkening mind – 'But you will be alone – Jessie!'

Miss Jessie had been feeling this all during the silence, I think; for the tears rolled down her cheeks like rain, at these words; and she could not answer at first. Then she put her hands together tight, and lifted them up, and said – but not to us –

'Though He slay me, yet will I trust in Him.'

In a few moments more Miss Brown lay calm and still; never to sorrow or murmur more.

After this second funeral, Miss Jenkyns insisted that Miss Jessie should come to stay with her, rather than go back to the desolate house; which, in fact, we learned from Miss Jessie, must now be given up, as she had not wherewithal to maintain it. She had something above twenty pounds a-year, besides the interest of the money for which the furniture would sell; but she could not live upon that: and so we talked over her qualifications for earning money.

'I can sew neatly,' said she, 'and I like nursing. I think, too, I could manage a house, if any one would try me as housekeeper; or I would go into a shop, as saleswoman, if they would have patience with me at first.'

Miss Jenkyns declared, in an angry voice, that she should do no such thing; and talked to herself about 'some people having no idea of their rank as a Captain's daughter,' nearly an hour afterwards, when she brought Miss Jessie up a basin of delicately-made arrowroot, and stood over her like a dragoon until the last spoonful was finished: then she disappeared. Miss Jessie began to tell me some more of the plans which had suggested themselves to her, and insensibly fell into talking of the days that were past and gone, and interested me so much, I neither knew nor heeded how time passed. We were both startled when Miss Jenkyns reappeared, and caught us crying. I was afraid lest she would be displeased, as she often said that crying hindered digestion, and I knew she wanted Miss Jessie to get strong; but, instead, she looked queer and excited, and fidgeted round us without saying anything. At last she spoke. 'I have been so much startled – no, I've not been at all startled – don't mind me, my dear Miss Jessie – I've been very much surprised – in fact, I've had a caller, whom you knew once, my dear Miss Jessie – '

Miss Jessie went very white, then flushed scarlet, and looked eagerly at Miss Jenkyns –

'A gentleman, my dear, who wants to know if you would see him.'

'Is it? – it is not – ' stammered out Miss Jessie – and got no farther.

'This is his card,' said Miss Jenkyns, giving it to Miss Jessie; and while her head was bent over it, Miss Jenkyns went through a series of winks and odd faces to me, and formed her lips into a long sentence, of which, of course, I could not understand a word.

'May he come up?' asked Miss Jenkyns at last.

'Oh, yes! certainly!' said Miss Jessie, as much as to say, this is your house, you may show any visitor where you like. She took up some knitting of Miss Matty's and began to be very busy, though I could see how she trembled all over.

Miss Jenkyns rang the bell, and told the servant who answered it to show Major Gordon up-stairs; and, presently, in walked a tall, fine, frank-looking man of forty, or upwards. He shook hands with Miss Jessie; but he could not see her eyes, she kept them so fixed on the ground. Miss Jenkyns asked me if I would come and help her to tie up the preserves in the store-room; and, though Miss Jessie plucked at my gown, and even looked up at me with begging eye, I durst not refuse to go where Miss Jenkyns asked. Instead of tying up preserves in the store-room, however, we went to talk in the dining-room; and there Miss Jenkyns told me what Major Gordon had told her; – how he had served in the same regiment with Captain Brown, and had become acquainted with Miss Jessie, then a sweet-looking, blooming girl of eighteen; how the acquaintance had grown into love, on his part, though it had been some years before he had spoken; how, on becoming possessed, through the will of an uncle, of a good estate in Scotland, he had offered, and been refused, though with so much agitation, and evident distress, that he was sure she was not indifferent to him; and how he had discovered that the obstacle was the fell disease which was, even then, too surely threatening her sister. She had mentioned that the surgeons foretold intense suffering; and there was no one but herself to nurse her poor Mary, or cheer and comfort her father during the time of illness. They had had long discussions; and, on her refusal to pledge herself to him as his wife, when all should be over, he had grown angry, and broken off entirely, and gone abroad, believing that she was a cold-hearted person, whom he would do well to forget. He had been travelling in the East, and was on his return home when, at Rome, he saw the account of Captain Brown's death in 'Galignani.'

Just then Miss Matty, who had been out all the morning, and had only lately returned to the house, burst in with a face of dismay and outraged propriety:

'Oh, goodness me!' she said. 'Deborah, there's a gentleman sitting in the drawing-room, with his arm round Miss Jessie's waist!' Miss Matty's eyes looked large with terror.

Miss Jenkyns snubbed her down in an instant:

'The most proper place in the world for his arm to be in. Go away, Matilda, and mind your own business.' This from her sister, who had hitherto been a model of feminine decorum, was a blow for poor Miss Matty, and with a double shock she left the room.

The last time I ever saw poor Miss Jenkyns was many years after this. Mrs Gordon had kept up a warm and affectionate intercourse with all at Cranford. Miss Jenkyns, Miss Matty, and Miss Pole had all been to visit her, and returned with wonderful accounts of her house, her husband, her dress, and her looks. For, with happiness, something of her early bloom returned; she had been a year or two younger than we had taken her for. Her eyes were always lovely, and, as Mrs Gordon, her dimples were not out of place. At the time to which I have referred, when I last saw Miss Jenkyns, that lady was old and feeble, and had lost something of her strong mind. Little Flora Gordon was staying with the Misses Jenkyns, and when I came in she was reading aloud to Miss Jenkyns, who lay feeble and changed on the sofa. Flora put down the 'Rambler' when I came in.

'Ah!' said Miss Jenkyns, 'you find me changed, my dear. I can't see as I used to do. If Flora were not here to read to me, I hardly know how I should get through the day. Did you ever read the "Rambler"? It's a wonderful book – wonderful! and the most improving book for Flora' – (which I dare say it would have been, if she could have read half the words without spelling, and could have understood the meaning of a third) – 'better than that strange old book, with the queer name, poor Captain Brown was killed for reading – that book by Mr Boz, you know – "Old Poz"; when I was a girl – but that's a long time ago – I acted Lucy in "Old Poz."' – She babbled on long enough for Flora to get a good long spell at the 'Christmas Carol,' which Miss Matty had left on the table.

Chapter III

A LOVE AFFAIR OF LONG AGO

I thought that probably my connexion with Cranford would cease after Miss Jenkyns's death; at least, that it would have to be kept up by correspondence, which bears much the same relation to personal intercourse that the books of dried plants I sometimes see ('Hortus Siccus,' I think they call the thing) do to the living and fresh flowers in the lanes and meadows. I was pleasantly surprised, therefore, by receiving a letter from Miss Pole (who had always come in for a supplementary week, after my annual visit to Miss Jenkyns) proposing that I should go and stay with her; and then, in a couple of days after my acceptance, came a note from Miss Matty, in which, in a rather circuitous and very humble manner, she told me how much pleasure I should confer, if I could spend a week or two with her, either before or after I had been at Miss Pole's; 'for,' she said, 'since my dear sister's death, I am well aware I have no attractions to offer; it is only to the kindness of my friends that I can owe their company.'

Of course, I promised to come to dear Miss Matty, as soon as I had ended my visit to Miss Pole; and the day after my arrival at Cranford, I went to see her, much wondering what the house would be like without Miss Jenkyns, and rather dreading the changed aspect of things. Miss Matty began to cry as soon as she saw me. She was evidently nervous from having anticipated my call. I comforted her as well as I could; and I found the best consolation I could give was the honest praise that came from my heart as I spoke of the deceased. Miss Matty slowly shook her head over each virtue as it was named and attributed to her sister; and at last she could not restrain the tears which had long been silently flowing, but hid her face behind her handkerchief, and sobbed aloud.

'Dear Miss Matty!' said I, taking her hand – for indeed I did not know in what way to tell her how sorry I was for her, left deserted in the world. She put down her handkerchief, and said:

'My dear, I'd rather you did not call me Matty. *She* did not like it; but I did many a thing she did not like, I'm afraid – and now she's gone! If you please, my love, will you call me Matilda?'

I promised faithfully, and began to practise the new name with Miss Pole that very day; and, by degrees, Miss Matilda's feeling on the subject was known through Cranford, and we all tried to drop the more familiar name, but with so little success that by and by we gave up the attempt.

My visit to Miss Pole was very quiet. Miss Jenkyns had so long taken the lead in Cranford, that, now she was gone, they hardly knew how to give a party. The Honourable Mrs Jamieson, to whom Miss Jenkyns herself had always yielded the post of honour, was fat and inert, and very much at the mercy of her old servants. If they chose that she should give a party, they reminded her of the necessity for so doing; if not, she let it alone. There was all the more time for me to hear old-world stories from Miss Pole, while she sat knitting, and I making my father's shirts. I always took a quantity of plain sewing to Cranford; for, as we did not read much, or walk much, I found it a capital time to get through my work. One of Miss Pole's stories related to a shadow of a love affair that was dimly perceived or suspected long years before.

Presently, the time arrived when I was to remove to Miss Matilda's house. I found her timid and anxious about the arrangements for my comfort. Many a time, while I was unpacking, did she come backwards and forwards to stir the fire, which burned all the worse for being so frequently poked.

'Have you drawers enough, dear?' asked she. 'I don't know exactly how my sister used to arrange them. She had capital methods. I am sure she would have trained a servant in a week to make a better fire than this, and Fanny has been with me four months.'

This subject of servants was a standing grievance, and I could not wonder much at it; for if gentlemen were scarce, and almost unheard of in the 'genteel society' of Cranford, they or their counterparts – handsome young men – abounded in the lower classes. The pretty neat servant-maids had their choice of desirable 'followers;' and their mistresses, without having the sort of mysterious dread of men and matrimony that Miss Matilda had, might well feel a little anxious, lest the heads of their comely maids should be turned by the joiner, or the butcher, or the gardener; who were obliged, by their callings, to come to the house; and who, as ill-luck would have it, were generally handsome and unmarried. Fanny's lovers, if she had any – and Miss Matilda suspected her of so many flirtations, that, if she had not been very pretty, I should have doubted her having one – were a constant anxiety to her mistress. She was forbidden, by the articles of her engagement, to have 'followers;' and though she had answered innocently enough, doubling up the hem of her apron as she spoke, 'Please, ma'am, I never had more than one at a time,' Miss Matty prohibited that one. But a vision of a man seemed to haunt the kitchen. Fanny assured me that it was all fancy; or else I should have said myself that I had seen a man's coat-tails whisk into the scullery once, when I went on an errand into the store-room at night; and another evening, when, our watches having stopped, I went to look at the clock, there was a very odd appearance, singularly like a young man squeezed up between the clock and the back of the open kitchen-door: and I thought Fanny snatched up the candle very hastily, so as to throw the shadow on the clock-face, while she very positively told me the time half an hour too early, as we found out afterwards by the church-clock. But I did not add to Miss Matty's anxieties by naming my suspicions, especially as Fanny said to me the next day, that it was such a queer kitchen for having odd shadows about it, she really was almost afraid to stay; 'for you know, miss,' she added, 'I don't see a creature from six o'clock tea, till Missus rings the bell for prayers at ten.'

However, it so fell out that Fanny had to leave; and Miss Matilda begged me to stay and 'settle her' with the new maid; to which I consented, after I had heard from my father that he did not want me at home. The new servant was a rough, honest-looking country girl, who had only lived in a farm place before; but I liked her looks when she came to be hired; and I promised Miss Matilda to put her in the ways of the house. The said ways were religiously such as Miss Matilda thought her sister would approve. Many a domestic rule and regulation had been a subject of plaintive whispered murmur to me, during Miss Jenkyns's life; but now that she was gone, I do not think that even I, who was a favourite, durst have suggested an alteration. To give an instance: we constantly adhered to the forms which were observed, at meal times, in 'my father, the Rector's house.' Accordingly, we had always wine and dessert; but the decanters were only filled when there was a party; and what remained was seldom touched, though we had two wine glasses apiece every day after dinner, until the next festive occasion arrived; when the state of the remainder wine was examined into, in a family council. The dregs were often given to the poor; but occasionally, when a good deal had been left at the last party (five months ago, it might be), it was added to some of a fresh bottle, brought up from the cellar. I fancy poor Captain Brown did not much like wine; for I noticed he never finished his first glass, and most military men take several. Then, as to our dessert, Miss Jenkyns used to gather currants and gooseberries for it herself, which I sometimes thought would have tasted better fresh from the trees; but then, as Miss Jenkyns observed, there would have been nothing for dessert in summer-time. As it was, we felt very genteel with our two glasses apiece, and a dish of gooseberries at the top, of currants and biscuits at the sides, and two decanters at the bottom. When oranges came in, a curious proceeding was gone through. Miss Jenkyns did not like to cut the fruit; for, as she observed, the juice all ran out, nobody knew where; sucking (only I think she used some more recondite word) was in fact the only way of enjoying oranges; but then there was the unpleasant association with a ceremony frequently gone through by little babies; and so, after dessert, in orange season, Miss Jenkyns and Miss Matty used to rise up, possess themselves each of an orange in silence, and withdraw to the privacy of their own rooms, to indulge in sucking oranges.

I had once or twice tried, on such occasions, to prevail on Miss Matty to stay; and had succeeded in her sister's lifetime. I held up a screen, and did not look, and, as she said, she tried not to make the noise very offensive; but now that she was left alone, she seemed quite horrified when I begged her to remain with me in the warm dining-parlour, and enjoy her orange as she liked best. And so it was in everything. Miss Jenkyns's rules were made more stringent than ever, because the framer of them was gone where there could be no appeal. In all things else Miss Matilda was meek and undecided to a fault. I have heard Fanny turn her round twenty times in a morning about dinner, just as the little hussy chose; and I sometimes fancied she worked on Miss Matilda's weakness in order to bewilder her, and to make her feel more in the power of her clever servant. I determined that I would not leave her till I had seen what sort of a person Martha was; and, if I found her trustworthy, I would tell her not to trouble her mistress with every little decision.

Martha was blunt and plain-spoken to a fault; otherwise she was a brisk, well-meaning, but very ignorant girl. She had not been with us a week before Miss Matilda and I were astounded one morning by the receipt of a letter from a cousin of hers, who had been twenty or thirty years in India, and who had lately, as we had seen by the 'Army List,' returned to England, bringing with him an invalid wife, who had never been introduced to her English relations. Major Jenkyns wrote to propose that he and his wife should spend a night at Cranford, on his way to Scotland – at the inn, if it did not suit Miss Matilda to receive them into her house; in which case they should hope to be with her as much as possible during the day. Of course, it *must* suit her, as she said; for all Cranford knew that she had her sister's bedroom at liberty; but I am sure she wished the Major had stopped in India and forgotten his cousins out and out.

'Oh! how must I manage?' asked she, helplessly. 'If Deborah had been alive, she would have known what to do with a gentleman-visitor. Must I put razors in his dressing-room? Dear! dear! and I've got none. Deborah would have had them. And slippers, and coat-brushes?' I suggested that probably he would bring all these things with him. 'And after dinner, how am I to know when to get up, and leave him to his wine? Deborah would have done it so well; she would have been quite in her element. Will he want coffee, do you think?' I undertook the management of the coffee, and told her I would instruct Martha in the art of waiting, in which it must be owned she was terribly deficient; and that I had no doubt Major and Mrs Jenkyns would understand the quiet mode in which a lady lived by herself in a country town. But she was sadly fluttered. I made her empty her decanters, and bring up two fresh bottles of wine. I wished I could have prevented her being present at my instructions to Martha; for she frequently cut in with some fresh direction, muddling the poor girl's mind, as she stood open-mouthed, listening to us both.

'Hand the vegetables round,' said I (foolishly, I see now – for it was aiming at more than we could accomplish with quietness and simplicity): and then, seeing her look bewildered, I added, 'Take the vegetables round to people, and let them help themselves.'

'And mind you go first to the ladies,' put in Miss Matilda. 'Always go to the ladies before gentlemen, when you are waiting.'

'I'll do it as you tell me, ma'am,' said Martha; 'but I like lads best.'

We felt very uncomfortable and shocked at this speech of Martha's; yet I don't think she meant any harm; and, on the whole, she attended very well to our directions, except that she 'nudged' the major, when he did not help himself as soon as she expected, to the potatoes, while she was handing them round.

The major and his wife were quiet, unpretending people enough when they did come; languid, as all East Indians are, I suppose. We were rather dismayed at their bringing two servants with them, a Hindoo body-servant for the major, and a steady elderly maid for his wife; but they slept at the inn, and took off a good deal of the responsibility by attending carefully to their master's and mistress's comfort. Martha, to be sure, had never ended her staring at the East Indian's white turban and brown complexion, and I saw that Miss Matilda shrunk away from him a little as he waited at dinner. Indeed, she asked me, when they were gone, if he did not remind me of Blue Beard? On the whole, the visit was most satisfactory, and is a subject of conversation even now with Miss Matilda; at the time it greatly excited Cranford, and even stirred up the apathetic and Honourable Mrs Jamieson to some expression of interest, when I went to call and thank her for the kind answers she had vouchsafed to Miss Matilda's inquiries as to the arrangement of a gentleman's dressing-room – answers which I must confess she had given in the wearied manner of the Scandinavian prophetess –

'Leave me, leave me to repose.'

And *now* I come to the love affair.

It seems that Miss Pole had a cousin, once or twice removed, who had offered to Miss Matty long ago. Now, this cousin lived four or five miles from Cranford on his own estate; but his property was not large enough to entitle him to rank higher than a yeoman; or rather, with something of the 'pride which apes humility,' he had refused to push himself on, as so many of his class had done, into the ranks of the squires. He would not allow himself to be called Thomas Holbrook, *Esq.*; he even sent back letters with this address, telling the postmistress at Cranford that his name was *Mr* Thomas Holbrook, yeoman. He rejected all domestic innovations; he would have the house door stand open in summer, and shut in winter, without knocker or bell to summon a servant. The closed fist or the knob of the stick did this office for him, if he found the door locked. He despised every refinement which had not its root deep down in humanity. If people were not ill, he saw no necessity for moderating his voice. He spoke the dialect of the country in perfection, and constantly used it in conversation; although Miss Pole (who gave me these particulars) added, that he read aloud more beautifully and with more feeling than any one she had ever heard, except the late rector.

'And how came Miss Matilda not to marry him?' asked I.

'Oh, I don't know. She was willing enough, I think; but you know Cousin Thomas would not have been enough of a gentleman for the rector, and Miss Jenkyns.'

'Well! but they were not to marry him,' said I, impatiently.

'No; but they did not like Miss Matty to marry below her rank. You know she was the rector's daughter, and somehow they are related to Sir Peter Arley: Miss Jenkyns thought a deal of that.'

'Poor Miss Matty!' said I.

'Nay, now, I don't know anything more than that he offered and was refused. Miss Matty might not like him – and Miss Jenkyns might never have said a word – it is only a guess of mine.'

'Has she never seen him since?' I inquired.

'No, I think not. You see, Woodley, Cousin Thomas's house, lies half-way between Cranford and Misselton; and I know he made Misselton his market town very soon after he had offered to Miss Matty; and I don't think he has been into Cranford above once or twice since – once, when I was walking with Miss Matty, in High Street; and suddenly she darted from me, and went up Shire Lane. A few minutes after, I was startled by meeting Cousin Thomas.'

'How old is he?' I asked, after a pause of castle-building.

'He must be about seventy, I think, my dear,' said Miss Pole, blowing up my castle, as if by gunpowder, into small fragments.

Very soon after – at least during my long visit to Miss Matilda – I had the opportunity of seeing Mr Holbrook; seeing, too, his first encounter with his former love, after thirty or forty years' separation. I was helping to decide whether any of the new assortment of coloured silks which they had just received at the shop, would do to match a grey and black mousseline-de-laine that wanted a new breadth, when a tall, thin, Don Quixote-looking old man came into the shop for some woollen gloves. I had never seen the person (who was rather striking) before, and I watched him rather attentively, while Miss Matty listened to the shopman. The stranger wore a blue coat with brass buttons, drab breeches, and gaiters, and drummed with his fingers on the counter until he was attended to. When he answered the shop-boy's question, 'What can I have the pleasure of showing you to-day, Sir?' I saw Miss Matilda start, and then suddenly sit down; and instantly I guessed who it was. She had made some inquiry which had to be carried round to the other shopman.

'Miss Jenkyns wants the black sarsenet two-and-twopence the yard'; and Mr Holbrook had caught the name, and was across the shop in two strides.

'Matty – Miss Matilda – Miss Jenkyns! God bless my soul! I should not have known you. How are you? how are you?' He kept shaking her hand in a way which proved the warmth of his friendship; but he repeated so often, as if to himself, 'I should not have known you!' that any sentimental romance which I might be inclined to build, was quite done away with by his manner. However, he kept talking to us all the time we were in the shop; and then waving the shopman with the unpurchased gloves on one side, with 'Another time, sir! another time!' he walked home with us. I am happy to say my client, Miss Matilda, also left the shop in an equally bewildered state, not having purchased either green or red silk. Mr Holbrook was evidently full with honest, loud-spoken joy at meeting his old love again; he touched on the changes that had taken place; he even spoke of Miss Jenkyns as 'Your poor sister! Well, well! we all have our faults'; and bade us good-bye with many a hope that he should soon see Miss Matty again. She went straight to her room; and never came back till our early tea-time, when I thought she looked as if she had been crying.

Chapter IV

A VISIT TO AN OLD BACHELOR

A few days after, a note came from Mr Holbrook, asking us – impartially asking both of us – in a formal, old-fashioned style, to spend a day at his house – a long June day – for it was June now. He named that he had also invited his cousin, Miss Pole; so that we might join in a fly, which could be put up at his house.

I expected Miss Matty to jump at this invitation; but, no! Miss Pole and I had the greatest difficulty in persuading her to go. She thought it was improper; and was even half annoyed when we utterly ignored the idea of any impropriety in her going with two other ladies to see her old lover. Then came a more serious difficulty. She did not think Deborah would have liked her to go. This took us half a day's good hard talking to get over; but, at the first sentence of relenting, I seized the opportunity, and wrote and despatched an acceptance in her name – fixing day and hour, that all might be decided and done with.

The next morning she asked me if I would go down to the shop with her; and there, after much hesitation, we chose out three caps to be sent home and tried on, that the most becoming might be selected to take with us on Thursday.

She was in a state of silent agitation all the way to Woodley. She had evidently never been there before; and, although she little dreamt I knew anything of her early story, I could perceive she was in a tremor at the thought of seeing the place which might have been her home, and round which it is probable that many of her innocent girlish imaginations had clustered. It was a long drive there, through paved jolting lanes. Miss Matilda sat bolt upright, and looked wistfully out of the windows, as we drew near the end of our journey. The aspect of the country was quiet and pastoral. Woodley stood among fields; and there was an old-fashioned garden, where roses and currant-bushes touched each other, and where the feathery asparagus formed a pretty background to the pinks and gilly-flowers; there was no drive up to the door: we got out at a little gate, and walked up a straight box-edged path.

'My cousin might make a drive, I think,' said Miss Pole, who was afraid of ear-ache, and had only her cap on.

'I think it is very pretty,' said Miss Matty, with a soft plaintiveness in her voice, and almost in a whisper; for just then Mr Holbrook appeared at the door, rubbing his hands in very effervescence of hospitality. He looked more like my idea of Don Quixote than ever, and yet the likeness was only external. His respectable housekeeper stood modestly at the door to bid us welcome; and, while she led the elder ladies up-stairs to a bedroom, I begged to look about the garden. My request evidently pleased the old gentleman; who took me all round the place, and showed me his six-and-twenty cows, named after the different letters of the alphabet. As we went along, he surprised me occasionally by repeating apt and beautiful quotations from the poets, ranging easily from Shakespeare and George Herbert to those of our own day. He did this as naturally as if he were thinking aloud, and their true and beautiful words were the best expression he could find for what he was thinking or feeling. To be sure, he called Byron 'my Lord Byrron,' and pronounced the name of Goethe strictly in accordance with the English sound of the letters – 'As Goethe says, "Ye ever-verdant palaces,"' &c. Altogether, I never met with a man, before or since, who had spent so long a life in a secluded and not impressive country, with ever-increasing delight in the daily and yearly change of season and beauty.

When he and I went in, we found that dinner was nearly ready in the kitchen – for so I suppose the room ought to be called, as there were oak dressers and cupboards all round, all over by the side of the fireplace, and only a small Turkey carpet in the middle of the flag-floor. The room might have been easily made into a handsome dark oak dining-parlour, by removing the oven, and a few other appurtenances of a kitchen, which were evidently never used; the real cooking place being at some distance. The room in which we were expected to sit was a stiffly furnished, ugly apartment; but that in which we did sit was what Mr Holbrook called the counting-house, when he paid his labourers their weekly wages, at a great desk near the door. The rest of the pretty sitting-room – looking into the orchard, and all covered over with dancing tree-shadows – was filled with books. They lay on the ground, they covered the walls, they strewed the table. He was evidently half ashamed and half proud of his extravagance in this respect. They were of all kinds, poetry and wild weird tales prevailing. He evidently chose his books in accordance with his own tastes, not because such and such were classical, or established favourites.

'Ah!' he said, 'we farmers ought not to have much time for reading; yet somehow one can't help it.'

'What a pretty room!' said Miss Matty, *sotto voce*.

'What a pleasant place!' said I, aloud, almost simultaneously.

'Nay! if you like it,' replied he; 'but can you sit on these great black leather three-cornered chairs? I like it better than the best parlour; but I thought ladies would take that for the smarter place.'

It was the smarter place; but, like most smart things, not at all pretty, or pleasant, or home-like; so, while we were at dinner, the servant girl dusted and scrubbed the counting-house chairs, and we sat there all the rest of the day.

We had pudding before meat; and I thought Mr Holbrook was going to make some apology for his old-fashioned ways, for he began –

'I don't know whether you like new-fangled ways.'

'Oh, not at all!' said Miss Matty.

'No more do I,' said he. 'My housekeeper *will* have these in her new fashion; or else I tell her that, when I was a young man, we used to keep strictly to my father's rule, "No broth, no ball; no ball, no beef"; and always began dinner with broth. Then we had suet puddings, boiled in the broth with the beef; and then the meat itself. If we did not sup our broth, we had no ball, which we liked a deal better; and the beef came last of all, and only those had it who had done justice to the broth and the ball. Now folks begin with sweet things, and turn their dinners topsy-turvy.'

When the ducks and green peas came, we looked at each other in dismay; we had only two-pronged, black-handled forks. It is true, the steel was as bright as silver; but what were we to do? Miss Matty picked up her peas, one by one, on the point of the prongs, much as Aminé ate her grains of rice after her previous feast with the Ghoul. Miss Pole sighed over her delicate young peas as she left them on one side of her plate untasted; for they *would* drop between the prongs. I looked at my host: the peas were going wholesale into his capacious mouth, shovelled up by his large round-ended knife. I saw, I imitated, I survived! My friends, in spite of my precedent, could not muster up courage enough to do an ungenteel thing; and, if Mr Holbrook had not been so heartily hungry, he would probably have seen that the good peas went away almost untouched.

After dinner, a clay pipe was brought in, and a spittoon; and, asking us to retire to another room, where he would soon join us, if we disliked tobacco-smoke, he presented his pipe to Miss Matty, and requested her to fill the bowl. This was a compliment to a lady in his youth; but it was rather inappropriate to propose it as an honour to Miss Matty, who had been trained by her sister to hold smoking of every kind in utter abhorrence. But if it was a shock to her refinement, it was also a gratification to her feelings to be thus selected; so she daintily stuffed the strong tobacco into the pipe; and then we withdrew.

'It is very pleasant dining with a bachelor,' said Miss Matty, softly, as we settled ourselves in the counting-house. 'I only hope it is not improper; so many pleasant things are!'

'What a number of books he has!' said Miss Pole, looking round the room. 'And how dusty they are!'

'I think it must be like one of the great Dr Johnson's rooms,' said Miss Matty. 'What a superior man your cousin must be!'

'Yes!' said Miss Pole; 'he's a great reader; but I am afraid he has got into very uncouth habits with living alone.'

'Oh! uncouth is too hard a word. I should call him eccentric; very clever people always are!' replied Miss Matty.

When Mr Holbrook returned, he proposed a walk in the fields; but the two elder ladies were afraid of damp and dirt; and had only very unbecoming calashes to put on over their caps; so they declined; and I was again his companion in a turn which he said he was obliged to take, to see after his men. He strode along, either wholly forgetting my existence, or soothed into silence by his pipe – and yet it was not silence exactly. He walked before me, with a stooping gait, his hands clasped behind him; and, as some tree or cloud, or glimpse of distant upland pastures, struck him, he quoted poetry to himself; saying it out loud in a grand sonorous voice, with just the emphasis that true feeling and appreciation give. We came upon an old cedar-tree, which stood at one end of the house: –

'The cedar spreads his dark-green layers of shade.'

'Capital term – "layers!" Wonderful man!' I did not know whether he was speaking to me or not; but I put in an assenting 'wonderful,' although I knew nothing about it; just because I was tired of being forgotten, and of being consequently silent.

He turned sharp round. 'Ay! you may say "wonderful." Why, when I saw the review of his poems in "Blackwood," I set off within an hour, and walked seven miles to Misselton (for the horses were not in the way) and ordered them. Now, what colour are ash-buds in March?'

Is the man going mad? thought I. He is very like Don Quixote.

'What colour are they, I say?' repeated he, vehemently.

'I am sure I don't know, sir,' said I, with the meekness of ignorance.

'I knew you didn't. No more did I – an old fool that I am! – till this young man comes and tells me. Black as ash-buds in March. And I've lived all my life in the country; more shame for me not to know. Black: they are jet-black, madam.' And he went off again, swinging along to the music of some rhyme he had got hold of.

When we came back, nothing would serve him but he must read us the poems he had been speaking of; and Miss Pole encouraged him in his proposal, I thought, because she wished me to hear his beautiful reading, of which she had boasted; but she afterwards said it was because she had got to a difficult part of her crochet, and wanted to count her stitches without having to talk. Whatever he had proposed would have been right to Miss Matty; although she did fall sound asleep within five minutes after he had begun a long poem, called 'Locksley Hall,' and had a comfortable nap, unobserved, till he ended; when the cessation of his voice wakened her up, and she said, feeling that something was expected, and that Miss Pole was counting:

'What a pretty book!'

'Pretty, madam! it's beautiful! Pretty, indeed!'

'Oh yes! I meant beautiful!' said she, fluttered at his disapproval of her word. 'It is so like that beautiful poem of Dr Johnson's my sister used to read – I forget the name of it; what was it, my dear?' turning to me.

'Which do you mean, ma'am? What was it about?'

'I don't remember what it was about, and I've quite forgotten what the name of it was; but it was written by Dr Johnson, and was very beautiful, and very like what Mr Holbrook has just been reading.'

'I don't remember it,' said he, reflectively. 'But I don't know Dr Johnson's poems well. I must read them.'

As we were getting into the fly to return, I heard Mr Holbrook say he should call on the ladies soon, and inquire how they got home; and this evidently pleased and fluttered Miss Matty at the time he said it; but after we had lost sight of the old house among the trees, her sentiments towards the master of it were gradually absorbed into a distressing wonder as to whether Martha had broken her word, and seized on the opportunity of her mistress's absence to have a 'follower.' Martha looked good, and steady, and composed enough, as she came to help us out; she was always careful of Miss Matty, and to-night she made use of this unlucky speech:

'Eh! dear ma'am, to think of your going out in an evening in such a thin shawl! It's no better than muslin. At your age, ma'am, you should be careful.'

'My age!' said Miss Matty, almost speaking crossly, for her; for she was usually gentle. 'My age! Why, how old do you think I am, that you talk about my age?'

'Well, ma'am! I should say you were not far short of sixty; but folks' looks is often against them – and I'm sure I meant no harm.'

'Martha, I'm not yet fifty-two!' said Miss Matty, with grave emphasis; for probably the remembrance of her youth had come very vividly before her this day, and she was annoyed at finding that golden time so far away in the past.

But she never spoke of any former and more intimate acquaintance with Mr Holbrook. She had probably met with so little sympathy in her early love, that she had shut it up close in her heart; and it was only by a sort of watching, which I could hardly avoid, since Miss Pole's confidence, that I saw how faithful her poor heart had been in its sorrow and its silence.

She gave me some good reason for wearing her best cap every day, and sat near the window, in spite of her rheumatism, in order to see, without being seen, down into the street.

He came. He put his open palms upon his knees, which were far apart, as he sat with his head bent down, whistling, after we had replied to his inquiries about our safe return. Suddenly, he jumped up:

'Well, madam! have you any commands for Paris? I am going there in a week or two.'

'To Paris!' we both exclaimed.

'Yes, madam! I've never been there, and always had a wish to go; and I think if I don't go soon, I mayn't go at all; so as soon as the hay is got in I shall go, before harvest-time.'

We were so much astonished, that we had no commissions.

Just as he was going out of the room, he turned back, with his favourite exclamation:

'God bless my soul, madam! but I nearly forgot half my errand. Here are the poems for you, you admired so much the other evening at my house.' He tugged away at a parcel in his coat-pocket. 'Good-bye, miss,' said he; 'good-bye, Matty! take care of yourself.' And he was gone. But he had given her a book, and he had called her Matty, just as he used to do thirty years ago.

'I wish he would not go to Paris,' said Miss Matilda, anxiously. 'I don't believe frogs will agree with him; he used to have to be very careful what he ate, which was curious in so strong-looking a young man.'

Soon after this I took my leave, giving many an injunction to Martha to look after her mistress, and to let me know if she thought that Miss Matilda was not so well; in which case I would volunteer a visit to my old friend, without noticing Martha's intelligence to her.

Accordingly I received a line or two from Martha every now

and then; and, about November, I had a note to say her mistress was 'very low and sadly off her food'; and the account made me so uneasy, that, although Martha did not decidedly summon me, I packed up my things and went.

I received a warm welcome, in spite of the little flurry produced by my impromptu visit, for I had only been able to give a day's notice. Miss Matilda looked miserably ill; and I prepared to comfort and cosset her.

I went down to have a private talk with Martha.

'How long has your mistress been so poorly?' I asked, as I stood by the kitchen fire.

'Well! I think it's better than a fortnight; it is, I know: it was one Tuesday, after Miss Pole had been, that she went into this moping way. I thought she was tired, and it would go off with a night's rest; but, no! she has gone on and on ever since, till I thought it my duty to write to you, ma'am.'

'You did quite right, Martha. It is a comfort to think she has so faithful a servant about her. And I hope you find your place comfortable?'

'Well, ma'am, missus is very kind, and there's plenty to eat and drink, and no more work but what I can do easily – but – ' Martha hesitated.

'But what, Martha?'

'Why, it seems so hard of missus not to let me have any followers; there's such lots of young fellows in the town; and many a one has as much as offered to keep company with me; and I may never be in such a likely place again, and it's like wasting an opportunity. Many a girl as I know would have 'em unbeknownst to missus; but I've given my word, and I'll stick to it; or else this is just the house for missus never to be the wiser if they did come: and it's such a capable kitchen – there's such good dark corners in it – I'd be bound to hide any one. I counted up last Sunday night – for I'll not deny I was crying because I had to shut the door in Jem Hearn's face; and he's a steady young man, fit for any girl;

132

only I had given missus my word.' Martha was all but crying again; and I had little comfort to give her, for I knew, from old experience, of the horror with which both the Miss Jenkynses looked upon 'followers'; and in Miss Matty's present nervous state this dread was not likely to be lessened.

I went to see Miss Pole the next day, and took her completely by surprise; for she had not been to see Miss Matilda for two days.

'And now I must go back with you, my dear, for I promised to let her know how Thomas Holbrook went on; and, I'm sorry to say, his housekeeper has sent me word to-day that he hasn't long to live. Poor Thomas! That journey to Paris was quite too much for him. His housekeeper says he has hardly ever been round his fields since; but just sits with his hands on his knees in the counting-house, not reading or anything, but only saying, what a wonderful city Paris was! Paris has much to answer for, if it's killed my cousin Thomas, for a better man never lived.'

'Does Miss Matilda know of his illness?' asked I; – a new light as to the cause of her indisposition dawning upon me.

'Dear! to be sure, yes! Has not she told you? I let her know a fortnight ago, or more, when first I heard of it. How odd, she shouldn't have told you!'

Not at all, I thought; but I did not say anything. I felt almost guilty of having spied too curiously into that tender heart, and I was not going to speak of its secrets – hidden, Miss Matty believed, from all the world. I ushered Miss Pole into Miss Matilda's little drawing-room; and then left them alone. But I was not surprised when Martha came to my bedroom door, to ask me to go down to dinner alone, for that missus had one of her bad headaches. She came into the drawing-room at tea-time; but it was evidently an effort to her; and, as if to make up for some reproachful feeling against her late sister, Miss Jenkyns, which had been troubling her all the afternoon, and for which she now felt penitent, she kept telling me how good and how clever Deborah was in her youth; how she used to settle what gowns they were to wear at all the parties (faint, ghostly ideas of grim parties, far away in the distance, when Miss Matty and Miss Pole were young!); and how Deborah and her mother had started the benefit society for the poor, and taught girls cooking and plain sewing; and how Deborah had once danced with a lord; and how she used to visit at Sir Peter Arley's, and try to remodel the quiet rectory establishment on the plans of Arley Hall, where they kept thirty servants; and how she had nursed Miss Matty through a long, long illness, of which I had never heard before, but which I now dated in my own mind as following the dismissal of the suit of Mr Holbrook. So we talked softly and quietly of old times, through the long November evening.

The next day Miss Pole brought us word that Mr Holbrook was dead. Miss Matty heard the news in silence; in fact, from the account of the previous day, it was only what we had to expect. Miss Pole kept calling upon us for some expression of regret, by asking if it was not sad that he was gone, and saying:

'To think of that pleasant day last June, when he seemed so well! And he might have lived this dozen years if he had not gone to that wicked Paris, where they are always having Revolutions.'

She paused for some demonstration on our part. I saw Miss Matty could not speak, she was trembling so nervously; so I said what I really felt: and after a call of some duration – all the time of which I have no doubt Miss Pole thought Miss Matty received the news very calmly – our visitor took her leave.

Miss Matty made a strong effort to conceal her feelings – a concealment she practised even with me, for she has never alluded to Mr Holbrook again, although the book he gave her lies with her Bible on the little table by her bedside. She did not think I heard her when she asked the little milliner of Cranford to make her caps something like the Honourable Mrs Jamieson's, or that I noticed the reply:

'But she wears widows' caps, ma'am?'

'Oh! I only meant something in that style; not widows', of course, but rather like Mrs Jamieson's.'

This effort at concealment was the beginning of the tremulous motion of head and hands which I have seen ever since in Miss Matty.

The evening of the day of which we heard of Mr Holbrook's death, Miss Matilda was very silent and thoughtful; after prayers she called Martha back, and then she stood uncertain what to say.

'Martha!' she said at last; 'you are young,' – and then she made so long a pause that Martha, to remind her of her half-finished sentence, dropped a courtesy, and said:

'Yes, please, ma'am; two-and-twenty last third of October, please, ma'am.'

'And perhaps, Martha, you may some time meet with a young man you like, and who likes you. I did say you were not to have followers; but if you meet with such a young man, and tell me, and I find he is respectable, I have no objection to his coming to see you once a week. God forbid!' said she, in a low voice, 'that I should grieve any young hearts.' She spoke as if she were providing for some distant contingency, and was rather startled when Martha made her ready eager answer:

'Please, ma'am, there's Jem Hearn, and he's a joiner, making three-and-sixpence a day, and six foot one in his stocking-feet, please, ma'am; and if you'll ask about him to-morrow morning, every one will give him a character for steadiness; and he'll be glad enough to come to-morrow night, I'll be bound.'

Though Miss Matty was startled, she submitted to Fate and Love.

Chapter V

OLD LETTERS

I have often noticed that almost every one has his own individual small economies – careful habits of saving fractions of pennies in some one peculiar direction – any disturbance of which annoys him more than spending shillings or pounds on some real extravagance. An old gentleman of my acquaintance, who took the intelligence of the failure of a Joint-Stock Bank, in which some of his money was invested, with stoical mildness, worried his family all through a long summer's day, because one of them had torn (instead of cutting) out the written leaves of his now useless bank-book; of course, the corresponding pages at the other end came out as well; and this little unnecessary waste of paper (his private economy) chafed him more than all the loss of his money. Envelopes fretted his soul terribly when they first came in; the only way in which he could reconcile himself to such waste of his cherished article was by patiently turning inside out all that were sent to him, and so making them serve again. Even now, though tamed by age, I see him casting wistful glances at his daughters when they send a whole instead of a half sheet of note-paper, with the three lines of acceptance to an invitation, written on only one of the sides. I am not above owning that I have this human weakness myself. String is my foible. My pockets get full of little hanks of it, picked up and twisted together, ready for uses that never come. I am seriously annoyed if any one cuts the string of a parcel, instead of patiently and faithfully undoing it fold by fold. How people can bring themselves to use India-rubber rings, which are a sort of deification of string, as lightly as they do, I cannot imagine. To me an India-rubber ring is a precious treasure. I have one which is not new; one that I picked up off the floor, nearly six years ago. I have really tried to use it; but my heart failed me, and I could not commit the extravagance.

Small pieces of butter grieve others. They cannot attend to conversation, because of the annoyance occasioned by the habit which some people have of invariably taking more butter than they want. Have you not seen the anxious look (almost mesmeric) which such persons fix on the article? They would feel it a relief if they might bury it out of their sight by popping it into their own mouths, and swallowing it down; and they are really made happy if the person on whose plate it lies unused, suddenly breaks off a piece of toast (which he does not want at all) and eats up his butter. They think that this is not waste.

Now Miss Matty Jenkyns was chary of candles. We had many devices to use as few as possible. In the winter afternoons she would sit knitting for two or three hours; she could do this in the dark, or by firelight; and when I asked if I might not ring for candles to finish stitching my wristbands, she told me to 'keep blind man's holiday.' They were usually brought in with tea; but we only burnt one at a time. As we lived in constant preparation for a friend who might come in any evening (but who never did), it required some contrivance to keep our two candles of the same length, ready to be lighted, and to look as if we burnt two always. The candles took it in turns; and, whatever we might be talking about or doing, Miss Matty's eyes were habitually fixed upon the candle, ready to jump up and extinguish it, and to light the other before they had become too uneven in length to be restored to equality in the course of the evening.

One night, I remember this candle economy particularly annoyed me. I had been very much tired of my compulsory 'blind man's holiday,' – especially as Miss Matty had fallen asleep, and I did not like to stir the fire and run the risk of awakening her; so I could not even sit on the rug, and scorch myself with sewing by fire-light, according to my usual custom. I fancied Miss Matty must be dreaming of her early life; for she spoke one or two words, in her uneasy sleep, bearing reference to persons who were dead long before. When Martha brought in the lighted candle and tea, Miss Matty started into wakefulness, with a strange bewildered look around, as if we were not the people she expected to see about her. There was a little sad expression that shadowed her face as she recognized me; but immediately afterwards she tried to give me her usual smile. All through tea-time her talk ran upon the days of her childhood and youth. Perhaps this reminded her of the desirableness of looking over all the old family letters, and destroying such as ought not to be allowed to fall into the hands of strangers; for she had often spoken of the necessity of this task, but had always shrunk from it, with a timid dread of something painful. Tonight, however, she rose up after tea and went for them – in the dark; for she piqued herself on the precise neatness of all her chamber arrangements, and used to look uneasily at me when I lighted a bed-candle to go to another room for anything. When she returned, there was a faint smell of Tonquin beans in the room. I had always noticed this scent about any of the things which had belonged to her mother; and many of the letters were addressed to her – yellow bundles of love-letters, sixty or seventy years old.

Miss Matty undid the packet with a sigh; but she stifled it directly, as if it were hardly right to regret the flight of time, or of life either. We agreed to look them over separately, each taking a different letter out of the same bundle, and describing its contents to the other, before destroying it. I never knew what sad work the reading of old letters was before that evening, though I could hardly tell why. The letters were as happy as letters could be – at least those early letters were. There was in them a vivid and intense sense of the present time, which seemed so strong and full, as if it could never pass away, and as if the warm, living hearts that so expressed themselves could never die, and be as nothing to the sunny earth. I should have felt less melancholy, I believe, if the letters had been more so. I saw the tears stealing down the well-worn furrows of Miss Matty's cheeks, and her spectacles often wanted wiping. I trusted at last that she would light the other candle, for my own eyes were rather dim, and I wanted more light to see the pale, faded ink; but no – even through her tears, she saw and remembered her little economical ways.

The earliest set of letters were two bundles tied together, and ticketed (in Miss Jenkyns's handwriting), 'Letters interchanged between my ever-honoured father and my dearly-beloved mother, prior to their marriage, in July, 1774.' I should guess that the Rector of Cranford was about twenty-seven years of age when he wrote those letters; and Miss Matty told me that her mother was just eighteen at the time of her wedding. With my idea of the Rector, derived from a picture in the dining-parlour, stiff and stately, in a huge full-bottomed wig, with gown, cassock, and bands, and his hand upon a copy of the only sermon he ever published – it was strange to read these letters. They were full of eager, passionate ardour; short homely sentences, right fresh from the heart – (very different from the grand Latinised, Johnsonian style of the printed sermon, preached before some judge at assize time). His letters were a curious contrast to those of his girl-bride. She was evidently rather annoyed at his demands upon her for expressions of love, and could not quite understand what he meant by repeating the same thing over in so many different ways; but what she was quite clear about was her longing for a white 'Paduasoy' – whatever that might be; and six or seven letters were principally occupied in asking her lover to use his influence with her parents (who evidently kept her in good order) to obtain this or that article of dress, more especially the white 'Paduasoy.' He cared nothing how she was dressed; she was always lovely enough for him, as he took pains to assure her, when she begged him to express in his answers a predilection for particular pieces of finery, in order that she might show what he said to her parents. But at length he seemed to find out that she would not be married till she had a 'trousseau' to her mind; and then he sent her a letter, which had evidently accompanied a whole box full of finery, and in which he requested that she might be dressed in everything her heart desired. This was the first letter, ticketed in a frail, delicate hand, 'From my dearest John.' Shortly afterwards they were married – I suppose, from the intermission in their correspondence.

'We must burn them, I think,' said Miss Matty, looking doubtfully at me. 'No one will care for them when I am gone.' And one by one she dropped them into the middle of the fire; watching each blaze up, die out, and rise away, in faint, white, ghostly semblance, up the chimney, before she gave another to the same fate. The room was light enough now; but I, like her, was fascinated into watching the destruction of those letters, into which the honest warmth of a manly heart had been poured forth.

The next letter, likewise docketed by Miss Jenkyns, was endorsed, 'Letter of pious congratulation and exhortation from my venerable grandfather to my beloved mother, on occasion of my own birth. Also some practical remarks on the desirability of keeping warm the extremities of infants, from my excellent grandmother.'

The first part was, indeed, a severe and forcible picture of the responsibilities of mothers, and a warning against the evils that were in the world, and lying in ghastly wait for the little baby of two days old. His wife did not write, said the old gentleman, because he had forbidden it, she being indisposed with a sprained ankle, which (he said) quite incapacitated her from holding a pen. However, at the foot of the page was a small 'T.O.,' and on turning it over, sure enough, there was a letter to 'my dear, dearest Molly,' begging her, when she left her room, whatever she did, to go *up* stairs before going *down*: and telling her to wrap her baby's feet up in flannel, and keep it warm by the fire, although it was summer, for babies were so tender.

It was pretty to see from the letters, which were evidently exchanged with some frequency, between the young mother and the grandmother, how the girlish vanity was being weeded out of her heart by love for her baby. The white 'Paduasoy' figured again in the letters, with almost as much vigour as before. In one, it was being made into a christening cloak for the baby. It decked it when it went with its parents to spend a day or two at Arley Hall. It added to its charms when it was 'the prettiest little baby that ever was seen. Dear mother, I wish you could see her! Without any parshality, I do think she will grow up a regular bewty!' I thought of Miss Jenkyns, grey, withered, and wrinkled; and I wondered if her mother had known her in the courts of heaven; and then I knew that she had, and that they stood there in angelic guise.

There was a great gap before any of the Rector's letters appeared. And then his wife had changed her mode of endorsement. It was no longer from 'My dearest John'; it was from 'My honoured Husband.' The letters were written on the occasion of the publication of the same Sermon which was represented in the picture. The preaching before 'My Lord Judge,' and the 'publishing by request,' was evidently the culminating point – the event of his life. It had been necessary for him to go up to London to superintend it through the press. Many friends had to be called upon, and consulted, before he could decide on any printer fit for so onerous a task; and at length it was arranged that J. & J. Rivingtons were to have the honourable responsibility. The worthy Rector seemed to be strung up by the occasion to a high literary pitch, for he could hardly write a letter to his wife without cropping out into Latin. I remember the end of one of his letters ran thus: 'I shall ever hold the virtuous qualities of my Molly in remembrance, *dum memor ipse mei, dum spiritus regit artus,*' which, considering that the English of his correspondent was sometimes at fault in grammar, and often in spelling, might be taken as a proof of how much he 'idealised his Molly;' and, as Miss Jenkyns used to say, 'People talk a great deal about idealising now-a-days, whatever that may mean.' But this was nothing to a fit of writing classical poetry, which soon seized him; in which his Molly figured away as 'Maria.' The letter containing the *carmen* was endorsed by termination of the lives of most of the grandfather's friends and acquaintance; and I was not surprised at the way in which he spoke of this life being 'a vale of tears.'

It seemed curious that I should never have heard of this brother before; but I concluded that he had died young; or else surely his name would have been alluded to by his sisters.

By-and-by we came to packets of Miss Jenkyns's letters. These, Miss Matty did regret to burn. She said all the others had been only interesting to those who loved the writers; and that it seemed as if it would have hurt her to allow them to fall into the hands of strangers, who had not known her dear mother, and how good she was, although she did not always spell quite in the modern fashion; but Deborah's letters were so very superior! Any one might profit by reading them. It was a long time since she had read Mrs Chapone, but she knew she used to think that Deborah could have said the same things quite as well; and as for Mrs Carter! people thought a deal of her letters, just because she had written *Epictetus,* but she was quite sure Deborah would never have made use of such a common expression as 'I canna be fashed!'

Miss Matty did grudge burning these letters, it was evident. She would not let them be carelessly passed over with any quiet reading, and skipping, to myself. She took them from me, and even lighted the second candle, in order to read them aloud with a proper emphasis, and without stumbling over the big words. Oh, dear! how I wanted facts instead of reflections, before those letters were concluded! They lasted us two nights; and I won't deny that I made use of the time to think of many other things, and yet I was always at my post at the end of each sentence.

The Rector's letters, and those of his wife and mother-in-law, had all been tolerably short and pithy, written in a straight hand, with the lines very close together. Sometimes the whole letter was contained on a mere scrap of paper. The paper was very yellow, and the ink very brown; some of the sheets were (as Miss Matty made me observe) the old original Post, with the stamp in the corner, representing a post-boy riding for life and twanging his horn. The letters of Mrs Jenkyns and her mother were fastened with a great round red wafer; for it was before Miss Edgeworth's 'Patronage' had banished wafers from polite society. It was evident, from the tenor of what was said, that franks were in great request, and were even used as a means of paying debts by needy Members of Parliament. The Rector sealed his epistles with an immense coat of arms, and showed by the care with which he had performed this ceremony that he expected they should be cut open, not broken by any thoughtless or impatient hand. Now, Miss Jenkyns's letters were of a later date in form and writing. She wrote on the square sheet, which we have learned to call old-fashioned. Her hand was admirably calculated, together with her use of many-syllabled words, to fill up a sheet, and then came the pride and delight of crossing. Poor Miss Matty got sadly puzzled with this, for the words gathered size like snow-balls, and towards the end of her letter Miss Jenkyns used to become quite sesquipedalian. In one to her father, slightly theological and controversial in its tone, she had spoken of Herod, Tetrarch of Idumea. Miss Matty read it 'Herod Petrarch of Etruria,' and was just as well pleased as if she had been right.

I can't quite remember the date, but I think it was in 1805 that Miss Jenkyns wrote the longest series of letters; on occasion of her absence on a visit to some friends near Newcastle-upon-Tyne. These friends were intimate with the commandant of the garrison there, and heard from him of all the preparations that were being made to repel the invasion of Buonaparte, which some people imagined might take place at the mouth of the Tyne. Miss Jenkyns was evidently very much alarmed; and the first part of her letters was often written in pretty intelligible English, conveying particulars of the preparations which were made in the family with whom she was residing against the dreaded event; the bundles of clothes that were packed up ready for a flight to Alston Moor (a wild hilly piece of ground between Northumberland and

Cumberland); the signal that was to be given for this flight, and for the simultaneous turning out of the volunteers under arms; which said signal was to consist (if I remember rightly) in ringing the church bells in a particular and ominous manner. One day, when Miss Jenkyns and her hosts were at a dinner-party in Newcastle, this warning summons was actually given (not a very wise proceeding, if there be any truth in the moral attached to the fable of the Boy and the Wolf; but so it was), and Miss Jenkyns, hardly recovered from her fright, wrote the next day to describe the sound, the breathless shock, the hurry and alarm; and then, taking breath, she added, 'How trivial, my dear father, do all our apprehensions of the last evening appear, at the present moment, to calm and inquiring minds!' And here Miss Matty broke in with –

'But, indeed, my dear, they were not at all trivial or trifling at the time. I know I used to wake up in the night many a time, and think I heard the tramp of the French entering Cranford. Many people talked of hiding themselves in the salt-mines; and meat would have kept capitally down there, only perhaps we should have been thirsty. And my father preached a whole set of sermons on the occasion; one set in the mornings, all about David and Goliath, to spirit up the people to fighting with spades or bricks, if need were; and the other set in the afternoons, proving that Napoleon (that was another name for Bony, as we used to call him) was all the same as an Apollyon and Abaddon. I remember my father rather thought he should be asked to print this last set; but the parish had, perhaps, had enough of them with hearing.'

Peter Marmaduke Arley Jenkyns ('poor Peter!' as Miss Matty began to call him) was at school at Shrewsbury by this time. The Rector took up his pen, and rubbed up his Latin, once more, to correspond with his boy. It was very clear that the lad's were what are called show-letters. They were of a highly mental description, giving an account of his studies, and his intellectual hopes of various kinds, with an occasional quotation from the classics; but, now and then, the animal nature broke out in such a little sentence

He was to win honours at Shrewsbury School, and carry them thick to Cambridge, and after that, a living awaited him, the gift of his godfather, Sir Peter Arley. Poor Peter! his lot in life was very different to what his friends had hoped and planned. Miss Matty told me all about it, and I think it was a relief to her when she had done so.

He was the darling of his mother, who seemed to dote on all her children, though she was, perhaps, a little afraid of Deborah's superior acquirements. Deborah was the favourite of her father, and when Peter disappointed him, she became his pride. The sole honour Peter brought away from Shrewsbury was the reputation of being the best good fellow that ever was, and of being the captain of the school in the art of practical joking. His father was disappointed, but set about remedying the matter in a manly way. He could not afford to send Peter to read with any tutor, but he could read with him himself; and Miss Matty told me much of the awful preparations in the way of dictionaries and lexicons that were made in her father's study the morning Peter began.

'My poor mother!' said she. 'I remember how she used to stand in the hall, just near enough the study door to catch the tone of my father's voice. I could tell in a moment if all was going right, by her face. And it did go right for a long time.'

'What went wrong at last?' said I. 'That tiresome Latin, I dare say.'

'No! it was not the Latin. Peter was in high favour with my father, for he worked up well for him. But he seemed to think that the Cranford people might be joked about, and made fun of, and they did not like it; nobody does. He was always hoaxing them; "hoaxing" is not a pretty word, my dear, and I hope you won't tell your father I used it, for I should not like him to think that I was not choice in my language, after living with such a woman as Deborah. And be sure you never use it yourself. I don't know how it slipped out of my mouth, except it was that I was thinking of poor Peter, and it was always his expression. But he was a very gentlemanly boy in many things. He was like dear Captain Brown in always being ready to help any old person or a child. Still, he did like joking and making fun; and he seemed to think the old ladies in Cranford would believe anything. There were many old ladies living here then; we are principally ladies now, I know; but we are not so old as the ladies used to be when I was a girl. I could laugh to think of some of Peter's jokes. No! my dear, I won't tell you of them, because they might not shock you as they ought to do; and they were very shocking. He even took in my father once, by dressing himself up as a lady that was passing through the town and wished to see the Rector of Cranford, "who had published that admirable Assize Sermon." Peter said, he was awfully frightened himself when he saw how my father took it all in, and even offered to copy out all his Napoleon Buonaparte sermons for her – him, I mean – no, her, for Peter was a lady then. He told me he was more terrified than he ever was before, all the time my father was speaking. He did not think my father would have believed him; and yet if he had not, it would have been a sad thing for Peter. As it was, he was none so glad of it, for my father kept him hard at work copying out all those twelve Buonaparte sermons for the lady – that was for Peter himself, you know. He was the lady. And once when he wanted to go fishing, Peter said, "Confound the woman!" – very bad language, my dear; but Peter was not always so guarded as he should have been; my father was so angry with him, it nearly frightened me out of my wits: and yet I could hardly keep from laughing at the little curtseys Peter kept making, quite slyly, whenever my father spoke of the lady's excellent taste and sound discrimination.'

'Did Miss Jenkyns know of these tricks?' said I.

'Oh, no! Deborah would have been too much shocked. No! no one knew but me. I wish I had always known of Peter's plans; but sometimes he did not tell me. He used to say, the old ladies in the town wanted something to talk about; but I don't think they did. They had the *St James's Chronicle* three times a-week, just as we

have now, and we have plenty to say; and I remember the clacking
noise there always was when some of the ladies got together. But,
probably, schoolboys talk more than ladies. At last there was a
terrible sad thing happened.' Miss Matty got up, went to the door,
and opened it; no one was there. She rang the bell for Martha; and
when Martha came, her mistress told her to go for eggs to a farm
at the other end of the town.

'I will lock the door after you, Martha. You are not afraid to go,
are you?'

'No, ma'am, not at all; Jem Hearn will be only too proud to go
with me.'

Miss Matty drew herself up, and, as soon as we were alone, she
wished that Martha had more maidenly reserve.

'We'll put out the candle, my dear. We can talk just as well by
fire-light, you know. There! well! you see, Deborah had gone
from home for a fortnight or so; it was a very still, quiet day, I
remember, overhead; and the lilacs were all in flower, so I suppose
it was spring. My father had gone out to see some sick people in
the parish; I recollect seeing him leave the house, with his wig and
shovel-hat, and cane. What possessed our poor Peter I don't
know; he had the sweetest temper, and yet he always seemed to
like to plague Deborah. She never laughed at his jokes, and
thought him ungenteel, and not careful enough about improving
his mind; and that vexed him.

'Well! he went to her room, it seems, and dressed himself in her
old gown, and shawl, and bonnet; just the things she used to wear
in Cranford, and was known by everywhere; and he made the
pillow into a little – you are sure you locked the door, my dear,
for I should not like any one to hear – into – into – a little baby,
with white long clothes. It was only, as he told me afterwards, to
make something to talk about in the town: he never thought of it
as affecting Deborah. And he went and walked up and down in
the Filbert walk – just half hidden by the rails, and half seen; and
he cuddled his pillow, just like a baby; and talked to it all the

nonsense people do. Oh dear! and my father came stepping stately up the street, as he always did; and what should he see but a little black crowd of people – I dare say as many as twenty – all peeping through his garden rails. So he thought, at first, they were only looking at a new rhododendron that was in full bloom, and that he was very proud of; and he walked slower, that they might have more time to admire. And he wondered if he could make out a sermon from the occasion, and thought, perhaps, there was some relation between the rhododendrons and the lilies of the field. My poor father! When he came nearer, he began to wonder that they did not see him; but their heads were all so close together, peeping and peeping! My father was amongst them, meaning, he said, to ask them to walk into the garden with him, and admire the beautiful vegetable production, when – oh, my dear! I tremble to think of it – he looked through the rails himself, and saw – I don't know what he thought he saw, but old Clare told me his face went quite grey-white with anger, and his eyes blazed out under his frowning black brows; and he spoke out – oh, so terribly! – and bade them all stop where they were – not one of them to go, not one to stir a step; and, swift as light, he was in at the garden door, and down the Filbert walk, and seized hold of poor Peter, and tore his clothes off his back – bonnet, shawl, gown, and all – and threw the pillow among the people over the railings: and then he was very, very angry indeed; and before all the people he lifted up his cane, and flogged Peter!

'My dear! that boy's trick, on that sunny day, when all seemed going straight and well, broke my mother's heart, and changed my father for life. It did, indeed. Old Clare said, Peter looked as white as my father; and stood as still as a statue to be flogged; and my father struck hard! When my father stopped to take breath, Peter said, "Have you done enough, Sir?" quite hoarsely, and still standing quite quiet. I don't know what my father said – or if he said anything. But old Clare said, Peter turned to where the people outside the railing were, and made them a low bow, as grand and as grave as any gentleman; and then walked slowly into the house. I was in the store-room helping my mother to make cowslip wine. I cannot abide the wine now, nor the scent of the flowers; they turn me sick and faint, as they did that day, when Peter came in, looking as haughty as any man – indeed, looking like a man, not like a boy. "Mother!" he said, "I am come to say, God bless you for ever." I saw his lips quiver as he spoke; and I think he durst not say anything more loving, for the purpose that was in his heart. She looked at him rather frightened, and wondering, and asked him what was to do? He did not smile or speak, but put his arms round her, and kissed her as if he did not know how to leave off; and before she could speak again, he was gone. We talked it over, and could not understand it, and she bade me go and seek my father, and ask what it was all about. I found him walking up and down, looking very highly displeased.

"Tell your mother I have flogged Peter, and that he richly deserved it."

'I durst not ask any more questions. When I told my mother, she sat down, quite faint, for a minute. I remember, a few days after, I saw the poor, withered cowslip flowers thrown out to the leaf-heap, to decay and die there. There was no making of cowslip wine that year at the Rectory – nor, indeed, ever after.

'Presently, my mother went to my father. I know I thought of Queen Esther and King Ahasuerus; for my mother was very pretty and delicate-looking, and my father looked as terrible as King Ahasuerus. Some time after they came out together; and then my mother told me what had happened, and that she was going up to Peter's room, at my father's desire – though she was not to tell Peter this – to talk the matter over with him. But no Peter was there. We looked over the house; no Peter was there! Even my father, who had not liked to join in the search at first, helped us before long. The Rectory was a very old house: steps up into a room, steps down into a room, all through. At first, my mother went calling low and soft – as if to reassure the poor boy – "Peter!

Peter, dear! it's only me"; but, by and by, as the servants came back from the errands my father had sent them, in different directions, to find where Peter was – as we found he was not in the garden, nor the hayloft, nor anywhere about – my mother's cry grew louder and wilder – "Peter! Peter, my darling! where are you?" for then she felt and understood that that long kiss meant some sad kind of "good-bye." The afternoon went on – my mother never resting, but seeking again and again in every possible place that had been looked into twenty minutes before; nay, that she had looked into over and over again herself. My father sat with his head in his hands, not speaking, except when his messengers came in, bringing no tidings; then he lifted up his face so strong and sad, and told them to go again in some new direction. My mother kept passing from room to room, in and out of the house, moving noiselessly, but never ceasing. Neither she nor my father durst leave the house, which was the meeting-place for all the messengers. At last (and it was nearly dark), my father rose up. He took hold of my mother's arm, as she came with wild, sad pace, through one door, and quickly towards another. She started at the touch of his hand, for she had forgotten all in the world but Peter.

'"Molly!" said he, "I did not think all this would happen." He looked into her face for comfort – her poor face, all wild and white; for neither she nor my father had dared to acknowledge – much less act upon – the terror that was in their hearts, lest Peter should have made away with himself. My father saw no conscious look in his wife's hot, dreary eyes, and he missed the sympathy that she had always been ready to give him – strong man as he was; and at the dumb despair in her face, his tears began to flow. But when she saw this, a gentle sorrow came over her countenance, and she said, "Dearest John! don't cry; come with me, and we'll find him," almost as cheerfully as if she knew where he was. And she took my father's great hand in her little soft one, and led him along, the tears dropping, as he walked on that same unceasing, weary walk, from room to room, through house and garden.

'Oh, how I wished for Deborah! I had no time for crying, for now all seemed to depend on me. I wrote for Deborah to come home. I sent a message privately to that same Mr Holbrook's house – poor Mr Holbrook! – you know who I mean. I don't mean I sent a message to him, but I sent one that I could trust, to know if Peter was at his house. For at one time Mr Holbrook was an occasional visitor at the Rectory – you know he was Miss Pole's cousin – and he had been very kind to Peter, and taught him how to fish – he was very kind to everybody, and I thought Peter might have gone off there. But Mr Holbrook was from home, and Peter had never been seen. It was night now; but the doors were all wide open, and my father and mother walked on and on; it was more than an hour since he had joined her, and I don't believe they had ever spoken all that time. I was getting the parlour fire lighted, and one of the servants was preparing tea, for I wanted them to have something to eat and drink and warm them, when old Clare asked to speak to me.

' "I have borrowed the nets from the weir, Miss Matty. Shall we drag the ponds to-night, or wait for the morning?"

'I remember staring in his face to gather his meaning; and when I did, I laughed out loud. The horror of that new thought – our bright, darling Peter, cold, and stark, and dead! I remember the ring of my own laugh now.

'The next day Deborah was at home before I was myself again. She would not have been so weak as to give way as I had done; but my screams (my horrible laughter had ended in crying) had roused my sweet dear mother, whose poor wandering wits were called back and collected, as soon as a child needed her care. She and Deborah sat by my bedside; I knew by the looks of each that there had been no news of Peter – no awful, ghastly news, which was what I most had dreaded in my dull state between sleeping and waking.

'The same result of all the searching had brought something of the same relief to my mother, to whom, I am sure, the thought that Peter might even then be hanging dead in some of the familiar home places, had caused that never-ending walk of yesterday. Her soft eyes never were the same again after that; they had always a restless craving look, as if seeking for what they could not find. Oh! it was an awful time; coming down like a thunderbolt on the still sunny day, when the lilacs were all in bloom.'

'Where was Mr Peter?' said I.

'He had made his way to Liverpool; and there was war then; and some of the king's ships lay off the mouth of the Mersey; and they were only too glad to have a fine likely boy such as him (five foot nine he was) come to offer himself. The captain wrote to my father, and Peter wrote to my mother. Stay! those letters will be somewhere here.'

We lighted the candle, and found the captain's letter, and Peter's too. And we also found a little simple begging letter from Mrs Jenkyns to Peter, addressed to him at the house of an old school fellow, whither she fancied he might have gone. They had returned it unopened; and unopened it had remained ever since, having been inadvertently put by among the other letters of that time. This is it:

'My dearest Peter,

'You did not think we should be so sorry as we are, I know, or you would never have gone away. You are too good. Your father sits and sighs till my heart aches to hear him. He cannot hold up his head for grief; and yet he only did what he thought was right. Perhaps he has been too severe, and perhaps I have not been kind enough; but God knows how we love you, my dear only boy. Don looks so sorry you are gone. Come back, and make us happy, who love you so much. I *know* you will come back.'

But Peter did not come back. That spring day was the last time he ever saw his mother's face. The writer of the letter – the last – the only person who had ever seen what was written in it, was dead long ago – and I, a stranger, not born at the time when this occurrence took place, was the one to open it.

The captain's letter summoned the father and mother to Liverpool instantly, if they wished to see their boy; and by some of the wild chances of life, the captain's letter had been detained some where, somehow.

Miss Matty went on: 'And it was race-time, and all the post-horses at Cranford were gone to the races; but my father and mother set off in our own gig – and oh! my dear, they were too late – the ship was gone! And now, read Peter's letter to my mother!'

It was full of love, and sorrow, and pride in his new profession, and a sore sense of his disgrace in the eyes of the people at Cranford; but ending with a passionate entreaty that she would come and see him before he left the Mersey: 'Mother! We may go into battle. I hope we shall, and lick those French; but I must see you again before that time.'

'And she was too late,' said Miss Matty; 'too late!'

We sat in silence, pondering on the full meaning of those sad, sad words. At length I asked Miss Matty to tell me how her mother bore it.

'Oh!' she said, 'she was patience itself. She had never been strong, and this weakened her terribly. My father used to sit looking at her: far more sad than she was. He seemed as if he could look at nothing else when she was by; and he was so humble – so very gentle now. He would, perhaps, speak in his old way – laying down the law, as it were – and then, in a minute or two, he would come round and put his hand on our shoulders, and ask us in a low voice if he had said anything to hurt us? I did not wonder at his speaking so to Deborah, for she was so clever; but I could not bear to hear him talking so to me.

'But, you see, he saw what we did not – that it was killing my mother. Yes! killing her – (put out the candle, my dear; I can talk better in the dark) – for she was but a frail woman, and ill fitted to stand the fright and shock she had gone through; and she would smile at him and comfort him, not in words but in her looks and tones, which were always cheerful when he was there. And she would speak of how she thought Peter stood a good chance of being admiral very soon – he was so brave and clever; and how she thought of seeing him in his navy uniform, and what sort of hats admirals wore; and how much more fit he was to be a sailor than a clergyman; and all in that way, just to make my father think she was quite glad of what came of that unlucky morning's work, and the flogging which was always in his mind, as we all knew. But, oh, my dear! the bitter, bitter crying she had when she was alone; – and at last, as she grew weaker, she could not keep her tears in when Deborah or me was by, and would give us message after message for Peter – (his ship had gone to the Mediterranean, or somewhere down there, and then he was ordered off to India, and there was no overland route then); – but she still said that no one knew where their death lay in wait, and that we were not to think hers was near. We did not think it, but we knew it, as we saw her fading away.

'Well, my dear, it's very foolish of me, I know, when in all likelihood I am so near seeing her again.

'And only think, love! the very day after her death – for she did not live quite a twelvemonth after Peter went away – the very day after – came a parcel for her from India – from her poor boy. It was a large, soft, white India shawl, with just a little narrow border all round; just what my mother would have liked.

'We thought it might rouse my father, for he had sat with her hand in his all night long; so Deborah took it in to him, and Peter's letter to her, and all. At first he took no notice; and we tried to make a kind of light careless talk about the shawl, opening it out and admiring it. Then, suddenly, he got up, and spoke: "She shall be buried in it," he said; "Peter shall have that comfort; and she would have liked it."

'Well! perhaps it was not reasonable, but what could we do or say? One gives people in grief their own way. He took it up and felt it – "It is just such a shawl as she wished for when she was married, and her mother did not give it her. I did not know of it till after, or she should have had it – she should; but she shall have it now."

'My mother looked so lovely in her death! She was always pretty, and now she looked fair, and waxen, and young – younger than Deborah as she stood trembling and shivering by her. We decked her in the long soft folds; she lay, smiling, as if pleased; and people came – all Cranford came – to beg to see her, for they had loved her dearly – as well they might; and the countrywomen brought posies; old Clare's wife brought some white violets, and begged they might lie on her breast.

'Deborah said to me, the day of my mother's funeral, that if she had a hundred offers, she never would marry and leave my father. It was not very likely she would have so many – I don't know that she had one; but it was not less to her credit to say so. She was such a daughter to my father, as I think there never was before, or since. His eyes failed him, and she read book after book, and wrote, and copied, and was always at his service in any parish business. She could do many more things than my poor mother could; she even once wrote a letter to the bishop for my father. But he missed my mother sorely; the whole parish noticed it. Not that he was less active; I think he was more so, and more patient in helping every one. I did all I could to set Deborah at liberty to be with him; for I knew I was good for little, and that my best work in the world was to do odd jobs quietly and set others at liberty. But my father was a changed man.'

'Did Mr Peter ever come home?'

'Yes, once. He came home a Lieutenant; he did not get to be Admiral. And he and my father were such friends! My father took him into every house in the parish, he was so proud of him. He never walked out without Peter's arm to lean upon. Deborah used to smile (I don't think we ever laughed again after my mother's death), and say she was quite put in a corner. Not but what my father always wanted her when there was letter-writing, or reading to be done, or anything to be settled.'

'And then?' said I, after a pause.

'Then Peter went to sea again; and by-and-by, my father died, blessing us both, and thanking Deborah for all she had been to him; and, of course, our circumstances were changed; and, instead of living at the Rectory, and keeping three maids and a man, we had to come to this small house, and be content with a servant-of-all-work; but, as Deborah used to say, we have always lived genteelly, even if circumstances have compelled us to simplicity. – Poor Deborah!'

'And Mr Peter?' asked I.

'Oh, there was some great war in India – I forget what they call it – and we have never heard of Peter since then. I believe he is dead myself; and it sometimes fidgets me that we have never put on mourning for him. And then, again, when I sit by myself, and all the house is still, I think I hear his step coming up the street, and my heart begins to flutter and beat; but the sound always goes past – and Peter never comes.

'That's Martha back? No! *I'll* go, my dear; I can always find my way in the dark, you know. And a blow of fresh air at the door will do my head good, and it's rather got a trick of aching.'

So she pattered off. I had lighted the candle, to give the room a cheerful appearance against her return.

'Was it Martha?' asked I.

'Yes. And I am rather uncomfortable, for I heard such a strange noise just as I was opening the door.'

'Where?' I asked, for her eyes were round with affright.

'In the street – just outside – it sounded like – '

'Talking?' I put in, as she hesitated a little.

'No! kissing – '

enabled the proprietor to go straight to (Paris, he said, until he found his customers too patriotic and John Bullish to wear what the Mounseers wore) London; where, as he often told his customers, Queen Adelaide had appeared, only the very week before, in a cap exactly like the one he showed them, trimmed with yellow and blue ribbons, and had been complimented by King William on the becoming nature of her head-dress.

Miss Barkers, who confined themselves to truth, and did not approve of miscellaneous customers throve notwithstanding. They were self-denying, good people. Many a time have I seen the eldest of them (she that had been maid to Mrs Jamieson) carrying out some delicate mess to a poor person. They only aped their betters in having 'nothing to do' with the class immediately below theirs. And when Miss Barker died, their profits and income were found to be such that Miss Betty was justified in shutting up shop and retiring from business. She also (as I think I have before said) set up her cow; a mark of respectability in Cranford almost as decided as setting up a gig is among some people. She dressed finer than any lady in Cranford; and we did not wonder at it; for it was understood that she was wearing out all the bonnets and caps, and outrageous ribbons, which had once formed her stock-in-trade. It was five or six years since she had given up shop: so in any other place than Cranford her dress might have been considered *passée*.

And now, Miss Betty Barker had called to invite Miss Matty to tea at her house on the following Tuesday. She gave me also an impromptu invitation, as I happened to be a visitor; though I could see she had a little fear lest, since my father had gone to live in Drumble, he might have engaged in that 'horrid cotton trade,' and so dragged his family down out of 'aristocratic society.' She prefaced this invitation with so many apologies, that she quite excited my curiosity. 'Her presumption' was to be excused. What had she been doing? She seemed so overpowered by it, I could only think that she had been writing to Queen Adelaide, to ask for a receipt for washing lace; but the act which she so characterised was only an invitation she had carried to her sister's former mistress, Mrs Jamieson. 'Her former occupation considered, could Miss Matty excuse the liberty?' Ah! thought I, she has found out that double cap, and is going to rectify Miss Matty's head-dress. No! it was simply to extend her invitation to Miss Matty and to me. Miss Matty bowed acceptance; and I wondered that, in the graceful action, she did not feel the unusual weight and extraordinary height of her head-dress. But I do not think she did; for she recovered her balance, and went on talking to Miss Betty in a kind, condescending manner, very different from the fidgety way she would have had, if she had suspected how singular her appearance was.

'Mrs Jamieson is coming, I think you said?' asked Miss Matty.

'Yes. Mrs Jamieson most kindly and condescendingly said she would be happy to come. One little stipulation she made, that she should bring Carlo. I told her that if I had a weakness, it was for dogs.'

'And Miss Pole?' questioned Miss Matty, who was thinking of her pool at Preference, in which Carlo would not be available as a partner.

'I am going to ask Miss Pole. Of course, I could not think of asking her until I had asked you, madam – the Rector's daughter, madam. Believe me, I do not forget the situation my father held under yours.'

'And Mrs Forrester, of course?'

'And Mrs Forrester. I thought, in fact, of going to her before I went to Miss Pole. Although her circumstances are changed, madam, she was born a Tyrrell, and we can never forget her alliance to the Bigges, of Bigelow Hall.'

Miss Matty cared much more for the little circumstance of her being a very good card-player.

'Mrs Fitz-Adam – I suppose – '

'No, madam. I must draw a line somewhere. Mrs Jamieson would not, I think, like to meet Mrs Fitz-Adam. I have the greatest respect for Mrs Fitz-Adam – but I cannot think her fit society for such ladies as Mrs Jamieson and Miss Matilda Jenkyns.'

Miss Betty Barker bowed low to Miss Matty, and pursed up her mouth. She looked at me with sidelong dignity, as much as to say, although a retired milliner, she was no democrat, and understood the difference of ranks.

'May I beg you to come as near half-past six, to my little dwelling, as possible, Miss Matilda? Mrs Jamieson dines at five, but has kindly promised not to delay her visit beyond that time – half-past six.' And with a swimming curtsey Miss Betty Barker took her leave.

My prophetic soul foretold a visit that afternoon from Miss Pole, who usually came to call on Miss Matilda after any event – or indeed in sight of any event – to talk it over with her.

'Miss Betty told me it was to be a choice and select few,' said Miss Pole, as she and Miss Matty compared notes.

'Yes, so she said. Not even Mrs Fitz-Adam.'

Now Mrs Fitz-Adam was the widowed sister of the Cranford surgeon, whom I have named before. Their parents were respectable farmers, content with their station. The name of these good people was Hoggins. Mr Hoggins was the Cranford doctor now; we disliked the name, and considered it coarse; but, as Miss Jenkyns said, if he changed it to Piggins it would not be much better. We had hoped to discover a relationship between him and that Marchioness of Exeter whose name was Molly Hoggins; but the man, careless of his own interests, utterly ignored and denied any such relationship; although, as dear Miss Jenkyns had said, he had a sister called Mary, and the same Christian names were very apt to run in families.

Soon after Miss Mary Hoggins married Mr Fitz-Adam, she disappeared from the neighbourhood for many years. She did not move in a sphere in Cranford society sufficiently high to make any of us care to know what Mr Fitz-Adam was. He died and was gathered to his fathers, without our ever having thought about him at all. And then Mrs Fitz-Adam reappeared in Cranford ('as bold as a lion,' Miss Pole said) a well-to-do widow, dressed in rustling black silk, so soon after her husband's death, that poor Miss Jenkyns was justified in the remark she made, that 'bombazine would have shown a deeper sense of her loss.'

I remember the convocation of ladies, who assembled to decide whether or not Mrs Fitz-Adam should be called upon by the old blue-blooded inhabitants of Cranford. She had taken a large rambling house, which had been usually considered to confer a patent of gentility upon its tenant; because, once upon a time, seventy or eighty years before, the spinster daughter of an earl had resided in it. I am not sure if the inhabiting this house was not also believed to convey some unusual power of intellect; for the earl's daughter, Lady Jane, had a sister, Lady Anne, who had married a general officer in the time of the American War; and this general officer had written one or two comedies, which were still acted on the London boards; and which, when we saw them advertised, made us all draw up, and feel that Drury Lane was paying a very pretty compliment to Cranford. Still, it was not at all a settled thing that Mrs Fitz-Adam was to be visited, when dear Miss Jenkyns died; and, with her, something of the clear knowledge of the strict code of gentility went out too. As Miss Pole observed, 'As most of the ladies of good family in Cranford were elderly spinsters, or widows without children, if we did not relax a little, and become less exclusive, by-and-by we should have no society at all.'

Mrs Forrester continued on the same side.

'She had always understood that Fitz meant something aristocratic; there was Fitz-Roy – she thought that some of the King's children had been called Fitz-Roy; and there was Fitz-Clarence now – they were the children of dear good King William the Fourth. Fitz-Adam! – it was a pretty name; and she thought it very probably meant "Child of Adam." No one, who had not some good blood in their veins, would dare to be called Fitz; there was a deal in a name – she had had a cousin who spelt his name with two little ff's – ffoulkes – and he always looked down upon capital letters, and said they belonged to lately-invented families. She had been afraid he would die a bachelor, he was so very choice. When he met with a Mrs ffaringdon, at a watering-place, he took to her immediately; and a very pretty genteel woman she was – a widow with a very good fortune; and "my cousin," Mr ffoulkes, married her; and it was all owing to her two little ff's.'

Mrs Fitz-Adam did not stand a chance of meeting with a Mr Fitz-anything in Cranford, so that could not have been her motive for settling there. Miss Matty thought it might have been the hope of being admitted in the society of the place, which would certainly be a very agreeable rise for *ci-devant* Miss Hoggins; and if this had been her hope, it would be cruel to disappoint her.

So everybody called upon Mrs Fitz-Adam – everybody but Mrs Jamieson, who used to show how honourable she was by never seeing Mrs Fitz-Adam, when they met at the Cranford parties. There would be only eight or ten ladies in the room, and Mrs Fitz-Adam was the largest of all, and she invariably used to stand up when Mrs Jamieson came in, and curtsey very low to her whenever she turned in her direction – so low, in fact, that I think Mrs Jamieson must have looked at the wall above her, for she never moved a muscle of her face, no more than if she had not seen her. Still Mrs Fitz-Adam persevered.

The spring evenings were getting bright and long, when three or four ladies in calashes met at Miss Barker's door. Do you know what a calash is? It is a covering worn over caps, not unlike the heads fastened on old-fashioned gigs; but sometimes it is not quite so large. This kind of headgear always made an awful impression on the children in Cranford; and now two or three left off their play in the quiet sunny little street, and gathered, in wondering silence, round Miss Pole, Miss Matty, and myself. We were silent too, so that, we could hear loud, suppressed whispers inside Miss Barker's house: 'Wait, Peggy! wait till I've run upstairs and washed my hands. When I cough, open the door; I'll not be a minute.'

And, true enough, it was not a minute before we heard a noise, between a sneeze and a crow; on which the door flew open. Behind it stood a round-eyed maiden, all aghast at the honourable company of calashes, who marched in without a word. She recovered presence of mind enough to usher us into a small room, which had been the shop, but was now converted into a temporary dressing-room. There we unpinned and shook ourselves, and arranged our features before the glass into a sweet and gracious company-face; and then, bowing backwards with 'After you, ma'am,' we allowed Mrs Forrester to take precedence up the narrow staircase that led to Miss Barker's drawing-room. There she sat, as stately and composed as though we had never heard that odd-sounding cough, from which her throat must have been even then sore and rough. Kind, gentle, shabbily-dressed Mrs Forrester was immediately conducted to the second place of honour – a seat arranged something like Prince Albert's near the Queen's – good, but not so good. The place of pre-eminence was, of course, reserved for the Honourable Mrs Jamieson, who presently came panting up the stairs – Carlo rushing round her on her progress, as if he meant to trip her up.

And now, Miss Betty Barker was a proud and happy woman! She stirred the fire, and shut the door, and sat as near to it as she could, quite on the edge of her chair. When Peggy came in, tottering under the weight of the tea-tray, I noticed that Miss Barker was sadly afraid lest Peggy should not keep her distance sufficiently. She and her mistress were on very familiar terms in their everyday intercourse, and Peggy wanted now to make several little confidences to her, which Miss Barker was on thorns to hear; but which she thought it her duty, as a lady, to repress. So she turned away from all Peggy's asides and signs; but she made one or two very mal-apropos answers to what was said; and at last, seized with a bright idea, she exclaimed, 'Poor sweet Carlo! I'm forgetting him. Come down stairs with me, poor ittie doggie, and it shall have its tea, it shall!'

In a few minutes she returned, bland and benignant as before; but I thought she had forgotten to give the 'poor ittie doggie' anything to eat; judging by the avidity with which he swallowed down chance pieces of cake. The tea-tray was abundantly loaded. I was pleased to see it, I was so hungry; but I was afraid the ladies present might think it vulgarly heaped up. I know they would have done at their own houses; but somehow the heaps disappeared here. I saw Mrs Jamieson eating seed-cake, slowly and considerately, as she did everything; and I was rather surprised, for I knew she had told us, on the occasion of her last party, that she never had it in her house, it reminded her so much of scented soap. She always gave us Savoy biscuits. However, Mrs Jamieson was kindly indulgent to Miss Barker's want of knowledge of the customs of high life; and, to spare her feelings, ate three large pieces of seed-cake, with a placid, ruminating expression of countenance, not unlike a cow's.

After tea there was some little demur and difficulty. We were six in number; four could play at Preference, and for the other two there was Cribbage. But all, except myself – (I was rather afraid of the Cranford ladies at cards, for it was the most earnest and serious business they ever engaged in) – were anxious to be of the 'pool.' Even Miss Barker, while declaring she did not know Spadille from Manille, was evidently hankering to take a hand. The dilemma was soon put an end to by a singular kind of noise. If a Baron's daughter-in-law could ever be supposed to snore, I should have said Mrs Jamieson did so then; for, overcome by the heat of the room, and inclined to doze by nature, the temptation of that very comfortable arm-chair had been too much for her, and Mrs Jamieson was nodding. Once or twice she opened her eyes with an effort, and calmly but unconsciously smiled upon us; but, by-and-by, even her benevolence was not equal to this exertion, and she was sound asleep.

'It is very gratifying to me,' whispered Miss Barker at the card-table to her three opponents, whom, notwithstanding her ignorance of the game, she was 'basting' most unmercifully – 'very gratifying indeed, to see how completely Mrs Jamieson feels at home in my poor little dwelling; she could not have paid me a greater compliment.'

Miss Barker provided me with some literature in the shape of three or four handsomely bound fashion-books ten or twelve years old, observing, as she put a little table and a candle for my especial benefit, that she knew young people liked to look at pictures. Carlo lay, and snorted, and started at his mistress's feet. He, too, was quite at home.

The card-table was an animated scene to watch; four ladies' heads, with niddle-noddling caps, all nearly meeting over the middle of the table, in their eagerness to whisper quick enough and loud enough: and every now and then came Miss Barker's 'Hush, ladies! if you please, hush! Mrs Jamieson is asleep.'

It was very difficult to steer clear between Mrs Forrester's deafness and Mrs Jamieson's sleepiness. But Miss Barker managed her arduous task well. She repeated the whisper to Mrs Forrester, distorting her face considerably, in order to show, by the motions of her lips, what was said; and then she smiled kindly all round at us, and murmured to herself, 'Very gratifying, indeed; I wish my poor sister had been alive to see this day.'

Presently the door was thrown wide open; Carlo started to his feet, with a loud snapping bark, and Mrs Jamieson awoke: or, perhaps, she had not been asleep – as she said almost directly, the room had been so light she had been glad to keep her eyes shut, but had been listening with great interest to all our amusing and agreeable conversation. Peggy came in once more, red with importance. Another tray! 'Oh, gentility!' thought I, 'can you endure this last shock?' For Miss Barker had ordered (nay, I doubt not, prepared, although she did say, 'Why! Peggy, what have you brought us?' and looked pleasantly surprised at the unexpected pleasure) all sorts of good things for supper – scalloped oysters, potted lobsters, jelly, a dish called 'little Cupids' (which was in great favour with the Cranford ladies, although too expensive to be given, except on solemn and state occasions – macaroons sopped in brandy, I should have called it, if I had not known its more refined and classical name). In short, we were evidently to be feasted with all that was sweetest and best; and we thought it better to submit graciously, even at the cost of our gentility – which never ate suppers in general – but which, like most non-supper-eaters, was particularly hungry on all special occasions.

Miss Barker, in her former sphere, had, I dare say, been made acquainted with the beverage they call cherry-brandy. We none of us had ever seen such a thing, and rather shrunk back when she proffered it us – 'just a little, leetle glass, ladies; after the oysters and lobsters, you know. Shell-fish are sometimes thought not very wholesome.' We all shook our heads like female mandarins; but, at last, Mrs Jamieson suffered herself to be persuaded, and we followed her lead. It was not exactly unpalatable, though so hot and so strong that we thought ourselves bound to give evidence that we were not accustomed to such things, by coughing terribly – almost as strangely as Miss Barker had done, before we were admitted by Peggy.

'It's very strong,' said Miss Pole, as she put down her empty glass; 'I do believe there's spirit in it.'

'Only a little drop – just necessary to make it keep,' said Miss Barker. 'You know we put brandy-paper over preserves to make them keep. I often feel tipsy myself from eating damson tart.'

I question whether damson tart would have opened Mrs Jamieson's heart as the cherry-brandy did; but she told us of a coming event, respecting which she had been quite silent till that moment.

'My sister-in-law, Lady Glenmire, is coming to stay with me.'

There was a chorus of 'Indeed!' and then a pause. Each one rapidly reviewed her wardrobe, as to its fitness to appear in the presence of a Baron's widow; for, of course, a series of small festivals were always held in Cranford on the arrival of a visitor at any of our friends' houses. We felt very pleasantly excited on the present occasion.

Not long after this, the maids and the lanterns were announced. Mrs Jamieson had the sedan chair, which had squeezed itself into Miss Barker's narrow lobby with some difficulty, and most literally 'stopped the way.' It required some skilful manoeuvring on the part of the old chairmen (shoemakers by day; but, when summoned to carry the sedan, dressed up in a strange old livery – long great-coats, with small capes, coeval with the sedan, and similar to the dress of the class in Hogarth's pictures) to edge, and back, and try at it again, and finally to succeed in carrying their burden out of Miss Barker's front door. Then we heard their quick pit-a-pat along the quiet little street, as we put on our calashes, and pinned up our gowns; Miss Barker hovering about us with offers of help, which, if she had not remembered her former occupation, and wished us to forget it, would have been much more pressing.

Chapter VIII

'YOUR LADYSHIP'

Early the next morning – directly after twelve – Miss Pole made her appearance at Miss Matty's. Some very trifling piece of business was alleged as a reason for the call; but there was evidently something behind. At last out it came.

'By the way, you'll think I'm strangely ignorant; but, do you really know, I am puzzled how we ought to address Lady Glenmire. Do you say "Your ladyship," where you would say "you" to a common person? I have been puzzling all morning; and are we to say "My lady" instead of "Ma'am"? Now, you knew Lady Arley – will you kindly tell me the most correct way of speaking to the Peerage?'

Poor Miss Matty! she took off her spectacles, and she put them on again – but how Lady Arley was addressed she could not remember.

'It is so long ago,' she said. 'Dear! dear! how stupid I am! I don't think I ever saw her more than twice. I know we used to call Sir Peter "Sir Peter," – but he came much oftener to see us than Lady Arley did. Deborah would have known in a minute. "My lady – your ladyship." It sounds very strange, and as if it was not natural. I never thought of it before; but, now you have named it, I am all in a puzzle.'

It was very certain Miss Pole would obtain no wise decision from Miss Matty, who got more bewildered every moment, and more perplexed as to etiquettes of address.

'Well, I really think,' said Miss Pole, 'I had better just go and tell Mrs Forrester about our little difficulty. One sometimes grows nervous; and yet one would not have Lady Glenmire think we were quite ignorant of the etiquettes of high life in Cranford.'

'And will you just step in here, dear Miss Pole, as you come back, please; and tell me what you decide upon. Whatever you and Mrs Forrester fix upon will be quite right, I'm sure. "Lady Arley," "Sir Peter,"' said Miss Matty to herself, trying to recall the old forms of words.

'Who is Lady Glenmire?' asked I.

'Oh, she's the widow of Mr Jamieson – that's Mrs Jamieson's late husband, you know – widow of his eldest brother. Mrs Jamieson was a Miss Walker, daughter of Governor Walker. "Your ladyship." My dear, if they fix on that way of speaking, you must just let me practise a little on you first, for I shall feel so foolish and hot, saying it the first time to Lady Glenmire.'

It was really a relief to Miss Matty when Mrs Jamieson came on a very unpolite errand. I notice that apathetic people have more quiet impertinence than any others; and Mrs Jamieson came now to insinuate pretty plainly that she did not particularly wish that the Cranford ladies should call upon her sister-in-law. I can hardly say how she made this clear; for I grew very indignant and warm, while with slow deliberation she was explaining her wishes to Miss Matty, who, a true lady herself, could hardly understand the feeling which made Mrs Jamieson wish to appear to her noble sister-in-law as if she only visited 'county' families. Miss Matty remained puzzled and perplexed long after I had found out the object of Mrs Jamieson's visit.

When she did understand the drift of the honourable lady's call, it was pretty to see with what quiet dignity she received the intimation thus uncourteously given. She was not in the least hurt – she was of too gentle a spirit for that; nor was she exactly conscious of disapproving of Mrs Jamieson's conduct; but there was something of this feeling in her mind, I am sure, which made her pass from the subject to others, in a less flurried and more composed manner than usual. Mrs Jamieson was, indeed, the more flurried of the two, and I could see she was glad to take her leave.

A little while afterwards, Miss Pole returned, red and indignant. 'Well! to be sure! You've had Mrs Jamieson here, I find from Martha; and we are not to call on Lady Glenmire. Yes! I met Mrs Jamieson, half-way between here and Mrs Forrester's, and she told me; she took me so by surprise, I had nothing to say. I wish I had thought of something very sharp and sarcastic; I dare say I shall to-night. And Lady Glenmire is but the widow of a Scotch baron, after all! I went on to look at Mrs Forrester's Peerage, to see who this lady was, that is to be kept under a glass case: widow of a Scotch peer – never sat in the House of Lords – and as poor as Job, I daresay; and she – fifth daughter of some Mr Campbell or other. You are the daughter of a Rector, at any rate, and related to the Arleys; and Sir Peter might have been Viscount Arley, every one says.'

Miss Matty tried to soothe Miss Pole, but in vain. That lady, usually so kind and good-humoured, was now in a full flow of anger.

'And I went and ordered a cap this morning, to be quite ready,' said she, at last – letting out the secret which gave sting to Mrs Jamieson's intimation. 'Mrs Jamieson shall see if it is so easy to get me to make fourth at a pool, when she has none of her fine Scotch relations with her!'

In coming out of church, the first Sunday on which Lady Glenmire appeared in Cranford, we sedulously talked together, and turned our backs on Mrs Jamieson and her guest. If we might not call on her, we would not even look at her, though we were dying with curiosity to know what she was like. We had the comfort of questioning Martha in the afternoon. Martha did not belong to a sphere of society whose observation could be an implied compliment to Lady Glenmire, and Martha had made good use of her eyes.

'Well, ma'am! is it the little lady with Mrs Jamieson, you mean? I thought you would like more to know how young Mrs Smith was dressed, her being a bride.' (Mrs Smith was the butcher's wife.)

Miss Pole said, 'Good gracious me! as if we cared about a Mrs Smith'; but was silent as Martha resumed her speech.

'The little lady in Mrs Jamieson's pew had on, ma'am, rather an old black silk, and a shepherd's plaid cloak, ma'am, and very bright black eyes she had, ma'am, and a pleasant, sharp face; not over young, ma'am, but yet, I should guess, younger than Mrs Jamieson herself. She looked up and down the church, like a bird, and nipped up her petticoats when she came out, as quick and sharp as ever I see. I'll tell you what, ma'am, she's more like Mrs Deacon, at the "Coach and Horses," nor any one.'

'Hush, Martha!' said Miss Matty, 'that's not respectful.'

'Isn't it, ma'am? I beg pardon, I'm sure; but Jem Hearn said so as well. He said, she was just such a sharp, stirring sort of a body – '

'Lady,' said Miss Pole.

'Lady – as Mrs Deacon.'

Another Sunday passed away, and we still averted our eyes from

Mrs Jamieson and her guest, and made remarks to ourselves that we thought were very severe – almost too much so. Miss Matty was evidently uneasy at our sarcastic manner of speaking.

Perhaps by this time Lady Glenmire had found out that Mrs Jamieson's was not the gayest, liveliest house in the world; perhaps Mrs Jamieson had found out that most of the county families were in London, and that those who remained in the country were not so alive as they might have been to the circumstance of Lady Glenmire being in their neighbourhood. Great events spring out of small causes; so I will not pretend to say what induced Mrs Jamieson to alter her determination of excluding the Cranford ladies, and send notes of invitation all round for a small party, on the following Tuesday. Mr Mulliner himself brought them round. He *would* always ignore the fact of there being a back door to any house, and gave a louder rat-tat than his mistress, Mrs Jamieson. He had three little notes, which he carried in a large basket, in order to impress his mistress with an idea of their great weight, though they might easily have gone into his waistcoat pocket.

Miss Matty and I quietly decided we would have a previous engagement at home: – it was the evening on which Miss Matty usually made candle-lighters of all the notes and letters of the week; for on Mondays her accounts were always made straight – not a penny owing from the week before; so, by a natural arrangement, making candle-lighters fell upon a Tuesday evening, and gave us a legitimate excuse for declining Mrs Jamieson's invitation. But before our answer was written, in came Miss Pole with an open note in her hand.

'So!' she said. 'Ah! I see you have got your note, too. Better late than never. I could have told my Lady Glenmire she would be glad enough of our society before a fortnight was over.'

'Yes,' said Miss Matty, 'we're asked for Tuesday evening. And perhaps you would just kindly bring your work across and drink tea with us that night. It is my usual regular time for looking over the last week's bills, and notes, and letters, and making candle-lighters of them; but that does not seem quite reason enough for saying I have a previous engagement at home, though I meant to make it do. Now, if you would come, my conscience would be quite at ease, and luckily the note is not written yet.'

I saw Miss Pole's countenance change while Miss Matty was speaking.

'Don't you mean to go then?' asked she.

'Oh, no!' said Miss Matty, quietly. 'You don't either, I suppose?'

'I don't know,' replied Miss Pole. 'Yes, I think I do,' said she, rather briskly; and, on seeing Miss Matty look surprised, she added, 'You see, one would not like Mrs Jamieson to think that anything she could do, or say, was of consequence enough to give offence; it would be a kind of letting down of ourselves, that I, for one, should not like. It would be too flattering to Mrs Jamieson, if we allowed her to suppose that what she had said affected us a week, nay ten days afterwards.'

'Well! I suppose it is wrong to be hurt and annoyed so long about anything; and, perhaps, after all, she did not mean to vex us. But, I must say, I could not have brought myself to say the things Mrs Jamieson did about our not calling. I really don't think I shall go.'

'Oh, come! Miss Matty, you must go; you know our friend Mrs Jamieson is much more phlegmatic than most people, and does not enter into the little delicacies of feeling which you possess in so remarkable a degree.'

'I thought you possessed them, too, that day Mrs Jamieson called to tell us not to go,' said Miss Matty, innocently.

But Miss Pole, in addition to her delicacies of feeling, possessed a very smart cap, which she was anxious to show to an admiring world; and so she seemed to forget all her angry words uttered not a fortnight before, and to be ready to act on what she called the great Christian principle of 'Forgive and forget'; and she lectured dear Miss Matty so long on this head, that she absolutely ended by assuring her it was her duty, as a deceased rector's daughter, to buy a new cap, and go to the party at Mrs Jamieson's. So 'we were most happy to accept,' instead of 'regretting that we were obliged to decline.'

The expenditure on dress in Cranford was principally in that one article referred to. If the heads were buried in smart new caps, the ladies were like ostriches, and cared not what became of their bodies. Old gowns, white and venerable collars, any number of brooches, up and down and everywhere (some with dogs' eyes painted in them; some that were like small picture-frames with mausoleums and weeping-willows neatly executed in hair inside; some, again, with miniatures of ladies and gentlemen sweetly smiling out of a nest of stiff muslin) – old brooches for a permanent ornament, and new caps to suit the fashion of the day; the ladies of Cranford always dressed with chaste elegance and propriety, as Miss Barker once prettily expressed it.

And with three new caps, and a greater array of brooches than had ever been seen together at one time, since Cranford was a town, did Mrs Forrester, and Miss Matty, and Miss Pole appear on that memorable Tuesday evening. I counted seven brooches myself on Miss Pole's dress. Two were fixed negligently in her cap (one was a butterfly made of Scotch pebbles, which a vivid imagination might believe to be the real insect); one fastened her net neck-kerchief; one her collar; one ornamented the front of her gown, midway between her throat and waist; and another adorned the point of her stomacher. Where the seventh was I have forgotten, but it was somewhere about her, I am sure.

But I am getting on too fast, in describing the dresses of the company. I should first relate the gathering, on the way to Mrs Jamieson's. That lady lived in a large house just outside the town. A road, which had known what it was to be a street, ran right before the house, which opened out upon it, without any intervening garden or court. Whatever the sun was about, he never shone on the front of that house. To be sure, the living-rooms were at the back, looking on to a pleasant garden; the front windows only belonged to kitchens and housekeepers' rooms, and pantries; and in one of them Mr Mulliner was reported to sit. Indeed, looking askance, we often saw the back of a head, covered with hair-powder, which also extended itself over his coat-collar down to his very waist; and this imposing back was always engaged in reading the *St James's Chronicle,* opened wide, which, in some degree, accounted for the length of time the said newspaper was in reaching us – equal subscribers with Mrs Jamieson, though, in right of her honourableness, she always had the reading of it first. This very Tuesday, the delay in forwarding the last number had been particularly aggravating; just when both Miss Pole and Miss Matty, the former more especially, had been wanting to see it, in order to coach up the court news, ready for the evening's interview with aristocracy. Miss Pole told us she had absolutely taken time by the forelock and been dressed by five o'clock, in order to be ready, if the *St James's Chronicle* should come in at the last moment – the very *St James's Chronicle* which the powdered head was tranquilly and composedly reading as we passed the accustomed window this evening.

'The impudence of the man!' said Miss Pole, in a low indignant whisper. 'I should like to ask him, whether his mistress pays her quarter share for his exclusive use.'

We looked at her in admiration of the courage of her thought; for Mr Mulliner was an object of great awe to all of us. He seemed never to have forgotten his condescension in coming to live at Cranford. Miss Jenkyns, at times, had stood forth as the undaunted champion of her sex, and spoken to him on terms of equality; but even Miss Jenkyns could get no higher. In his pleasantest and most gracious moods he looked like a sulky cockatoo. He did not speak except in gruff monosyllables. He would wait in the hall when we begged him not to wait, and then looked deeply offended because we had kept him there, while, with trembling, hasty hands, we prepared ourselves for appearing in company.

Miss Pole ventured on a small joke as we went up-stairs, intended, though addressed to us, to afford Mr Mulliner some slight amusement. We all smiled, in order to seem as if we felt at our ease, and timidly looked for Mr Mulliner's sympathy. Not a muscle of that wooden face had relaxed, and we were grave in an instant.

Mrs Jamieson's drawing-room was cheerful; the evening sun came streaming into it, and the large square window was clustered round with flowers. The furniture was white and gold; not the later style, Louis Quatorze I think they call it, all shells and twirls; no, Mrs Jamieson's chairs and tables had not a curve or bend about them. The chair and table legs diminished as they neared the ground, and were straight and square in all their corners. The chairs were all a-row against the walls, with the exception of four or five which stood in a circle round the fire. They were railed with white bars across the back, and knobbed with gold; neither the railings nor the knobs invited to ease. There was a japanned table devoted to literature, on which lay a Bible, a Peerage, and a Prayer Book. There was another square Pembroke table dedicated to the Fine Arts, on which were a kaleidoscope, conversation-cards, puzzle-cards (tied together to an interminable length with faded pink satin ribbon), and a box painted in fond imitation of the drawings which decorate tea-chests. Carlo lay on the worsted-worked rug, and ungraciously barked at us as we entered. Mrs Jamieson stood up, giving us each a torpid smile of welcome, and looking helplessly beyond us at Mr Mulliner, as if she hoped he would place us in chairs, for if he did not, she never could. I suppose he thought we could find our way to the circle round the fire, which reminded me of Stonehenge, I don't know why. Lady Glenmire came to the rescue of our hostess; and, somehow or other, we found ourselves for the first time placed agreeably, and not formally, in Mrs Jamieson's house. Lady Glenmire, now we had time to look at her, proved to be a bright little woman of middle age, who had been very pretty in the days of her youth, and who was even yet very pleasant-looking. I saw Miss Pole

Mrs Jamieson, meanwhile, was absorbed in wonder why Mr Mulliner did not bring the tea; and at length the wonder oozed out of her mouth.

'I had better ring the bell, my dear, had not I?' said Lady Glenmire, briskly.

'No – I think not – Mulliner does not like to be hurried.'

We should have liked our tea, for we dined at an earlier hour than Mrs Jamieson. I suspect Mr Mulliner had to finish the *St James's Chronicle* before he chose to trouble himself about tea. His mistress fidgeted and fidgeted, and kept saying, 'I can't think why Mulliner does not bring tea. I can't think what he can be about.' And Lady Glenmire at last grew quite impatient, but it was a pretty kind of impatience after all; and she rang the bell rather sharply, on receiving a half permission from her sister-in-law to do so. Mr Mulliner appeared in dignified surprise. 'Oh!' said Mrs Jamieson, 'Lady Glenmire rang the bell; I believe it was for tea.'

In a few minutes tea was brought. Very delicate was the china, very old the plate, very thin the bread and butter, and very small the lumps of sugar. Sugar was evidently Mrs Jamieson's favourite economy. I question if the little filigree sugar-tongs, made something like scissors, could have opened themselves wide enough to take up an honest, vulgar, good-sized piece; and when I tried to seize two little minnikin pieces at once, so as not to be detected in too many returns to the sugar-basin, they absolutely dropped one, with a little sharp clatter, quite in a malicious and unnatural manner. But before this happened we had had a slight disappointment. In the little silver jug was cream, in the larger one was milk. As soon as Mr Mulliner came in, Carlo began to beg, which was a thing our manners forbade us to do, though I am sure we were just as hungry; and Mrs Jamieson said she was certain we would excuse her if she gave her poor dumb Carlo his tea first. She accordingly mixed a saucerful for him, and put it down for him to lap; and then she told us how intelligent and sensible the dear little fellow was; he knew cream quite well, and constantly refused tea with only milk in it: so the milk was left for us; but we silently thought we were quite as intelligent and sensible as Carlo, and felt as if insult were added to injury, when we were called upon to admire the gratitude evinced by his wagging his tail for the cream, which should have been ours.

After tea we thawed down into common-life subjects. We were thankful to Lady Glenmire for having proposed some more bread and butter, and this mutual want made us better acquainted with her than we should ever have been with talking about the Court, though Miss Pole did say she had hoped to know how the dear Queen was from some one who had seen her.

The friendship, begun over bread and butter, extended on to cards. Lady Glenmire played Preference to admiration, and was a complete authority as to Ombre and Quadrille. Even Miss Pole quite forgot to say 'my lady,' and 'your ladyship,' and said 'Basto! ma'am'; 'you have Spadille, I believe,' just as quietly as if we had never held the great Cranford parliament on the subject of the proper mode of addressing a peeress.

As a proof of how thoroughly we had forgotten that we were in the presence of one who might have sat down to tea with a coronet, instead of a cap, on her head, Mrs Forrester related a curious little fact to Lady Glenmire – an anecdote known to the circle of her intimate friends, but of which even Mrs Jamieson was not aware. It related to some fine old lace, the sole relic of better days, which Lady Glenmire was admiring on Mrs Forrester's collar.

'Yes,' said that lady, 'such lace cannot be got now for either love or money; made by the nuns abroad they tell me. They say that they can't make it now, even there. But perhaps they can now they've passed the Catholic Emancipation Bill. I should not wonder. But, in the meantime, I treasure up my lace very much. I daren't even trust the washing of it to my maid' (the little charity school-girl I have named before, but who sounded well as 'my maid'). 'I always wash it myself. And once it had a narrow escape.

Of course, your ladyship knows that such lace must never be starched or ironed. Some people wash it in sugar and water; and some in coffee, to make it the right yellow colour; but I myself have a very good receipt for washing it in milk, which stiffens it enough, and gives it a very good creamy colour. Well, ma'am, I had tacked it together (and the beauty of this fine lace is, that when it is wet, it goes into a very little space), and put it to soak in milk, when, unfortunately, I left the room; on my return I found pussy on the table, looking very like a thief, but gulping very uncomfortably, as if she was half-choked with something she wanted to swallow, and could not. And, would you believe it? At first I pitied her, and said, "Poor pussy! poor pussy!" till, all at once, I looked and saw the cup of milk empty – cleaned out! "You naughty cat!" said I; and I believe I was provoked enough to give her a slap, which did no good, but only helped the lace down – just as one slaps a choking child on the back. I could have cried, I was so vexed; but I determined I would not give the lace up without a struggle for it. I hoped the lace might disagree with her at any rate; but it would have been too much for Job, if he had seen, as I did, that cat come in, quite placid and purring, not a quarter of an hour after, and almost expecting to be stroked. "No, pussy!" said I; "if you have any conscience, you ought not to expect that!" And then a thought struck me; and I rang the bell for my maid, and sent her to Mr Hoggins, with my compliments, and would he be kind enough to lend me one of his top-boots for an hour? I did not think there was anything odd in the message; but Jenny said, the young men in the surgery laughed as if they would be ill, at my wanting a top-boot. When it came, Jenny and I put pussy in, with her fore-feet straight down, so that they were fastened, and could not scratch, and we gave her a teaspoonful of currant-jelly, in which (your ladyship must excuse me) I had mixed some tartar emetic. I shall never forget how anxious I was for the next half-hour. I took pussy to my own room, and spread a clean towel on the floor. I could have kissed her when she returned the lace to sight, very much as it had gone down. Jenny had boiling water ready, and we soaked it and soaked it, and spread it on a lavender bush in the sun, before I could touch it again, even to put it in milk. But now, your ladyship would never guess that it had been in pussy's inside.'

We found out, in the course of the evening, that Lady Glenmire was going to pay Mrs Jamieson a long visit, as she had given up her apartments in Edinburgh, and had no ties to take her back there in a hurry. On the whole, we were rather glad to hear this, for she had made a pleasant impression upon us; and it was also very comfortable to find, from things which dropped out in the course of conversation, that, in addition to many other genteel qualities, she was far removed from the vulgarity of wealth.

'Don't you find it very unpleasant walking?' asked Mrs Jamieson, as our respective servants were announced. It was a pretty regular question from Mrs Jamieson, who had her own carriage in the coach-house, and always went out in a sedan-chair to the very shortest distances. The answers were nearly as much a matter of course.

'Oh dear, no! it is so pleasant and still at night!' 'Such a refreshment after the excitement of a party!' 'The stars are so beautiful!' This last was from Miss Matty.

'Are you fond of astronomy?' Lady Glenmire asked.

'Not very,' replied Miss Matty, rather confused at the moment to remember which was astronomy and which was astrology – but the answer was true under either circumstance, for she read, and was slightly alarmed at, Francis Moore's astrological predictions; and, as to astronomy, in a private and confidential conversation, she had told me, she never could believe that the earth was moving constantly, and that she would not believe it if she could, it made her feel so tired and dizzy whenever she thought about it.

In our pattens, we picked our way home with extra care that night; so refined and delicate were our perceptions after drinking tea with 'my lady.'

Chapter IX

SIGNOR BRUNONI

Soon after the events of which I gave an account in my last paper, I was summoned home by my father's illness; and for a time I forgot, in anxiety about him, to wonder how my dear friends at Cranford were getting on, or how Lady Glenmire could reconcile herself to the dullness of the long visit which she was still paying to her sister-in-law, Mrs Jamieson. When my father grew a little stronger I accompanied him to the seaside, so that altogether I seemed banished from Cranford, and was deprived of the opportunity of hearing any chance intelligence of the dear little town for the greater part of that year.

Late in November – when we had returned home again, and my father was once more in good health – I received a letter from Miss Matty; and a very mysterious letter it was. She began many sentences without ending them, running them one into another, in much the same confused sort of way in which written words run together on blotting-paper. All I could make out was, that if my father was better (which she hoped he was), and would take warning and wear a great-coat from Michaelmas to Lady Day, if turbans were in fashion, could I tell her? such a piece of gaiety was going to happen as had not been seen or known of since Wombwell's lions came, when one of them ate a little child's arm; and she was, perhaps, too old to care about dress, but a new cap she must have; and, having heard that turbans were worn, and some of the county families likely to come, she would like to look tidy, if I would bring her a cap from the milliner I employed; and oh, dear! how careless of her to forget that she wrote to beg I would come and pay her a visit next Tuesday; when she hoped to have something to offer me in the way of amusement, which she would not now more particularly describe, only sea-green was her favourite colour. So she ended her letter; but in a P.S. she added, she thought she might as well tell me what was the peculiar attraction to Cranford just now; Signor Brunoni was going to exhibit his wonderful magic in the Cranford Assembly Rooms, on Wednesday and Friday evening in the following week.

I was very glad to accept the invitation from my dear Miss Matty, independently of the conjurer; and most particularly anxious to prevent her from disfiguring her small gentle mousey face with a great Saracen's-head turban; and accordingly, I bought her a pretty, neat, middle-aged cap, which, however, was rather a disappointment to her when, on my arrival, she followed me into my bedroom, ostensibly to poke the fire, but in reality, I do believe, to see if the sea-green turban was not inside the cap-box with which I had travelled. It was in vain that I twirled the cap round on my hand to exhibit back and side fronts; her heart had been set upon a turban and all she could do was to say, with resignation in her look and voice:

'I am sure you did your best, my dear. It is just like the caps all the ladies in Cranford are wearing, and they have had theirs for a year, I dare say. I should have liked something newer, I confess – something more like the turbans Miss Betty Barker tells me Queen Adelaide wears; but it is very pretty, my dear. And I dare say lavender will wear better than sea-green. Well, after all, what is dress, that we should care about it! You'll tell me if you want anything, my dear. Here is the bell. I suppose turbans have not got down to Drumble yet?'

So saying, the dear old lady gently bemoaned herself out of the room, leaving me to dress for the evening, when, as she informed me, she expected Miss Pole and Mrs Forrester, and she hoped I should not feel myself too much tired to join the party. Of course I should not; and I made some haste to unpack and arrange my dress; but, with all my speed, I heard the arrivals and the buzz of conversation in the next room before I was ready. Just as I opened the door, I caught the words – 'I was foolish to expect anything very genteel out of the Drumble shops – poor girl! she did her best, I've no doubt.' But for all that, I had rather that she blamed Drumble and me than disfigured herself with a turban.

Miss Pole was always the person, in the trio of Cranford ladies now assembled, to have had adventures. She was in the habit of spending the morning in rambling from shop to shop; not to purchase anything (except an occasional reel of cotton, or a piece of tape), but to see the new articles and report upon them, and to collect all the stray pieces of intelligence in the town. She had a way, too, of demurely popping hither and thither into all sorts of places to gratify her curiosity on any point; a way which, if she had not looked so very genteel and prim, might have been considered impertinent. And now, by the expressive way in which she cleared her throat, and waited for all minor subjects (such as caps and turbans) to be cleared off the course, we knew she had something very particular to relate, when the due pause came – and I defy any people, possessed of common modesty, to keep up a conversation long, where one among them sits up aloft in silence, looking down upon all the things they chance to say as trivial and contemptible compared to what they could disclose, if properly entreated. Miss Pole began:

'As I was stepping out of Gordon's shop to-day, I chanced to go into the George (my Betty has a second-cousin who is chambermaid there, and I thought Betty would like to hear how she was), and, not seeing any one about, I strolled up the staircase, and found myself in the passage leading to the Assembly Room – (you and I remember the Assembly Room, I am sure, Miss Matty! and the menuets de la cour!) – so I went on, not thinking of what I was about, when, all at once, I perceived that I was in the middle of the preparations for to-morrow night – the room being divided with great clothes-maids, over which Crosby's men were tacking red flannel; very dark and odd it seemed; it quite bewildered me, and I was going on behind the screens, in my absence of mind, when a gentleman (quite the gentleman, I can assure you) stepped forwards and asked if I had any business he could arrange for me. He spoke such pretty broken English, I could not help thinking of Thaddeus of Warsaw and the Hungarian Brothers, and Santo Sebastiani; and while I was busy picturing his past life to myself, he had bowed me out of the room. But wait a minute! You have not heard half my story yet! I was going downstairs, when who should I meet but Betty's second-cousin. So, of course, I stopped to speak to her for Betty's sake; and she told me that I had really seen the conjurer; the gentleman who spoke broken English was Signor Brunoni himself. Just at this moment he passed us on the stairs, making such a graceful bow! in reply to which I dropped a curtsey – all foreigners have such polite manners, one catches something of it. But when he had gone downstairs, I bethought me that I had dropped my glove in the Assembly Room (it was safe in my muff all the time, but I never found it till afterwards); so I went back, and, just as I was creeping up the passage left on one side of the great screen that goes nearly across the room, who should I see but the very same gentleman that had met me before, and passed me on the stairs, coming now forwards from the inner part of the room, to which there is no entrance – you remember, Miss Matty! – and just repeating, in his pretty broken English, the inquiry if I had any business there – I don't mean that he put it quite so bluntly, but he seemed very determined that I should not pass the screen – so, of course, I explained about my glove, which, curiously enough, I found at that very moment.'

Miss Pole then had seen the conjurer – the real live conjurer! and numerous were the questions we all asked her. 'Had he a beard?' 'Was he young or old?' 'Fair or dark?' 'Did he look' – (unable to shape my question prudently, I put it in another form) – 'How did he look?' In short, Miss Pole was the heroine of the evening, owing to her morning's encounter. If she was not the rose (that is to say the conjurer), she had been near it.

Conjuration, sleight of hand, magic, witchcraft, were the subjects of the evening. Miss Pole was slightly sceptical, and inclined to think there might be a scientific solution found for even the proceedings of the Witch of Endor. Mrs Forrester believed everything from ghosts to death-watches. Miss Matty ranged between the two – always convinced by the last speaker. I think she was naturally more inclined to Mrs Forrester's side, but a desire of proving herself a worthy sister to Miss Jenkyns kept her equally balanced – Miss Jenkyns, who would never allow a servant to call the little rolls of tallow that formed themselves round candles, 'winding-sheets,' but insisted on their being spoken of as 'roly-poleys'! A sister of hers to be superstitious! It would never do.

After tea I was despatched downstairs into the dining-parlour for that volume of the old Encyclopaedia which contained the nouns beginning with C, in order that Miss Pole might prime herself with scientific explanations for the tricks of the following evening. It spoilt the pool at Preference which Miss Matty and Mrs Forrester had been looking forward to, for Miss Pole became so much absorbed in her subject, and the plates by which it was illustrated, that we felt it would be cruel to disturb her, otherwise than by one or two well-timed yawns, which I threw in now and then, for I was really touched by the meek way in which the two ladies were bearing their disappointment. But Miss Pole only read the more zealously, imparting to us no more interesting information than this:

'Ah! I see; I comprehend perfectly. A represents the ball. Put A between B and D – no! between C and F, and turn the second joint of the third finger of your left hand over the wrist of your right H. Very clear indeed! My dear Mrs Forrester, conjuring and witchcraft is a mere affair of the alphabet. Do let me read you this one passage?'

Mrs Forrester implored Miss Pole to spare her, saying, from a child upwards, she never could understand being read aloud to; and I dropped the pack of cards, which I had been shuffling very audibly; and by this discreet movement, I obliged Miss Pole to

perceive that Preference was to have been the order of the
evening, and to propose, rather unwillingly, that the pool should
commence. The pleasant brightness that stole over the other two
ladies' faces on this! Miss Matty had one or two twinges of self-
reproach for having interrupted Miss Pole in her studies: and did
not remember her cards well, or give her full attention to the
game, until she had soothed her conscience by offering to lend the
volume of the Encyclopaedia to Miss Pole, who accepted it
thankfully, and said Betty should take it home when she came
with the lantern.

The next evening we were all in a little gentle flutter at the idea
of the gaiety before us. Miss Matty went up to dress betimes, and
hurried me until I was ready, when we found we had an hour and
a half to wait before the 'doors opened at seven precisely.' And we
had only twenty yards to go! However, as Miss Matty said, it
would not do to get too much absorbed in anything, and forget
the time; so, she thought we had better sit quietly, without
lighting the candles, till five minutes to seven. So Miss Matty
dozed, and I knitted.

At length we set off; and at the door, under the carriage-way at
the George, we met Mrs Forrester and Miss Pole: the latter was
discussing the subject of the evening with more vehemence than
ever, and throwing A's and B's at our heads like hail-stones. She
had even copied one or two of the 'receipts' – as she called them
– for the different tricks, on backs of letters, ready to explain and
to detect Signor Brunoni's arts.

We went into the cloak-room adjoining the Assembly Room;
Miss Matty gave a sigh or two to her departed youth, and the
remembrance of the last time she had been there, as she adjusted
her pretty new cap before the strange, quaint old mirror in the
cloak-room. The Assembly Room had been added to the inn
about a hundred years before, by the different county families,
who met together there once a month during the winter, to dance
and play at cards. Many a county beauty had first swam through

the minuet, that she afterwards danced before Queen Charlotte, in this very room. It was said that one of the Gunnings had graced the apartment with her beauty; it was certain that a rich and beautiful widow, Lady Williams, had here been smitten with the noble figure of a young artist, who was staying with some family in the neighbourhood for professional purposes, and accompanied his patrons to the Cranford Assembly. And a pretty bargain poor Lady Williams had of her handsome husband, if all tales were true! Now, no beauty blushed and dimpled along the sides of the Cranford Assembly Room; no handsome artist won hearts by his bow, *chapeau bras* in hand: the old room was dingy; the salmon-coloured paint had faded into a drab; great pieces of plaster had chipped off from the white wreaths and festoons on its walls; but still a mouldy odour of aristocracy lingered about the place, and a dusty recollection of the days that were gone made Miss Matty and Mrs Forrester bridle up as they entered, and walk mincingly up the room, as if there were a number of genteel observers, instead of two little boys, with a stick of toffy between them with which to beguile the time.

We stopped short at the second front row; I could hardly understand why, until I heard Miss Pole ask a stray waiter if any of the county families were expected; and when he shook his head, and believed not, Mrs Forrester and Miss Matty moved forwards, and our party represented a conversational square. The front row was soon augmented and enriched by Lady Glenmire and Mrs Jamieson. We six occupied the two front rows, and our aristocratic seclusion was respected by the groups of shopkeepers who strayed in from time to time, and huddled together on the back benches. At least I conjectured so, from the noise they made, and the sonorous bumps they gave in sitting down; but when, in weariness of the obstinate green curtain, that would not draw up, but would stare at me with two odd eyes, seen through holes, as in the old tapestry story, I would fain have looked round at the merry chattering people behind me, Miss Pole clutched my arm, and begged me not to turn, for 'it was not the thing.' What 'the thing' was, I never could find out, but it must have been something eminently dull and tiresome. However, we all sat eyes right, square front, gazing at the tantalizing curtain, and hardly speaking intelligibly, we were so afraid of being caught in the vulgarity of making any noise in a place of public amusement. Mrs Jamieson was the most fortunate, for she fell asleep.

At length the eyes disappeared – the curtain quivered – one side went up before the other, which stuck fast; it was dropped again, and, with a fresh effort, and a vigorous pull from some unseen hand, it flew up, revealing to our sight a magnificent gentleman in the Turkish costume, seated before a little table, gazing at us (I should have said with the same eyes that I had last seen through the hole in the curtain) with calm and condescending dignity, 'like a being of another sphere,' as I heard a sentimental voice ejaculate behind me.

'That's not Signor Brunoni!' said Miss Pole decidedly, and so audibly that I am sure he heard, for he glanced down over his flowing beard at our party with an air of mute reproach. 'Signor Brunoni had no beard – but perhaps he'll come soon.' So she lulled herself into patience. Meanwhile, Miss Matty had reconnoitred through her eye-glass; wiped it, and looked again. Then she turned round, and said to me, in a kind, mild, sorrowful tone:

'You see, my dear, turbans *are* worn.'

But we had no time for more conversation. The Grand Turk, as Miss Pole chose to call him, arose and announced himself as Signor Brunoni.

'I don't believe him!' exclaimed Miss Pole, in a defiant manner. He looked at her again, with the same dignified upbraiding in his countenance. 'I don't!' she repeated, more positively than ever. 'Signor Brunoni had not got that muffy sort of thing about his chin, but looked like a close-shaved Christian gentleman.'

Miss Pole's energetic speeches had the good effect of awakening up Mrs Jamieson, who opened her eyes wide, in sign of the deepest attention – a proceeding which silenced Miss Pole, and encouraged the Grand Turk to proceed, which he did in very broken English – so broken that there was no cohesion between the parts of his sentences; a fact which he himself perceived at last, and so he left off speaking and proceeded to action.

Now we *were* astonished. How he did his tricks I could not imagine; no, not even when Miss Pole pulled out her pieces of paper and began reading aloud – or at least in a very audible whisper – the separate 'receipts' for the most common of his tricks. If ever I saw a man frown, and look enraged, I saw the Grand Turk frown at Miss Pole; but, as she said, what could be expected but unchristian looks from a Mussulman? If Miss Pole was sceptical, and more engrossed with her receipts and diagrams than with his tricks, Miss Matty and Mrs Forrester were mystified and perplexed to the highest degree. Mrs Jamieson kept taking her spectacles off and wiping them, as if she thought it was something defective in them which made the legerdemain; and Lady Glenmire, who had seen many curious sights in Edinburgh, was very much struck with the tricks, and would not at all agree with Miss Pole, who declared that anybody could do them with a little practice – and that she would, herself, undertake to do all he did, with two hours given to study the Encyclopaedia and make her third finger flexible.

At last Miss Matty and Mrs Forrester became perfectly awe-struck. They whispered together. I sat just behind them, so I could not help hearing what they were saying. Miss Matty asked Mrs Forrester 'if she thought it was quite right to have come to see such things? She could not help fearing they were lending encouragement to something that was not quite – ' a little shake of the head filled up the blank. Mrs Forrester replied, that the same thought had crossed her mind; she, too, was feeling very uncomfortable; it was so very strange. She was quite certain that it was her pocket-handkerchief which was in that loaf just now; and it had been in her own hand not five minutes before. She wondered who had furnished the bread? She was sure it could not be Dakin, because he was the churchwarden. Suddenly, Miss Matty half turned towards me:

'Will you look, my dear – you are a stranger in the town, and it won't give rise to unpleasant reports – will you just look round and see if the Rector is here? If he is, I think we may conclude that this wonderful man is sanctioned by the Church, and that will be a great relief to my mind!'

I looked, and I saw the tall, thin, dry, dusty Rector, sitting surrounded by National School boys, guarded by troops of his own sex from any approach of the many Cranford spinsters. His kind face was all agape with broad smiles, and the boys around him were in chinks of laughing. I told Miss Matty that the Church was smiling approval, which set her mind at ease.

I have never named Mr Hayter, the rector, because I, as a well-to-do and happy young woman, never came in contact with him. He was an old bachelor, but as afraid of matrimonial reports getting abroad about him as any girl of eighteen: and he would rush into a shop, or dive down an entry, sooner than encounter any of the Cranford ladies in the street; and, as for the Preference parties, I did not wonder at his not accepting invitations to them. To tell the truth, I always suspected Miss Pole of having given very vigorous chase to Mr Hayter when he first came to Cranford; and not the less, because now she appeared to share so vividly in his dread lest her name should ever be coupled with his. He found all his interests among the poor and helpless; he had treated the National School boys this very night to the performance; and virtue was for once its own reward, for they guarded him right and left, and clung round him as if he had been the queen-bee, and they the swarm. He felt so safe in their environment, that he could even afford to give our party a bow as we filed out. Miss Pole ignored his presence, and pretended to be absorbed in convincing us that we had been cheated, and had not seen Signor Brunoni after all.

Chapter X

THE PANIC

I think a series of circumstances dated from Signor Brunoni's visit to Cranford, which seemed; at the time connected in our minds with him, though I don't know that he had anything really to do with them. All at once all sorts of uncomfortable rumours got afloat in the town. There were one or two robberies – real *bonâ-fide* robberies; men had up before the magistrates and committed for trial; and that seemed to make us all afraid of being robbed; and for a long time at Miss Matty's, I know, we used to make a regular expedition all round the kitchens and cellars every night, Miss Matty leading the way, armed with the poker, I following with the hearth-brush, and Martha carrying the shovel and fire-irons with which to sound the alarm; and by the accidental hitting together of them she often frightened us so much that we bolted ourselves up, all three together, in the back kitchen, or store-room, or wherever we happened to be, till, when our affright was over, we recollected ourselves, and set out afresh with double valiance. By day we heard strange stories from the shopkeepers and cottagers, of carts that went about in the dead of night, drawn by horses shod with felt, and guarded by men in dark clothes, going round the town, no doubt in search of some unwatched house or some unfastened door.

Miss Pole, who affected great bravery herself, was the principal person to collect and arrange these reports, so as to make them assume their most fearful aspect. But we discovered that she had begged one of Mr Hoggins's worn-out hats to hang up in her lobby, and we (at least I) had my doubts as to whether she really would enjoy the little adventure of having her house broken into, as she protested she should. Miss Matty made no secret of being an arrant coward; but she went regularly through her housekeeper's duty of inspection – only the hour for this became earlier and earlier, till at last we went the rounds at half-past six, and Miss Matty adjourned to bed soon after seven, 'in order to get the night over the sooner.'

Cranford had so long piqued itself on being an honest and moral town, that it had grown to fancy itself too genteel and well-bred to be otherwise, and felt the stain upon its character at this time doubly. But we comforted ourselves with the assurance which we gave to each other, that the robberies could never have been committed by any Cranford person; it must have been a stranger or strangers who brought this disgrace upon the town, and occasioned as many precautions as if we were living among the Red Indians or the French.

This last comparison of our nightly state of defence and fortification was made by Mrs Forrester, whose father had served under General Burgoyne in the American war, and whose husband had fought the French in Spain. She indeed inclined to the idea that, in some way, the French were connected with the small thefts, which were ascertained facts, and the burglaries and highway robberies, which were rumours. She had been deeply impressed with the idea of French spies, at some time in her life; and the notion could never be fairly eradicated, but sprung up again from time to time. And now her theory was this: the Cranford people respected themselves too much, and were too grateful to the aristocracy who were so kind as to live near the town, ever to disgrace their bringing up by being dishonest or immoral; therefore, we must believe that the robbers were strangers – if strangers, why not foreigners? – if foreigners, who so likely as the French? Signor Brunoni spoke broken English like a Frenchman, and, though he wore a turban like a Turk, Mrs Forrester had seen a print of Madame de Staël with a turban on, and another of Mr Denon in just such a dress as that in which the conjurer had made his appearance; showing clearly that the French, as well as the Turks, wore turbans: there could be no doubt Signor Brunoni was a Frenchman – a French spy, come to discover the weak and undefended places of England; and, doubtless, he had his accomplices; for her part, she, Mrs Forrester, had always had her own opinion of Miss Pole's adventure at the George Inn – seeing two men where only one was believed to be: French people had ways and means, which she was thankful to say, the English knew nothing about; and she had never felt quite easy in her mind about going to see that conjurer; it was rather too much like a forbidden thing, though the Rector was there. In short, Mrs Forrester grew more excited than we had ever known her before; and, being an officer's daughter and widow, we looked up to her opinion, of course.

Really I do not know how much was true or false in the reports which flew about like wildfire just at this time; but it seemed to me then that there was every reason to believe that at Mardon (a small town about eight miles from Cranford) houses and shops were entered by holes made in the walls, the bricks being silently carried away in the dead of the night, and all done so quietly that no sound was heard either in or out of the house. Miss Matty gave it up in despair when she heard of this. 'What was the use,' said she, 'of locks and bolts, and bells to the windows, and going round the house every night? That last trick was fit for a conjurer. Now she did believe that Signor Brunoni was at the bottom of it.'

One afternoon, about five o'clock, we were startled by a hasty knock at the door. Miss Matty bade me run and tell Martha on no account to open the door till she (Miss Matty) had reconnoitred through the window; and she armed herself with a footstool to drop down on the head of the visitor, in case he should show a face covered with black crape, as he looked up in answer to her inquiry of who was there. But it was nobody but Miss Pole and Betty. The former came upstairs, carrying a little hand-basket, and she was evidently in a state of great agitation.

'Take care of that!' said she to me, as I offered to relieve her of her basket. 'It's my plate. I am sure there is a plan to rob my house to-night. I am come to throw myself on your hospitality, Miss Matty. Betty is going to sleep with her cousin at the George. I can sit up here all night, if you will allow me; but my house is so far from any neighbours; and I don't believe we could be heard if we screamed ever so!'

'But,' said Miss Matty, 'what has alarmed you so much? Have you seen any men lurking about the house?'

'Oh yes!' answered Miss Pole. 'Two very bad-looking men have gone three times past the house, very slowly; and an Irish beggar-woman came not half an hour ago, and all but forced herself in past Betty, saying her children were starving, and she must speak to the mistress. You see, she said "mistress," though there was a hat hanging up in the hall, and it would have been more natural to have said "master." But Betty shut the door in her face, and came up to me, and we got the spoons together, and sat in the parlour-window watching, till we saw Thomas Jones going from his work, when we called to him and asked him to take care of us into the town.'

We might have triumphed over Miss Pole, who had professed such bravery until she was frightened; but we were too glad to perceive that she shared in the weaknesses of humanity to exult over her; and I gave up my room to her very willingly, and shared Miss Matty's bed for the night. But before we retired, the two ladies rummaged up, out of the recesses of their memory, such horrid stories of robbery and murder, that I quite quaked in my shoes. Miss Pole was evidently anxious to prove that such terrible events had occurred within her experience that she was justified in her sudden panic; and Miss Matty did not like to be outdone, and capped every story with one yet more horrible, till it reminded me, oddly enough, of an old story I had read somewhere, of a nightingale and a musician, who strove one against the other which could produce the most admirable music, till poor Philomel dropped down dead.

One of the stories that haunted me for a long time afterwards, was of a girl, who was left in charge of a great house in Cumberland, on some particular fair-day, when the other servants all went off to the gaieties. The family were away in London, and a pedlar came by, and asked to leave his large and heavy pack in the kitchen, saying he would call for it again at night; and the girl (a gamekeeper's daughter), roaming about in search of amusement, chanced to hit upon a gun hanging up in the hall, and took it down to look at the chasing; and it went off through the open kitchen door, hit the pack, and a slow dark thread of blood came oozing out. (How Miss Pole enjoyed this part of the story, dwelling on each word as if she loved it!) She rather hurried over the further account of the girl's bravery, and I have but a confused idea that, somehow, she baffled the robbers with Italian irons, heated red hot, and then restored to blackness by being dipped in grease.

We parted for the night with an awe-struck wonder as to what we should hear of in the morning – and, on my part, with a vehement desire for the night to be over and gone: I was so afraid lest the robbers should have seen, from some dark lurking-place, that Miss Pole had carried off her plate, and thus have a double motive for attacking our house.

But, until Lady Glenmire came to call next day, we heard of nothing unusual. The kitchen fire-irons were in exactly the same position against the back door, as when Martha and I had skilfully piled them up like spillikins, ready to fall with an awful clatter, if only a cat had touched the outside panels. I had wondered what we should all do if thus awakened and alarmed, and had proposed to Miss Matty that we should cover up our faces under the bed-clothes, so that there should be no danger of the robbers thinking that we could identify them; but Miss Matty, who was trembling very much, scouted this idea, and said we owed it to society to apprehend them, and that she should certainly do her best to lay hold of them, and lock them up in the garret till morning.

When Lady Glenmire came, we almost felt jealous of her. Mrs

Jamieson's house had really been attacked; at least there were men's footsteps to be seen on the flower-borders, underneath the kitchen windows, 'where nae men should be'; and Carlo had barked all through the night as if strangers were abroad. Mrs Jamieson had been awakened by Lady Glenmire, and they had rung the bell which communicated with Mr Mulliner's room in the third story, and when his night-capped head had appeared over the banisters, in answer to the summons, they had told him of their alarm, and the reasons for it; whereupon he retreated into his bedroom, and locked the door (for fear of draughts, as he informed them in the morning), and opened the window, and called out valiantly to say, if the supposed robbers would come to him he would fight them; but, as Lady Glenmire observed, that was but poor comfort, since they would have to pass by Mrs Jamieson's room and her own, before they could reach him, and must be of a very pugnacious disposition indeed, if they neglected the opportunities of robbery presented by the unguarded lower stories, to go up to a garret, and there force a door in order to get at the champion of the house. Lady Glenmire, after waiting and listening for some time in the drawing-room, had proposed to Mrs Jamieson that they should go to bed; but that lady said she should not feel comfortable unless she sat up and watched; and, accordingly, she packed herself warmly up on the sofa, where she was found by the housemaid, when she came into the room at six o'clock, fast asleep; but Lady Glenmire went to bed, and kept awake all night.

When Miss Pole heard of this, she nodded her head in great satisfaction. She had been sure we should hear of something happening in Cranford that night; and we had heard. It was clear enough they had first proposed to attack her house; but when they saw that she and Betty were on their guard, and had carried off the plate, they had changed their tactics and gone to Mrs Jamieson's, and no one knew what might have happened if Carlo had not barked, like a good dog as he was!

Poor Carlo! his barking days were nearly over. Whether the gang who infested the neighbourhood were afraid of him; or whether they were revengeful enough, for the way in which he had baffled them on the night in question, to poison him; or whether, as some among the more uneducated people thought, he died of apoplexy, brought on by too much feeding and too little exercise; at any rate, it is certain that, two days after this eventful night, Carlo was found dead, with his poor little legs stretched out stiff in the attitude of running, as if by such unusual exertion he could escape the sure pursuer, Death.

We were all sorry for Carlo, the old familiar friend who had snapped at us for so many years; and the mysterious mode of his death made us very uncomfortable. Could Signor Brunoni be at the bottom of this? He had apparently killed a canary with only a word of command; his will seemed of deadly force; who knew but what he might yet be lingering in the neighbourhood willing all sorts of awful things!

We whispered these fancies among ourselves in the evenings; but in the mornings our courage came back with the daylight, and in a week's time we had got over the shock of Carlo's death; all but Mrs Jamieson. She, poor thing, felt it as she had felt no event since her husband's death; indeed Miss Pole said, that as the Honourable Mr Jamieson drank a good deal, and occasioned her much uneasiness, it was possible that Carlo's death might be the greater affliction. But there was always a tinge of cynicism in Miss Pole's remarks. However, one thing was clear and certain: it was necessary for Mrs Jamieson to have some change of scene; and Mr Mulliner was very impressive on this point, shaking his head whenever we inquired after his mistress, and speaking of her loss of appetite and bad nights very ominously; and with justice too, for if she had two characteristics in her natural state of health, they were a facility of eating and sleeping. If she could neither eat nor sleep, she must be indeed out of spirits and out of health.

Lady Glenmire (who had evidently taken very kindly to

Cranford) did not like the idea of Mrs Jamieson's going to Cheltenham, and more than once insinuated pretty plainly that it was Mr Mulliner's doing, who had been much alarmed on the occasion of the house being attacked, and since had said, more than once, that he felt it a very responsible charge to have to defend so many women. Be that as it might, Mrs Jamieson went to Cheltenham, escorted by Mr Mulliner; and Lady Glenmire remained in possession of the house, her ostensible office being to take care that the maid-servants did not pick up followers. She made a very pleasant-looking dragon: and, as soon as it was arranged for her stay in Cranford, she found out that Mrs Jamieson's visit to Cheltenham was just the best thing in the world. She had let her house in Edinburgh, and was for the time houseless, so the charge of her sister-in-law's comfortable abode was very convenient and acceptable.

Miss Pole was very much inclined to instal herself as a heroine, because of the decided steps she had taken in flying from the two men and one woman, whom she entitled 'that murderous gang.' She described their appearance in glowing colours, and I noticed that every time she went over the story some fresh trait of villainy was added to their appearance. One was tall – he grew to be gigantic in height before we had done with him; he of course had black hair – and by-and-by, it hung in elf-locks over his forehead and down his back. The other was short and broad – and a hump sprouted out on his shoulder before we heard the last of him; he had red hair – which deepened into carroty; and she was almost sure he had a cast in his eye – a decided squint. As for the woman, her eyes glared, and she was masculine-looking – a perfect virago; most probably a man dressed in woman's clothes: afterwards, we heard of a beard on her chin, and a manly voice and a stride.

If Miss Pole was delighted to recount the events of that afternoon to all inquirers, others were not so proud of their adventures in the robbery line. Mr Hoggins, the surgeon, had been attacked at his own door by two ruffians, who were concealed in the shadow of the porch, and so effectually silenced him, that he was robbed in the interval between ringing his bell and the servant's answering it. Miss Pole was sure it would turn out that this robbery had been committed by 'her men,' and went the very day she heard of the report to have her teeth examined, and to question Mr Hoggins. She came to us afterwards; so we heard what she had heard, straight and direct from the source, while we were yet in the excitement and flutter of the agitation caused by the first intelligence; for the event had only occurred the night before.

'Well!' said Miss Pole, sitting down with the decision of a person who has made up her mind as to the nature of life and the world – (and such people never tread lightly, or seat themselves without a bump) – 'Well, Miss Matty! men will be men. Every mother's son of them wishes to be considered Samson and Solomon rolled into one – too strong ever to be beaten or discomfited – too wise ever to be outwitted. If you will notice, they have always foreseen events, though they never tell one for one's warning before the events happen; my father was a man, and I know the sex pretty well.'

She had talked herself out of breath, and we should have been very glad to fill up the necessary pause as chorus, but we did not exactly know what to say, or which man had suggested this diatribe against the sex; so we only joined in generally, with a grave shake of the head, and a soft murmur of 'They are very incomprehensible, certainly!'

'Now only think,' said she. 'There I have undergone the risk of having one of my remaining teeth drawn (for one is terribly at the mercy of any surgeon-dentist; and I, for one, always speak them fair till I have got my mouth out of their clutches), and after all, Mr Hoggins is too much of a man to own that he was robbed last night.'

'Not robbed!' exclaimed the chorus.

'Don't tell me!' Miss Pole exclaimed, angry that we could be for a moment imposed upon. 'I believe he was robbed, just as Betty told me, and he is ashamed to own it: and, to be sure, it was very silly of him to be robbed just at his own door; I dare say he feels that such a thing won't raise him in the eyes of Cranford society, and is anxious to conceal it – but he need not have tried to impose upon me, by saying I must have heard an exaggerated account of some petty theft of a neck of mutton, which, it seems, was stolen out of the safe in his yard last week; he had the impertinence to add, he believed that that was taken by the cat. I have no doubt, if I could get at the bottom of it, it was that Irishman dressed up in woman's clothes, who came spying about my house, with the story about the starving children.'

After we had duly condemned the want of candour which Mr Hoggins had evinced, and abused men in general, taking him for the representative and type, we got round to the subject about which we had been talking when Miss Pole came in – namely, how far, in the present disturbed state of the country, we could venture to accept an invitation which Miss Matty had just received from Mrs Forrester, to come as usual and keep the anniversary of her wedding-day, by drinking tea with her at five o'clock, and playing a quiet pool afterwards. Mrs Forrester had said, that she asked us with some diffidence, because the roads were, she feared, very unsafe. But she suggested that perhaps one of us would not object to take the sedan; and that the others, by walking briskly, might keep up with the long trot of the chairmen, and so we might all arrive safely at Over Place, a suburb of the town. (No. That is too large an expression: a small cluster of houses separated from Cranford by about two hundred yards of a dark and lonely lane.) There was no doubt but that a similar note was awaiting Miss Pole at home; so her call was a very fortunate affair, as it enabled us to consult together. We would all much rather have declined this invitation; but we felt that it would not be quite kind to Mrs Forrester, who would otherwise be left to a solitary retrospect of her not very happy or fortunate life. Miss Matty and

Miss Pole had been visitors on this occasion for many years; and now they gallantly determined to nail their colours to the mast, and to go through Darkness Lane rather than fail in loyalty to their friend.

But when the evening came, Miss Matty (for it was she who was voted into the chair, as she had a cold), before being shut down in the sedan, like jack-in-a-box, implored the chairmen, whatever might befall, not to run away and leave her fastened up there, to be murdered; and even after they had promised, I saw her tighten her features into the stern determination of a martyr, and she gave me a melancholy and ominous shake of the head through the glass. However, we got there safely, only rather out of breath, for it was who could trot hardest through Darkness Lane, and I am afraid poor Miss Matty was sadly jolted.

Mrs Forrester had made extra preparations, in acknowledgement of our exertion in coming to see her through such dangers. The usual forms of genteel ignorance as to what her servants might send up were all gone through; and harmony and Preference seemed likely to be the order of the evening, but for an interesting conversation that began I don't know how, but which had relation, of course, to the robbers who infested the neighbourhood of Cranford.

Having braved the dangers of Darkness Lane, and thus having a little stock of reputation for courage to fall back upon; and also, I dare say, desirous of proving ourselves superior to men (*videlicet* Mr Hoggins) in the article of candour, we began to relate our individual fears, and the private precautions we each of us took. I owned that my pet apprehension was eyes – eyes looking at me, and watching me, glittering out from some dull flat wooden surface; and that if I dared to go up to my looking-glass when I was panic-stricken, I should certainly turn it round, with its back towards me, for fear of seeing eyes behind me looking out of the darkness. I saw Miss Matty nerving herself up for a confession; and at last out it came. She owned that, ever since she had been a girl, she had dreaded being caught by her last leg, just as she was getting into bed, by some one concealed under it. She said, when she was younger and more active, she used to take a flying leap from a distance, and so bring both her legs up safely into bed at once; but that this had always annoyed Deborah, who piqued herself upon getting into bed gracefully, and she had given it up in consequence. But now the old terror would often come over her, especially since Miss Pole's house had been attacked (we had got quite to believe in the fact of the attack having taken place), and yet it was very unpleasant to think of looking under a bed, and seeing a man concealed, with a great fierce face staring out at you; so she had bethought herself of something – perhaps I had noticed that she had told Martha to buy her a penny ball, such as children play with – and now she rolled this ball under the bed every night; if it came out on the other side, well and good; if not, she always took care to have her hand on the bell-rope, and meant to call out John and Harry, just as if she expected men-servants to answer her ring.

We all applauded this ingenious contrivance, and Miss Matty sank back into satisfied silence, with a look at Mrs Forrester as if to ask for *her* private weakness.

Mrs Forrester looked askance at Miss Pole, and tried to change the subject a little, by telling us that she had borrowed a boy from one of the neighbouring cottages, and promised his parents a hundredweight of coals at Christmas, and his supper every evening for the loan of him at nights. She had instructed him in his possible duties when he first came; and, finding him sensible, she had given him the Major's sword (the Major was her late husband), and desired him to put it very carefully behind his pillow at night, turning the edge towards the head of the pillow. He was a sharp lad, she was sure; for, spying out the Major's cocked hat, he had said, if he might have that to wear he was sure he could frighten two Englishmen, or four Frenchmen, any day. But she had impressed upon him anew that he was to lose no time in putting on hats or anything else; but, if he heard any noise, he was to run at it with his drawn sword. On my suggesting that some accident might occur from such slaughterous and indiscriminate directions, and that he might rush on Jenny getting up to wash, and have spitted her before he had discovered that she was not a Frenchman, Mrs Forrester said she did not think that that was likely, for he was a very sound sleeper, and generally had to be well shaken, or cold-pigged in a morning before they could rouse him. She sometimes thought such dead sleep must be owing to the hearty suppers the poor lad ate, for he was half-starved at home, and she told Jenny to see that he got a good meal at night.

Still this was no confession of Mrs Forrester's peculiar timidity, and we urged her to tell us what she thought would frighten her more than anything. She paused, and stirred the fire, and snuffed the candles, and then she said, in a sounding whisper,

'Ghosts!'

She looked at Miss Pole, as much as to say she had declared it, and would stand by it. Such a look was a challenge in itself. Miss Pole came down upon her with indigestion, spectral illusions, optical delusions, and a great deal out of Dr Ferrier and Dr Hibbert besides. Miss Matty had rather a leaning to ghosts, as I have mentioned before, and what little she did say, was all on Mrs Forrester's side, who, emboldened by sympathy, protested that ghosts were a part of her religion; that surely she, the widow of a Major in the army, knew what to be frightened at, and what not; in short, I never saw Mrs Forrester so warm either before or since, for she was a gentle, meek, enduring old lady in most things. Not all the elder-wine that ever was mulled could this night wash out the remembrance of this difference between Miss Pole and her hostess. Indeed, when the elder-wine was brought in, it gave rise to a new burst of discussion; for Jenny, the little maiden who staggered under the tray, had to give evidence of having seen a ghost with her own eyes, not so many nights ago, in Darkness Lane – the very lane we were to go through on our way home.

In spite of the uncomfortable feeling which this last consideration gave me, I could not help being amused at Jenny's position, which was exceedingly like that of a witness being examined and cross-examined by two counsel who are not at all scrupulous about asking leading questions. The conclusion I arrived at was, that Jenny had certainly seen something beyond what a fit of indigestion would have caused. A lady all in white, and without her head, was what she deposed and adhered to, supported by a consciousness of the secret sympathy of her mistress under the withering scorn with which Miss Pole regarded her. And not only she, but many others, had seen this headless lady, who sat by the roadside wringing her hands as in deep grief. Mrs Forrester looked at us from time to time, with an air of conscious triumph; but then she had not to pass through Darkness Lane before she could bury herself beneath her own familiar bedclothes.

We preserved a discreet silence as to the headless lady while we were putting on our things to go home, for there was no knowing how near the ghostly head and ears might be, or what spiritual connexion they might be keeping up with the unhappy body in Darkness Lane; and therefore, even Miss Pole felt that it was as well not to speak lightly on such subjects, for fear of vexing or insulting that woe-begone trunk. At least, so I conjecture; for, instead of the busy clatter usual in the operation, we tied on our cloaks as sadly as mutes at a funeral. Miss Matty drew the curtains round the windows of the chair to shut out disagreeable sights; and the men (either because they were in spirits that their labours were so nearly ended, or because they were going down hill) set off at such a round and merry pace, that it was all Miss Pole and I could do to keep up with them. She had breath for nothing beyond an imploring 'Don't leave me!' uttered as she clutched my arm so tightly that I could not have quitted her, ghost or no ghost. What a relief it was when the men, weary of their burden and their quick trot, stopped just where Headingley-causeway branches off from Darkness Lane!

the adventure – the real adventure they had met with on their morning's walk. They had been perplexed about the exact path which they were to take across the fields, in order to find the knitting old woman, and had stopped to inquire at a little wayside public-house, standing on the high road to London, about three miles from Cranford. The good woman had asked them to sit down and rest themselves, while she fetched her husband, who could direct them better than she could; and, while they were sitting in the sanded parlour, a little girl came in. They thought that she belonged to the landlady, and began some trifling conversation with her; but, on Mrs Roberts's return, she told them that the little thing was the only child of a couple who were staying in the house. And then she began a long story, out of which Lady Glenmire and Miss Pole could only gather one or two decided facts; which were that, about six weeks ago, a light spring cart had broken down just before their door, in which there were two men, one woman, and this child. One of the men was seriously hurt – no bones broken, only 'shaken,' the landlady called it; but he had probably sustained some severe internal injury, for he had languished in their house ever since, attended by his wife, the mother of this little girl. Miss Pole had asked what he was, what he looked like. And Mrs Roberts had made answer that he was not like a gentleman, nor yet like a common person; if it had not been that he and his wife were such decent, quiet people, she could almost have thought he was a mountebank, or something of that kind, for they had a great box in the cart, full of she did not know what. She had helped to unpack it, and take out their linen and clothes, when the other man – the twin brother, she believed he was – had gone off with the horse and cart.

Miss Pole had begun to have her suspicions at this point, and expressed her idea that it was rather strange that the box and cart and horse and all should have disappeared; but good Mrs Roberts seemed to have become quite indignant at Miss Pole's implied suggestion; in fact, Miss Pole said, she was as angry as if Miss Pole had told her that she herself was a swindler. As the best way of convincing the ladies, she bethought her of begging them to see the wife; and, as Miss Pole said, there was no doubting the honest, worn, bronze face of the woman, who, at the first tender word from Lady Glenmire, burst into tears, which she was too weak to check, until some word from the landlady made her swallow down her sobs, in order that she might testify to the Christian kindness shown by Mr and Mrs Roberts. Miss Pole came round with a swing to as vehement a belief in the sorrowful tale as she had been sceptical before; and, as a proof of this, her energy in the poor sufferer's behalf was nothing daunted when she found out that he, and no other, was our Signor Brunoni, to whom all Cranford had been attributing all manner of evil this six weeks past! Yes! his wife said his proper name was Samuel Brown – 'Sam,' she called him – but to the last we preferred calling him 'the Signor;' it sounded so much better.

The end of their conversation with the Signora Brunoni was, that it was agreed that he should be placed under medical advice, and for any expense incurred in procuring this Lady Glenmire promised to hold herself responsible; and had accordingly gone to Mr Hoggins to beg him to ride over to the Rising Sun that very afternoon, and examine into the Signor's real state; and as Miss Pole said, if it was desirable to remove him to Cranford to be more immediately under Mr Hoggins's eye, she would undertake to see for lodgings, and arrange about the rent. Mrs Roberts had been as kind as could be all throughout; but it was evident that their long residence there had been a slight inconvenience.

Before Miss Pole left us, Miss Matty and I were as full of the morning's adventure as she was. We talked about it all the evening, turning it in every possible light, and we went to bed anxious for the morning, when we should surely hear from some one what Mr Hoggins thought and recommended. For, as Miss Matty observed, though Mr Hoggins did say 'Jack's up,' 'a fig for his heels,' and call Preference 'Pref,' she believed he was a very worthy man, and a very clever surgeon. Indeed, we were rather proud of our doctor at Cranford, as a doctor. We often wished, when we heard of Queen Adelaide or the Duke of Wellington being ill, that they would send for Mr Hoggins; but, on consideration, we were rather glad they did not, for if we were ailing, what should we do if Mr Hoggins had been appointed physician-in-ordinary to the Royal Family? As a surgeon we were proud of him; but as a man – or rather, I should say, as a gentleman – we could only shake our heads over his name and himself, and wished that he had read Lord Chesterfield's Letters in the days when his manners were susceptible of improvement. Nevertheless, we all regarded his dictum in the Signor's case as infallible; and when he said, that with care and attention he might rally, we had no more fear for him.

But although we had no more fear, everybody did as much as if there was great cause for anxiety – as indeed there was, until Mr Hoggins took charge of him. Miss Pole looked out clean and comfortable, if homely, lodgings; Miss Matty sent the sedan-chair for him; and Martha and I aired it well before it left Cranford, by holding a warming-pan full of red-hot coals in it, and then shutting it up close, smoke and all, until the time when he should get into it at the Rising Sun. Lady Glenmire undertook the medical department under Mr Hoggins's directions; and rummaged up all Mrs Jamieson's medicine glasses, and spoons, and bed tables, in a free and easy way, that made Miss Matty feel a little anxious as to what that lady and Mr Mulliner might say, if they knew. Mrs Forrester made some of the bread-jelly for which she was so famous, to have ready as a refreshment in the lodgings when he should arrive. A present of this bread-jelly was the highest mark of favour dear Mrs Forrester could confer. Miss Pole had once asked her for the receipt, but she had met with a very decided rebuff; that lady told her that she could not part with it to any one during her life, and that after her death it was bequeathed, as her executors would find, to Miss Matty. What Miss Matty –

or, as Mrs Forrester called her (remembering the clause in her will, and the dignity of the occasion), Miss Matilda Jenkyns – might choose to do with the receipt when it came into her possession – whether to make it public, or to hand it down as an heirloom – she did not know, nor would she dictate. And a mould of this admirable, digestible, unique bread-jelly was sent by Mrs Forrester to our poor sick conjurer. Who says that the aristocracy are proud? Here was a lady, by birth a Tyrrell, and descended from the great Sir Walter that shot King Rufus, and in whose veins ran the blood of him who murdered the little Princes in the Tower, going every day to see what dainty dishes she could prepare for Samuel Brown, a mountebank! But, indeed, it was wonderful to see what kind feelings were called out by this poor man's coming among us. And also wonderful to see how the great Cranford panic, which had been occasioned by his first coming in his Turkish dress, melted away into thin air on his second coming – pale and feeble, and with his heavy filmy eyes, that only brightened a very little when they fell upon the countenance of his faithful wife, or their pale and sorrowful little girl.

Somehow, we all forgot to be afraid. I dare say it was that finding out that he, who had first excited our love of the marvellous by his unprecedented arts, had not sufficient everyday gifts to manage a shying horse, made us feel as if we were ourselves again. Miss Pole came with her little basket at all hours of the evening, as if her lonely house, and the unfrequented road to it, had never been infested by that 'murderous gang'; Mrs Forrester said, she thought that neither Jenny nor she need mind the headless lady who wept and wailed in Darkness Lane, for surely the power was never given to such beings to harm those who went about to try to do what little good was in their power; to which Jenny, trembling, assented; but the mistress's theory had little effect on the maid's practice, until she had sewed two pieces of red flannel, in the shape of a cross, on her inner garment.

I found Miss Matty covering her penny ball – the ball that she used to roll under her bed – with gay-coloured worsted in rainbow stripes.

'My dear,' said she, 'my heart is sad for that little careworn child. Although her father is a conjurer, she looks as if she had never had a good game of play in her life. I used to make very pretty balls in this way when I was a girl, and I thought I would try if I could not make this one smart and take it to Phoebe this afternoon. I think "the gang" must have left the neighbourhood, for one does not hear any more of their violence and robbery now.'

We were all of us far too full of the Signor's precarious state to talk about either robbers or ghosts. Indeed, Lady Glenmire said, she never had heard of any actual robberies, except that two little boys had stolen some apples from Farmer Benson's orchard, and that some eggs had been missed on a market-day off Widow Hayward's stall. But that was expecting too much of us; we could not acknowledge that we had only had this small foundation for all our panic. Miss Pole drew herself up at this remark of Lady Glenmire's, and said 'that she wished she could agree with her as to the very small reason we had had for alarm; but, with the recollection of a man disguised as a woman, who had endeavoured to force himself into her house, while his confederates waited outside; with the knowledge gained from Lady Glenmire herself, of the footprints seen on Mrs Jamieson's flower borders; with the fact before her of the audacious robbery committed on Mr Hoggins at his own door – ' But here Lady Glenmire broke in with a very strong expression of doubt as to whether this last story was not an entire fabrication, founded upon the theft of a cat; she grew so red while she was saying all this, that I was not surprised at Miss Pole's manner of bridling up, and I am certain if Lady Glenmire had not been 'her ladyship,' we should have had a more emphatic contradiction than the 'Well, to be sure!' and similar fragmentary ejaculations, which were all that she ventured upon in my lady's presence. But when she was gone, Miss Pole began a long congratulation to Miss Matty that so far they had escaped marriage, which she noticed always made people credulous to the last degree; indeed, she thought it argued great natural credulity in a woman if she could not keep herself from being married; and in what Lady Glenmire had said about Mr Hoggins's robbery, we had a specimen of what people came to, if they gave way to such a weakness; evidently, Lady Glenmire would swallow anything, if she could believe the poor vamped-up story about a neck of mutton and a pussy, with which he had tried to impose on Miss Pole, only she had always been on her guard against believing too much of what men said.

We were thankful, as Miss Pole desired us to be, that we had never been married; but I think, of the two, we were even more thankful that the robbers had left Cranford; at least I judge so from a speech of Miss Matty's that evening, as we sat over the fire, in which she evidently looked upon a husband as a great protector against thieves, burglars, and ghosts; and said, that she did not think that she should dare to be always warning young people against matrimony, as Miss Pole did continually; – to be sure, marriage was a risk, as she saw now she had had some experience; but she remembered the time when she had looked forward to being married as much as any one.

'Not to any particular person, my dear,' said she, hastily checking herself up as if she were afraid of having admitted too much; 'only the old story, you know, of ladies always saying, "*When* I marry," and gentlemen, "*If* I marry."' It was a joke spoken in rather a sad tone, and I doubt if either of us smiled; but I could not see Miss Matty's face by the flickering fire-light. In a little while she continued:

'But after all I have not told you the truth. It is so long ago, and no one ever knew how much I thought of it at the time, unless, indeed, my dear mother guessed; but I may say that there was a time when I did not think I should have been only Miss Matty Jenkyns all my life; for even if I did meet with any one who wished to marry me now (and as Miss Pole says, one is never too safe), I could not take him – I hope he would not take it too much to heart, but I could *not* take him – or any one but the person I once thought I should be married to, and he is dead and gone, and he never knew how it all came about that I said "No," when I had thought many and many a time – Well, it's no matter what I thought. God ordains it all, and I am very happy, my dear. No one has such kind friends as I,' continued she, taking my hand and holding it in hers.

If I had never known of Mr Holbrook, I could have said something in this pause, but as I had, I could not think of anything that would come in naturally, and so we both kept silence for a little time.

'My father once made us,' she began, 'keep a diary, in two columns; on one side we were to put down in the morning what we thought would be the course and events of the coming day, and at night we were to put down on the other side what really had happened. It would be to some people rather a sad way of telling their lives' – (a tear dropped upon my hand at these words) – 'I don't mean that mine has been sad, only so very different to what I expected. I remember, one winter's evening, sitting over our bedroom fire with Deborah – I remember it as if it were yesterday – and we were planning our future lives – both of us were planning, though only she talked about it. She said she should like to marry an archdeacon, and write his charges; and you know, my dear, she never was married, and, for aught I know, she never spoke to an unmarried archdeacon in her life. I never was ambitious, nor could I have written charges, but I thought I could manage a house (my mother used to call me her right hand), and I was always so fond of little children – the shyest babies would stretch out their little arms to come to me; when I was a girl, I was half my leisure time nursing in the neighbouring cottages – but I don't know how it was, when I grew sad and grave – which I did a year or two after this time – the little things drew back from me, and I am afraid I lost the knack, though I am just as fond of children as ever, and have a strange yearning at my heart whenever I see a mother with her baby in her arms. Nay, my dear' – (and by a sudden blaze which sprang up from a fall of the unstirred coals, I saw that her eyes were full of tears – gazing intently on some vision of what might have been) – 'do you know, I dream sometimes that I have a little child – always the same – a little girl of about two years old; she never grows older, though I have dreamt about her for many years. I don't think I ever dream of any words or sound she makes; she is very noiseless and still, but she comes to me when she is very sorry or very glad, and I have wakened with the clasp of her dear little arms round my neck. Only last night – perhaps because I had gone to sleep thinking of this ball for Phoebe – my little darling came in my dream, and put up her mouth to be kissed, just as I have seen real babies do to real mothers before going to bed. But all this is nonsense, dear! only don't be frightened by Miss Pole from being married. I can fancy it may be a very happy state, and a little credulity helps one on through life very smoothly – better than always doubting and doubting, and seeing difficulties and disagreeables in everything.'

If I had been inclined to be daunted from matrimony, it would not have been Miss Pole to do it; it would have been the lot of poor Signor Brunoni and his wife. And yet again, it was an encouragement to see how, through all their cares and sorrows, they thought of each other and not of themselves; and how keen were their joys, if they only passed through each other, or through the little Phoebe.

The Signora told me, one day, a good deal about their lives up to this period. It began by my asking her whether Miss Pole's story of the twin-brothers was true; it sounded so wonderful a likeness, that I should have had my doubts, if Miss Pole had not been unmarried. But the Signora, or (as we found out she preferred to be called) Mrs Brown, said it was quite true; that her brother-in-law was by many taken for her husband, which was of great assistance to them in their profession; 'though,' she continued, 'how people can mistake Thomas for the real Signor Brunoni, I can't conceive; but he says they do; so I suppose I must believe him. Not but what he is a very good man; I am sure I don't know how we should have paid our bill at the Rising Sun but for the money he sends; but people must know very little about art, if they can take him for my husband. Why, Miss, in the ball trick, where my husband spreads his fingers wide, and throws out his little finger with quite an air and a grace, Thomas just clumps up his hand like a fist, and might have ever so many balls hidden in it. Besides, he has never been in India, and knows nothing of the proper sit of a turban.'

'Have you been in India?' said I, rather astonished.

'Oh, yes! many a year, ma'am. Sam was a sergeant in the 31st; and when the regiment was ordered to India, I drew a lot to go, and I was more thankful than I can tell; for it seemed as if it would only be a slow death to me to part from my husband. But, indeed, ma'am, if I had known all, I don't know whether I would not rather have died there and then, than gone through what I have done since. To be sure, I've been able to comfort Sam, and to be with him; but, ma'am, I've lost six children,' said she, looking up at me with those strange eyes that I have never noticed but in mothers of dead children – with a kind of wild look in them, as if seeking for what they never more might find. 'Yes! Six children died off, like little buds nipped untimely, in that cruel India. I thought, as each died, I never could – I never would – love a child again; and when the next came, it had not only its own love, but the deeper love that came from the thoughts of its little dead brothers and sisters. And when Phoebe was coming, I said to my husband, "Sam, when the child is born, and I am strong, I shall leave you; it will cut my heart cruel; but if this baby dies too, I shall go mad; the madness is in me now; but if you let me go down to Calcutta, carrying my baby step by step, it will may-be work itself off; and I will save, and I will hoard, and I will beg – and I will die, to get a passage home to England, where our baby may live!" God bless him! he said I might go; and he saved up his pay, and I saved every pice I could get for washing or any way; and when Phoebe came, and I grew strong again, I set off. It was very lonely; through the thick forests, dark again with their heavy trees – along by the river's side – (but I had been brought up near the Avon in Warwickshire, so that flowing noise sounded like home) – from station to station, from Indian village to village, I went along, carrying my child. I had seen one of the officers' ladies with a little picture, ma'am – done by a Catholic foreigner, ma'am – of the Virgin and the little Saviour, ma'am. She had him on her arm, and her form was softly curled round him, and their cheeks touched. Well, when I went to bid good-bye to this lady, for whom I had washed, she cried sadly; for she, too, had lost her children, but she had not another to save, like me; and I was bold enough to ask her, would she give me that print? And she cried the more, and said *her* children were with that little blessed Jesus; and gave it me, and told me she had heard it had been painted on the bottom of a cask, which made it have that round shape. And when my body was very weary, and my heart was sick – (for there were times when I misdoubted if I could ever reach my home, and there were times when I thought of my husband; and one time when I thought my baby was dying) – I took out that picture and looked at it, till I could have thought the mother spoke to me, and comforted me. And the natives were very kind. We could not understand one another; but they saw my baby on my breast, and they came out to me, and brought me rice and milk, and sometimes flowers – I have got some of the flowers dried. Then, the next morning, I was so tired! and they wanted me to stay with them – I could tell that – and tried to frighten me from going into the deep woods, which, indeed, looked very strange and dark; but it seemed to me as if Death was following me to take my baby away from me; and as if I must go on, and on – and I thought how God had cared for mothers ever since the world was made, and

Jenkyns be the lost Peter? True, he was reported by many to be dead. But, equally true, some had said that he had arrived at the dignity of Great Lama of Thibet. Miss Matty thought he was alive. I would make further inquiry.

Chapter XII

ENGAGED TO BE MARRIED

Was the 'poor Peter' of Cranford the Aga Jenkyns of Chunderabaddad, or was he not? As somebody says, that was the question.

In my own home, whenever people had nothing else to do, they blamed me for want of discretion. Indiscretion was my bugbear fault. Everybody has a bugbear fault; a sort of standing characteristic – a *pièce de résistance* for their friends to cut at; and in general they cut and come again. I was tired of being called indiscreet and incautious; and I determined for once to prove myself a model of prudence and wisdom. I would not even hint my suspicions respecting the Aga. I would collect evidence and carry it home to lay before my father, as the family friend of the two Miss Jenkynses.

In my search after facts, I was often reminded of a description my father had once given of a Ladies' Committee that he had had to preside over. He said he could not help thinking of a passage in Dickens, which spoke of a chorus in which every man took the tune he knew best, and sang it to his own satisfaction. So, at this charitable committee, every lady took the subject uppermost in her mind, and talked about it to her own great contentment, but not much to the advancement of the subject they had met to discuss. But even that committee could have been nothing to the Cranford ladies when I attempted to gain some clear and definite information as to poor Peter's height, appearance, and when and where he was seen and heard of last. For instance, I remember asking Miss Pole – (and I thought the question was very opportune, for I put it when I met her at a call at Mrs Forrester's, and both the ladies had known Peter, and I imagined that they might refresh each other's memories) – I asked Miss Pole what was the very last thing they had ever heard about him; and then she named the absurd report to which I have alluded, about his having been elected Great Lama of Thibet; and this was a signal for each lady to go off on her separate idea. Mrs Forrester's start was made on the Veiled Prophet in Lalla Rookh – whether I thought he was meant for the Great Lama, though Peter was not so ugly, indeed rather handsome if he had not been freckled. I was thankful to see her double upon Peter; but, in a moment, the delusive lady was off upon Rowland's Kalydor, and the merits of cosmetics and hair oils in general, and holding forth so fluently that I turned to listen to Miss Pole, who (through the llamas, the beasts of burden) had got to Peruvian bonds, and the share market, and her poor opinion of joint-stock banks in general, and of that one in particular in which Miss Matty's money was invested. In vain I put in, 'When was it – in what year was it that you heard that Mr Peter was the Great Lama?' They only joined issue to dispute whether llamas were carnivorous animals or not; in which dispute they were not quite on fair grounds, as Mrs Forrester (after they had grown warm and cool again) acknowledged that she always confused carnivorous and graminivorous together, just as she did horizontal and perpendicular; but then she apologized for it very prettily, by saying that in her day the only use people made of four-syllabled words was to teach how they should be spelt.

The only fact I gained from this conversation was that certainly Peter had been last heard of in India, 'or that neighbourhood'; and that this scanty intelligence of his whereabouts had reached Cranford in the year when Miss Pole had bought her India muslin gown, long since worn out (we washed it and mended it, and traced its decline and fall into a window-blind, before we could go on); and in a year when Wombwell came to Cranford, because Miss Matty had wanted to see an elephant in order that she might the better imagine Peter riding on one; and had seen a boa-constrictor too, which was more than she wished to imagine in her fancy-pictures of Peter's locality; and in a year when Miss Jenkyns had learnt some piece of poetry off by heart, and used to say, at all the Cranford parties, how Peter was 'surveying mankind from China to Peru,' which everybody had thought very grand, and rather appropriate, because India was between China and Peru, if you took care to turn the globe to the left instead of the right.

I suppose, all these inquiries of mine, and the consequent curiosity excited in the minds of my friends, made us blind and deaf to what was going on around us. It seemed to me as if the sun rose and shone, and as if the rain rained on Cranford just as usual, and I did not notice any sign of the times that could be considered as a prognostic of any uncommon event; and, to the best of my belief, not only Miss Matty and Mrs Forrester, but even Miss Pole herself, whom we looked upon as a kind of prophetess, from the knack she had of foreseeing things before they came to pass – although she did not like to disturb her friends by telling them her foreknowledge – even Miss Pole herself was breathless with astonishment when she came to tell us of the astounding piece of news. But I must recover myself; the contemplation of it, even at this distance of time, has taken away my breath and my grammar, and unless I subdue my emotion, my spelling will go too.

We were sitting – Miss Matty and I – much as usual; she in the blue chintz easy-chair, with her back to the light, and her knitting in her hand – I reading aloud the *St James's Chronicle*. A few minutes more, and we should have gone to make the little alterations in dress usual before calling time (twelve o'clock) in Cranford. I remember the scene and the date well. We had been talking of the Signor's rapid recovery since the warmer weather had set in, and praising Mr Hoggins's skill, and lamenting his want of refinement and manner – (it seems a curious coincidence that this should have been our subject, but so it was) – when a knock was heard; a caller's knock – three distinct taps – and we were flying (that is to say, Miss Matty could not walk very fast, having had a touch of rheumatism) to our rooms, to change cap and collars, when Miss Pole arrested us by calling out as she came up the stairs, 'Don't go – I can't wait – it is not twelve, I know – but never mind your dress – I must speak to you.' We did our best to look as if it was not we who had made the hurried movement, the sound of which she had heard; for, of course, we did not like to have it supposed that we had any old clothes that it was convenient to wear out in the 'sanctuary of home,' as Miss Jenkyns once prettily called the back parlour, where she was tying up preserves. So we threw our gentility with double force into our manners, and very genteel we were for two minutes while Miss Pole recovered breath, and excited our curiosity strongly by lifting up her hands in amazement, and bringing them down in silence, as if what she had to say was too big for words, and could only be expressed by pantomime.

'What do you think, Miss Matty? What *do* you think? Lady Glenmire is to marry – is to be married, I mean – Lady Glenmire – Mr Hoggins – Mr Hoggins is going to marry Lady Glenmire!'

'Marry!' said we. 'Marry! Madness!'

'Marry!' said Miss Pole, with the decision that belonged to her character. '*I* said marry! as you do; and I also said, "What a fool my lady is going to make of herself!" I could have said "Madness!" but I controlled myself, for it was in a public shop that I heard of it. Where feminine delicacy is gone to, I don't know! You and I, Miss Matty, would have been ashamed to have known that our marriage was spoken of in a grocer's shop, in the hearing of shopmen!'

'But,' said Miss Matty, sighing as one recovering from a blow, 'perhaps it is not true. Perhaps we are doing her injustice.'

'No!' said Miss Pole. 'I have taken care to ascertain that. I went takes the surgery with it,' said Miss Pole, with a little dry laugh at her own joke. But, like many people who think they have made a severe and sarcastic speech, which yet is clever of its kind, she began to relax in her grimness from the moment when she made this allusion to the surgery; and we turned to speculate on the way in which Mrs Jamieson would receive the news. The person whom she had left in charge of her house to keep off followers from her maids, to set up a follower of her own! And that follower a man whom Mrs Jamieson had tabooed as vulgar, and inadmissible to Cranford society; not merely on account of his name, but because of his voice, his complexion, his boots, smelling of the stable, and himself, smelling of drugs. Had he ever been to see Lady Glenmire at Mrs Jamieson's? Chloride of lime would not purify the house in its owner's estimation if he had. Or had their interviews been confined to the occasional meetings in the chamber of the poor sick conjurer, to whom, with all our sense of the *mésalliance*, we could not help allowing that they had both been exceedingly kind? And now it turned out that a servant of Mrs Jamieson's had been ill, and Mr Hoggins had been attending her for some weeks. So the wolf had got into the fold, and now he was carrying off the shepherdess. What would Mrs Jamieson say? We looked into the darkness of futurity as a child gazes after a rocket up in the cloudy sky, full of wondering expectation of the rattle, the discharge, and the brilliant shower of sparks and light. Then we brought ourselves down to earth and the present time, by questioning each other (being all equally ignorant, and all equally without the slightest data to build any conclusions upon) as to when IT would take place? Where? How much a year Mr Hoggins had? Whether she would drop her title? And how Martha and the other correct servants in Cranford would ever be brought to announce a married couple as Lady Glenmire and Mr Hoggins? But would they be visited? Would Mrs Jamieson let us? Or must we choose between the Honourable Mrs Jamieson and the degraded Lady Glenmire? We all liked Lady Glenmire the best.

She was bright, and kind, and sociable, and agreeable; and Mrs Jamieson was dull, and inert, and pompous, and tiresome. But we had acknowledged the sway of the latter so long, that it seemed like a kind of disloyalty now even to meditate disobedience to the prohibition we anticipated.

Mrs Forrester surprised us in our darned caps and patched collars; and we forgot all about them in our eagerness to see how she would bear the information, which we honourably left to Miss Pole to impart, although, if we had been inclined to take unfair advantage, we might have rushed in ourselves, for she had a most out-of-place fit of coughing for five minutes after Mrs Forrester entered the room. I shall never forget the imploring expression of her eyes, as she looked at us over her pocket-handkerchief. They said, as plain as words could speak, 'Don't let nature deprive me of the treasure which is mine, although for a time I can make no use of it.' And we did not.

Mrs Forrester's surprise was equal to ours; and her sense of injury rather greater, because she had to feel for her Order, and saw more fully than we could do how such conduct brought stains on the aristocracy.

When she and Miss Pole left us we endeavoured to subside into calmness; but Miss Matty was really upset by the intelligence she had heard. She reckoned it up, and it was more than fifteen years since she had heard of any of her acquaintance going to be married, with the one exception of Miss Jessie Brown; and, as she said, it gave her quite a shock, and made her feel as if she could not think what would happen next.

I don't know whether it is a fancy of mine, or a real fact, but I have noticed that, just after the announcement of an engagement in any set, the unmarried ladies in that set flutter out in an unusual gaiety and newness of dress, as much as to say, in a tacit and unconscious manner, 'We also are spinsters.' Miss Matty and Miss Pole talked and thought more about bonnets, gowns, caps, and shawls, during the fortnight that succeeded this call, than I had known them do for years before. But it might be the spring weather, for it was a warm and pleasant March; and merinoes and beavers, and woollen materials of all sorts, were but ungracious receptacles of the bright sun's glancing rays. It had not been Lady Glenmire's dress that had won Mr Hoggins's heart, for she went about on her errands of kindness more shabby than ever. Although in the hurried glimpses I caught of her at church or elsewhere she appeared rather to shun meeting any of her friends, her face seemed to have almost something of the flush of youth in it; her lips looked redder, and more trembling full than in their old compressed state, and her eyes dwelt on all things with a lingering light, as if she was learning to love Cranford and its belongings. Mr Hoggins looked broad and radiant, and creaked up the middle aisle at church in a brand-new pair of top-boots – an audible, as well as visible, sign of his purposed change of state; for the tradition went, that the boots he had worn till now were the identical pair in which he first set out on his rounds in Cranford twenty-five years ago; only they had been new-pieced, high and low, top and bottom, heel and sole, black leather and brown leather, more times than any one could tell.

None of the ladies in Cranford chose to sanction the marriage by congratulating either of the parties. We wished to ignore the whole affair until our liege lady, Mrs Jamieson, returned. Till she came back to give us our cue, we felt that it would be better to consider the engagement in the same light as the Queen of Spain's legs – facts which certainly existed, but the less said about the better. This restraint upon our tongues – for you see if we did not speak about it to any of the parties concerned, how could we get answers to the questions that we longed to ask? – was beginning to be irksome, and our idea of the dignity of silence was paling before our curiosity, when another direction was given to our thoughts, by an announcement on the part of the principal shopkeeper of Cranford, who ranged the trades from grocer and cheesemonger to man-milliner, as occasion required, that the unusual occasions, such as Christmas Day, or Good Friday; and on those days the letters, which should have been delivered at eight in the morning, did not make their appearance until two or three in the afternoon; for every one liked poor Thomas, and gave him a welcome on these festive occasions. He used to say, 'He was welly stawed wi' eating, for there were three or four houses where nowt would serve 'em but he must share in their breakfast;' and by the time he had done his last breakfast, he came to some other friend who was beginning dinner; but come what might in the way of temptation, Tom was always sober, civil, and smiling; and, as Miss Jenkyns used to say, it was a lesson in patience, that she doubted not would call out that precious quality in some minds, where, but for Thomas, it might have lain dormant and undiscovered. Patience was certainly very dormant in Miss Jenkyns's mind. She was always expecting letters, and always drumming on the table till the post-woman had called or gone past. On Christmas Day and Good Friday she drummed from breakfast till church, from church-time till two o'clock – unless when the fire wanted stirring, when she invariably knocked down the fire-irons, and scolded Miss Matty for it. But equally certain was the hearty welcome and the good dinner for Thomas; Miss Jenkyns standing over him like a bold dragoon, questioning him as to his children – what they were doing – what school they went to; upbraiding him if another was likely to make its appearance, but sending even the little babies the shilling and the mince-pie which was her gift to all the children, with half-a-crown in addition for both father and mother. The post was not half of so much consequence to dear Miss Matty; but not for the world would she have diminished Thomas's welcome and his dole, though I could see that she felt rather shy over the ceremony, which had been regarded by Miss Jenkyns as a glorious opportunity of giving advice and benefiting her fellow-creatures. Miss Matty would steal the money all in a lump into his hand, as if she were ashamed of herself. Miss Jenkyns gave him each individual coin separate, with a 'There! that's for yourself; that's for Jenny,' &c. Miss Matty would even beckon Martha out of the kitchen while he ate his food: and once, to my knowledge, winked at its rapid disappearance into a blue cotton pocket-handkerchief. Miss Jenkyns almost scolded him if he did not leave a clean plate, however heaped it might have been, and gave an injunction with every mouthful.

I have wandered a long way from the two letters that awaited us on the breakfast-table that Tuesday morning. Mine was from my father. Miss Matty's was printed. My father's was just a man's letter; I mean it was very dull, and gave no information beyond that he was well, that they had had a good deal of rain, that trade was very stagnant, and there were many disagreeable rumours afloat. He then asked me if I knew whether Miss Matty still retained her shares in the Town and County Bank, as there were very unpleasant reports about it; though nothing more than he had always foreseen, and had prophesied to Miss Jenkyns years ago, when she would invest their little property in it – the only unwise step that clever woman had ever taken, to his knowledge – (the only time she ever acted against his advice, I knew). However, if anything had gone wrong, of course I was not to think of leaving Miss Matty while I could be of any use, &c.

'Who is your letter from, my dear? Mine is a very civil invitation, signed Edwin Wilson, asking me to attend an important meeting of the shareholders of the Town and County Bank, to be held in Drumble, on Thursday the twenty-first. I am sure, it is very attentive of them to remember me.'

I did not like to hear of this 'important meeting,' for though I did not know much about business, I feared it confirmed what my father said: however, I thought, ill news always came fast enough, so I resolved to say nothing about my alarm, and merely told her that my father was well, and sent his kind regards to her. She kept turning over and admiring her letter. At last she spoke –

'I remember their sending one to Deborah just like this; but that

229

I did not wonder at, for everybody knew she was so clear-headed. I am afraid I could not help them much; indeed, if they came to accounts, I should be quite in the way, for I never could do sums in my head. Deborah, I know, rather wished to go, and went so far as to order a new bonnet for the occasion; but when the time came, she had a bad cold; so they sent her a very polite account of what they had done. Chosen a Director, I think it was. Do you think they want me to help them to choose a Director? I am sure, I should choose your father at once.'

'My father has no shares in the Bank,' said I.

'Oh, no! I remember! He objected very much to Deborah's buying any, I believe. But she was quite the woman of business, and always judged for herself; and here, you see, they have paid eight per cent, all these years.'

It was a very uncomfortable subject to me, with my half knowledge; so I thought I would change the conversation, and I asked at what time she thought we had better go and see the fashions. 'Well, my dear,' she said, 'the thing is this: it is not etiquette to go till after twelve, but then, you see, all Cranford will be there, and one does not like to be too curious about dress and trimmings and caps, with all the world looking on. It is never genteel to be over-curious on these occasions. Deborah had the knack of always looking as if the latest fashion was nothing new to her; a manner she had caught from Lady Arley, who did see all the new modes in London, you know. So I thought we would just slip down this morning, soon after breakfast; for I do want half a pound of tea; and then we could go up and examine the things at our leisure, and see exactly how my new silk gown must be made; and then, after twelve, we could go with our minds disengaged, and free from thoughts of dress.'

We began to talk of Miss Matty's new silk gown. I discovered that it would be really the first time in her life that she had had to choose anything of consequence for herself: for Miss Jenkyns had always been the more decided character, whatever her taste might have been; and it is astonishing how such people carry the world before them by the mere force of will. Miss Matty anticipated the sight of the glossy folds with as much delight as if the five sovereigns, set apart for the purchase, could buy all the silks in the shop; and (remembering my own loss of two hours in a toy-shop before I could tell on what wonder to spend a silver threepence) I was very glad that we were going early that dear Miss Matty might have leisure for the delights of perplexity.

If a happy sea-green could be met with, the gown was to be sea-green: if not, she inclined to maize, and I to silver grey; and we discussed the requisite number of breadths until we arrived at the shop-door. We were to buy the tea, select the silk, and then clamber up the iron corkscrew stairs that led into what was once a loft, though now a fashion show-room.

The young men at Mr Johnson's had on their best looks, and their best cravats, and pivoted themselves over the counter with surprising activity. They wanted to show us upstairs at once; but on the principle of business first and pleasure afterwards, we stayed to purchase the tea. Here Miss Matty's absence of mind betrayed itself. If she was made aware that she had been drinking green tea at any time, she always thought it her duty to lie awake half through the night afterward – (I have known her take it in ignorance many a time without such effects) – and consequently green tea was prohibited the house; yet to-day she herself asked for the obnoxious article, under the impression that she was talking about the silk. However, the mistake was soon rectified; and then the silks were unrolled in good truth. By this time the shop was pretty well filled, for it was Cranford market-day, and many of the farmers and country people from the neighbourhood round came in, sleeking down their hair, and glancing shyly about from under their eyelids, as anxious to take back some notion of the unusual gaiety to the mistress or the lasses at home, and yet feeling that they were out of place among the smart shopmen and gay shawls and summer prints. One honest-looking man, however, made his way up to the counter at which we stood, and boldly asked to look at a shawl or two. The other country folk confined themselves to the grocery side; but our neighbour was evidently too full of some kind intention towards mistress, wife, or daughter, to be shy; and it soon became a question with me, whether he or Miss Matty would keep their shopman the longest time. He thought each shawl more beautiful than the last; and, as for Miss Matty, she smiled and sighed over each fresh bale that was brought out; one colour set off another, and the heap together would, as she said, make even a rainbow look poor.

'I am afraid,' said she, hesitating, 'whichever I choose I shall wish I had taken another. Look at this lovely crimson! it would be so warm in winter. But spring is coming on, you know. I wish I could have a gown for every season,' said she, dropping her voice – as we all did in Cranford whenever we talked of anything we wished for but could not afford. 'However,' she continued in a louder and more cheerful tone, 'it would give me a great deal of trouble to take care of them if I had them; so, I think, I'll only take one. But which must it be, my dear?'

And now she hovered over a lilac with yellow spots, while I pulled out a quiet sage-green, that had faded into insignificance under the more brilliant colours, but which was nevertheless a good silk in its humble way. Our attention was called off to our neighbour. He had chosen a shawl of about thirty shillings' value; and his face looked broadly happy, under the anticipation, no doubt, of the pleasant surprise he should give to some Molly or Jenny at home; he had tugged a leathern purse out of his breeches-pocket, and had offered a five-pound note in payment for the shawl, and for some parcels which had been brought round to him from the grocery counter; and it was just at this point that he attracted our notice. The shopman was examining the note with a puzzled, doubtful air:

'Town and County Bank! I am not sure, sir, but I believe we have received a warning against notes issued by this bank only this morning. I will just step and ask Mr Johnson, sir; but I'm afraid I must trouble you for payment in cash, or in a note of a different bank.'

I never saw a man's countenance fall so suddenly into dismay and bewilderment. It was almost piteous to see the rapid change.

'Dang it!' said he, striking his fist down on the table, as if to try which was the harder, 'the chap talks as if notes and gold were to be had for the picking up.'

Miss Matty had forgotten her silk gown in her interest for the man. I don't think she had caught the name of the bank, and in my nervous cowardice I was anxious that she should not; and so I began admiring the yellow-spotted lilac gown that I had been utterly condemning only a minute before. But it was of no use.

'What bank was it? I mean, what bank did your note belong to?'

'Town and County Bank.'

'Let me see it,' said she quietly to the shopman, gently taking it out of his hand, as he brought it back to return it to the farmer.

Mr Johnson was very sorry, but from information he had received, the notes issued by that bank were little better than waste paper.

'I don't understand it,' said Miss Matty to me in a low voice. 'That is our bank, is it not? – the Town and County Bank?'

'Yes,' said I. 'This lilac silk will just match the ribbons in your new cap, I believe,' I continued, holding up the folds so as to catch the light, and wishing that the man would make haste and be gone, and yet having a new wonder, that had only just sprung up, how far it was wise or right in me to allow Miss Matty to make this expensive purchase, if the affairs of the bank were really so bad as the refusal of the note implied.

But Miss Matty put on the soft dignified manner peculiar to her, rarely used, and yet which became her so well, and laying her hand gently on mine, she said:

'Never mind the silks for a few minutes, dear. I don't

understand you, sir,' turning now to the shopman, who had been attending to the farmer. 'Is this a forged note?'

'Oh, no, ma'am. It is a true note of its kind; but you see, ma'am, it is a joint-stock Bank, and there are reports out that it is likely to break. Mr Johnson is only doing his duty, ma'am, as I am sure Mr Dobson knows.'

But Mr Dobson could not respond to the appealing bow by any answering smile. He was turning the note absently over in his fingers, looking gloomily enough at the parcel containing the lately chosen shawl.

'It's hard upon a poor man,' said he, 'as earns every farthing with the sweat of his brow. How ever, there's no help for it. You must take back your shawl, my man; Lizzie must do on with her cloak for a while. And yon figs for the little ones – I promised them to 'em – I'll take them; but the 'bacco and the other things – '

'I will give you five sovereigns for your note, my good man,' said Miss Matty. 'I think there is some great mistake about it, for I am one of the shareholders, and I'm sure they would have told me if things had not been going on right.'

The shopman whispered a word or two across the table to Miss Matty. She looked at him with a dubious air.

'Perhaps so,' said she. 'But I don't pretend to understand business; I only know, that if it is going to fail, and if honest people are to lose their money because they have taken our notes – I can't explain myself,' said she, suddenly becoming aware that she had got into a long sentence with four people for audience – 'only I would rather exchange my gold for the note, if you please,' turning to the farmer, 'and then you can take your wife the shawl. It is only going without my gown a few days longer,' she continued, speaking to me. 'Then, I have no doubt, everything will be cleared up.'

'But if it is cleared up the wrong way?' said I.

'Why! then it will only have been common honesty in me, as a shareholder, to have given this good man the money. I am quite clear about it in my own mind; but, you know, I can never speak quite as comprehensibly as others can; – only you must give me your note, Mr Dobson, if you please, and go on with your purchases with these sovereigns.'

The man looked at her with silent gratitude – too awkward to put his thanks into words; but he hung back for a minute or two, fumbling with his note.

'I'm loth to make another one lose instead of me, if it is a loss; but, you see, five pounds is a deal of money to a man with a family; and, as you say, ten to one in a day or two the note will be as good as gold again.'

'No hope of that, my friend,' said the shopman.

'The more reason why I should take it,' said Miss Matty, quietly. She pushed her sovereigns towards the man, who slowly laid his note down in exchange. 'Thank you. I will wait a day or two before I purchase any of these silks; perhaps you will then have a greater choice. My dear! will you come upstairs?'

We inspected the fashions with as minute and curious an interest as if the gown to be made after them had been bought. I could not see that the little event in the shop below had in the least damped Miss Matty's curiosity as to the make of sleeves, or the sit of skirts. She once or twice exchanged congratulations with me on our private and leisurely view of the bonnets and shawls; but I was, all the time, not so sure that our examination was so utterly private, for I caught glimpses of a figure dodging behind the cloaks and mantles; and, by a dexterous move, I came face to face with Miss Pole, also in morning costume (the principal feature of which was her being without teeth, and wearing a veil to conceal the deficiency), come on the same errand as ourselves. But she quickly took her departure, because, as she said, she had a bad headache, and did not feel herself up to conversation.

As we came down through the shop, the civil Mr Johnson was awaiting us; he had been informed of the exchange of the note for gold, and with much good feeling and real kindness, but with a little want of tact, he wished to condole with Miss Matty, and impress upon her the true state of the case. I could only hope that he had heard an exaggerated rumour, for he said that her shares were worse than nothing, and that the bank could not pay a shilling in the pound. I was glad that Miss Matty seemed still a little incredulous; but I could not tell how much of this was real or assumed, with that self-control which seemed habitual to ladies of Miss Matty's standing in Cranford, who would have thought their dignity compromised by the slightest expression of surprise, dismay, or any similar feeling to an inferior in station, or in a public shop. However, we walked home very silently. I am ashamed to say, I believe I was rather vexed and annoyed at Miss Matty's conduct, in taking the note to herself so decidedly. I had so set my heart upon her having a new silk gown, which she wanted sadly; in general she was so undecided anybody might turn her round; in this case I had felt that it was no use attempting it, but I was not the less put out at the result.

Somehow, after twelve o'clock, we both acknowledged to a sated curiosity about the fashions, and to a certain fatigue of body (which was, in fact, depression of mind) that indisposed us to go out again. But still we never spoke of the note; till, all at once, something possessed me to ask Miss Matty if she would think it her duty to offer sovereigns for all the notes of the Town and County Bank she met with? I could have bitten my tongue out the minute I had said it. She looked up rather sadly, and as if I had thrown a new perplexity into her already distressed mind; and for a minute or two she did not speak. Then she said – my own dear Miss Matty – without a shade of reproach in her voice:

'My dear! I never feel as if my mind was what people call very strong; and it's often hard enough work for me to settle what I ought to do with the case right before me. I was very thankful to – I was very thankful that I saw my duty this morning, with the poor man standing by me; but it's rather a strain upon me to keep thinking and thinking what I should do if such and such a thing happened; and, I believe, I had rather wait and see what really does come; and I don't doubt I shall be helped then, if I don't fidget myself, and get too anxious beforehand. You know, love, I'm not like Deborah. If Deborah had lived, I've no doubt she would have seen after them, before they had got themselves into this state.'

We had neither of us much appetite for dinner, though we tried to talk cheerfully about indifferent things. When we returned into the drawing-room, Miss Matty unlocked her desk and began to look over her account-books. I was so penitent for what I had said in the morning, that I did not choose to take upon myself the presumption to suppose that I could assist her; I rather left her alone, as, with puzzled brow, her eye followed her pen up and down the ruled page. By-and-by she shut the book, locked her desk, and came and drew a chair to mine, where I sat in moody sorrow over the fire. I stole my hand into hers; she clasped it, but did not speak a word. At last she said, with forced composure in her voice, 'If that bank goes wrong, I shall lose one hundred and forty-nine pounds thirteen shillings and four-pence a year; I shall only have thirteen pounds a year left.' I squeezed her hand hard and tight. I did not know what to say. Presently (it was too dark to see her face) I felt her fingers work convulsively in my grasp; and I knew she was going to speak again. I heard the sobs in her voice as she said, 'I hope it's not wrong – not wicked – but oh! I am so glad poor Deborah is spared this. She could not have borne to come down in the world – she had such a noble, lofty spirit.'

This was all she said about the sister who had insisted upon investing their little property in that unlucky bank. We were later in lighting the candle than usual that night, and until that light shamed us into speaking, we sat together very silently and sadly.

However, we took to our work after tea with a kind of forced cheerfulness (which soon became real as far as it went), talking of that never-ending wonder, Lady Glenmire's engagement. Miss Matty was almost coming round to think it a good thing.

'I don't mean to deny that men are troublesome in a house. I don't judge from my own experience, for my father was neatness itself, and wiped his shoes on coming in as carefully as any woman; but still a man has a sort of knowledge of what should be done in difficulties, that it is very pleasant to have one at hand ready to lean upon. Now, Lady Glenmire, instead of being tossed about, and wondering where she is to settle, will be certain of a home among pleasant and kind people, such as our good Miss Pole and Mrs Forrester. And Mr Hoggins is really a very personable man; and as for his manners – why, if they are not very polished, I have known people with very good hearts, and very clever minds too, who were not what some people reckoned refined, but who were both true and tender.'

She fell off into a soft reverie about Mr Holbrook, and I did not interrupt her, I was so busy maturing a plan I had had in my mind for some days, but which this threatened failure of the bank had brought to a crisis. That night, after Miss Matty went to bed, I treacherously lighted the candle again, and sat down in the drawing-room to compose a letter to the Aga Jenkyns – a letter which should affect him if he were Peter, and yet seem a mere statement of dry facts if he were a stranger. The church clock pealed out two before I had done.

The next morning news came, both official and otherwise, that the Town and County Bank had stopped payment. Miss Matty was ruined.

She tried to speak quietly to me; but when she came to the actual fact, that she would have but about five shillings a week to live upon, she could not restrain a few tears.

'I am not crying for myself, dear,' said she, wiping them away; 'I believe I am crying for the very silly thought of how my mother would grieve if she could know – she always cared for us so much more than for herself. But many a poor person has less; and I am not very extravagant, and, thank God, when the neck of mutton, and Martha's wages, and the rent are paid, I have not a farthing owing. Poor Martha! I think she'll be sorry to leave me.'

Miss Matty smiled at me through her tears, and she would fain have had me see only the smile, not the tears.

Chapter XIV

FRIENDS IN NEED

It was an example to me, and I fancy it might be to many others, to see how immediately Miss Matty set about the retrenchment which she knew to be right under her altered circumstances. While she went down to speak to Martha, and break the intelligence to her, I stole out with my letter to the Aga Jenkyns, and went to the Signor's lodgings to obtain the exact address. I bound the Signora to secrecy; and, indeed, her military manners had a degree of shortness and reserve in them which made her always say as little as possible, except when under the pressure of strong excitement. Moreover – (which made my secret doubly sure) – the Signor was now so far recovered as to be looking forward to travelling and conjuring again in the space of a few days, when he, his wife, and little Phoebe, would leave Cranford. Indeed, I found him looking over a great black and red placard, in which the Signor Brunoni's accomplishments were set forth, and to which only the name of the town where he would next display them was wanting. He and his wife were so much absorbed in deciding where the red letters would come in with most effect (it might have been the Rubric for that matter), that it was some time before I could get my question asked privately, and not before I had given several decisions, the wisdom of which I questioned afterwards with equal sincerity as soon as the Signor threw in his doubts and reasons on the important subject. At last I got the

address, spelt by sound; and very queer it looked! I dropped it in
the post on my way home; and then for a minute I stood looking
at the wooden pane with a gaping slit which divided me from the
letter but a moment ago in my hand. It was gone from me like life
– never to be recalled. It would get tossed about on the sea, and
stained with sea-waves perhaps; and be carried among palm-trees,
and scented with all tropical fragrance; the little piece of paper, but
an hour ago so familiar and commonplace, had set out on its race
to the strange wild countries beyond the Ganges! But I could not
afford to lose much time on this speculation. I hastened home, that
Miss Matty might not miss me. Martha opened the door to me,
her face swollen with crying. As soon as she saw me she burst out
afresh, and taking hold of my arm she pulled me in, and banged
the door to, in order to ask me if indeed it was all true that Miss
Matty had been saying.

'I'll never leave her! No! I won't. I told her so, and said I could
not think how she could find in her heart to give me warning. I
could not have had the face to do it, if I'd been her. I might ha'
been just as good-for-nothing as Mrs Fitz-Adam's Rosy, who
struck for wages after living seven years and a half in one place. I
said I was not one to go and serve Mammon at that rate; that I
knew when I'd got a good missus, if she didn't know when she'd
got a good servant – '

'But, Martha,' said I, cutting in while she wiped her eyes.

'Don't "but Martha" me,' she replied to my deprecatory tone.
'Listen to reason – '

'I'll not listen to reason,' she said, now in full possession of her
voice, which had been rather choked with sobbing. 'Reason
always means what some one else has got to say. Now I think what
I've got to say is good enough reason. But, reason or not, I'll say
it, and I'll stick to it. I've money in the Savings Bank, and I've a
good stock of clothes, and I'm not going to leave Miss Matty. No!
not if she gives me warning every hour in the day!'

She put her arms akimbo, as much as to say she defied me; and, indeed, I could hardly tell how to begin to remonstrate with her, so much did I feel that Miss Matty, in her increasing infirmity, needed the attendance of this kind and faithful woman.

'Well! – ' said I at last.

'I'm thankful you begin with "well!" If you'd ha' begun with "but," as you did afore, I'd not ha' listened to you. Now you may go on.'

'I know you would be a great loss to Miss Matty, Martha – '

'I told her so. A loss she'd never cease to be sorry for,' broke in Martha, triumphantly.

'Still, she will have so little – so very little – to live upon, that I don't see just now how she could find you food – she will even be pressed for her own. I tell you this, Martha, because I feel you are like a friend to dear Miss Matty – but you know she might not like to have it spoken about.'

Apparently this was even a blacker view of the subject than Miss Matty had presented to her; for Martha just sat down on the first chair that came to hand, and cried out loud (we had been standing in the kitchen).

At last she put her apron down, and looking me earnestly in the face, asked, 'Was that the reason Miss Matty wouldn't order a pudding to-day? She said she had no great fancy for sweet things, and you and she would just have a mutton-chop. But I'll be up to her. Never you tell, but I'll make her a pudding, and a pudding she'll like, too, and I'll pay for it myself; so mind you see she eats it. Many a one has been comforted in their sorrow by seeing a good dish come upon the table.'

I was rather glad that Martha's energy had taken the immediate and practical direction of pudding-making, for it staved off the quarrelsome discussion as to whether she should or should not leave Miss Matty's service. She began to tie on a clean apron, and otherwise prepare herself for going to the shop for the butter, eggs, and what else she might require; she would not use a scrap of the articles already in the house for her cookery, but went to an old teapot in which her private store of money was deposited, and took out what she wanted.

I found Miss Matty very quiet, and not a little sad; but by-and-by she tried to smile for my sake. It was settled that I was to write to my father, and ask him to come over and hold a consultation; and as soon as this letter was despatched, we began to talk over future plans. Miss Matty's idea was to take a single room, and retain as much of her furniture as would be necessary to fit up this, and sell the rest; and there to quietly exist upon what would remain after paying the rent. For my part, I was more ambitious and less contented. I thought of all the things by which a woman, past middle age, and with the education common to ladies fifty years ago, could earn or add to a living, without materially losing caste; but at length I put even this last clause on one side, and wondered what in the world Miss Matty could do.

Teaching was, of course, the first thing that suggested itself. If Miss Matty could teach children anything, it would throw her among the little elves in whom her soul delighted. I ran over her accomplishments. Once upon a time I had heard her say she could play *'Ah! vous dirai-je, maman?'* on the piano; but that was long, long ago; that faint shadow of musical acquirement had died out years before. She had also once been able to trace out patterns very nicely for muslin embroidery, by dint of placing a piece of silver-paper over the design to be copied, and holding both against the window-pane, while she marked the scollop and eyelet-holes. But that was her nearest approach to the accomplishment of drawing, and I did not think it would go very far. Then again, as to the branches of a solid English education – fancy work and the use of the globes – such as the mistress of the Ladies' Seminary, to which all the tradespeople in Cranford sent their daughters, professed to teach; Miss Matty's eyes were failing her, and I doubted if she could discover the number of threads in a worsted-work pattern, or rightly appreciate the different shades required for Queen Adelaide's face, in the loyal wool-work now fashionable in Cranford. As for the use of the globes, I had never been able to find it out myself, so perhaps I was not a good judge of Miss Matty's capability of instructing in this branch of education; but it struck me that equators and tropics, and such mystical circles, were very imaginary lines indeed to her, and that she looked upon the signs of the Zodiac as so many remnants of the Black Art.

What she piqued herself upon, as arts in which she excelled, was making candle-lighters, or 'spills' (as she preferred calling them), of coloured paper, cut so as to resemble feathers, and knitting garters in a variety of dainty stitches. I had once said, on receiving a present of an elaborate pair, that I should feel quite tempted to drop one of them in the street, in order to have it admired; but I found this little joke (and it was a very little one) was such a distress to her sense of propriety, and was taken with such anxious, earnest alarm, lest the temptation might some day prove too strong for me, that I quite regretted having ventured upon it. A present of these delicately-wrought garters, a bunch of gay 'spills,' or a set of cards on which sewing-silk was wound in a mystical manner, were the well-known tokens of Miss Matty's favour. But would any one pay to have their children taught these arts? or, indeed, would Miss Matty sell, for filthy lucre, the knack and the skill with which she made trifles of value to those who loved her?

I had to come down to reading, writing, and arithmetic; and, in reading the chapter every morning, she always coughed before coming to long words. I doubted her power of getting through a genealogical chapter, with any number of coughs. Writing she did well and delicately; but spelling! She seemed to think that the more out-of-the-way this was, and the more trouble it cost her, the greater the compliment she paid to her correspondent; and words that she would spell quite correctly in her letters to me, became perfect enigmas when she wrote to my father.

No! there was nothing she could teach to the rising generation of Cranford; unless they had been quick learners and ready imitators of her patience, her humility, her sweetness, her quiet contentment with all that she could not do. I pondered and pondered until dinner was announced by Martha, with a face all blubbered and swollen with crying.

Miss Matty had a few little peculiarities, which Martha was apt to regard as whims below her attention, and appeared to consider as childish fancies, of which an old lady of fifty-eight should try and cure herself. But to-day everything was attended to with the most careful regard. The bread was cut to the imaginary pattern of excellence that existed in Miss Matty's mind, as being the way which her mother had preferred; the curtain was drawn so as to exclude the dead-brick wall of a neighbour's stables, and yet left so as to show every tender leaf of the poplar which was bursting into spring beauty. Martha's tone to Miss Matty was just such as that good, rough-spoken servant usually kept sacred for little children, and which I had never heard her use to any grown-up person.

I had forgotten to tell Miss Matty about the pudding, and I was afraid she might not do justice to it, for she had evidently very little appetite this day; so I seized the opportunity of letting her into the secret while Martha took away the meat. Miss Matty's eyes filled with tears, and she could not speak, either to express surprise or delight, when Martha returned, bearing it aloft, made in the most wonderful representation of a lion *couchant* that ever was moulded. Martha's face gleamed with triumph, as she set it down before Miss Matty with an exultant 'There!' Miss Matty wanted to speak her thanks, but could not; so she took Martha's hand and shook it warmly, which set Martha off crying, and I myself could hardly keep up the necessary composure. Martha burst out of the room; and Miss Matty had to clear her voice once or twice before she could speak. At last she said, 'I should like to keep this pudding under a glass shade, my dear!' and the notion of the lion *couchant*, with his currant eyes, being hoisted up to the place of honour on a mantelpiece, tickled my hysterical fancy, and I began to laugh, which rather surprised Miss Matty.

'I am sure, dear, I have seen uglier things under a glass shade before now,' said she.

So had I, many a time and oft; and I accordingly composed my countenance (and now I could hardly keep from crying), and we both fell to upon the pudding, which was indeed excellent – only every morsel seemed to choke us, our hearts were so full.

We had too much to think about to talk much that afternoon. It passed over very tranquilly. But when the tea-urn was brought in, a new thought came into my head. Why should not Miss Matty sell tea – be an agent to the East India Tea Company which then existed? I could see no objections to this plan, while the advantages were many – always supposing that Miss Matty could get over the degradation of condescending to anything like trade. Tea was neither greasy, nor sticky – grease and stickiness being two of the qualities which Miss Matty could not endure. No shop-window would be required. A small genteel notification of her being licensed to sell tea would, it is true, be necessary; but I hoped that it could be placed where no one would see it. Neither was tea a heavy article, so as to tax Miss Matty's fragile strength. The only thing against my plan was the buying and selling involved.

While I was giving but absent answers to the questions Miss Matty was putting – almost as absently – we heard a clumping sound on the stairs, and a whispering outside the door: which indeed once opened and shut as if by some invisible agency. After a little while Martha came in, dragging after her a great tall young man, all crimson with shyness, and finding his only relief in perpetually sleeking down his hair.

'Please, ma'am, he's only Jem Hearn,' said Martha, by way of an introduction; and so out of breath was she, that I imagine she had had some bodily struggle before she could overcome his reluctance to be presented on the courtly scene of Miss Matilda Jenkyns's drawing-room.

'And please, ma'am, he wants to marry me offhand. And please, ma'am, we want to take a lodger – just one quiet lodger, to make our two ends meet; and we'd take any house conformable; and, oh dear Miss Matty, if I may be so bold, would you have any objections to lodging with us? Jem wants it as much as I do.' [To Jem:] 'You great oaf! why can't you back me? – But he does want it, all the same, very bad – don't you, Jem? – only, you see, he's dazed at being called on to speak before quality.'

'It's not that,' broke in Jem. 'It's that you've taken me all on a sudden, and I didn't think for to get married so soon – and such quick work does flabbergast a man. It's not that I'm against it, ma'am' (addressing Miss Matty), 'only Martha has such quick ways with her, when once she takes a thing into her head; and marriage, ma'am – marriage nails a man, as one may say. I daresay I shan't mind it after it's once over.'

'Please, ma'am,' said Martha, who had plucked at his sleeve, and nudged him with her elbow, and otherwise tried to interrupt him all the time he had been speaking, 'don't mind him, he'll come to; 'twas only last night he was an-axing me, and an-axing me, and all the more because I said I could not think of it for years to come, and now he's only taken aback with the suddenness of the joy; but you know, Jem, you are just as full as me about wanting a lodger.' (Another great nudge.)

'Ay! if Miss Matty would lodge with us – otherwise I've no mind to be cumbered with strange folk in the house,' said Jem, with a want of tact which I could see enraged Martha, who was trying to represent a lodger as the great object they wished to obtain, and that, in fact, Miss Matty would be smoothing their path and conferring a favour, if she would only come and live with them.

Miss Matty herself was bewildered by the pair: their, or rather Martha's, sudden resolution in favour of matrimony staggered her, and stood between her and the contemplation of the plan which Martha had at heart. Miss Matty began:

'Marriage is a very solemn thing, Martha.'

'It is indeed, ma'am,' quoth Jem. 'Not that I've no objections to Martha.'

'You've never let me a-be for asking me for to fix when I would be married,' said Martha – her face all a-fire, and ready to cry with vexation – 'and now you're shaming me before my missus and all.'

'Nay, now! Martha, don't ee! don't ee! only a man likes to have breathing-time,' said Jem, trying to possess himself of her hand, but in vain. Then seeing that she was more seriously hurt than he had imagined, he seemed to try to rally his scattered faculties, and with more straightforward dignity than, ten minutes before, I should have thought it possible for him to assume, he turned to Miss Matty, and said, 'I hope, ma'am, you know that I am bound to respect every one who has been kind to Martha. I always looked on her as to be my wife – some time; and she has often and often spoken of you as the kindest lady that ever was; and though the plain truth is I would not like to be troubled with lodgers of the common run, yet if, ma'am, you'd honour us by living with us, I'm sure Martha would do her best to make you comfortable; and I'd keep out of your way as much as I could, which I reckon would be the best kindness such an awkward chap as me could do.'

Miss Matty had been very busy with taking off her spectacles, wiping them, and replacing them; but all she could say was, 'Don't let any thought of me hurry you into marriage: pray don't! Marriage is such a very solemn thing!'

'But Miss Matilda will think of your plan, Martha,' said I, struck with the advantages that it offered, and unwilling to lose the opportunity of considering about it. 'And I'm sure neither she nor I can ever forget your kindness; nor yours either, Jem.'

'Why, yes, ma'am! I'm sure I mean kindly, though I'm a bit fluttered by being pushed straight a-head into matrimony, as it were, and mayn't express myself conformable. But I'm sure I'm willing enough, and give me time to get accustomed; so, Martha, wench, what's the use of crying so, and slapping me if I come near?'

This last was *sotto voce*, and had the effect of making Martha bounce out of the room, to be followed and soothed by her lover. Whereupon Miss Matty sat down and cried very heartily, and accounted for it by saying that the thought of Martha being married so soon gave her quite a shock, and that she should never forgive herself if she thought she was hurrying the poor creature. I think my pity was more for Jem, of the two; but both Miss Matty and I appreciated to the full the kindness of the honest couple, although we said little about this, and a good deal about the chances and dangers of matrimony.

The next morning, very early, I received a note from Miss Pole, so mysteriously wrapped up, and with so many seals on it to secure secrecy, that I had to tear the paper before I could unfold it. And when I came to the writing I could hardly understand the meaning, it was so involved and oracular. I made out, however, that I was to go to Miss Pole's at eleven o'clock; the number *eleven* being written in full length as well as in numerals, and *A.M.* twice dashed under, as if I were very likely to come at eleven at night, when all Cranford was usually a-bed and asleep by ten. There was no signature except Miss Pole's initials, reversed, P. E.; but as Martha had given me the note, 'with Miss Pole's kind regards,' it needed no wizard to find out who sent it; and if the writer's name was to be kept secret, it was very well that I was alone when Martha delivered it.

I went, as requested, to Miss Pole's. The door was opened to me by her little maid Lizzy, in Sunday trim, as if some grand event was impending over this workday. And the drawing-room upstairs was arranged in accordance with this idea. The table was set out, with the best green card-cloth, and writing materials upon it. On the little chiffonier was a tray with a newly-decanted bottle of cowslip wine, and some ladies'-finger biscuits. Miss Pole herself was in solemn array, as if to receive visitors, although it was only eleven o'clock. Mrs Forrester was there, crying quietly and sadly, and my arrival seemed only to call forth fresh tears. Before we had finished our greetings, performed with lugubrious mystery and demeanour, there was another rat-tat-tat, and Mrs Fitz-Adam appeared, crimson with walking and excitement. It seemed as if this was all the company expected; for now Miss Pole made several demonstrations of being about to open the business of the meeting, by stirring the fire, opening and shutting the door, and coughing and blowing her nose. Then she arranged us all round the table, taking care to place me opposite to her; and last of all, she inquired of me if the sad report was true, as she feared it was, that Miss Matty had lost all her fortune?

Of course, I had but one answer to make; and I never saw more unaffected sorrow depicted on any countenances than I did there on the three before me.

'I wish Mrs Jamieson was here!' said Mrs Forrester at last; but to judge from Mrs Fitz-Adam's face, she could not second the wish.

'But without Mrs Jamieson,' said Miss Pole, with just a sound of offended merit in her voice 'we, the ladies of Cranford, in my drawing-room assembled, can resolve upon something. I imagine we are none of us what may be called rich, though we all possess a genteel competency, sufficient for tastes that are elegant and refined, and would not, if they could, be vulgarly ostentatious.' (Here I observed Miss Pole refer to a small card concealed in her hand, on which I imagine she had put down a few notes.)

'Miss Smith,' she continued, addressing me (familiarly known as 'Mary' to all the company assembled, but this was a state occasion), 'I have conversed in private – I made it my business to do so yesterday afternoon – with these ladies on the misfortune which has happened to our friend – and one and all of us have agreed that, while we have a superfluity, it is not only a duty but a pleasure – a true pleasure, Mary!' – her voice was rather choked just here, and she had to wipe her spectacles before she could go on – 'to give what we can to assist her – Miss Matilda Jenkyns. Only, in consideration of the feelings of delicate independence existing in the mind of every refined female' – I was sure she had got back to the card now – 'we wish to contribute our mites in a secret and concealed manner, so as not to hurt the feelings I have referred to. And our object in requesting you to meet us this morning is, that believing you are the daughter – that your father is, in fact, her confidential adviser in all pecuniary matters, we imagined that, by consulting with him, you might devise some mode in which our contribution could be made to appear the legal due which Miss Matilda Jenkyns ought to receive from —. Probably, your father, knowing her investments, can fill up the blank.'

Miss Pole concluded her address, and looked round for approval and agreement.

'I have expressed your meaning, ladies, have I not? And while Miss Smith considers what reply to make, allow me to offer you some little refreshment.'

I had no great reply to make; I had more thankfulness at my heart for their kind thoughts than I cared to put into words; and so I only mumbled out something to the effect 'that I would name what Miss Pole had said to my father, and that if anything could be arranged for dear Miss Matty' – and here I broke down utterly, and had to be refreshed with a glass of cowslip wine before I could check the crying which had been repressed for the last two or three days. The worst was, all the ladies cried in concert. Even Miss Pole cried, who had said a hundred times that to betray emotion before any one was a sign of weakness and want of self-control. She recovered herself into a slight degree of impatient anger, directed against me, as having set them all off; and, moreover, I think she was vexed that I could not make a speech back in return for hers; and if I had known beforehand what was to be said, and had a card on which to express the probable feelings that would rise in my heart, I would have tried to gratify her. As it was,

very little she had to live upon; a confession which she was brought to make from a dread lest we should think that the small contribution named in her paper bore any proportion to her love and regard for Miss Matty. And yet that sum which she so easily relinquished was, in truth, more than a twentieth part of what she had to live upon, and keep house, and a little serving-maid, all as became one born a Tyrrell. And when the whole income does not nearly amount to a hundred pounds, to give up a twentieth of it will necessitate many careful economies, and many pieces of self-denial – small and insignificant in the world's account, but bearing a different value in another account-book that I have heard of. She did so wish she was rich, she said; and this wish she kept repeating, with no thought of herself in it, only with a longing, yearning desire to be able to heap up Miss Matty's measure of comforts.

It was some time before I could console her enough to leave her; and then, on quitting the house, I was waylaid by Mrs Fitz-Adam, who had also her confidence to make of pretty nearly the opposite description. She had not liked to put down all that she could afford, and was ready to give. She told me she thought she never could look Miss Matty in the face again if she presumed to be giving her so much as she should like to do. 'Miss Matty!' continued she, 'that I thought was such a fine young lady, when I was nothing but a country girl, coming to market with eggs and butter and such like things. For my father, though well to do, would always make me go on as my mother had done before me; and I had to come into Cranford every Saturday and see after sales and prices, and what not. And one day, I remember, I met Miss Matty in the lane that leads to Combehurst; she was walking on the footpath, which, you know, is raised a good way above the road, and a gentleman rode beside her and was talking to her, and she was looking down at some primroses she had gathered and pulling them all to pieces, and I do believe she was crying. But after she had passed, she turned round and ran after me to ask – oh, so kindly – about my poor mother, who lay on her death-bed;

and when I cried, she took hold of my hand to comfort me; and the gentleman waiting for her all the time; and her poor heart very full of something, I am sure; and I thought it such an honour to be spoken to in that pretty way by the Rector's daughter, who visited at Arley Hall. I have loved her ever since, though perhaps I'd no right to do it; but if you can think of any way in which I might be allowed to give a little more without any one knowing it, I should be so much obliged to you, my dear. And my brother would be delighted to doctor her for nothing – medicines, leeches, and all. I know that he and her ladyship – (my dear! I little thought in the days I was telling you of that I should ever come to be sister-in-law to a ladyship!) – would do anything for her. We all would.'

I told her I was quite sure of it, and promised all sorts of things, in my anxiety to get home to Miss Matty, who might well be wondering what had become of me – absent from her two hours without being able to account for it. She had taken very little note of time, however, as she had been occupied in numberless little arrangements preparatory to the great step of giving up her house. It was evidently a relief to her to be doing something in the way of retrenchment; for, as she said, whenever she paused to think, the recollection of the poor fellow with his bad five-pound note came over her, and she felt quite dishonest; only if it made her so uncomfortable, what must it not be doing to the directors of the Bank, who must know so much more of the misery consequent upon this failure? She almost made me angry by dividing her sympathy between these directors (whom she imagined overwhelmed by self-reproach for the mismanagement of other people's affairs) and those who were suffering like her. Indeed, of the two, she seemed to think poverty a lighter burden than self-reproach; but I privately doubted if the directors would agree with her.

Old hoards were taken out and examined as to their money value, which luckily was small, or else I don't know how Miss Matty would have prevailed upon herself to part with such things as her mother's wedding-ring, the strange uncouth brooch with which her father had disfigured his shirt-frill, &c. However, we arranged things a little in order as to their pecuniary estimation, and were all ready for my father when he came the next morning.

I am not going to weary you with the details of all the business we went through; and one reason for not telling about them is, that I did not understand what we were doing at the time, and cannot recollect it now. Miss Matty and I sat assenting to accounts, and schemes, and reports, and documents, of which I do not believe we either of us understood a word; for my father was clear-headed and decisive, and a capital man of business, and if we made the slightest inquiry, or expressed the slightest want of comprehension, he had a sharp way of saying, 'Eh? eh? it's as clear as daylight. What's your objection?' And as we had not comprehended anything of what he had proposed, we found it rather difficult to shape our objections; in fact, we never were sure if we had any. So presently Miss Matty got into a nervously acquiescent state, and said 'Yes,' and 'Certainly,' at every pause, whether required or not: but when I once joined in as chorus to a 'Decidedly,' pronounced by Miss Matty in a tremblingly dubious tone, my father fired round at me and asked me 'What there was to decide?' And I am sure, to this day, I have never known. But, in justice to him, I must say he had come over from Drumble to help Miss Matty when he could ill spare the time, and when his own affairs were in a very anxious state.

While Miss Matty was out of the room, giving orders for luncheon – and sadly perplexed between her desire of honouring my father by a delicate dainty meal and her conviction that she had no right, now that all her money was gone, to indulge this desire – I told him of the meeting of the Cranford ladies at Miss Pole's the day before. He kept brushing his hand before his eyes as I spoke; – and when I went back to Martha's offer the evening before, of receiving Miss Matty as a lodger, he fairly walked away from me to the window and began drumming with his fingers upon it. Then he turned abruptly round, and said, 'See, Mary, how a good innocent life makes friends all around. Confound it! I could make a good lesson out of it if I were a parson; but as it is, I can't get a tail to my sentences – only I'm sure you feel what I want to say. You and I will have a walk after lunch, and talk a bit more about these plans.'

The lunch – a hot savoury mutton-chop, and a little of the cold lion sliced and fried – was now brought in. Every morsel of this last dish was finished, to Martha's great gratification. Then my father bluntly told Miss Matty he wanted to talk to me alone, and that he would stroll out and see some of the old places, and then I could tell her what plan we thought desirable. Just before we went out, she called me back and said, 'Remember, dear, I'm the only one left – I mean, there's no one to be hurt by what I do. I'm willing to do anything that's right and honest; and I don't think, if Deborah knows where she is, she'll care so very much if I'm not genteel; because, you see, she'll know all, dear. Only let me see what I can do, and pay the poor people as far as I'm able.'

I gave her a hearty kiss, and ran after my father. The result of our conversation was this. If all parties were agreeable, Martha and Jem were to be married with as little delay as possible, and they were to live on in Miss Matty's present abode; the sum which the Cranford ladies had agreed to contribute annually being sufficient to meet the greater part of the rent, and leaving Martha free to appropriate what Miss Matty should pay for her lodgings to any little extra comforts required. About the sale, my father was dubious at first. He said the old rectory furniture, however carefully used and reverently treated, would fetch very little; and that little would be but as a drop in the sea of the debts of the Town and County Bank. But when I represented how Miss Matty's tender conscience would be soothed by feeling that she had done what she could, he gave way; especially after I had told him the five-pound note adventure, and he had scolded me well for allowing it. I then alluded to my idea that she might add to her small income by selling tea; and, to my surprise (for I had nearly given up the plan), my father grasped at it with all the energy of a tradesman. I think he reckoned his chickens before they were hatched, for he immediately ran up the profits of the sales that she could effect in Cranford to more than twenty pounds a-year. The small dining parlour was to be converted into a shop, without any of its degrading characteristics; a table was to be the counter; one window was to be retained unaltered, and the other changed into a glass door. I evidently rose in his estimation for having made this bright suggestion. I only hoped we should not both fall in Miss Matty's.

But she was patient and content with all our arrangements. She knew, she said, that we should do the best we could for her; and she only hoped, only stipulated, that she should pay every farthing that she could be said to owe, for her father's sake, who had been so respected in Cranford. My father and I had agreed to say as little as possible about the Bank, indeed never to mention it again, if it could be helped. Some of the plans were evidently a little perplexing to her; but she had seen me sufficiently snubbed in the morning for want of comprehension to venture on too many inquiries now; and all passed over well, with a hope on her part that no one would be hurried into marriage on her account. When we came to the proposal that she should sell tea, I could see it was rather a shock to her; not on account of any personal loss of gentility involved, but only because she distrusted her own powers of action in a new line of life, and would timidly have preferred a little more privation to any exertion for which she feared she was unfitted. However, when she saw my father was bent upon it, she sighed, and said she would try; and if she did not do well, of course she might give it up. One good thing about it was, she did not think men ever bought tea; and it was of men particularly she was afraid. They had such sharp loud ways with them; and did up accounts, and counted their change so quickly! Now, if she might only sell comfits to children, she was sure she could please them!

Chapter XV

A HAPPY RETURN

Before I left Miss Matty at Cranford everything had been comfortably arranged for her. Even Mrs Jamieson's approval of her selling tea had been gained. That oracle had taken a few days to consider whether by so doing Miss Matty would forfeit her right to the privileges of society in Cranford. I think she had some little idea of mortifying Lady Glenmire by the decision she gave at last; which was to this effect: that whereas a married woman takes her husband's rank by the strict laws of precedence, an unmarried woman retains the station her father occupied. So Cranford was allowed to visit Miss Matty; and, whether allowed or not, it intended to visit Lady Glenmire.

But what was our surprise – our dismay – when we learnt that Mr and *Mrs Hoggins* were returning on the following Tuesday. Mrs Hoggins! Had she absolutely dropped her title, and so, in a spirit of bravado, cut the aristocracy to become a Hoggins! She, who might have been called Lady Glenmire to her dying day! Mrs Jamieson was pleased. She said it only convinced her of what she had known from the first, that the creature had a low taste. But 'the creature' looked very happy on Sunday at church; nor did we see it necessary to keep our veils down on that side of our bonnets on which Mr and Mrs Hoggins sat, as Mrs Jamieson did; thereby missing all the smiling glory of his face, and all the becoming blushes of hers. I am not sure if Martha and Jem looked more radiant in the afternoon, when they too made their first appearance. Mrs Jamieson soothed the turbulence of her soul by having the blinds of her windows drawn down, as if for a funeral, on the day when Mr and Mrs Hoggins received callers; and it was with some difficulty that she was prevailed upon to continue the *St James's Chronicle* – so indignant was she with its having inserted the announcement of the marriage.

Miss Matty's sale went off famously. She retained the furniture of her sitting-room and bedroom; the former of which she was to occupy till Martha could meet with a lodger who might wish to take it; and into this sitting-room and bedroom she had to cram all sorts of things, which were (the auctioneer assured her) bought in for her at the sale by an unknown friend. I always suspected Mrs Fitz-Adam of this; but she must have had an accessory, who knew what articles were particularly regarded by Miss Matty on account of their associations with her early days. The rest of the house looked rather bare, to be sure; all except one tiny bedroom, of which my father allowed me to purchase the furniture for my occasional use in case of Miss Matty's illness.

I had expended my own small store in buying all manner of comfits and lozenges, in order to tempt the little people whom Miss Matty loved so much, to come about her. Tea in bright green canisters – and comfits in tumblers – Miss Matty and I felt quite proud as we looked round us on the evening before the shop was to be opened. Martha had scoured the boarded floor to a white cleanness, and it was adorned with a brilliant piece of oil-cloth, on which customers were to stand before the table-counter. The wholesome smell of plaster and whitewash pervaded the apartment. A very small 'Matilda Jenkyns, licensed to sell tea,' was hidden under the lintel of the new door, and two boxes of tea with cabalistic inscriptions all over them stood ready to disgorge their contents into the canisters.

Miss Matty, as I ought to have mentioned before, had had some scruples of conscience at selling tea when there was already Mr Johnson in the town, who included it among his numerous commodities; and, before she could quite reconcile herself to the adoption of her new business, she had trotted down to his shop, unknown to me, to tell him of the project that was entertained, and to inquire if it was likely to injure his business. My father called this idea of hers 'great nonsense,' and 'wondered how tradespeople were to get on if there was to be a continual consulting of each other's interests, which would put a stop to all competition directly.' And, perhaps, it would not have done in Drumble, but in Cranford it answered very well; for not only did Mr Johnson kindly put at rest all Miss Matty's scruples, and fear of injuring his business, but, I have reason to know, he repeatedly sent customers to her, saying that the teas he kept were of a common kind, but that Miss Jenkyns had all the choice sorts. And expensive tea is a very favourite luxury with well-to-do tradespeople and rich farmers' wives, who turn up their noses at the Congou and Souchong prevalent at many tables of gentility, and will have nothing else than Gunpowder and Pekoe for themselves.

But to return to Miss Matty. It was really very pleasant to see how her unselfishness and simple sense of justice called out the same good qualities in others. She never seemed to think any one would impose upon her, because she should be so grieved to do it to them. I have heard her put a stop to the asseverations of the man who brought her coals, by quietly saying, 'I am sure you would be sorry to bring me wrong weight;' and if the coals were short measure that time, I don't believe they ever were again. People would have felt as much ashamed of presuming on her good faith as they would have done on that of a child. But my father says, 'such simplicity might be very well in Cranford, but would never do in the world.' And I fancy the world must be very bad, for with all my father's suspicion of every one with whom he has dealings, and in spite of all his many precautions, he lost upwards of a thousand pounds by roguery only last year.

I just stayed long enough to establish Miss Matty in her new mode of life, and to pack up the library, which the Rector had purchased. He had written a very kind letter to Miss Matty, saying 'how glad he should be to take a library so well selected as he knew that the late Mr Jenkyns's must have been, at any valuation put upon them.' And when she agreed to this, with a touch of sorrowful gladness that they would go back to the Rectory, and be arranged on the accustomed walls once more, he sent word that he feared that he had not room for them all, and perhaps Miss Matty would kindly allow him to leave some volumes on her shelves. But Miss Matty said that she had her Bible and Johnson's Dictionary, and should not have much time for reading, she was afraid. Still I retained a few books out of consideration for the Rector's kindness.

The money which he had paid, and that produced by the sale, was partly expended in the stock of tea, and part of it was invested against a rainy day – *i.e.* old age or illness. It was but a small sum, it is true; and it occasioned a few evasions of truth and white lies (all of which I think very wrong indeed – in theory – and would rather not put them in practice), for we knew Miss Matty would be perplexed as to her duty if she were aware of any little reserve-fund being made for her while the debts of the Bank remained unpaid. Moreover, she had never been told of the way in which her friends were contributing to pay the rent. I should have liked to tell her this; but the mystery of the affair gave a piquancy to their deed of kindness which the ladies were unwilling to give up; and at first Martha had to shirk many a perplexed question as to her ways and means of living in such a house; but by-and-by Miss Matty's prudent uneasiness sank down into acquiescence with the existing arrangement.

I left Miss Matty with a good heart. Her sales of tea during the first two days had surpassed my most sanguine expectations. The whole country round seemed to be all out of tea at once. The only alteration I could have desired in Miss Matty's way of doing business was, that she should not have so plaintively entreated some of her customers not to buy green tea – running it down as slow poison, sure to destroy the nerves, and produce all manner of evil. Their pertinacity in taking it, in spite of all her warnings, distressed her so much that I really thought she would relinquish the sale of it, and so lose half her custom; and I was driven to my wits' end for instances of longevity entirely attributable to a persevering use of green tea. But the final argument, which settled the question, was a happy reference of mine to the train oil and tallow candles which the Esquimaux not only enjoy but digest. After that she acknowledged that 'one man's meat might be another man's poison,' and contented herself thenceforward with an occasional remonstrance, when she thought the purchaser was too young and innocent to be acquainted with the evil effects green tea produced on some constitutions; and an habitual sigh when people old enough to choose more wisely would prefer it.

I went over from Drumble once a quarter at least, to settle the accounts, and see after the necessary business letters. And, speaking of letters, I began to be very much ashamed of remembering my letter to the Aga Jenkyns, and very glad I had never named my writing to any one. I only hoped the letter was lost. No answer came. No sign was made.

About a year after Miss Matty set up shop, I received one of Martha's hieroglyphics, begging me to come to Cranford very soon. I was afraid that Miss Matty was ill and went off that very afternoon, and took Martha by surprise when she saw me on opening the door. We went into the kitchen, as usual, to have our confidential conference; and then Martha told me she was expecting her confinement very soon – in a week or two; and she did not think Miss Matty was aware of it; and she wanted me to break the news to her, 'for indeed, Miss!' continued Martha, crying hysterically, 'I'm afraid she won't approve of it; and I'm sure I don't know who is to take care of her as she should be taken care of, when I am laid up.'

I comforted Martha by telling her that I would remain till she was about again; and only wished she had told me her reason for this sudden summons, as then I would have brought the requisite stock of clothes. But Martha was so tearful and tender-spirited, and unlike her usual self, that I said as little as possible about myself, and endeavoured rather to comfort Martha under all the probable and possible misfortunes which came crowding upon her imagination.

I then stole out of the house-door, and made my appearance, as if I were a customer, in the shop, just to take Miss Matty by surprise, and gain an idea of how she looked in her new situation. It was warm May weather, so only the little half-door was closed; and Miss Matty sat behind her counter, knitting an elaborate pair of garters: elaborate they seemed to me, but the difficult stitch was no weight upon her mind, for she was singing in a low voice to herself as her needles went rapidly in and out. I call it singing, but I dare say a musician would not use that word to the tuneless yet sweet humming of the low worn voice. I found out from the words, far more than from the attempt at the tune, that it was the Old Hundredth she was crooning to herself: but the quiet continuous sound told of content, and gave me a pleasant feeling, as I stood in the street just outside the door, quite in harmony with that soft May morning. I went in. At first she did not catch who it was, and stood up as if to serve me; but in another minute watchful pussy had clutched her knitting, which was dropped in eager joy at seeing me. I found, after we had had a little conversation, that it was as Martha said, and that Miss Matty had no idea of the approaching household event. So I thought I would let things take their course, secure that when I went to her with the baby in my arms I should obtain that forgiveness for Martha which she was needlessly frightening herself into believing that Miss Matty would withhold, under some notion that the new claimant would require attentions from its mother that it would be faithless treason to Miss Matty to render.

But I was right. I think that must be an hereditary quality, for my father says he is scarcely ever wrong. One morning, within a week after I arrived, I went to call Miss Matty, with a little bundle of flannel in my arms. She was very much awe-struck when I showed her what it was, and asked for her spectacles off the

the employment, which brought her into kindly intercourse with many of the people round about. If she gave them good weight, they, in their turn, brought many a little country present to the 'old rector's daughter;' – a cream cheese, a few new-laid eggs, a little fresh ripe fruit, a bunch of flowers. The counter was quite loaded with these offerings sometimes, as she told me.

As for Cranford in general, it was going on much as usual. The Jamieson and Hoggins feud still raged, if a feud it could be called, when only one side cared much about it. Mr and Mrs Hoggins were very happy together; and, like most very happy people, quite ready to be friendly: indeed, Mrs Hoggins was really desirous to be restored to Mrs Jamieson's good graces, because of the former intimacy. But Mrs Jamieson considered their very happiness an insult to the Glenmire family, to which she had still the honour to belong; and she doggedly refused and rejected every advance. Mr Mulliner, like a faithful clans man, espoused his mistress's side with ardour. If he saw either Mr or Mrs Hoggins, he would cross the street, and appear absorbed in the contemplation of life in general, and his own path in particular, until he had passed them by. Miss Pole used to amuse herself with wondering what in the world Mrs Jamieson would do, if either she or Mr Mulliner, or any other member of her household, was taken ill; she could hardly have the face to call in Mr Hoggins after the way she had behaved to them. Miss Pole grew quite impatient for some indisposition or accident to befall Mrs Jamieson or her dependants, in order that Cranford might see how she would act under the perplexing circumstances.

Martha was beginning to go about again, and I had already fixed a limit, not very far distant, to my visit, when one afternoon, as I was sitting in the shop-parlour with Miss Matty – I remember the weather was colder now than it had been in May, three weeks before, and we had a fire, and kept the door fully closed – we saw a gentleman go slowly past the window, and then stand opposite to the door, as if looking out for the name which we had so carefully hidden. He took out a double eye-glass and peered about for some time before he could discover it. Then he came in. And, all on a sudden, it flashed across me that it was the Aga himself! For his clothes had an out-of-the-way foreign cut about them; and his face was deep brown, as if tanned and retanned by the sun. His complexion contrasted oddly with his plentiful snow-white hair; his eyes were dark and piercing, and he had an odd way of contracting them, and puckering up his cheeks into innumerable wrinkles when he looked earnestly at objects. He did so to Miss Matty when he first came in. His glance had first caught and lingered a little upon me; but then turned, with the peculiar searching look I have described, to Miss Matty. She was a little fluttered and nervous, but no more so than she always was when any man came into her shop. She thought that he would probably have a note, or a sovereign at least, for which she would have to give change, which was an operation she very much disliked to perform. But the present customer stood opposite to her, without asking for anything, only looking fixedly at her as he drummed upon the table with his fingers, just for all the world as Miss Jenkyns used to do. Miss Matty was on the point of asking him what he wanted (as she told me afterwards), when he turned sharp to me: 'Is your name Mary Smith?'

'Yes!' said I.

All my doubts as to his identity were set at rest; and I only wondered what he would say or do next, and how Miss Matty would stand the joyful shock of what he had to reveal. Apparently he was at a loss how to announce himself; for he looked round at last in search of something to buy, so as to gain time; and, as it happened, his eye caught on the almond comfits, and he boldly asked for a pound of 'those things.' I doubt if Miss Matty had a whole pound in the shop; and besides the unusual magnitude of the order, she was distressed with the idea of the indigestion they would produce, taken in such unlimited quantities. She looked up to remonstrate. Something of tender relaxation in his face struck home to her heart. She said, 'It is – oh sir! can you be Peter?' and trembled from head to foot. In a moment he was round the table, and had her in his arms, sobbing the tearless cries of old age. I brought her a glass of wine; for indeed her colour had changed so as to alarm me, and Mr Peter, too. He kept saying, 'I have been too sudden for you, Matty – I have, my little girl.'

I proposed that she should go at once up into the drawing-room, and lie down on the sofa there; she looked wistfully at her brother, whose hand she had held tight, even when nearly fainting; but on his assuring her that he would not leave her, she allowed him to carry her upstairs.

I thought that the best I could do was to run and put the kettle on the fire for early tea, and then to attend to the shop, leaving the brother and sister to exchange some of the many thousand things they must have to say. I had also to break the news to Martha, who received it with a burst of tears, which nearly infected me. She kept recovering herself to ask if I was sure it was indeed Miss Matty's brother; for I had mentioned that he had grey hair, and she had always heard that he was a very handsome young man. Something of the same kind perplexed Miss Matty at tea-time, when she was installed in the great easy-chair opposite to Mr Jenkyns's, in order to gaze her fill. She could hardly drink for looking at him; and as for eating, that was out of the question.

'I suppose hot climates age people very quickly,' said she, almost to herself. 'When you left Cranford you had not a grey hair in your head.'

'But how many years ago is that?' said Mr Peter, smiling.

'Ah! true! yes! I suppose you and I are getting old. But still I did not think we were so very old! But white hair is very becoming to you, Peter,' she continued – a little afraid lest she had hurt him by revealing how his appearance had impressed her.

'I suppose I forgot dates too, Matty, for what do you think I have brought for you from India? I have an Indian muslin gown and a pearl necklace for you somewhere in my chest at Portsmouth.' He smiled as if amused at the idea of the incongruity of his presents with the appearance of his sister; but this did not strike her all at once, while the elegance of the articles did. I could see that for a moment her imagination dwelt complacently on the idea of herself thus attired; and instinctively she put her hand up to her throat – that little delicate throat which (as Miss Pole had told me) had been one of her youthful charms; but the hand met the touch of folds of soft muslin, in which she was always swathed up to the chin; and the sensation recalled a sense of the unsuitableness of a pearl necklace to her age. She said, 'I'm afraid I'm too old; but it was very kind of you to think of it. They are just what I should have liked years ago – when I was young.'

'So I thought, my little Matty. I remembered your tastes; they were so like my dear mother's.' At the mention of that name, the brother and sister clasped each other's hands yet more fondly; and although they were perfectly silent, I fancied they might have something to say if they were unchecked by my presence, and I got up to arrange my room for Mr Peter's occupation that night, intending myself to share Miss Matty's bed. But at my movement he started up. 'I must go and settle about my room at the George. My carpet-bag is there too.'

'No!' said Miss Matty, in great distress – 'you must not go; please, dear Peter – pray, Mary – oh, you must not go!'

She was so much agitated that we both promised everything she wished. Peter sat down again, and gave her his hand, which, for better security, she held in both of hers, and I left the room to accomplish my arrangements.

Long, long into the night, far, far into the morning, did Miss Matty and I talk. She had much to tell me of her brother's life and adventures, which he had communicated to her, as they had sat alone. She said all was thoroughly clear to her, but I never quite understood the whole story; and when in after days I lost my awe of Mr Peter enough to question him myself, he laughed at my curiosity, and told me stories that sounded so very much like Baron Munchausen's, that I was sure he was making fun of me.

What I heard from Miss Matty was that he had been a volunteer at the siege of Rangoon; had been taken prisoner by the Burmese; had somehow obtained favour and eventual freedom from knowing how to bleed the chief of the small tribe in some case of dangerous illness; that on his release from years of captivity he had had his letters returned from England with the ominous word 'Dead' marked upon them; and, believing himself to be the last of his race, he had settled down as an indigo planter, and had proposed to spend the remainder of his life in the country to whose inhabitants and modes of life he had become habituated, when my letter had reached him; and with the odd vehemence which characterized him in age as it had done in youth, he had sold his land and all his possessions to the first purchaser, and come home to the poor old sister, who was more glad and rich than any princess when she looked at him. She talked me to sleep at last, and then I was awakened by a slight sound at the door, for which she begged my pardon as she crept penitently into bed; but it seems that when I could no longer confirm her belief that the long-lost was really here – under the same roof – she had begun to fear lest it was only a waking dream of hers; that there never had been a Peter sitting by her all that blessed evening – but that the real Peter lay dead far away beneath some wild sea-wave, or under some strange Eastern tree. And so strong had this nervous feeling of hers become, that she was fain to get up and go and convince herself that he was really there by listening through the door to his even regular breathing – I don't like to call it snoring, but I heard it myself through two closed doors – and by-and-by it soothed Miss Matty to sleep.

I don't believe Mr Peter came home from India as rich as a Nabob; he even considered himself poor, but neither he nor Miss Matty cared much about that. At any rate, he had enough to live upon 'very genteelly' at Cranford; he and Miss Matty together. And a day or two after his arrival the shop was closed, while troops of little urchins gleefully awaited the showers of comfits and lozenges that came from time to time down upon their faces as they stood up-gazing at Miss Matty's drawing-room windows. Occasionally Miss Matty would say to them (half hidden behind the curtains), 'My dear children, don't make yourselves ill;' but a strong arm pulled her back, and a more rattling shower than ever succeeded. A part of the tea was sent in presents to the Cranford ladies; and some of it was distributed among the old people who remembered Mr Peter in the days of his frolicsome youth. The India muslin gown was reserved for darling Flora Gordon (Miss Jessie Brown's daughter). The Gordons had been on the Continent for the last few years, but were now expected to return very soon; and Miss Matty, in her sisterly pride, anticipated great delight in the joy of showing them Mr Peter. The pearl necklace disappeared; and about that time many handsome and useful presents made their appearance in the households of Miss Pole and Mrs Forrester; and some rare and delicate Indian ornaments graced the drawing-rooms of Mrs Jamieson and Mrs Fitz-Adam. I myself was not forgotten. Among other things, I had the handsomest bound and best edition of Dr Johnson's works that could be procured; and dear Miss Matty, with tears in her eyes, begged me to consider it as a present from her sister as well as herself. In short, no one was forgotten; and what was more, every one, however insignificant, who had shown kindness to Miss Matty at any time, was sure of Mr Peter's cordial regard.

Chapter XVI

PEACE TO CRANFORD

It was not surprising that Mr Peter became such a favourite at Cranford. The ladies vied with each other who should admire him most; and no wonder; for their quiet lives were astonishingly stirred up by the arrival from India – especially as the person arrived told more wonderful stories than Sindbad the Sailor; and, as Miss Pole said, was quite as good as an Arabian Night any evening. For my own part, I had vibrated all my life between Drumble and Cranford, and I thought it was quite possible that all Mr Peter's stories might be true although wonderful; but when I found, that if we swallowed an anecdote of tolerable magnitude one week, we had the dose considerably increased the next, I began to have my doubts; especially as I noticed that when his sister was present the accounts of Indian life were comparatively tame; not that she knew more than we did, perhaps less. I noticed also that when the Rector came to call, Mr Peter talked in a different way about the countries he had been in. But I don't think the ladies in Cranford would have considered him such a wonderful traveller if they had only heard him talk in the quiet way he did to him. They liked him the better, indeed, for being what they called 'so very Oriental.'

One day, at a select party in his honour, which Miss Pole gave, and from which, as Mrs Jamieson honoured it with her presence, and had even offered to send Mr Mulliner to wait, Mr and Mrs Hoggins and Mrs Fitz-Adam were necessarily excluded – one day at Miss Pole's, Mr Peter said he was tired of sitting upright against the hard-backed uneasy chairs, and asked if he might not indulge himself in sitting cross-legged. Miss Pole's consent was eagerly given, and down he went with the utmost gravity. But when Miss Pole asked me, in an audible whisper, 'if he did not remind me of the Father of the Faithful?' I could not help thinking of poor Simon Jones the lame tailor; and while Mrs Jamieson slowly commented on the elegance and convenience of the attitude, I remembered how we had all followed that lady's lead in condemning Mr Hoggins for vulgarity because he simply crossed his legs as he sat still on his chair. Many of Mr Peter's ways of eating were a little strange amongst such ladies as Miss Pole, and Miss Matty, and Mrs Jamieson, especially when I recollected the untasted green peas and two-pronged forks at poor Mr Holbrook's dinner.

The mention of that gentleman's name recalls to my mind a conversation between Mr Peter and Miss Matty one evening in the summer after he returned to Cranford. The day had been very hot, and Miss Matty had been much oppressed by the weather; in the heat of which her brother revelled. I remember that she had been unable to nurse Martha's baby; which had become her favourite employment of late, and which was as much at home in her arms as in its mother's, as long as it remained a light weight – portable by one so fragile as Miss Matty. This day to which I refer, Miss Matty had seemed more than usually feeble and languid, and only revived when the sun went down, and her sofa was wheeled to the open window, through which, although it looked into the principal street of Cranford, the fragrant smell of the neighbouring hayfields came in every now and then, borne by the soft breezes that stirred the dull air of the summer twilight, and then died away. The silence of the sultry atmosphere was lost in the murmuring noises which came in from many an open window and door; even the children were abroad in the street, late as it was (between ten and eleven), enjoying the game of play for which they had not had spirits during the heat of the day. It was a source of satisfaction to Miss Matty to see how few candles were lighted even in the apartments of those houses from which issued the greatest signs of life. Mr Peter, Miss Matty, and I had all been quiet, each with a separate reverie, for some little time, when Mr Peter broke in:

'Do you know, little Matty, I could have sworn you were on the high road to matrimony when I left England that last time! If anybody had told me you would have lived and died an old maid then, I should have laughed in their faces.'

Miss Matty made no reply; and I tried in vain to think of some subject which should effectually turn the conversation; but I was very stupid, and before I spoke, he went on:

'It was Holbrook; that fine manly fellow who lived at Woodley, that I used to think would carry off my little Matty. You would not think it now, I dare say, Mary! but this sister of mine was once a very pretty girl – at least I thought so; and so I've a notion did poor Holbrook. What business had he to die before I came home to thank him for all his kindness to a good-for-nothing cub as I was? It was that that made me first think he cared for you; for in all our fishing expeditions it was Matty, Matty, we talked about. Poor Deborah! What a lecture she read me on having asked him home to lunch one day, when she had seen the Arley carriage in the town, and thought that my lady might call. Well, that's long years ago; more than half a lifetime! and yet it seems like yesterday! I don't know a fellow I should have liked better as a brother-in-law. You must have played your cards badly, my little Matty, somehow or another – wanted your brother to be a good go-between, eh, little one?' said he, putting out his hand to take hold of hers as she lay on the sofa – 'Why, what's this? you're shivering and shaking, Matty, with that confounded open window. Shut it, Mary, this minute!'

I did so, and then stooped down to kiss Miss Matty, and see if she really were chilled. She caught at my hand, and gave it a hard squeeze – but unconsciously I think – for in a minute or two she spoke to us quite in her usual voice, and smiled our uneasiness away; although she patiently submitted to the prescriptions we enforced of a warm bed, and a glass of weak negus. I was to leave Cranford the next day, and before I went I saw that all the effects of the open window had quite vanished. I had superintended most of the alterations necessary in the house and household during the latter weeks of my stay. The shop was once more a parlour; the empty resounding rooms again furnished up to the very garrets.

There has been some talk of establishing Martha and Jem in another house; but Miss Matty would not hear of this. Indeed, I never saw her so much roused as when Miss Pole had assumed it to be the most desirable arrangement. As long as Martha would remain with Miss Matty, Miss Matty was only too thankful to have her about her; yes, and Jem too, who was a very pleasant man to have in the house, for she never saw him from week's end to week's end. And as for the probable children, if they would all turn out such little darlings as her god-daughter Matilda, she should not mind the number, if Martha didn't. Besides, the next was to be called Deborah; a point which Miss Matty had reluctantly yielded to Martha's stubborn determination that her first-born was to be Matilda. So Miss Pole had to lower her colours, and even her voice, as she said to me that as Mr and Mrs Hearn were still to go on living in the same house with Miss Matty, we had certainly done a wise thing in hiring Martha's niece as an auxiliary.

I left Miss Matty and Mr Peter most comfortable and contented; the only subject for regret to the tender heart of the one and the social friendly nature of the other being the unfortunate quarrel between Mrs Jamieson and the plebeian Hogginses and their following. In joke I prophesied one day that this would only last until Mrs Jamieson or Mr Mulliner were ill, in which case they would only be too glad to be friends with Mr Hoggins; but Miss Matty did not like my looking forward to anything like illness in so light a manner; and, before the year was out, all had come round in a far more satisfactory way.

I received two Cranford letters on one auspicious October morning. Both Miss Pole and Miss Matty wrote to ask me to come over and meet the Gordons, who had returned to England alive and well, with their two children, now almost grown up. Dear Jessie Brown had kept her old kind nature, although she had changed her name and station; and she wrote to say that she and Major Gordon expected to be in Cranford on the fourteenth, and she hoped and begged to be remembered to Mrs Jamieson (named first, as became her honourable station), Miss Pole, and Miss Matty – could she ever forget their kindness to her poor father and sister? – Mrs Forrester, Mr Hoggins (and here again came in an allusion to kindness shown to the dead long ago), his new wife, who as such must allow Mrs Gordon to desire to make her acquaintance, and who was moreover an old Scotch friend of her husband's. In short, every one was named, from the Rector – who had been appointed to Cranford in the interim between Captain Brown's death and Miss Jessie's marriage, and was now associated with the latter event – down to Miss Betty Barker; all were asked to the luncheon; all except Mrs Fitz-Adam, who had come to live in Cranford since Miss Jessie Brown's days, and whom I found rather moping on account of the omission. People wondered at Miss Betty Barker's being included in the honourable list; but then, as Miss Pole said, we must remember the disregard of the genteel proprieties of life in which the poor Captain had educated his girls; and for his sake we swallowed our pride; indeed, Mrs Jamieson rather took it as a compliment, as putting Miss Betty (formerly *her* maid) on a level with 'those Hogginses.'

But when I arrived in Cranford, nothing was as yet ascertained of Mrs Jamieson's own intentions; would the honourable lady go, or would she not? Mr Peter declared that she should and she would; Miss Pole shook her head and desponded. But Mr Peter was a man of resources. In the first place, he persuaded Miss Matty to write to Mrs Gordon, and to tell her of Mrs Fitz-Adam's existence, and to beg that one so kind, and cordial, and generous, might be included in the pleasant invitation. An answer came back by return of post, with a pretty little note for Mrs Fitz-Adam, and a request that Miss Matty would deliver it herself and explain the previous omission. Mrs Fitz-Adam was as pleased as could be, and thanked Miss Matty over and over again. Mr Peter had said, 'Leave Mrs Jamieson to me'; so we did; especially as we knew nothing that we could do to alter her determination if once formed.

I did not know, nor did Miss Matty, how things were going on, until Miss Pole asked me, just the day before Mrs Gordon came, if I thought there was anything between Mr Peter and Mrs

Jamieson in the matrimonial line, for that Mrs Jamieson was really going to the lunch at the George. She had sent Mr Mulliner down to desire that there might be a footstool put to the warmest seat in the room, as she meant to come, and knew that their chairs were very high. Miss Pole had picked this piece of news up, and from it she conjectured all sorts of things, and bemoaned yet more. 'If Peter should marry, what would become of poor dear Miss Matty! And Mrs Jamieson of all people!' Miss Pole seemed to think there were other ladies in Cranford who would have done more credit to his choice, and I think she must have had some one who was unmarried in her head, for she kept saying, 'It was so wanting in delicacy in a widow to think of such a thing.'

When I got back to Miss Matty's, I really did begin to think that Mr Peter might be thinking of Mrs Jamieson for a wife; and I was as unhappy as Miss Pole about it. He had the proof-sheet of a great placard in his hand. 'Signor Brunoni, Magician to the King of Delhi, the Rajah of Oude, and the Great Lama of Thibet, etc., etc.' was going to 'perform in Cranford for one night only' – the very next night; and Miss Matty, exultant, showed me a letter from the Gordons, promising to remain over this gaiety, which Miss Matty said was entirely Peter's doing. He had written to ask the Signor to come, and was to be at all the expenses of the affair. Tickets were to be sent gratis to as many as the room would hold. In short, Miss Matty was charmed with the plan, and said that to-morrow Cranford would remind her of the Preston Guild, to which she had been in her youth – a luncheon at the George, with the dear Gordons, and the Signor in the Assembly Room in the evening. But I – I looked only at the fatal words:

'*Under the Patronage of the* HONOURABLE
MRS JAMIESON.'

She, then, was chosen to preside over this entertainment of Mr Peter's, she was perhaps going to displace my dear Miss Matty in his heart, and make her life lonely once more! I could not look forward to the morrow with any pleasure; and every innocent anticipation of Miss Matty's only served to add to my annoyance.

So, angry, and irritated, and exaggerating every little incident which could add to my irritation, I went on till we were all assembled in the great parlour at the George. Major and Mrs Gordon and pretty Flora and Mr Ludovic were all as bright and handsome and friendly as could be; but I could hardly attend to them for watching Mr Peter, and I saw that Miss Pole was equally busy. I had never seen Mrs Jamieson so roused and animated before; her face looked full of interest in what Mr Peter was saying. I drew near to listen. My relief was great when I caught that his words were not words of love, but that, for all his grave face, he was at his old tricks. He was telling her of his travels in India, and describing the wonderful height of the Himalaya mountains: one touch after another added to their size; and each exceeded the former in absurdity; but Mrs Jamieson really enjoyed all in perfect good faith. I suppose she required strong stimulants to excite her to come out of her apathy. Mr Peter wound up his account by saying that, of course, at that altitude there were none of the animals to be found that existed in the lower regions; the game – everything was different. Firing one day at some flying creature, he was very much dismayed, when it fell, to find that he had shot a cherubim! Mr Peter caught my eye at this moment, and gave me such a funny twinkle, that I felt sure he had no thoughts of Mrs Jamieson as a wife from that time. She looked uncomfortably amazed:

'But, Mr Peter – shooting a cherubim – don't you think – I am afraid that was sacrilege!'

Mr Peter composed his countenance in a moment, and appeared shocked at the idea! which, as he said truly enough, was now presented to him for the first time; but then Mrs Jamieson must remember that he had been living for a long time among savages – all of whom were heathens – some of them, he was afraid, were downright Dissenters. Then, seeing Miss Matty draw near, he hastily changed the conversation, and after a little while, turning to me, he said, 'Don't be shocked, prim little Mary, at all my wonderful stories. I consider Mrs Jamieson fair game, and besides, I am bent on propitiating her, and the first step towards it is keeping her well awake. I bribed her here by asking her to let me have her name as patroness for my poor conjurer this evening; and I don't want to give her time enough to get up her rancour against the Hogginses, who are just coming in. I want everybody to be friends, for it harasses Matty so much to hear of these quarrels. I shall go at it again by-and-by, so you need not look shocked. I intend to enter the Assembly Room to-night with Mrs Jamieson on one side, and my lady Mrs Hoggins on the other. You see if I don't.'

Somehow or another he did; and fairly got them into conversation together. Major and Mrs Gordon helped at the good work with their perfect ignorance of any existing coolness between any of the inhabitants of Cranford.

Ever since that day there has been the old friendly sociability in Cranford society; which I am thankful for, because of my dear Miss Matty's love of peace and kindliness. We all love Miss Matty, and I somehow think we are all of us better when she is near us.

My Lady Ludlow

these ruffles – but we were all taught as children to feel rather proud when my mother put them on, and to hold up our heads as became the descendants of the lady who had first possessed the lace. Not but what my dear father often told us that pride was a great sin; we were never allowed to be proud of anything but my mother's ruffles: and she was so innocently happy when she put them on – often, poor dear creature, to a very worn and threadbare gown – that I still think, even after all my experience of life, they were a blessing to the family. You will think that I am wandering away from my Lady Ludlow. Not at all. The lady who had owned the lace, Ursula Hanbury, was a common ancestress of both my mother and my Lady Ludlow. And so it fell out, that when my poor father died, and my mother was sorely pressed to know what to do with her nine children, and looked far and wide for signs of willingness to help, Lady Ludlow sent her a letter, proffering aid and assistance. I see that letter now: a large sheet of thick yellow paper, with a straight broad margin left on the left-hand side of the delicate Italian writing – writing which contained far more in the same space of paper than all the sloping, or masculine handwritings of the present day. It was sealed with a coat of arms, – a lozenge – for Lady Ludlow was a widow. My mother made us notice the motto, 'Foy et Loy,' and told us where to look for the quarterings of the Hanbury arms before she opened the letter. Indeed, I think she was rather afraid of what the contents might be; for, as I have said, in her anxious love for her fatherless children, she had written to many people upon whom, to tell truly, she had but little claim; and their cold, hard answers had many a time made her cry, when she thought none of us were looking. I do not even know if she had ever seen Lady Ludlow: all I knew of her was that she was a very grand lady, whose grandmother had been half-sister to my mother's great-grandmother; but of her character and circumstances I had heard nothing, and I doubt if my mother was acquainted with them.

I looked over my mother's shoulder to read the letter; it began,

'Dear Cousin Margaret Dawson,' and I think I felt hopeful from the moment I saw those words. She went on to say – stay, I think I can remember the very words: –

'DEAR COUSIN MARGARET DAWSON – I have been much grieved to hear of the loss you have sustained in the death of so good a husband, and so excellent a clergyman as I have always heard that my late cousin Richard was esteemed to be.'

'There!' said my mother, laying her finger on the passage, 'read that aloud to the little ones. Let them hear how their father's good report travelled far and wide, and how well he is spoken of by one whom he never saw. COUSIN Richard, how prettily her ladyship writes! Go on, Margaret!' She wiped her eyes as she spoke: and laid her finger on her lips, to still my little sister, Cecily, who, not understanding anything about the important letter, was beginning to talk and make a noise.

'You say you are left with nine children. I too should have had nine, if mine had all lived. I have none left but Rudolph, the present Lord Ludlow. He is married, and lives, for the most part, in London. But I entertain six young gentlewomen at my house at Connington, who are to me as daughters – save that, perhaps, I restrict them in certain indulgences in dress and diet that might be befitting in young ladies of a higher rank, and of more probable wealth. These young persons – all of condition, though out of means – are my constant companions, and I strive to do my duty as a Christian lady towards them. One of these young gentle-women died (at her own home, whither she had gone upon a visit) last May. Will you do me the favour to allow your eldest daughter to supply her place in my household? She is, as I make out, about sixteen years of age. She will find companions here who are but a little older than herself. I dress my young friends myself, and make each of them a small allowance for pocket-money. They have but few opportunities for matrimony, as Connington is far removed from any town. The clergyman is a deaf old widower; my agent is married; and as for the neighbouring farmers, they are, of course, below the notice of the young gentlewomen under my protection. Still, if any young woman wishes to marry, and has conducted herself to my satisfaction, I give her a wedding dinner, her clothes, and her house-linen. And such as remain with me to my death, will find a small competency provided for them in my will. I reserve to myself the option of paying their travelling expenses – disliking gadding women, on the one hand; on the other, not wishing by too long absence from the family home to weaken natural ties.

'If my proposal pleases you and your daughter – or rather, if it pleases you, for I trust your daughter has been too well brought up to have a will in opposition to yours – let me know, dear cousin Margaret Dawson, and I will make arrangements for meeting the young gentlewoman at Cavistock, which is the nearest point to which the coach will bring her.'

My mother dropped the letter, and sat silent.
'I shall not know what to do without you, Margaret.'
A moment before, like a young untried girl as I was, I had been pleased at the notion of seeing a new place, and leading a new life. But now – my mother's look of sorrow, and the children's cry of remonstrance: 'Mother, I won't go,' I said.

'Nay! but you had better,' replied she, shaking her head. 'Lady Ludlow has much power. She can help your brothers. It will not do to slight her offer.'

So we accepted it, after much consultation. We were rewarded – or so we thought – for afterwards, when I came to know Lady

Ludlow, I saw that she would have done her duty by us, as helpless relations, however we might have rejected her kindness – by a presentation to Christ's Hospital for one of my brothers.

And this was how I came to know my Lady Ludlow.

I remember well the afternoon of my arrival at Hanbury Court. Her ladyship had sent to meet me at the nearest post-town at which the mail-coach stopped. There was an old groom inquiring for me, the ostler said, if my name was Dawson – from Hanbury Court, he believed. I felt it rather formidable; and first began to understand what was meant by going among strangers, when I lost sight of the guard to whom my mother had entrusted me. I was perched up in a high gig with a hood to it, such as in those days was called a chair, and my companion was driving deliberately through the most pastoral country I had ever yet seen. By-and-by we ascended a long hill, and the man got out and walked at the horse's head. I should have liked to walk, too, very much indeed; but I did not know how far I might do it; and, in fact, I dared not speak to ask to be helped down the deep steps of the gig. We were at last at the top – on a long, breezy, sweeping, unenclosed piece of ground, called, as I afterwards learnt, a Chase. The groom stopped, breathed, patted his horse, and then mounted again to my side.

'Are we near Hanbury Court?' I asked.

'Near! Why, Miss! we've a matter of ten mile yet to go.'

Once launched into conversation, we went on pretty glibly. I fancy he had been afraid of beginning to speak to me, just as I was to him; but he got over his shyness with me sooner than I did mine with him. I let him choose the subjects of conversation, although very often I could not understand the points of interest in them: for instance, he talked for more than a quarter of an hour of a famous race which a certain dog-fox had given him, above thirty years before; and spoke of all the covers and turns just as if I knew them as well as he did; and all the time I was wondering what kind of an animal a dog-fox might be.

After we left the Chase, the road grew worse. No one in these days, who has not seen the byroads of fifty years ago, can imagine what they were. We had to quarter, as Randal called it, nearly all the way along the deep-rutted, miry lanes; and the tremendous jolts I occasionally met with made my seat in the gig so unsteady that I could not look about me at all, I was so much occupied in holding on. The road was too muddy for me to walk without dirtying myself more than I liked to do, just before my first sight of my Lady Ludlow. But by-and-by, when we came to the fields in which the lane ended, I begged Randal to help me down, as I saw that I could pick my steps among the pasture grass without making myself unfit to be seen; and Randal, out of pity for his steaming horse, wearied with the hard struggle through the mud, thanked me kindly, and helped me down with a springing jump.

The pastures fell gradually down to the lower land, shut in on either side by rows of high elms, as if there had been a wide grand avenue here in former times. Down the grassy gorge we went, seeing the sunset sky at the end of the shadowed descent. Suddenly we came to a long flight of steps.

'If you'll run down there, Miss, I'll go round and meet you, and then you'd better mount again, for my lady will like to see you drive up to the house.'

'Are we near the house?' said I, suddenly checked by the idea.

'Down there, Miss,' replied he, pointing with his whip to certain stacks of twisted chimneys rising out of a group of trees, in deep shadow against the crimson light, and which lay just beyond a great square lawn at the base of the steep slope of a hundred yards, on the edge of which we stood.

I went down the steps quietly enough. I met Randal and the gig at the bottom; and, falling into a side road to the left, we drove sedately round, through the gateway, and into the great court in front of the house.

The road by which we had come lay right at the back.

Hanbury Court is a vast red-brick house – at least, it is cased in part with red bricks; and the gate-house and walls about the place are of brick – with stone facings at every corner, and door, and window, such as you see at Hampton Court. At the back are the gables, and arched doorways, and stone mullions, which show (so Lady Ludlow used to tell us) that it was once a priory. There was a prior's parlour, I know – only we called it Mrs Medlicott's room; and there was a tithe-barn as big as a church, and rows of fish-ponds, all got ready for the monks' fasting-days in old time. But all this I did not see till afterwards. I hardly noticed, this first night, the great Virginian Creeper (said to have been the first planted in England by one of my lady's ancestors) that half-covered the front of the house. As I had been unwilling to leave the guard of the coach, so did I now feel unwilling to leave Randal, a known friend of three hours. But there was no help for it; in I must go; past the grand-looking old gentleman holding the door open for me, on into the great hall on the right hand, into which the sun's last rays were sending in glorious red light – the gentleman was now walking before me – up a step on to the dais, as I afterwards learned that it was called – then again to the left, through a series of sitting-rooms, opening one out of another, and all of them looking into a stately garden, glowing, even in the twilight, with the bloom of flowers. We went up four steps out of the last of these rooms, and then my guide lifted up a heavy silk curtain, and I was in the presence of my Lady Ludlow.

She was very small of stature, and very upright. She wore a great lace cap, nearly half her own height, I should think, that went round her head (caps which tied under the chin, and which we called 'mobs,' came in later, and my lady held them in great contempt, saying people might as well come down in their nightcaps). In front of my lady's cap was a great bow of white satin ribbon; and a broad band of the same ribbon was tied tight round her head, and served to keep the cap straight. She had a fine Indian muslin shawl folded over her shoulders and across her chest, and an apron of the same; a black silk mode gown, made with short sleeves and ruffles, and with the tail thereof pulled through the pocket-hole, so as to shorten it to a useful length: beneath it she wore, as I could plainly see, a quilted lavender satin petticoat. Her hair was snowy white, but I hardly saw it, it was so covered with her cap: her skin, even at her age, was waxen in texture and tint; her eyes were large and dark blue, and must have been her great beauty when she was young, for there was nothing particular, as far as I can remember, either in mouth or nose. She had a great gold-headed stick by her chair; but I think it was more as a mark of state and dignity than for use; for she had as light and brisk a step when she chose as any girl of fifteen, and, in her private early walk of meditation in the mornings, would go as swiftly from garden alley to garden alley as any one of us.

She was standing up when I went in. I dropped my curtsy at the door, which my mother had always taught me as a part of good manners, and went up instinctively to my lady. She did not put out her hand, but raised herself a little on tiptoe, and kissed me on both cheeks.

'You are cold, my child. You shall have a dish of tea with me.' She rang a little hand-bell on the table by her, and her waiting-maid came in from a small anteroom; and, as if all had been prepared, and was awaiting my arrival, brought with her a small china-service with tea ready made, and a plate of delicately-cut bread-and-butter, every morsel of which I could have eaten, and been none the better for it, so hungry was I after my long ride. The waiting-maid took off my cloak, and I sat down, sorely alarmed at the silence, the hushed foot-falls of the subdued maiden over the thick carpet, and the soft voice and clear pronunciation of my Lady Ludlow. My tea-spoon fell against my cup with a sharp noise, that seemed so out of place and season that I blushed deeply. My lady caught my eye with hers – both keen and sweet were those dark-blue eyes of her ladyship's: –

'Your hands are very cold, my dear; take off those gloves' (I wore thick serviceable doeskin, and had been too shy to take them off unbidden), 'and let me try and warm them – the evenings are very chilly.' And she held my great red hands in hers – soft, warm, white, ring-laden. Looking at last a little wistfully into my face, she said – 'Poor child! And you're the eldest of nine! I had a daughter who would have been just your age; but I cannot fancy her the eldest of nine.' Then came a pause of silence; and then she rang her bell, and desired her waiting-maid, Adams, to show me to my room.

It was so small that I think it must have been a cell. The walls were whitewashed stone; the bed was of white dimity. There was a small piece of red stair-carpet on each side of the bed, and two chairs. In a closet adjoining were my washstand and toilet-table. There was a text of Scripture painted on the wall right opposite to my bed; and below hung a print, common enough in those days, of King George and Queen Charlotte, with all their numerous children, down to the little Princess Amelia in a go-cart. On each side hung a small portrait, also engraved: on the left, it was Louis the Sixteenth, on the other, Marie Antoinette. On the chimney-piece there was a tinder-box and a Prayer-book. I do not remember anything else in the room. Indeed, in those days people did not dream of writing-tables, and inkstands, and portfolios, and easy chairs, and what not. We were taught to go into our bedrooms for the purposes of dressing, and sleeping, and praying.

Presently I was summoned to supper. I followed the young lady who had been sent to call me, down the wide shallow stairs, into the great hall, through which I had first passed on my way to my Lady Ludlow's room. There were four other young gentlewomen, all standing, and all silent, who curtsied to me when I first came in. They were dressed in a kind of uniform: muslin caps bound round their heads with blue ribbons, plain muslin handkerchiefs, lawn aprons, and drab-coloured stuff gowns. They were all gathered together at a little distance from the table, on which were placed a couple of cold chickens, a salad, and a fruit-tart. On the dais there was a smaller round table, on which stood a silver jug filled with milk, and a small roll. Near that was set a carved chair, with a countess's coronet surmounting the back of it. I thought that some one might have spoken to me; but they were shy, and I was shy; or else there was some other reason; but, indeed, almost the minute after I had come into the hall by the door at the lower end, her ladyship entered by the door opening upon the dais; whereupon we all curtsied very low; I, because I saw the others do it. She stood, and looked at us for a moment.

'Young gentlewomen,' said she, 'make Margaret Dawson welcome among you;' and they treated me with the kind politeness due to a stranger, but still without any talking beyond what was required for the purposes of the meal. After it was over, and grace was said by one of our party, my lady rang her hand-bell, and the servants came in and cleared away the supper things: then they brought in a portable reading-desk, which was placed on the dais, and, the whole household trooping in, my lady called to one of my companions to come up and read the Psalms and Lessons for the day. I remember thinking how afraid I should have been had I been in her place. There were no prayers. My lady thought it schismatic to have any prayers excepting those in the Prayer-book; and would as soon have preached a sermon herself in the parish church, as have allowed any one not a deacon at the least to read prayers in a private dwelling-house. I am not sure that even then she would have approved of his reading them in an unconsecrated place.

She had been maid of honour to Queen Charlotte: a Hanbury of that old stock that flourished in the days of the Plantagenets, and heiress of all the land that remained to the family, of the great estates which had once stretched into four separate counties. Hanbury Court was hers by right. She had married Lord Ludlow, and had lived for many years at his various seats, and away from her ancestral home. She had lost all her children but one, and most of them had died at these houses of Lord Ludlow's; and, I dare say, that gave my lady a distaste to the places, and a longing to come back to Hanbury Court, where she had been so happy as a girl. I imagine her girlhood had been the happiest time of her life; for, now I think of it, most of her opinions, when I knew her in later life, were singular enough then, but had been universally prevalent fifty years before. For instance, while I lived at Hanbury Court, the cry for education was beginning to come up: Mr Raikes had set up his Sunday Schools; and some clergymen were all for teaching writing and arithmetic, as well as reading. My lady would have none of this; it was levelling and revolutionary, she said. When a young woman came to be hired, my lady would have her in, and see if she liked her looks and her dress, and question her about her family. Her ladyship laid great stress upon this latter point, saying that a girl who did not warm up when any interest or curiosity was expressed about her mother, or the 'baby' (if there was one), was not likely to make a good servant. Then she would make her put out her feet, to see if they were well and neatly shod. Then she would bid her say the Lord's Prayer and the Creed. Then she inquired if she could write. If she could, and she had liked all that had gone before, her face sank – it was a great disappointment, for it was an all but inviolable rule with her never to engage a servant who could write. But I have known her ladyship break through it, although in both cases in which she did so she put the girl's principles to a further and unusual test in asking her to repeat the Ten Commandments. One pert young woman – and yet I was sorry for her too, only she afterwards married a rich draper in Shrewsbury – who had got through her trials pretty tolerably, considering she could write, spoilt all, by saying glibly, at the end of the last Commandment, 'An't please your ladyship, I can cast accounts.'

'Go away, wench,' said my lady in a hurry, 'you're only fit for trade; you will not suit me for a servant.' The girl went away crestfallen: in a minute, however, my lady sent me after her to see that she had something to eat before leaving the house; and, indeed, she sent for her once again, but it was only to give her a

Bible, and to bid her beware of French principles, which had led the French to cut off their king's and queen's heads.

The poor, blubbering girl said, 'Indeed, my lady, I wouldn't hurt a fly, much less a king, and I cannot abide the French, nor frogs neither, for that matter.'

But my lady was inexorable, and took a girl who could neither read nor write, to make up for her alarm about the progress of education towards addition and subtraction; and, afterwards, when the clergyman who was at Hanbury parish when I came there, had died, and the bishop had appointed another, and a younger man, in his stead, this was one of the points on which he and my lady did not agree. While good old deaf Mr Mountford lived, it was my lady's custom, when indisposed for a sermon, to stand up at the door of her large square pew – just opposite to the reading-desk – and to say (at that part of the morning service where it is decreed that, in quires and places where they sing, here followeth the Anthem): 'Mr Mountford, I will not trouble you for a discourse this morning.' And we all knelt down to the Litany with great satisfaction; for Mr Mountford, though he could not hear, had always his eyes open about this part of the service, for any of my lady's movements. But the new clergyman, Mr Gray, was of a different stamp. He was very zealous in all his parish work; and my lady, who was just as good as she could be to the poor, was often crying him up as a godsend to the parish, and he never could send amiss to the Court when he wanted broth, or wine, or jelly, or sago for a sick person. But he needs must take up the new hobby of education; and I could see that this put my lady sadly about one Sunday, when she suspected, I know not how, that there was something to be said in his sermon about a Sunday-school which he was planning. She stood up, as she had not done since Mr Mountford's death, two years and better before this time, and said –

'Mr Gray, I will not trouble you for a discourse this morning.'

But her voice was not well-assured and steady; and we knelt down with more of curiosity than satisfaction in our minds. Mr

Gray preached a very rousing sermon, on the necessity of establishing a Sabbath-school in the village. My lady shut her eyes, and seemed to go to sleep; but I don't believe she lost a word of it, though she said nothing about it that I heard until the next Saturday, when two of us, as was the custom, were riding out with her in her carriage, and we went to see a poor bed-ridden woman, who lived some miles away at the other end of the estate and of the parish: and as we came out of the cottage we met Mr Gray walking up to it, in a great heat, and looking very tired. My lady beckoned him to her, and told him she should wait and take him home with her, adding that she wondered to see him there, so far from his home, for that it was beyond a Sabbath-day's journey, and, from what she had gathered from his sermon the last Sunday, he was all for Judaism against Christianity. He looked as if he did not understand what she meant; but the truth was that, besides the way in which he had spoken up for schools and schooling, he had kept calling Sunday the Sabbath: and, as her ladyship said, 'The Sabbath is the Sabbath, and that's one thing – it is Saturday; and if I keep it, I'm a Jew, which I'm not. And Sunday is Sunday; and that's another thing; and if I keep it, I'm a Christian, which I humbly trust I am.'

But when Mr Gray got an inkling of her meaning in talking about a Sabbath-day's journey, he only took notice of a part of it: he smiled and bowed, and said no one knew better than her ladyship what were the duties that abrogated all inferior laws regarding the Sabbath; and that he must go in and read to old Betty Brown, so that he would not detain her ladyship.

'But I shall wait for you, Mr Gray,' said she. 'Or I will take a drive round by Oakfield, and be back in an hour's time.' For, you see, she would not have him feel hurried or troubled with a thought that he was keeping her waiting, while he ought to be comforting and praying with old Betty.

'A very pretty young man, my dears,' said she, as we drove away. 'But I shall have my pew glazed all the same.'

We did not know what she meant at the time; but the next Sunday but one we did. She had the curtains all round the grand old Hanbury family seat taken down, and, instead of them, there was glass up to the height of six or seven feet. We entered by a door, with a window in it that drew up or down just like what you see in carriages. This window was generally down, and then we could hear perfectly; but if Mr Gray used the word 'Sabbath,' or spoke in favour of schooling and education, my lady stepped out of her corner, and drew up the window with a decided clang and clash.

I must tell you something more about Mr Gray. The presentation to the living of Hanbury was vested in two trustees, of whom Lady Ludlow was one: Lord Ludlow had exercised this right in the appointment of Mr Mountford, who had won his lordship's favour by his excellent horsemanship. Nor was Mr Mountford a bad clergyman, as clergymen went in those days. He did not drink, though he liked good eating as much as any one. And if any poor person was ill, and he heard of it, he would send them plates from his own dinner of what he himself liked best; sometimes of dishes which were almost as bad as poison to sick people. He meant kindly to everybody except dissenters, whom Lady Ludlow and he united in trying to drive out of the parish; and among dissenters he particularly abhorred Methodists – some one said, because John Wesley had objected to his hunting. But that must have been long ago, for when I knew him he was far too stout and too heavy to hunt; besides, the bishop of the diocese disapproved of hunting, and had intimated his disapprobation to the clergy. For my own part, I think a good run would not have come amiss, even in a moral point of view, to Mr Mountford. He ate so much, and took so little exercise, that we young women often heard of his being in terrible passions with his servants, and the sexton and clerk. But they none of them minded him much, for he soon came to himself, and was sure to make them some present or other – some said in proportion to his anger; so that the sexton, who was a bit of a wag (as all sextons are, I think), said that the vicar's saying, 'the Devil take you,' was worth a shilling any day, whereas 'the Deuce' was a shabby sixpenny speech, only fit for a curate.

There was a great deal of good in Mr Mountford, too. He could not bear to see pain, or sorrow, or misery of any kind; and, if it came under his notice, he was never easy till he had relieved it, for the time, at any rate. But he was afraid of being made uncomfortable; so, if he possibly could, he would avoid seeing any one who was ill or unhappy; and he did not thank any one for telling him about them.

'What would your ladyship have me to do?' he once said to my Lady Ludlow, when she wished him to go and see a poor man who had broken his leg. 'I cannot piece the leg as the doctor can; I cannot nurse him as well as his wife does; I may talk to him, but he no more understands me than I do the language of the alchemists. My coming puts him out; he stiffens himself into an uncomfortable posture, out of respect to the cloth, and dare not take the comfort of kicking, and swearing, and scolding his wife, while I am there. I hear him, with my figurative ears, my lady, heave a sigh of relief when my back is turned, and the sermon that he thinks I ought to have kept for the pulpit, and have delivered to his neighbours (whose case, as he fancies, it would just have fitted, as it seemed to him to be addressed to the sinful), is all ended, and done for the day. I judge others as myself; I do to them as I would be done to. That's Christianity, at any rate. I should hate – saving your ladyship's presence – to have my Lord Ludlow coming and seeing me, if I were ill. 'Twould be a great honour, no doubt; but I should have to put on a clean nightcap for the occasion; and sham patience, in order to be polite, and not weary his lordship with my complaints. I should be twice as thankful to him if he would send me game, or a good fat haunch, to bring me up to that pitch of health and strength one ought to be in, to appreciate the honour of a visit from a nobleman. So I shall send

Jerry Butler a good dinner every day till he is strong again; and spare the poor old fellow my presence and advice.'

My lady would be puzzled by this, and by many other of Mr Mountford's speeches. But he had been appointed by my lord, and she could not question her dead husband's wisdom; and she knew that the dinners were always sent, and often a guinea or two to help to pay the doctor's bills; and Mr Mountford was true blue, as we call it, to the backbone; hated the dissenters and the French; and could hardly drink a dish of tea without giving out the toast of 'Church and King, and down with the Rump.' Moreover, he had once had the honour of preaching before the King and Queen, and two of the Princesses, at Weymouth; and the King had applauded his sermon audibly with – 'Very good; very good;' and that was a seal put upon his merit in my lady's eyes.

Besides, in the long winter Sunday evenings, he would come up to the Court, and read a sermon to us girls, and play a game of picquet with my lady afterwards; which served to shorten the tedium of the time. My lady would, on those occasions, invite him to sup with her on the dais; but as her meal was invariably bread and milk only, Mr Mountford preferred sitting down amongst us, and made a joke about its being wicked and heterodox to eat meagre on Sunday, a festival of the Church. We smiled at this joke just as much the twentieth time we heard it as we did at the first; for we knew it was coming, because he always coughed a little nervously before he made a joke, for fear my lady should not approve: and neither she nor he seemed to remember that he had ever hit upon the idea before.

Mr Mountford died quite suddenly at last. We were all very sorry to lose him. He left some of his property (for he had a private estate) to the poor of the parish, to furnish them with an annual Christmas dinner of roast-beef and plum-pudding, for which he wrote out a very good receipt in the codicil to his will.

Moreover, he desired his executors to see that the vault, in which the vicars of Hanbury were interred, was well aired, before his coffin was taken in; for, all his life long, he had had a dread of damp, and latterly he kept his rooms to such a pitch of warmth that some thought it hastened his end.

Then the other trustee, as I have said, presented the living to Mr Gray, Fellow of Lincoln College, Oxford. It was quite natural for us all, as belonging in some sort to the Hanbury family, to disapprove of the other trustee's choice. But when some ill-natured person circulated the report that Mr Gray was a Moravian Methodist, I remember my lady said, 'She could not believe anything so bad, without a great deal of evidence.'

Chapter II

Before I tell you about Mr Gray, I think I ought to make you understand something more of what we did all day long at Hanbury Court. There were five of us at the time of which I am speaking, all young women of good descent, and allied (however distantly) to people of rank. When we were not with my lady, Mrs Medlicott looked after us; a gentle little woman, who had been companion to my lady for many years, and was indeed, I have been told, some kind of relation to her. Mrs Medlicott's parents had lived in Germany, and the consequence was, she spoke English with a very foreign accent. Another consequence was, that she excelled in all manner of needlework, such as is not known even by name in these days. She could darn either lace, table-linen, India muslin, or stockings, so that no one could tell where the hole or rent had been. Though a good Protestant, and never missing Guy Faux' day at church, she was as skilful at fine work as any nun in a Papist convent. She would take a piece of French cambric, and by drawing out some threads, and working in others, it became delicate lace in a very few hours. She did the same by Hollands cloth, and made coarse strong lace, with which all my

297

lady's napkins and table-linen were trimmed. We worked under her during a great part of the day, either in the still-room, or at our sewing in a chamber that opened out of the great hall. My lady despised every kind of work that would now be called Fancy-work. She considered that the use of coloured threads or worsted was only fit to amuse children; but that grown women ought not to be taken with mere blues and reds, but to restrict their pleasure in sewing to making small and delicate stitches. She would speak of the old tapestry in the hall as the work of her ancestresses, who lived before the Reformation, and were consequently unacquainted with pure and simple tastes in work, as well as in religion. Nor would my lady sanction the fashion of the day, which, at the beginning of this century, made all the fine ladies take to making shoes. She said that such work was a consequence of the French Revolution, which had done much to annihilate all distinctions of rank and class, and hence it was, that she saw young ladies of birth and breeding handling lasts, and awls, and dirty cobblers'-wax, like shoemakers' daughters.

Very frequently one of us would be summoned to my lady to read aloud to her, as she sat in her small withdrawing-room, some improving book. It was generally Mr Addison's 'Spectator'; but one year, I remember, we had to read 'Sturm's Reflections', translated from a German book Mrs Medlicott recommended. Mr Sturm told us what to think about for every day in the year; and very dull it was. But I believe Queen Charlotte had liked the book very much, and the thought of her royal approbation kept my lady awake during the reading. 'Mrs Chapone's Letters' and 'Dr Gregory's Advice to Young Ladies' composed the rest of our library for week-day reading. I, for one, was glad to leave my fine sewing, and even my reading aloud (though this last did keep me with my dear lady), to go to the still-room and potter about among the preserves and the medicated waters. There was no doctor for many miles round, and with Mrs Medlicott to direct us, and Dr Buchan to go by for recipes, we sent out many a bottle of physic, which, I dare say, was as good as what comes out of the druggist's shop. At any rate, I do not think we did much harm; for if any of our physics tasted stronger than usual, Mrs Medlicott would bid us let it down with cochineal and water, to make all safe, as she said. So our bottles of medicine had very little real physic in them at last; but we were careful in putting labels on them, which looked very mysterious to those who could not read, and helped the medicine to do its work. I have sent off many a bottle of salt-and-water coloured red; and whenever we had nothing else to do in the still-room, Mrs Medlicott would set us to making bread-pills by way of practice, and, as far as I can say, they were very efficacious, as before we gave out a box Mrs Medlicott always told the patient what symptoms to expect; and I hardly ever inquired without hearing that they had produced their effect. There was one old man, who took six pills a-night, of any kind we liked to give him, to make him sleep; and if, by any chance, his daughter had forgotten to let us know that he was out of his medicine, he was so restless and miserable that, as he said, he thought he was like to die. I think ours was what would be called homoeopathic practice now-a-days. Then we learnt to make all the bakes and dishes of the season in the still-room. We had plum-porridge and mince-pies at Christmas, fritters and pancakes on Shrove Tuesday, furmenty on Mothering Sunday, violet-cakes in Passion Week, tansy-pudding on Easter Sunday, three-cornered cakes on Trinity Sunday, and so on through the year: all made from good old Church receipts, handed down from one of my lady's earliest Protestant ancestresses. Every one of us passed a portion of the day with Lady Ludlow; and now and then we rode out with her in her coach-and-four. She did not like to go out with a pair of horses, considering this rather beneath her rank; and, indeed, four horses were very often needed to pull her heavy coach through the stiff mud. But it was rather a cumbersome equipage through the narrow Warwickshire lanes; and I used often to think it was well that countesses were not plentiful, or else we might have met another lady of quality in another coach-and-four where there would have been no possibility of turning, or passing each other, and very little chance of backing. Once when the idea of this danger of meeting another countess in a narrow deep-rutted lane was very prominent in my mind, I ventured to ask Mrs Medlicott what would have to be done on such an occasion; and she told me that 'de latest creation must back, for sure,' which puzzled me a good deal at the time, although I understand it now. I began to find out the use of the 'Peerage,' a book which had seemed to me rather dull before; but, as I was always a coward in a coach, I made myself well acquainted with the dates of creation of our three Warwickshire earls, and was happy to find that Earl Ludlow ranked second, the oldest earl being a hunting widower, and not likely to drive out in a carriage.

All this time I have wandered from Mr Gray. Of course, we first saw him in church when he read himself in. He was very red-faced, the kind of redness which goes with light hair, and a blushing complexion; he looked slight and short, and his bright light frizzy hair had hardly a dash of powder in it. I remember my lady making this observation, and sighing over it; for, though since the famine in seventeen hundred and ninety-nine and eighteen hundred, there had been a tax on hair-powder, yet it was reckoned very revolutionary and Jacobin not to wear a good deal of it. My lady hardly liked the opinions of any man who wore his own hair; but this she would say was rather a prejudice: only in her youth none but the mob had gone wigless, and she could not get over the association of wigs with birth and breeding; a man's own hair with that class of people who had formed the rioters in seventeen hundred and eighty, when Lord George Gordon had been one of the bugbears of my lady's life. Her husband and his brothers, she told us, had been put into breeches, and had their heads shaved on their seventh birthday, each of them; a handsome little wig of the newest fashion forming the old Lady Ludlow's invariable birthday present to her sons as they each arrived at that age; and afterwards, to the day of their death, they never saw their own hair. To be without powder, as some underbred people were talking of being now, was in fact to insult the proprieties of life, by being undressed. It was English sans-culottism. But Mr Gray did wear a little powder, enough to save him in my lady's good opinion; but not enough to make her approve of him decidedly.

The next time I saw him was in the great hall. Mary Mason and I were going to drive out with my lady in her coach, and when we went downstairs with our best hats and cloaks on, we found Mr Gray awaiting my lady's coming. I believe he had paid his respects to her before, but we had never seen him; and he had declined her invitation to spend Sunday evening at the Court (as Mr Mountford used to do pretty regularly – and play a game of picquet too –), which, Mrs Medlicott told us, had caused my lady to be not over well pleased with him.

He blushed redder than ever at the sight of us, as we entered the hall, and dropped him our curtsies. He coughed two or three times, as if he would have liked to speak to us, if he could but have found something to say; and every time he coughed, he became hotter-looking than ever. I am ashamed to say, we were nearly laughing at him; half because we, too, were so shy that we understood what his awkwardness meant.

My lady came in, with her quick active step – she always walked quickly when she did not bethink herself of her cane – as if she were sorry to have kept us waiting – and, as she entered, she gave us all round one of those graceful sweeping curtsies, of which I think the art must have died out with her – it implied so much courtesy; – this time it said, as well as words could do, 'I am sorry to have kept you all waiting – forgive me.'

She went up to the mantelpiece, near which Mr Gray had been standing until her entrance, and curtsying afresh to him, and pretty deeply this time, because of his cloth, and her being hostess, and he, a new guest. She asked him if he would not prefer speaking to her in her own private parlour, and looked as though she would have conducted him there. But he burst out with his errand, of which he was full even to choking, and which sent the glistening tears into his large blue eyes, which stood farther and farther out with his excitement.

'My lady, I want to speak to you, and to persuade you to exert your kind interest with Mr Lathom – Justice Lathom of Hathaway Manor' –

'Harry Lathom?' inquired my lady – as Mr Gray stopped to take the breath he had lost in his hurry – 'I did not know he was in the commission.'

'He is only just appointed; he took the oaths not a month ago – more's the pity!'

'I do not understand why you should regret it. The Lathoms have held Hathaway since Edward the First, and Mr Lathom bears a good character, although his temper is hasty – '

'My lady! he has committed Job Gregson for stealing – a fault of which he is as innocent as I – and all the evidence goes to prove it, now that the case is brought before the Bench; only the Squires hang so together that they can't be brought to see justice, and are all for sending Job to gaol, out of compliment to Mr Lathom, saying it is his first committal, and it won't be civil to tell him there is no evidence against his man. For God's sake, my lady, speak to the gentlemen; they will attend to you, while they only tell me to mind my own business.'

Now my lady was always inclined to stand by her order, and the Lathoms of Hathaway Court were cousins to the Hanburys. Besides, it was rather a point of honour in those days to encourage a young magistrate, by passing a pretty sharp sentence on his first committals; and Job Gregson was the father of a girl who had been lately turned away from her place as scullery-maid for sauciness to Mrs Adams, her ladyship's own maid; and Mr Gray had not said a word of the reasons why he believed the man innocent – for he was in such a hurry, I believe he would have had my lady drive off to the Henley Court-house then and there;

– so there seemed a good deal against the man, and nothing but Mr Gray's bare word for him; and my lady drew herself a little up, and said:

'Mr Gray! I do not see what reason either you or I have to interfere. Mr Harry Lathom is a sensible kind of young man, well capable of ascertaining the truth without our help – '

'But more evidence has come out since,' broke in Mr Gray.

My lady went a little stiffer, and spoke a little more coldly:

'I suppose this additional evidence is before the justices; men of good family, and of honour and credit, well known in the county. They naturally feel that the opinion of one of themselves must have more weight than the words of a man like Job Gregson, who bears a very indifferent character – has been strongly suspected of poaching, coming from no one knows where, squatting on Hareman's Common – which, by the way, is extra-parochial, I believe; consequently you, as a clergyman, are not responsible for what goes on there; and, although impolitic, there might be some truth in what the magistrates said, in advising you to mind your own business,' – said her ladyship, smiling – 'and they might be tempted to bid me mind mine, if I interfered, Mr Gray; might they not?'

He looked extremely uncomfortable, half angry. Once or twice he began to speak, but checked himself, as if his words would not have been wise or prudent. At last he said: 'It may seem presumptuous in me – a stranger of only a few weeks' standing – to set up my judgement as to men's character against that of residents' – ' Lady Ludlow gave a little bow of acquiescence, which was, I think, involuntary on her part, and which I don't think he perceived – 'but I am convinced that the man is innocent of this offence – and besides, the justices themselves allege this ridiculous custom of paying a compliment to a newly-appointed magistrate as their only reason.'

That unlucky word 'ridiculous!' It undid all the good his modest beginning had done him with my lady. I knew, as well as words could have told me, that she was affronted at the expression being used by a man inferior in rank to those whose actions he applied it to – and, truly, it was a great want of tact, considering to whom he was speaking.

Lady Ludlow spoke very gently and slowly; she always did so when she was annoyed; it was a certain sign, the meaning of which we had all learnt.

'I think, Mr Gray, we will drop the subject. It is one on which we are not likely to agree.'

Mr Gray's ruddy colour grew purple, and then faded away, and his face became pale. I think both my lady and he had forgotten our presence; and we were beginning to feel too awkward to wish to remind them of it. And yet we could not help watching and listening with the greatest interest.

Mr Gray drew himself up to his full height, with an unconscious feeling of dignity. Little as was his stature, and awkward and embarrassed as he had been only a few minutes before, I remember thinking he looked almost as grand as my lady when he spoke.

'Your ladyship must remember that it may be my duty to speak to my parishioners on many subjects on which they do not agree with me. I am not at liberty to be silent, because they differ in opinion from me.'

Lady Ludlow's great blue eyes dilated with surprise, and – I do think – anger, at being thus spoken to. I am not sure whether it was very wise in Mr Gray. He himself looked afraid of the consequences, but as if he was determined to bear them without flinching. For a minute there was silence. Then my lady replied:

'Mr Gray, I respect your plain speaking, although I may wonder whether a young man of your age and position has any right to assume that he is a better judge than one with the experience which I have naturally gained at my time of life, and in the station I hold.'

'If I, madam, as the clergyman of this parish, am not to shrink from telling what I believe to be the truth to the poor and lowly, no more am I to hold my peace in the presence of the rich and titled.' Mr Gray's face showed that he was in that state of excitement which in a child would have ended in a good fit of crying. He looked as if he had nerved himself up to doing and saying things, which he disliked above everything, and which nothing short of serious duty could have compelled him to do and say. And at such times every minute circumstance which could add to pain comes vividly before one. I saw that he became aware of our presence, and that it added to his discomfiture.

My lady flushed up. 'Are you aware, sir,' asked she, 'that you have gone far astray from the original subject of conversation? But as you talk of your parish, allow me to remind you that Hareman's Common is beyond the bounds, and that you are really not responsible for the characters and lives of the squatters on that unlucky piece of ground.'

'Madam, I see I have only done harm in speaking to you about the affair at all. I beg your pardon, and take my leave.'

He bowed, and looked very sad. Lady Ludlow caught the expression of his face.

'Good morning!' she cried, in rather a louder and quicker way than that in which she had been speaking. 'Remember Job Gregson is a notorious poacher and evildoer, and you really are not responsible for what goes on at Hareman's Common.'

He was near the hall-door, and said something – half to himself, which we heard (being nearer to him), but my lady did not; although she saw that he spoke. 'What did he say?' she asked, in a somewhat hurried manner, as soon as the door was closed – 'I did not hear.' We looked at each other, and then I spoke:

'He said, my lady, that "God help him! he was responsible for all the evil he did not strive to overcome."'

My lady turned sharp round away from us, and Mary Mason said afterwards she thought her ladyship was much vexed with both of us, for having been present, and with me for having repeated what Mr Gray had said. But it was not our fault that we were in the hall, and when my lady asked what Mr Gray had said, I thought it right to tell her.

In a few minutes she bade us accompany her in her ride in the coach.

Lady Ludlow always sat forwards by herself, and we girls backwards. Somehow this was a rule, which we never thought of questioning. It was true that riding backwards made some of us feel very uncomfortable and faint; and to remedy this my lady always drove with both windows open, which occasionally gave her the rheumatism; but we always went on in the old way. This day she did not pay any great attention to the road by which we were going, and Coachman took his own way. We were very silent, as my lady did not speak, and looked very serious. Or else, in general, she made these rides very pleasant (to those who were not qualmish with riding backwards), by talking to us in a very agreeable manner, and telling us of the different things which had happened to her at various places – at Paris and Versailles, where she had been in her youth – at Windsor and Kew and Weymouth, where she had been with the Queen, when maid-of-honour – and so on. But this day she did not talk at all. All at once she put her head out of the window.

'John Footman,' said she, 'where are we? Surely this is Hareman's Common.'

'Yes, an't please my lady,' said John Footman, and waited for further speech or orders. My lady thought awhile, and then said she would have the steps put down and get out.

As soon as she was gone, we looked at each other, and then without a word began to gaze after her. We saw her pick her dainty way, in the little high-heeled shoes she always wore (because they had been in fashion in her youth), among the yellow pools of stagnant water that had gathered in the clayey soil. John Footman followed, stately, after; afraid too, for all his stateliness, of splashing his pure white stockings. Suddenly my lady turned round, and said something to him, and he returned to the carriage with a half-pleased, half-puzzled air.

My lady went on to a cluster of rude mud houses at the higher end of the Common; cottages built, as they were occasionally at that day, of wattles and clay, and thatched with sods. As far as we could make out from dumb show, Lady Ludlow saw enough of the interiors of these places to make her hesitate before entering or even speaking to any of the children who were playing about in the puddles. After a pause, she disappeared into one of the cottages. It seemed to us a long time before she came out; but I dare say it was not more than eight or ten minutes. She came back with her head hanging down, as if to choose her way – but we saw it was more in thought and bewilderment than for any such purpose.

She had not made up her mind where we should drive to when she got into the carriage again. John Footman stood, bare-headed, waiting for orders.

'To Hathaway. My dears, if you are tired, or if you have anything to do for Mrs Medlicott, I can drop you at Barford Corner, and it is but a quarter of an hour's brisk walk home.'

But luckily we could safely say that Mrs Medlicott did not want us; and as we had whispered to each other, as we sat alone in the coach, that surely my lady must have gone to Job Gregson's, we were far too anxious to know the end of it all to say that we were tired. So we all set off to Hathaway. Mr Harry Lathom was a bachelor squire, thirty or thirty-five years of age, more at home in the field than in the drawing-room, and with sporting men than with ladies.

My lady did not alight, of course; it was Mr Lathom's place to wait upon her, and she bade the butler – who had a smack of the gamekeeper in him, very unlike our own powdered venerable fine gentleman at Hanbury – tell his master, with her compliments, that she wished to speak to him. You may think how pleased we were to find that we should hear all that was said; though, I think, afterwards we were half sorry when we saw how our presence confused the squire, who would have found it bad enough to answer my lady's questions, even without two eager girls for audience.

'Pray, Mr Lathom,' began my lady, something abruptly for her – but she was very full of her subject – 'what is this I hear about Job Gregson?'

Mr Lathom looked annoyed and vexed, but dared not show it in his words.

'I gave out a warrant against him, my lady, for theft, that is all. You are doubtless aware of his character; a man who sets nets and springes in long cover, and fishes wherever he takes a fancy. It is but a short step from poaching to thieving.'

'That is quite true,' replied Lady Ludlow (who had a horror of poaching for this very reason): 'but I imagine you do not send a man to gaol on account of his bad character.'

'Rogues and vagabonds,' said Mr Lathom. 'A man may be sent to prison for being a vagabond; for no specific act, but for his general mode of life.'

He had the better of her ladyship for one moment; but then she answered:

'But in this case, the charge on which you committed him was theft; now his wife tells me he can prove he was some miles distant from Holmwood, where the robbery took place, all that afternoon; she says you had the evidence before you.'

Mr Lathom here interrupted my lady, by saying, in a somewhat sulky manner –

'No such evidence was brought before me when I gave the warrant. I am not answerable for the other magistrates' decision, when they had more evidence before them. It was they who committed him to gaol. I am not responsible for that.'

My lady did not often show signs of impatience; but we knew she was feeling irritated by the little perpetual tapping of her high-heeled shoe against the bottom of the carriage. About the same time we, sitting backwards, caught a glimpse of Mr Gray through the open door, standing in the shadow of the hall. Doubtless Lady Ludlow's arrival had interrupted a conversation between Mr Lathom and Mr Gray. The latter must have heard every word of what she was saying; but of this she was not aware, and caught at Mr Lathom's disclaimer of responsibility with pretty much the same argument which she had heard (through our repetition) that Mr Gray had used not two hours before.

'And do you mean to say, Mr Lathom, that you don't consider yourself responsible for all injustice or wrong-doing that you might have prevented, and have not? Nay, in this case the first germ of injustice was your own mistake. I wish you had been with me a little while ago, and seen the misery in that poor fellow's cottage.' She spoke lower, and Mr Gray drew near, in a sort of involuntary manner; as if to hear all she was saying. We saw him, and doubtless Mr Lathom heard his footstep, and knew who it was that was listening behind him, and approving of every word that was said. He grew yet more sullen in manner; but still my lady was my lady, and he dared not speak out before her, as he would have done to Mr Gray. Lady Ludlow, however, caught the look of stubbornness in his face, and it roused her as I had never seen her roused.

'I am sure you will not refuse, sir, to accept my bail. I offer to bail the fellow out, and to be responsible for his appearance at the sessions. What say you to that, Mr Lathom?'

'The offence of theft is not bailable, my lady.'

'Not in ordinary cases, I dare say. But I imagine this is an extraordinary case. The man is sent to prison out of compliment to you, and against all evidence, as far as I can learn. He will have to rot in gaol for two months, and his wife and children to starve. I, Lady Ludlow, offer to bail him out, and pledge myself for his appearance at next quarter-sessions.'

'It is against the law, my lady.'

'Bah! Bah! Bah! Who makes laws? Such as I, in the House of Lords – such as you, in the House of Commons. We, who make the laws in St Stephen's may break the mere forms of them, when we have right on our sides, on our own land, and amongst our own people.'

'The lord-lieutenant may take away my commission, if he heard of it.'

'And a very good thing for the county, Harry Lathom; and for you too, if he did – if you don't go on more wisely than you have begun. A pretty set you and your brother magistrates are to administer justice through the land! I always said a good despotism was the best form of government; and I am twice as much in favour of it now I see what a quorum is! My dears!' suddenly turning round to us, 'if it would not tire you to walk home, I would beg Mr Lathom to take a seat in my coach, and we would drive to Henley Gaol, and have the poor man out at once.'

'A walk over the fields at this time of day is hardly fitting for young ladies to take alone,' said Mr Lathom, anxious no doubt to escape from his tête-à-tête drive with my lady, and possibly not quite prepared to go to the illegal length of prompt measures, which she had in contemplation.

But Mr Gray now stepped forward, too anxious for the release of the prisoner to allow any obstacle to intervene which he could do away with. To see Lady Ludlow's face when she first perceived whom she had had for auditor and spectator of her interview with Mr Lathom, was as good as a play. She had been doing and saying the very things she had been so much annoyed at Mr Gray's saying and proposing only an hour or two ago. She had been setting down Mr Lathom pretty smartly, in the presence of the very man to whom she had spoken of that gentleman as so sensible, and of such a standing in the county, that it was presumption to question his doings. But before Mr Gray had finished his offer of escorting us back to Hanbury Court, my lady had recovered herself. There was neither surprise nor displeasure in her manner, as she answered:

'I thank you, Mr Gray. I was not aware that you were here, but

I think I can understand on what errand you came. And seeing you here, recalls me to a duty I owe Mr Lathom. Mr Lathom, I have spoken to you pretty plainly – forgetting, until I saw Mr Gray, that only this very afternoon I differed from him on this very question; taking completely, at that time, the same view of the whole subject which you have done; thinking that the county would be well rid of such a man as Job Gregson, whether he had committed this theft or not. Mr Gray and I did not part quite friends,' she continued, bowing towards him; 'but it so happened that I saw Job Gregson's wife and home – I felt that Mr Gray had been right and I had been wrong, so, with the famous incon-sistency of my sex, I came hither to scold you,' smiling towards Mr Lathom, who looked half-sulky yet, and did not relax a bit of his gravity at her smile, 'for holding the same opinions that I had done an hour before. Mr Gray,' (again bowing towards him) 'these young ladies will be very much obliged to you for your escort, and so shall I. Mr Lathom, may I beg of you to accompany me to Henley?'

Mr Gray bowed very low, and went very red; Mr Lathom said something which we none of us heard, but which was, I think, some remonstrance against the course he was, as it were, compelled to take. Lady Ludlow, however, took no notice of his murmur, but sat in an attitude of polite expectancy; and as we turned off on our walk, I saw Mr Lathom getting into the coach with the air of a whipped hound. I must say, considering my lady's feeling, I did not envy him his ride – though, I believe, he was quite in the right as to the object of the ride being illegal.

Our walk home was very dull. We had no fears; and would far rather have been without the awkward, blushing young man, into which Mr Gray had sunk. At every stile he hesitated – sometimes he half got over it, thinking that he could assist us better in that way; then he would turn back, unwilling to go before ladies. He had no ease of manner, as my lady once said of him, though on any occasion of duty, he had an immense deal of dignity.

311

Chapter III

As far as I can remember, it was very soon after this that I first began to have the pain in my hip, which has ended in making me a cripple for life. I hardly recollect more than one walk after our return under Mr Gray's escort from Mr Lathom's. Indeed, at the time, I was not without suspicions (which I never named) that the beginning of all the mischief was a great jump I had taken from the top of one of the stiles on that very occasion.

Well, it is a long while ago, and God disposes of us all, and I am not going to tire you out with telling you how I thought and felt, and how, when I saw what my life was to be, I could hardly bring myself to be patient, but rather wished to die at once. You can every one of you think for yourselves what becoming all at once useless and unable to move, and by-and-by growing hopeless of cure, and feeling that one must be a burden to some one all one's life long, would be to an active, wilful, strong girl of seventeen, anxious to get on in the world, so as, if possible, to help her brothers and sisters. So I shall only say, that one among the blessings which arose out of what seemed at the time a great, black sorrow was, that Lady Ludlow for many years took me, as it were, into her own especial charge; and now, as I lie still and alone in my old age, it is such a pleasure to think of her!

Mrs Medlicott was great as a nurse, and I am sure I can never be grateful enough to her memory for all her kindness. But she was puzzled to know how to manage me in other ways. I used to have long, hard fits of crying; and, thinking that I ought to go home – and yet what could they do with me there? – and a hundred and fifty other anxious thoughts, some of which I could tell to Mrs Medlicott, and others I could not. Her way of comforting me was hurrying away for some kind of tempting or strengthening food – a basin of melted calves'-foot jelly was, I am sure she thought, a cure for every woe.

'There! take it, dear, take it!' she would say; 'and don't go on fretting for what can't be helped.'

But, I think, she got puzzled at length at the non-efficacy of good things to eat; and one day, after I had limped down to see the doctor, in Mrs Medlicott's sitting-room – a room lined with cupboards, containing preserves and dainties of all kinds, which she perpetually made, and never touched herself – when I was returning to my bed-room to cry away the afternoon, under pretence of arranging my clothes, John Footman brought me a message from my lady (with whom the doctor had been having a conversation) to bid me go to her in that private sitting-room at the end of the suite of apartments, about which I spoke in describing the day of my first arrival at Hanbury. I had hardly been in it since; as, when we read to my lady, she generally sat in the small withdrawing-room out of which this private room of hers opened. I suppose great people do not require what we smaller people value so much – I mean privacy. I do not think that there was a room which my lady occupied that had not two doors, and some of them had three or four. Then my lady had always Adams waiting upon her in her bed-chamber; and it was Mrs Medlicott's duty to sit within call, as it were, in a sort of anteroom that led out of my lady's own sitting-room, on the opposite side to the drawing-room door. To fancy the house, you must take a great square, and halve it by a line; at one end of this line was the hall-door, or public-entrance; at the opposite the private entrance from a terrace, which was terminated at one end by a sort of postern door in an old gray stone wall, beyond which lay the farm buildings and offices; so that people could come in this way to my lady on business, while, if she were going into the garden from her own room, she had nothing to do but to pass through Mrs Medlicott's apartment, out into the lesser hall, and then turning to the right as she passed on to the terrace, she could go down the flight of broad, shallow steps at the corner of the house into the lovely garden, with stretching, sweeping lawns, and gay flower-beds, and beautiful, bossy laurels, and other blooming or massy shrubs, with full-grown beeches, or larches feathering down to the ground a little farther off. The whole was set in a frame, as it were, by the more distant woodlands. The house had been modernized in the days of Queen Anne, I think; but the money had fallen short that was requisite to carry out all the improvements, so it was only the suite of withdrawing-rooms and the terrace-rooms, as far as the private entrance, that had the new, long, high windows put in, and these were old enough by this time to be draped with roses, and honeysuckles, and pyracanthus, winter and summer long.

Well, to go back to that day when I limped into my lady's sitting-room, trying hard to look as if I had not been crying, and not to walk as if I was in much pain. I do not know whether my lady saw how near my tears were to my eyes, but she told me she had sent for me, because she wanted some help in arranging the drawers of her bureau, and asked me – just as if it was a favour I was to do her – if I could sit down in the easy chair near the window – (all quietly arranged before I came in, with a footstool, and a table quite near) – and assist her. You will wonder, perhaps, why I was not bidden to sit or lie on the sofa; but (although I found one there a morning or two afterwards, when I came down) the fact was, that there was none in the room at this time. I have even fancied that the easy-chair was brought in on purpose for me, for it was not the chair in which I remembered my lady sitting the first time I saw her. That chair was very much carved and gilded, with a countess's coronet at the top. I tried it one day, some time afterwards, when my lady was out of the room, and I had a fancy for seeing how I could move about, and very uncomfortable it was. Now my chair (as I learnt to call it, and to think it) was soft and luxurious, and seemed somehow to give one's body rest just in that part where one most needed it.

I was not at my ease that first day, nor indeed for many days afterwards, notwithstanding my chair was so comfortable. Yet I forgot my sad pain in silently wondering over the meaning of many of the things we turned out of those curious old drawers. I was puzzled to know why some were kept at all; a scrap of writing maybe, with only half-a-dozen commonplace words written on it, or a bit of broken riding-whip, and here and there a stone, of which I thought I could have picked up twenty just as good in the first walk I took. But it seems that was just my ignorance; for my lady told me they were pieces of valuable marble, used to make the floors of the great Roman emperors' palaces long ago; and that when she had been a girl, and made the grand tour long ago, her cousin, Sir Horace Mann, the Ambassador or Envoy at Florence, had told her to be sure to go into the fields inside the walls of ancient Rome, when the farmers were preparing the ground for the onion-sowing, and had to make the soil fine, and pick up what bits of marble she could find. She had done so, and meant to have had them made into a table; but somehow that plan fell through, and there they were with all the dirt out of the onion-field upon them; but once when I thought of cleaning them with soap and water, at any rate, she bade me not to do so, for it was Roman dirt – earth, I think, she called it – but it was dirt all the same.

Then, in this bureau, were many other things, the value of which I could understand – locks of hair carefully ticketed, which my lady looked at very sadly; and lockets and bracelets with miniatures in them – very small pictures to what they make now-a-days, and call miniatures; some of them had even to be looked at through a microscope before you could see the individual expression of the faces, or how beautifully they were painted. I don't think that looking at these made my lady seem so melancholy, as the seeing and touching of the hair did. But, to be sure, the hair was, as it were, a part of some beloved body which she might never touch and caress again, but which lay beneath the turf, all faded and disfigured, except perhaps the very hair, from which the lock she held had been dissevered; whereas the pictures were but pictures after all – likenesses, but not the very things themselves. This is only my own conjecture, mind. My lady rarely spoke out her feelings. For, to begin with, she was of rank: and I have heard her say that people of rank do not talk about their feelings except to their equals, and even to them they conceal them, except upon rare occasions. Secondly – and this is my own reflection – she was an only child and an heiress; and as such was more apt to think than to talk, as all well-brought-up heiresses must be, I think. Thirdly, she had long been a widow, without any companion of her own age with whom it would have been natural for her to refer to old associations, past pleasures, or mutual sorrows. Mrs Medlicott came nearest to her as a companion of this sort; and her ladyship talked more to Mrs Medlicott, in a kind of familiar way, than she did to all the rest of the household put together. But Mrs Medlicott was silent by nature, and did not reply at any great length. Adams, indeed, was the only one who spoke much to Lady Ludlow.

After we had worked away about an hour at the bureau, her ladyship said we had done enough for one day; and as the time was come for her afternoon ride, she left me, with a volume of engravings from Mr Hogarth's pictures on one side of me (I don't like to write down the names of them, though my lady thought nothing of it, I am sure), and upon a stand her great prayer-book open at the evening-psalms for the day, on the other. But as soon as she was gone, I troubled myself little with either, but amused myself with looking round the room at my leisure. The side on which the fire-place stood, was all panelled – part of the old ornaments of the house, for there was an Indian paper with birds and beasts and insects on it, on all the other sides. There were coats of arms, of the various families with whom the Hanburys had intermarried, all over these panels, and up and down the ceiling as well. There was very little looking-glass in the room, though one of the great drawing-rooms was called the 'Mirror Room,' because it was lined with glass, which my lady's great-grandfather had brought from Venice when he was ambassador there. There were china jars of all shapes and sizes round and about the room, and some china monsters, or idols, of which I could never bear the sight, they were so ugly, though I think my lady valued them more than all. There was a thick carpet on the middle of the floor, which was made of small pieces of rare wood fitted into a pattern; the doors were opposite to each other, and were composed of two heavy tall wings, and opened in the middle, moving on brass grooves inserted into the floor – they would not have opened over a carpet. There were two windows reaching up nearly to the ceiling, but very narrow, and with deep window-seats in the thickness of the wall. The room was full of scent, partly from the flowers outside, and partly from the great jars of pot-pourri inside. The choice of odours was what my lady piqued herself upon, saying nothing showed birth like a keen susceptibility of smell. We never named musk in her presence, her antipathy to it was so well understood through the household: her opinion on the subject was believed to be, that no scent derived from an animal could ever be of a sufficiently pure nature to give pleasure to any person of good family, where, of course, the delicate perception of the senses had been cultivated for generations. She would instance the way in which sportsmen preserve the breed of dogs who have shown keen scent; and how such gifts descend for generations amongst animals, who cannot be supposed to have anything of ancestral pride, or hereditary fancies about them. Musk, then, was never mentioned at Hanbury Court. No more were bergamot or southernwood, although vegetable in their nature. She considered these two latter as betraying a vulgar taste in the person who chose to gather or wear them. She was sorry to notice sprigs of them in the button-hole of any young man in whom she took an interest, either because he was engaged to a servant of hers or otherwise, as he came out of church on a Sunday afternoon. She was afraid that he liked coarse pleasures; and I am not sure if she did not think that his preference for these coarse sweetnesses did not imply a probability that he would take to drinking. But she distinguished

by the Blue Drawing-room windows; that is the old musk-rose, Shakespeare's musk-rose, which is dying out through the kingdom now. But to return to my Lord Bacon: "Then the strawberry leaves, dying with a most excellent cordial smell." Now the Hanburys can always smell this excellent cordial odour, and very delicious and refreshing it is. You see, in Lord Bacon's time, there had not been so many intermarriages between the court and the city as there have been since the needy days of his Majesty Charles the Second; and altogether in the time of Queen Elizabeth, the great old families of England were a distinct race, just as a cart-horse is one creature, and very useful in its place, and Childers or Eclipse is another creature, though both are of the same species. So the old families have gifts and powers of a different and higher class to what the other orders have. My dear, remember that you try if you can smell the scent of dying strawberry-leaves in this next autumn. You have some of Ursula Hanbury's blood in you, and that gives you a chance.'

But when October came, I sniffed and sniffed, and all to no purpose; and my lady – who had watched the little experiment rather anxiously – had to give me up as a hybrid. I was mortified, I confess, and thought that it was in some ostentation of her own powers that she ordered the gardener to plant a border of strawberries on that side the terrace that lay under her windows.

I have wandered away from time and place. I tell you all the remembrances I have of those years just as they come up, and I hope that, in my old age, I am not getting too like a certain Mrs Nickleby, whose speeches were once read out aloud to me.

I came by degrees to be all day long in this room which I have been describing; sometimes sitting in the easy chair, doing some little piece of dainty work for my lady, or sometimes arranging flowers, or sorting letters according to their handwriting, so that she could arrange them afterwards, and destroy or keep, as she planned, looking ever onward to her death. Then, after the sofa was brought in, she would watch my face, and if she saw my colour change, she would bid me lie down and rest. And I used to try to walk upon the terrace every day for a short time: it hurt me very much, it is true, but the doctor had ordered it, and I knew her ladyship wished me to obey.

Before I had seen the background of a great lady's life, I had thought it all play and fine doings. But whatever other grand people are, my lady was never idle. For one thing, she had to superintend the agent for the large Hanbury estate. I believe it was mortgaged for a sum of money which had gone to improve the late lord's Scotch lands; but she was anxious to pay off this before her death, and so to leave her own inheritance free of encumbrance to her son, the present Earl; whom, I secretly think, she considered a greater person, as being the heir of the Hanburys (though through a female line), than as being my Lord Ludlow with half-a-dozen other minor titles.

With this wish of releasing her property from the mortgage, skilful care was much needed in the management of it: and as far as my lady could go, she took every pains. She had a great book, in which every page was ruled into three divisions; on the first column was written the date and the name of the tenant who addressed any letter on business to her; on the second was briefly stated the subject of the letter, which generally contained a request of some kind. This request would be surrounded and enveloped in so many words, and often inserted amidst so many odd reasons and excuses, that Mr Horner (the steward) would sometimes say it was like hunting through a bushel of chaff to find a grain of wheat. Now, in the second column of this book, the grain of meaning was placed, clean and dry, before her ladyship every morning. She sometimes would ask to see the original letter; sometimes she simply answered the request by a 'Yes,' or a 'No;' and often she would send for leases and papers, and examine them well, with Mr Horner at her elbow, to see if such petitions, as to be allowed to plough up pasture fields, &c., were provided for in the terms of the original agreement. On every Thursday she made herself at liberty to see her tenants, from four to six in the afternoon. Mornings would have suited my lady better, as far as convenience went, and I believe the old custom had been to have these levées (as her ladyship used to call them) held before twelve. But, as she said to Mr Horner, when he urged returning to the former hours, it spoilt a whole day for a farmer, if he had to dress himself in his best and leave his work in the forenoon (and my lady liked to see her tenants come in their Sunday-clothes; she would not say a word, maybe, but she would take her spectacles slowly out, and put them on with silent gravity, and look at a dirty or raggedly-dressed man so solemnly and earnestly, that his nerves must have been pretty strong if he did not wince, and resolve that, however poor he might be, soap and water, and needle and thread should be used before he again appeared in her ladyship's anteroom). The outlying tenants had always a supper provided for them in the servants'-hall on Thursdays, to which, indeed, all comers were welcome to sit down. For my lady said, though there were not many hours left of a working-man's day when their business with her was ended, yet that they needed food and rest, and that she should be ashamed if they sought either at the 'Fighting Lion' (called at this day the 'Hanbury Arms'). They had as much beer as they could drink while they were eating; and when the food was cleared away, they had a cup a-piece of good ale, in which the oldest tenant present, standing up, gave Madam's health; and after that was drunk, they were expected to set off homewards; at any rate, no more liquor was given them. The tenants one and all called her 'Madam;' for they recognised in her the married heiress of the Hanburys, not the widow of a Lord Ludlow, of whom they and their forefathers knew nothing; and against whose memory, indeed, there rankled a dim unspoken grudge, the cause of which was accurately known to the very few who understood the nature of a mortgage, and were therefore aware that Madam's money had been taken to enrich my lord's poor land in Scotland. I am sure – for you can understand I was behind the scenes, as it were, and had many an opportunity of seeing and hearing, as I lay or sat motionless in my lady's room, with the double doors open between it and the anteroom beyond, where Lady Ludlow saw her steward, and gave audience to her tenants – I am certain, I say, that Mr Horner was silently as much annoyed at the money that was swallowed up by this mortgage as any one; and, some time or other, he had probably spoken his mind out to my lady; for there was a sort of offended reference on her part, and respectful submission to blame on his, while every now and then there was an implied protest – whenever the payments of the interest became due, or whenever my lady stinted herself of any personal expense, such as Mr Horner thought was only decorous and becoming in the heiress of the Hanburys. Her carriages were old and cumbrous, wanting all the improvements which had been adopted by those of her rank throughout the county. Mr Horner would fain have had the ordering of a new coach. The carriage-horses, too, were getting past their work; yet all the promising colts bred on the estate were sold for ready money; and so on. My lord, her son, was ambassador at some foreign place; and very proud we all were of his glory and dignity; but I fancy it cost money, and my lady would have lived on bread and water sooner than have called upon him to help her in paying off the mortgage, although he was the one who was to benefit by it in the end.

Mr Horner was a very faithful steward, and very respectful to my lady; although, sometimes, I thought she was sharper to him than to any one else; perhaps because she knew that, although he never said anything, he disapproved of the Hanburys being made to pay for the Earl Ludlow's estates and state.

The late lord had been a sailor, and had been as extravagant in his habits as most sailors are, I am told – for I never saw the sea; and yet he had a long sight to his own interests; but whatever he was, my lady loved him and his memory, with about as fond and proud a love as ever wife gave husband, I should think.

For a part of his life Mr Horner, who was born on the Hanbury property, had been a clerk to an attorney in Birmingham; and these few years had given him a kind of worldly wisdom, which, though always exerted for her benefit, was antipathetic to her ladyship, who thought that some of her steward's maxims savoured of trade and commerce. I fancy that if it had been possible, she would have preferred a return to the primitive system of living on the produce of the land, and exchanging the surplus for such articles as were needed, without the intervention of money.

But Mr Horner was bitten with new-fangled notions, as she would say, though his new-fangled notions were what folk at the present day would think sadly behindhand; and some of Mr Gray's ideas fell on Mr Horner's mind like sparks on tow, though they started from two different points. Mr Horner wanted to make every man useful and active in this world, and to direct as much activity and usefulness as possible to the improvement of the Hanbury estates, and the aggrandisement of the Hanbury family, and therefore he fell into the new cry for education.

Mr Gray did not care much – Mr Horner thought not enough – for this world, and where any man or family stood in their earthly position; but he would have every one prepared for the world to come, and capable of understanding and receiving certain doctrines, for which latter purpose, it stands to reason, he must have heard of these doctrines; and therefore Mr Gray wanted education. The answer in the catechism that Mr Horner was most fond of calling upon a child to repeat, was that to, 'What is thy duty towards thy neighbour?' The answer Mr Gray liked best to hear repeated with unction, was that to the question, 'What is the inward and spiritual grace?' The reply to which Lady Ludlow bent her head the lowest, as we said our Catechism to her on Sundays, was to, 'What is thy duty towards God?' But neither Mr Horner nor Mr Gray had heard many answers to the Catechism as yet.

Up to this time there was no Sunday-school in Hanbury. Mr

Gray's desires were bounded by that object. Mr Horner looked farther on: he hoped for a day-school at some future time, to train up intelligent labourers for working on the estate. My lady would hear of neither one nor the other: indeed, not the boldest man whom she ever saw would have dared to name the project of a day-school within her hearing.

So Mr Horner contented himself with quietly teaching a sharp, clever lad to read and write, with a view to making use of him as a kind of foreman in process of time. He had his pick of the farm-lads for this purpose; and, as the brightest and sharpest, although by far the raggedest and dirtiest, singled out Job Gregson's son. But all this – as my lady never listened to gossip, or indeed, was spoken to unless she spoke first – was quite unknown to her, until the unlucky incident took place which I am going to relate.

Chapter IV

I think my lady was not aware of Mr Horner's views on education (as making men into more useful members of society) or the practice to which he was putting his precepts in taking Harry Gregson as pupil and protégé; if, indeed, she were aware of Harry's distinct existence at all, until the following unfortunate occasion. The anteroom, which was a kind of business-place for my lady to receive her steward and tenants in, was surrounded by shelves. I cannot call them book-shelves, though there were many books on them; but the contents of the volumes were principally manuscript, and relating to details connected with the Hanbury property. There were also one or two dictionaries, gazetteers, works of reference on the management of property; all of a very old date (the dictionary was Bailey's, I remember; we had a great Johnson in my lady's room, but where lexicographers differed, she generally preferred Bailey).

In this antechamber a footman generally sat, awaiting orders from my lady; for she clung to the grand old customs, and despised any bells, except her own little hand-bell, as modern inventions; she would have her people always within summons of this silvery bell, or her scarce less silvery voice. This man had not the sinecure you might imagine. He had to reply to the private entrance; what we should call the back door in a smaller house. As none came to the front door but my lady, and those of the county whom she honoured by visiting, and her nearest acquaintance of this kind lived eight miles (of bad road) off, the majority of comers knocked at the nail-studded terrace-door; not to have it opened (for open it stood, by my lady's orders, winter and summer, so that the snow often drifted into the back-hall, and lay there in heaps when the weather was severe), but to summon some one to receive their message, or carry their request to be allowed to speak to my lady. I remember it was long before Mr Gray could be made to understand that the great door was only opened on state occasions, and even to the last he would as soon come in by that as the terrace entrance. I had been received there on my first setting foot over my lady's threshold; every stranger was led in by that way the first time they came; but after that (with the exceptions I have named) they went round by the terrace, as it were by instinct. It was an assistance to this instinct to be aware that from time immemorial, the magnificent and fierce Hanbury wolf-hounds, which were extinct in every other part of the island, had been and still were kept chained in the front quadrangle, where they bayed through a great part of the day and night, and were always ready with their deep, savage growl at the sight of every person and thing, excepting the man who fed them, my lady's carriage-and-four, and my lady herself. It was pretty to see her small figure go up to the great, crouching brutes, thumping the flags with their heavy, wagging tails, and slobbering in an ecstacy of delight, at her light approach and soft caress. She had no fear of them; but she was a Hanbury born, and the tale went, that they and their kind knew all Hanburys instantly, and acknowledged their supremacy, ever since the ancestors of the breed had been brought from the East by the great Sir Urian Hanbury, who lay with his legs crossed on the altar-tomb in the church. Moreover, it was reported that, not fifty years before, one of these dogs had eaten up a child, which had inadvertently strayed within reach of its chain. So you may imagine how most people preferred the terrace-door. Mr Gray did not seem to care for the dogs. It might be absence of mind, for I have heard of his starting away from their sudden spring when he had unwittingly walked within reach of their chains; but it could hardly have been absence of mind when one day he went right up to one of them, and patted him in the most friendly manner, the dog meanwhile looking pleased, and affably wagging his tail, just as if Mr Gray had been a Hanbury. We were all very much puzzled by this, and to this day I have not been able to account for it.

But now let us go back to the terrace-door, and the footman sitting in the antechamber.

One morning we heard a parleying which rose to such a vehemence, and lasted for so long, that my lady had to ring her hand-bell twice before the footman heard it.

'What is the matter, John?' asked she, when he entered.

'A little boy, my lady, who says he comes from Mr Horner, and must see your ladyship. Impudent little lad!' (this last to himself).

'What does he want?'

'That's just what I have asked him, my lady, but he won't tell me, please your ladyship.'

'It is, probably, some message from Mr Horner,' said Lady Ludlow, with just a shade of annoyance in her manner; for it was against all etiquette to send a message to her, and by such a messenger too!

'No! please your ladyship, I asked him if he had any message, and he said no, he had none; but he must see your ladyship for all that.'

'You had better show him in then, without more words,' said her ladyship, quietly, but still, as I have said, rather annoyed.

As if in mockery of the humble visitor, the footman threw open both battants of the door, and in the opening there stood a lithe, wiry lad, with a thick head of hair, standing out in every direction, as if stirred by some electrical current, a short, brown face, red now from affright and excitement, wide, resolute mouth, and bright, deep-set eyes; which glanced keenly and rapidly round the room, as if taking in everything (and all was new and strange) to be thought and puzzled over at some future time. He knew enough of manners not to speak first to one above him in rank, or else he was afraid.

'What do you want with me?' asked my lady, in so gentle a tone that it seemed to surprise and stun him.

'An't please your ladyship?' said he, as if he had been deaf.

'You come from Mr Horner's: why do you want to see me?' again asked she, a little more loudly.

'An't please your ladyship, Mr Horner was sent for all on a sudden to Warwick this morning.'

His face began to work; but he felt it, and closed his lips into a resolute form.

'Well?'

'And he went off all on a sudden-like.'

'Well?'

'And he left a note for your ladyship with me, your ladyship.'

'Is that all? You might have given it to the footman.'

'Please your ladyship, I've clean gone and lost it.'

He never took his eyes off her face. If he had not kept his look fixed, he would have burst out crying.

'That was very careless,' said my lady, gently. 'But I am sure you are very sorry for it. You had better try and find it. It may have been of consequence.'

'Please, Mum – please your ladyship – I can say it off by heart.'

'You! What do you mean?' I was really afraid now. My lady's

blue eyes absolutely gave out light, she was so much displeased, and, moreover, perplexed. The more reason he had for affright, the more his courage rose. He must have seen – so sharp a lad must have perceived her displeasure, but he went on quickly and steadily.

'Mr Horner, my lady, has taught me to read, write, and cast accounts, my lady. And he was in a hurry, and he folded his paper up, but he did not seal it; and I read it, my lady; and now, my lady, it seems like as if I had got it off by heart;' and he went on with a high pitched voice, saying out very loud what, I have no doubt, were the identical words of the letter, date, signature and all: it was merely something about a deed, which required my lady's signature.

When he had done, he stood almost as if he expected commendation for his accurate memory.

My lady's eyes contracted till the pupils were as needle-points; it was a way she had when much disturbed. She looked at me, and said:

'Margaret Dawson, what will this world come to?' And then she was silent.

The lad, beginning to perceive he had given deep offence, stood stock still – as if his brave will had brought him into this presence, and impelled him to confession, and the best amends he could make, but had now deserted him, or was extinct, and left his body motionless, until some one else with word or deed made him quit the room. My lady looked again at him, and saw the frowning, dumb-foundering terror at his misdeed, and the manner in which his confession had been received.

'My poor lad!' said she, the angry look leaving her face, 'into whose hands have you fallen?'

The boy's lips began to quiver.

'Don't you know what tree we read of in Genesis? – No! I hope you have not got to read so easily as that.' A pause. 'Who has taught you to read and write?'

'Please, my lady, I meant no harm, my lady.' He was fairly blubbering, overcome by her evident feeling of dismay and regret, the soft repression of which was more frightening to him than any strong or violent words would have been.

'Who taught you, I ask?'

'It were Mr Horner's clerk who learned me, my lady.'

'And did Mr Horner know of it?'

'Yes, my lady. And I am sure I thought for to please him.'

'Well! perhaps you were not to blame for that. But I wonder at Mr Horner. However, my boy, as you have got possession of edge-tools, you must have some rules how to use them. Did you never hear that you were not to open letters?'

'Please, my lady, it were open. Mr Horner forgot for to seal it, in his hurry to be off.'

'But you must not read letters that are not intended for you. You must never try to read any letters that are not directed to you, even if they be open before you.'

'Please, my lady, I thought it were good for practice, all as one as a book.'

My lady looked bewildered as to what way she could farther explain to him the laws of honour as regarded letters.

'You would not listen, I am sure,' said she, 'to anything you were not intended to hear?'

He hesitated for a moment, partly because he did not fully comprehend the question. My lady repeated it. The light of intelligence came into his eager eyes, and I could see that he was not certain if he could tell the truth.

'Please, my lady, I always hearken when I hear folk talking secrets; but I mean no harm.'

My poor lady sighed: she was not prepared to begin a long way off in morals. Honour was, to her, second nature, and she had never tried to find out on what principle its laws were based. So, telling the lad that she wished to see Mr Horner when he returned from Warwick, she dismissed him with a despondent look; he, meanwhile, right glad to be out of the awful gentleness of her presence.

'What is to be done?' said she, half to herself and half to me. I could not answer, for I was puzzled myself.

'It was a right word,' she continued, 'that I used, when I called reading and writing "edge-tools." If our lower orders have these edge-tools given to them, we shall have the terrible scenes of the French Revolution acted over again in England. When I was a girl, one never heard of the rights of men, one only heard of the duties. Now, here was Mr Gray, only last night, talking of the right every child had to instruction. I could hardly keep my patience with him, and at length we fairly came to words; and I told him I would have no such thing as a Sunday-school (or a Sabbath-school, as he calls it, just like a Jew) in my village.'

'And what did he say, my lady?' I asked; for the struggle that seemed now to have come to a crisis, had been going on for some time in a quiet way.

'Why, he gave way to temper, and said he was bound to remember he was under the bishop's authority, not under mine; and implied that he should persevere in his designs, notwithstanding my expressed opinion.'

'And your ladyship – ' I half inquired.

'I could only rise and curtsy, and civilly dismiss him. When two persons have arrived at a certain point of expression on a subject, about which they differ as materially as I do from Mr Gray, the wisest course, if they wish to remain friends, is to drop the conversation entirely and suddenly. It is one of the few cases where abruptness is desirable.'

I was sorry for Mr Gray. He had been to see me several times, and had helped me to bear my illness in a better spirit than I should have done without his good advice and prayers. And I had gathered, from little things he said, how much his heart was set upon this new scheme. I liked him so much, and I loved and respected my lady so well, that I could not bear them to be on the cool terms to which they were constantly getting. Yet I could do nothing but keep silence.

I suppose my lady understood something of what was passing in my mind; for, after a minute or two, she went on: –

'If Mr Gray knew all I know – if he had my experience, he would not be so ready to speak of setting up his new plans in opposition to my judgement. Indeed,' she continued, lashing herself up with her own recollections, 'times are changed when the parson of a village comes to beard the liege lady in her own house. Why, in my grandfather's days, the parson was family chaplain too, and dined at the Hall every Sunday. He was helped last, and expected to have done first. I remember seeing him take up his plate and knife and fork, and say, with his mouth full all the time he was speaking: "If you please, Sir Urian, and my Lady, I'll follow the beef into the housekeeper's room;" for, you see, unless he did so, he stood no chance of a second helping. A greedy man, that parson was, to be sure! I recollect his once eating up the whole of some little bird at dinner, and by way of diverting attention from his greediness, he told how he had heard that a rook soaked in vinegar and then dressed in a particular way, could not be distinguished from the bird he was then eating. I saw by the grim look of my grandfather's face that the parson's doing and saying displeased him; and, child as I was, I had some notion what was coming, when, as I was riding out on my little, white pony, by my grandfather's side, the next Friday, he stopped one of the gamekeepers, and bade him shoot one of the oldest rooks he could find. I knew no more about it till Sunday, when a dish was set right before the parson, and Sir Urian said: "Now, Parson Hemming, I have had a rook shot, and soaked in vinegar, and dressed as you described last Sunday. Fall to, man, and eat it with as good an appetite as you had last Sunday. Pick the bones clean, or by —, no more Sunday dinners shall you eat at my table!" I gave one look at poor Mr Hemming's face, as he tried to swallow the first morsel, and make believe as though he thought it very good; but I could not look again, for shame, although my grandfather laughed, and kept asking us all round if we knew what could have become of the parson's appetite.'

'And did he finish it?' I asked.

'O yes, my dear. What my grandfather said was to be done, was done always. He was a terrible man in his anger! But to think of the difference between Parson Hemming and Mr Gray! or even of poor, dear Mr Mountford and Mr Gray. Mr Mountford would never have withstood me as Mr Gray did!'

'And your ladyship really thinks that it would not be right to have a Sunday-school?' I asked, feeling very timid as I put the question.

'Certainly not. As I told Mr Gray, I consider a knowledge of the Creed, and of the Lord's Prayer, as essential to salvation; and that any child may have, whose parents bring it regularly to church. Then there are the Ten Commandments, which teach simple duties in the plainest language. Of course, if a lad is taught to read and write (as that unfortunate boy has been who was here this morning) his duties become complicated, and his temptations much greater, while, at the same time, he has no hereditary principles and honourable training to serve as safeguards. I might take up my old simile of the race-horse and cart-horse. I am distressed,' continued she, with a break in her ideas, 'about that boy. The whole thing reminds me so much of a story of what happened to a friend of mine – Clément de Créquy. Did I ever tell you about him?'

'No, your ladyship,' I replied.

'Poor Clément! More than twenty years ago, Lord Ludlow and I spent a winter in Paris. He had many friends there; perhaps not very good or very wise men, but he was so kind that he liked every one, and every one liked him. We had an apartment, as they call it there, in the Rue de Lille; we had the first-floor of a grand hotel, with the basement for our servants. On the floor above us the owner of the house lived, a Marquise de Créquy, a widow.

They tell me that the Créquy coat-of-arms is still emblazoned, after all these terrible years, on a shield above the arched *porte-cochère*, just as it was then, though the family is quite extinct. Madame de Créquy had only one son, Clément, who was just the same age as my Urian – you may see his portrait in the great hall – Urian's, I mean.' I knew that Master Urian had been drowned at sea; and often had I looked at the presentment of his bonny hopeful face, in his sailor's dress, with right hand outstretched to a ship on the sea in the distance as if he had just said, 'Look at her! all her sails are set, and I'm just off.' Poor Master Urian! he went down in this very ship not a year after the picture was taken! But now I will go back to my lady's story. 'I can see those two boys playing now,' continued she, softly, shutting her eyes, as if the better to call up the vision, 'as they used to do five-and-twenty years ago in those old-fashioned French gardens behind our hotel. Many a time have I watched them from my windows. It was, perhaps, a better play-place than an English garden would have been, for there were but few flower-beds, and no lawn at all to speak about; but instead, terraces and balustrades, and vases and flights of stone steps more in the Italian style; and there were jets-d'eau, and little fountains that could be set playing by turning water-cocks that were hidden here and there. How Clément delighted in turning the water on to surprise Urian, and how gracefully he did the honours, as it were, to my dear, rough, sailor lad! Urian was as dark as a gypsy boy, and cared little for his appearance, and resisted all my efforts at setting off his black eyes and tangled curls; but Clément, without ever showing that he thought about himself and his dress, was always dainty and elegant, even though his clothes were sometimes but threadbare. He used to be dressed in a kind of hunter's green suit, open at the neck and half-way down the chest to beautiful old lace frills; his long golden curls fell behind just like a girl's, and his hair in front was cut over his straight dark eyebrows in a line almost as straight. Urian learnt more of a gentleman's carefulness and propriety of appearance

knees went Clément, hands crossed, eyes bent down: while Urian stood looking on in respectful thought.

'What a friendship that might have been! I never dream of Urian without seeing Clément too – Urian speaks to me, or does something – but Clément only flits round Urian, and never seems to see any one else!

'But I must not forget to tell you, that the next morning, before he was out of his room, a footman of Madame de Créquy's brought Urian the starling's nest.

'Well! we came back to England, and the boys were to correspond; and Madame de Créquy and I exchanged civilities; and Urian went to sea.

'After that, all seemed to drop away. I cannot tell you all. However, to confine myself to the De Créquys. I had a letter from Clément; I knew he felt his friend's death deeply; but I should never have learnt it from the letter he sent. It was formal, and seemed like chaff to my hungering heart. Poor fellow! I dare say he had found it hard to write. What could he – or any one – say to a mother who has lost her child? The world does not think so, and, in general, one must conform to the customs of the world; but, judging from my own experience, I should say that reverent silence at such times is the tenderest balm. Madame de Créquy wrote too. But I knew she could not feel my loss so much as Clément, and therefore her letter was not such a disappointment. She and I went on being civil and polite in the way of commissions, and occasionally introducing friends to each other, for a year or two, and then we ceased to have any intercourse. Then the terrible Revolution came. No one who did not live at those times can imagine the daily expectation of news – the hourly terror of rumours affecting the fortunes and lives of those whom most of us had known as pleasant hosts, receiving us with peaceful welcome in their magnificent houses. Of course, there was sin enough and suffering enough behind the scenes; but we English visitors to Paris had seen little or nothing of that – and I had sometimes thought, indeed, how even Death seemed loth to choose his victims out of that brilliant throng whom I had known. Madame de Créquy's one boy lived; while three out of my six were gone since we had met! I do not think all lots are equal, even now that I know the end of her hopes; but I do say, that whatever our individual lot is, it is our duty to accept it, without comparing it with that of others.

'The times were thick with gloom and terror. "What next?" was the question we asked of every one who brought us news from Paris. Where were these demons hidden when, so few years ago, we danced and feasted, and enjoyed the brilliant salons and the charming friendships of Paris?

'One evening, I was sitting alone in Saint James's Square; my lord off at the club with Mr Fox and others: he had left me, thinking that I should go to one of the many places to which I had been invited for that evening; but I had no heart to go anywhere, for it was poor Urian's birthday, and I had not even rung for lights, though the day was fast closing in, but was thinking over all his pretty ways, and on his warm affectionate nature, and how often I had been too hasty in speaking to him, for all I loved him so dearly; and how I seemed to have neglected and dropped his dear friend Clément, who might even now be in need of help in that cruel, bloody Paris. I say I was thinking reproachfully of all this, and particularly of Clément de Créquy in connection with Urian, when Fenwick brought me a note, sealed with a coat-of-arms I knew well, though I could not remember at the moment where I had seen it. I puzzled over it, as one does sometimes, for a minute or more, before I opened the letter. In a moment I saw it was from Clément de Créquy. "My mother is here," he said: "she is very ill, and I am bewildered in this strange country. May I entreat you to receive me for a few minutes?" The bearer of the note was the woman of the house where they lodged. I had her brought up into the anteroom, and questioned her myself, while my carriage was being brought round. They had arrived in London a fortnight or so before: she had not known their quality, judging them (according to her kind) by their dress and their luggage; poor enough, no doubt. The lady had never left her bedroom since her arrival; the young man waited upon her, did everything for her, never left her, in fact; only she (the messenger) had promised to stay within call, as soon as she returned, while he went out somewhere. She could hardly understand him, he spoke English so badly. He had never spoken it, I dare say, since he had talked to my Urian.

Chapter V

'In the hurry of the moment I scarce knew what I did. I bade the housekeeper put up every delicacy she had, in order to tempt the invalid, whom yet I hoped to bring back with me to our house. When the carriage was ready, I took the good woman with me to show us the exact way, which my coachman professed not to know; for, indeed, they were staying at but a poor kind of place at the back of Leicester Square, of which they had heard, as Clément told me afterwards, from one of the fishermen who had carried them across from the Dutch coast in their disguises as a Friesland peasant and his mother. They had some jewels of value concealed round their persons; but their ready money was all spent before I saw them, and Clément had been unwilling to leave his mother, even for the time necessary to ascertain the best mode of disposing of the diamonds. For, overcome with distress of mind and bodily fatigue, she had reached London only to take to her bed in a sort of low, nervous fever, in which her chief and only idea seemed to be, that Clément was about to be taken from her to some prison or other; and if he were out of her sight, though but for a minute, she cried like a child, and could not be pacified or comforted. The landlady was a kind, good woman, and though she but half understood the case, she was truly sorry for them, as foreigners, and the mother sick in a strange land.

'I sent her forwards to request permission for my entrance. In a moment I saw Clément – a tall, elegant young man, in a curious dress of coarse cloth, standing at the open door of a room, and evidently – even before he accosted me – striving to soothe the terrors of his mother inside. I went towards him, and would have taken his hand, but he bent down and kissed mine.

' "May I come in, madame?" I asked, looking at the poor sick lady, lying in the dark, dingy bed, her head propped up on coarse and dirty pillows, and gazing with affrighted eyes at all that was going on.

' "Clément! Clément! come to me!" she cried; and when he went to the bedside she turned on one side, and took his hand in both of hers, and began stroking it, and looking up in his face. I could scarce keep back my tears.

'He stood there quite still, except that from time to time he spoke to her in a low tone. At last I advanced into the room, so that I could talk to him, without renewing her alarm. I asked for the doctor's address; for I had heard that they had called in some one, at their landlady's recommendation: but I could hardly understand Clément's broken English, and mispronunciation of our proper names, and was obliged to apply to the woman herself. I could not say much to Clément, for his attention was perpetually needed by his mother, who never seemed to perceive that I was there. But I told him not to fear, however long I might be away, for that I would return before night; and, bidding the woman take charge of all the heterogeneous things the housekeeper had put up, and leaving one of my men in the house, who could understand a few words of French, with directions that he was to hold himself at Madame de Créquy's orders until I sent or gave him fresh commands, I drove off to the doctor's. What I wanted was his permission to remove Madame de Créquy to my own house, and to learn how it best could be done; for I saw that every movement in the room, every sound, except Clément's voice, brought on a fresh access of trembling and nervous agitation.

'The doctor was, I should think, a clever man; but he had that kind of abrupt manner which people get who have much to do with the lower orders.

'I told him the story of his patient, the interest I had in her, and the wish I entertained of removing her to my own house.

' "It can't be done," said he. "Any change will kill her."

' "But it must be done," I replied. "And it shall not kill her."

' "Then I have nothing more to say," said he, turning away from the carriage-door, and making as though he would go back into the house.

' "Stop a moment. You must help me; and, if you do, you shall have reason to be glad, for I will give you fifty pounds down with pleasure. If you won't do it, another shall."

'He looked at me, then (furtively) at the carriage, hesitated, and then said: "You do not mind expense, apparently. I suppose you are a rich lady of quality. Such folks will not stick at such trifles as the life or death of a sick woman to get their own way. I suppose I must e'en help you, for if I don't, another will."

'I did not mind what he said, so that he would assist me. I was pretty sure that she was in a state to require opiates; and I had not forgotten Christopher Sly, you may be sure, so I told him what I had in my head. That in the dead of night – the quiet time in the streets – she should be carried in a hospital litter, softly and warmly covered over, from the Leicester Square lodging-house to rooms that I would have in perfect readiness for her. As I planned, so it was done. I let Clément know, by a note, of my design. I had all prepared at home, and we walked about my house as though shod with velvet, while the porter watched at the open door. At last, through the darkness, I saw the lanterns carried by my men, who were leading the little procession. The litter looked like a hearse; on one side walked the doctor, on the other Clément: they came softly and swiftly along. I could not try any farther experiment; we dared not change her clothes; she was laid in the bed in the landlady's coarse night-gear, and covered over warmly, and left in the shaded, scented room, with a nurse and the doctor watching by her, while I led Clément to the dressing-room adjoining, in which I had had a bed placed for him. Farther than that he would not go; and there I had refreshments brought. Meanwhile, he had shown his gratitude by every possible action (for we none of us dared to speak): he had kneeled at my feet, and kissed my hand, and left it wet with his tears. He had thrown up his arms to Heaven, and prayed earnestly, as I could see by the movement of his lips. I allowed him to relieve himself by these dumb expressions, if I may so call them – and then I left him, and went to my own rooms to sit up for my lord, and tell him what I had done.

'Of course, it was all right; and neither my lord nor I could sleep for wondering how Madame de Créquy would bear her awakening. I had engaged the doctor, to whose face and voice she was accustomed, to remain with her all night: the nurse was experienced, and Clément was within call. But it was with the greatest relief that I heard from my own woman, when she brought me my chocolate, that Madame de Créquy (Monsieur had said) had awakened more tranquil than she had been for many days. To be sure, the whole aspect of the bed-chamber must have been more familiar to her than the miserable place where I had found her, and she must have intuitively felt herself among friends.

'My lord was scandalized at Clément's dress, which, after the first moment of seeing him, I had forgotten, in thinking of other things, and for which I had not prepared Lord Ludlow. He sent for his own tailor, and bade him bring patterns of stuffs, and engage his men to work night and day till Clément could appear as became his rank. In short, in a few days so much of the traces of their flight were removed, that we had almost forgotten the terrible causes of it, and rather felt as if they had come on a visit to us than that they had been compelled to fly their country. Their diamonds, too, were sold well by my lord's agents, though the London shops were stocked with jewellery, and such portable valuables, some of rare and curious fashion, which were sold for half their real value by emigrants who could not afford to wait. Madame de Créquy was recovering her health, although her strength was sadly gone, and she would never be equal to such another flight as the perilous one which she had gone through, and to which she could not bear the slightest reference. For some time things continued in this state; – the De Créquys still our honoured visitors – many houses besides our own, even among our own friends, open to receive the poor flying nobility of France, driven from their country by the brutal republicans, and every freshly-arrived emigrant bringing new tales of horror, as if these revolutionists were drunk with blood, and mad to devise new atrocities. One day Clément – I should tell you he had been presented to our good King George and the sweet Queen, and they had accosted him most graciously, and his beauty and elegance, and some of the circumstances attendant on his flight, made him be received in the world quite like a hero of romance: he might have been on intimate terms in many a distinguished house, had he cared to visit much; but he accompanied my lord and me with an air of indifference and languor, which I sometimes fancied, made him be all the more sought after: Monkshaven (that was the title my eldest son bore) tried in vain to interest him in all young men's sports. But no! it was the same through all. His mother took far more interest in the *on-dits* of the London world, into which she was far too great an invalid to venture, than he did in the absolute events themselves, in which he might have been an actor. One day, as I was saying, an old Frenchman of a humble class presented himself to our servants, several of whom understood French; and, through Medlicott, I learnt that he was in some way connected with the De Créquys; not with their Paris life; but I fancy he had been intendant of their estates in the country; estates which were more useful as hunting-grounds than as adding to their income. However, there was the old man; and with him, wrapped round his person, he had brought the long parchment rolls, and deeds relating to their property. These he would deliver up to none but Monsieur de Créquy, the rightful owner; and Clément was out with Monkshaven, so the old man waited; and when Clément came in, I told him of the steward's arrival, and how he had been cared for by my people. Clément went directly to see him. He was a long time away, and I was waiting for him to drive out with me, for some purpose or another, I scarce know what, but I remember I was tired of waiting, and was just in the act of ringing the bell to desire that he might be reminded of his engagement with me, when he came in, his face as white as the powder in his hair, his beautiful eyes dilated with horror. I saw that he had heard something that touched him even more closely than the usual tales which every fresh emigrant brought.

'"What is it, Clément?" I asked.

'He clasped his hands, and looked as though he tried to speak, but could not bring out the words.

'"They have guillotined my uncle!" said he at last. Now, I knew that there was a Count de Créquy; but I had always understood that the elder branch held very little communication with him; in fact, that he was a vaurien of some kind, and rather a disgrace than otherwise to the family. So, perhaps, I was hardhearted; but I was a little surprised at this excess of emotion, till I saw that peculiar look in his eyes that many people have when there is more terror in their hearts than they dare put into words. He wanted me to understand something without his saying it; but how could I? I had never heard of a Mademoiselle de Créquy.

'"Virginie!" at last he uttered. In an instant I understood it all, and remembered that, if Urian had lived, he too might have been in love.

'"Your uncle's daughter?" I inquired.

'"My cousin," he replied.

'I did not say, "your betrothed," but I had no doubt of it. I was mistaken, however.

' "O madame!" he continued, "her mother died long ago – her father now – and she is in daily fear – alone, deserted."

' "Is she in the Abbaye?" asked I.

' "No! She is in hiding with the widow of her father's old concierge. Any day they may search the house for aristocrats. They are seeking them everywhere. Then, not her life alone, but that of the old woman, her hostess, is sacrificed. The old woman knows this, and trembles with fear. Even if she is brave enough to be faithful, her fears would betray her, should the house be searched. Yet there is no one to help Virginie to escape. She is alone in Paris."

'I saw what was in his mind. He was fretting and chafing to go to his cousin's assistance; but the thought of his mother restrained him. I would not have kept back Urian from such an errand at such a time. How should I restrain him? And yet, perhaps, I did wrong in not urging the chances of danger more. Still, if it was danger to him, was it not the same or even greater danger to her? – for the French spared neither age nor sex in those wicked days of terror. So I rather fell in with his wish, and encouraged him to think how best and most prudently it might be fulfilled; never doubting, as I have said, that he and his cousin were troth-plighted.

'But when I went to Madame de Créquy – after he had imparted his, or rather our plan to her – I found out my mistake. She, who was in general too feeble to walk across the room save slowly, and with a stick, was going from end to end with quick, tottering steps; and, if now and then she sank upon a chair, it seemed as if she could not rest, for she was up again in a moment, pacing along, wringing her hands, and speaking rapidly to herself. When she saw me, she stopped: "Madame," she said, "you have lost your own boy. You might have left me mine."

'I was so astonished – I hardly knew what to say. I had spoken to Clément as if his mother's consent were secure (as I had felt my own would have been if Urian had been alive to ask it). Of course, both he and I knew that his mother's consent must be asked and obtained, before he could leave her to go on such an undertaking; but, somehow, my blood always rose at the sight or sound of danger; perhaps, because my life had been so peaceful. Poor Madame de Créquy! it was otherwise with her; she despaired while I hoped, and Clément trusted.

'"Dear Madame de Créquy," said I, "he will return safely to us; every precaution shall be taken, that either he or you, or my lord, or Monkshaven can think of; but he cannot leave a girl – his nearest relation save you – his betrothed, is she not?"

'"His betrothed!" cried she, now at the utmost pitch of her excitement. "Virginie betrothed to Clément? – no! thank heaven, not so bad as that! Yet it might have been. But Mademoiselle scorned my son! She would have nothing to do with him. Now is the time for him to have nothing to do with her!"

'Clément had entered at the door behind his mother as she thus spoke. His face was set and pale, till it looked as gray and immovable as if it had been carved in stone. He came forward and stood before his mother. She stopped her walk, threw back her haughty head, and the two looked each other steadily in the face. After a minute or two in this attitude, her proud and resolute gaze never flinching or wavering, he went down upon one knee, and, taking her hand – her hard, stony hand, which never closed on his, but remained straight and stiff:

'"Mother," he pleaded, "withdraw your prohibition. Let me go!"

'"What were her words?" Madame de Créquy replied, slowly, as if forcing her memory to the extreme of accuracy. "'My cousin,' she said, 'when I marry, I marry a man, not a petit-maître. I marry a man who, whatever his rank may be, will add dignity to the human race by his virtues, and not be content to live in an effeminate court on the traditions of past grandeur.' She borrowed

Marquis expressed his wish for the marriage of the cousins. The Count had had some interest in the management of the De Créquy property during her son's minority. Indeed, I remembered then that it was through Count de Créquy that Lord Ludlow had first heard of the apartment which we afterwards took in the Hotel de Créquy; and then the recollection of a past feeling came distinctly out of the mist, as it were; and I called to mind how, when we first took up our abode in the Hotel de Créquy, both Lord Ludlow and I imagined that the arrangement was displeasing to our hostess; and how it had taken us a considerable time before we had been able to establish relations of friendship with her. Years after our visit, she began to suspect that Clément (whom she could not forbid to visit at his uncle's house, considering the terms on which his father had been with his brother; though she herself never set foot over the Count de Créquy's threshold) was attaching himself to Mademoiselle, his cousin; and she made cautious inquiries as to the appearance, character, and disposition of the young lady. Mademoiselle was not handsome, they said; but of a fine figure, and generally considered as having a very noble and attractive presence. In character she was daring and wilful (said one set); original and independent (said another). She was much indulged by her father, who had given her something of a man's education, and selected for her intimate friend a young lady below her in rank, one of the Bureaucracie, a Mademoiselle Necker, daughter of the Minister of Finance. Mademoiselle de Créquy was thus introduced into all the free-thinking salons of Paris; among people who were always full of plans for subverting society. "And did Clément affect such people?" Madame de Créquy had asked, with some anxiety. No! Monsieur de Créquy had neither eyes nor ears nor thought for anything but his cousin, while she was by. And she? She hardly took notice of his devotion, so evident to every one else. The proud creature! But perhaps that was her haughty way of concealing what she felt. And so Madame de Créquy listened, and questioned, and learnt nothing decided, until one day she surprised Clément with the note in his hand, of which she remembered the stinging words so well, in which Virginie had said, in reply to a proposal Clément had sent her through her father, that "When she married she married a man, not a petit-maître."

'Clément was justly indignant at the insulting nature of the answer Virginie had sent to a proposal, respectful in its tone, and which was, after all, but the cool, hardened lava over a burning heart. He acquiesced in his mother's desire, that he should not again present himself in his uncle's salons; but he did not forget Virginie, though he never mentioned her name.

'Madame de Créquy and her son were among the earliest proscrits, as they were of the strongest possible royalists, and aristocrats, as it was the custom of the horrid Sansculottes to term those who adhered to the habits of expression and action in which it was their pride to have been educated. They had left Paris some weeks before they had arrived in England, and Clément's belief at the time of quitting the Hôtel de Créquy had certainly been that his uncle was not merely safe, but rather a popular man with the party in power. And, as all communication having relation to private individuals of a reliable kind was intercepted, Monsieur de Créquy had felt but little anxiety for his uncle and cousin, in comparison with what he did for many other friends of very different opinions in politics, until the day when he was stunned by the fatal information that even his progressive uncle was guillotined, and learnt that his cousin was imprisoned by the licence of the mob, whose rights (as she called them) she was always advocating.

'When I had heard all this story, I confess I lost in sympathy for Clément what I gained for his mother. Virginie's life did not seem to me worth the risk that Clément's would run. But when I saw him – sad, depressed, nay, hopeless – going about like one oppressed by a heavy dream which he cannot shake off; caring neither to eat, drink, nor sleep, yet bearing all with silent dignity, and even trying to force a poor, faint smile when he caught my anxious eyes; I turned round again, and wondered how Madame de Créquy could resist this mute pleading of her son's altered appearance. As for my Lord Ludlow and Monkshaven, as soon as they understood the case, they were indignant that any mother should attempt to keep a son out of honourable danger; and it was honourable, and a clear duty (according to them), to try to save the life of a helpless orphan girl, his next of kin. None but a Frenchman, said my lord, would hold himself bound by an old woman's whimsies and fears, even though she were his mother. As it was, he was chafing himself to death under the restraint. If he went, to be sure, the — wretches might make an end of him, as they had done of many a fine fellow; but my lord would take heavy odds that, instead of being guillotined, he would save the girl, and bring her safe to England, just desperately in love with her preserver, and then we would have a jolly wedding down at Monkshaven. My lord repeated his opinion so often, that it became a certain prophecy in his mind of what was to take place; and, one day seeing Clément look even paler and thinner than he had ever done before, he sent a message to Madame de Créquy, requesting permission to speak to her in private.

' "For, by George!" said he, "she shall hear my opinion, and not let that lad of hers kill himself by fretting. He's too good for that. If he had been an English lad, he would have been off to his sweetheart long before this, without saying with your leave or by your leave; but being a Frenchman, he is all for Aeneas and filial piety – filial fiddle-sticks!" (My lord had run away to sea, when a boy, against his father's consent, I am sorry to say; and, as all had ended well, and he had come back to find both his parents alive, I do not think he was ever as much aware of his fault as he might have been under other circumstances.) "No, my lady," he went on, "don't come with me. A woman can manage a man best when he has a fit of obstinacy, and a man can persuade a woman out of her tantrums, when all her own sex, the whole army of them, would fail. Allow me to go alone to my tête-à-tête with madame."

'What he said, what passed, he never could repeat; but he came back graver than he went. However, the point was gained; Madame de Créquy withdrew her prohibition, and had given him leave to tell Clément as much.

'"But she is an old Cassandra," said he. "Don't let the lad be much with her; her talk would destroy the courage of the bravest man; she is so given over to superstition." Something that she had said had touched a chord in my lord's nature which he inherited from his Scotch ancestors. Long afterwards, I heard what this was. Medlicott told me.

'However, my lord shook off all fancies that told against the fulfilment of Clément's wishes. All that afternoon we three sat together, planning; and Monkshaven passed in and out, executing our commissions, and preparing everything. Towards nightfall all was ready for Clément's start on his journey towards the coast.

'Madame had declined seeing any of us since my lord's stormy interview with her. She sent word that she was fatigued, and desired repose. But, of course, before Clément set off, he was bound to wish her farewell, and to ask for her blessing. In order to avoid an agitating conversation between mother and son, my lord and I resolved to be present at the interview. Clément was already in his travelling-dress, that of a Norman fisherman, which Monkshaven had, with infinite trouble, discovered in the possession of one of the émigrés who thronged London, and who had made his escape from the shores of France in this disguise. Clément's plan was to go down to the coast of Sussex, and get some of the fishing or smuggling boats to take him across to the French Coast near Dieppe. There again he would have to change his dress. O, it was so well planned! His mother was startled by his disguise (of which we had not thought to forewarn her) as he entered her apartment. And either that, or the being suddenly roused from the heavy slumber into which she was apt to fall when she was left alone, gave her manner an air of wildness that was almost like insanity.

'"Go, go!" she said to him, almost pushing him away as he knelt to kiss her hand. "Virginie is beckoning to you, but you don't see what kind of a bed it is –"

'"Clément, make haste!" said my lord, in a hurried manner, as if to interrupt madame. "The time is later than I thought, and you must not miss the morning's tide. Bid your mother good-bye at once, and let us be off." For my lord and Monkshaven were to ride with him to an inn near the shore, from whence he was to walk to his destination. My lord almost took him by the arm to pull him away; and they were gone, and I was left alone with Madame de Créquy. When she heard the horses' feet, she seemed to find out the truth, as if for the first time. She set her teeth together. "He has left me for her!" she almost screamed. "Left me for her!" she kept muttering; and then, as the wild look came back into her eyes, she said, almost with exultation, "But I did not give him my blessing!"

Chapter VI

'All night Madame de Créquy raved in delirium. If I could, I would have sent for Clément back again. I did send off one man, but I suppose my directions were confused, or they were wrong, for he came back after my lord's return, on the following afternoon. By this time Madame de Créquy was quieter: she was, indeed, asleep from exhaustion when Lord Ludlow and Monkshaven came in. They were in high spirits, and their hopefulness brought me round to a less dispirited state. All had gone well: they had accompanied Clément on foot along the shore, until they had met with a lugger, which my lord had hailed in good nautical language. The captain had responded to these freemason terms by sending a boat to pick up his passenger, and by an invitation to breakfast sent through a speaking-trumpet. Monkshaven did not approve of either the meal or the company, and had returned to the inn, but my lord had gone with Clément, and breakfasted on board, upon grog, biscuit, fresh-caught fish – "the best breakfast he ever ate," he said, but that was probably owing to the appetite his night's ride had given him. However, his good fellowship had evidently won the captain's heart, and Clément had set sail under the best auspices. It was agreed that I should tell all this to Madame de Créquy, if she inquired; otherwise, it would be wiser not to renew her agitation by alluding to her son's journey.

'I sat with her constantly for many days; but she never spoke of Clément. She forced herself to talk of the little occurrences of Parisian society in former days: she tried to be conversational and agreeable, and to betray no anxiety or even interest in the object of Clément's journey; and, as far as unremitting efforts could go, she succeeded. But the tones of her voice were sharp and yet piteous, as if she were in constant pain; and the glance of her eye hurried and fearful, as if she dared not let it rest on any object.

'In a week we heard of Clément's safe arrival on the French coast. He sent a letter to this effect by the captain of the smuggler, when the latter returned. We hoped to hear again; but week after week elapsed, and there was no news of Clément. I had told Lord Ludlow, in Madame de Créquy's presence, as he and I had arranged, of the note I had received from her son, informing us of his landing in France. She heard, but she took no notice. Yet now, evidently, she began to wonder that we did not mention any further intelligence of him in the same manner before her; and daily I began to fear that her pride would give way, and that she would supplicate for news before I had any to give her.

'One morning, on my awakening, my maid told me that Madame de Créquy had passed a wretched night, and had bidden Medlicott (whom, as understanding French, and speaking it pretty well, though with that horrid German accent, I had put about her) request that I would go to Madame's room as soon as I was dressed.

'I knew what was coming, and I trembled all the time they were doing my hair, and otherwise arranging me. I was not encouraged by my lord's speeches. He had heard the message, and kept declaring that he would rather be shot than have to tell her that there was no news of her son; and yet he said, every now and then, when I was at the lowest pitch of uneasiness, that he never expected to hear again: that some day soon we should see him walking in, and introducing Mademoiselle de Créquy to us.

'However, at last I was ready, and go I must.

'Her eyes were fixed on the door by which I entered. I went up to the bedside. She was not rouged – she had left it off now for several days – she no longer attempted to keep up the vain show of not feeling and loving and fearing.

'For a moment or two she did not speak, and I was glad of the respite.

' "Clément?" she said at length, covering her mouth with a handkerchief the minute she had spoken, that I might not see it quiver.

' "There has been no news since the first letter, saying how well the voyage was performed, and how safely he had landed – near Dieppe, you know," I replied as cheerfully as possible. "My lord does not expect that we shall have another letter; he thinks that we shall see him soon."

'There was no answer. As I looked, uncertain whether to do or say more, she slowly turned herself in bed, and lay with her face to the wall; and, as if that did not shut out the light of day and the busy, happy world enough, she put out her trembling hands, and covered her face with her handkerchief. There was no violence: hardly any sound.

'I told her what my lord had said about Clément's coming in some day, and taking us all by surprise. I did not believe it myself, but it was just possible – and I had nothing else to say. Pity, to one who was striving so hard to conceal her feelings, would have been impertinent. She let me talk; but she did not reply. She knew that my words were vain and idle, and had no root in my belief, as well as I did myself.

'I was very thankful when Medlicott came in with Madame's breakfast, and gave me an excuse for leaving.

'But I think that conversation made me feel more anxious and impatient than ever. I felt almost pledged to Madame de Créquy for the fulfilment of the vision I had held out. She had taken entirely to her bed by this time; not from illness, but because she had no hope within her to stir her up to the effort of dressing. In the same way she hardly cared for food. She had no appetite – why eat to prolong a life of despair? But she let Medlicott feed her, sooner than take the trouble of resisting.

'And so it went on – for weeks, months – I could hardly count the time, it seemed so long. Medlicott told me she noticed a preternatural sensitiveness of ear in Madame de Créquy, induced by the habit of listening silently for the slightest unusual sound in the house. Medlicott was always a minute watcher of any one whom she cared about; and, one day, she made me notice by a sign madame's acuteness of hearing, although the quick expectation was but evinced for a moment in the turn of the eye, the hushed breath – and then, when the unusual footstep turned into my lord's apartments, the soft quivering sigh, and the closed eyelids.

'At length the intendant of the De Créquy estates – the old man, you will remember, whose information respecting Virginie de Créquy first gave Clément the desire to return to Paris – came to St James's Square, and begged to speak to me. I made haste to go down to him in the housekeeper's room, sooner than that he should be ushered into mine, for fear of Madame hearing any sound.

'The old man stood – I see him now – with his hat held before him in both his hands; he slowly bowed till his face touched it when I came in. Such long excess of courtesy augured ill. He waited for me to speak.

'"Have you any intelligence?" I inquired. He had been often to the house before, to ask if we had received any news; and once or twice I had seen him, but this was the first time he had begged to see me.

'"Yes, madame," he replied, still standing with his head bent down, like a child in disgrace.

'"And it is bad!" I exclaimed.

'"It is bad." For a moment I was angry at the cold tone in which my words were echoed; but directly afterwards I saw the large, slow, heavy tears of age falling down the old man's cheeks, and on to the sleeves of his poor, thread-bare coat.

'I asked him how he had heard it: it seemed as though I could not all at once bear to hear what it was. He told me that the night before, in crossing Long Acre, he had stumbled upon an old acquaintance of his; one who, like himself, had been a dependant upon the De Créquy family, but had managed their Paris affairs, while Fléchier had taken charge of their estates in the country. Both were now emigrants, and living on the proceeds of such small available talents as they possessed. Fléchier, as I knew, earned a very fair livelihood by going about to dress salads for dinner parties. His compatriot, Le Fèbvre, had begun to give a few lessons as a dancing-master. One of them took the other home to his lodgings; and there, when their most immediate personal adventures had been hastily talked over, came the inquiry from Fléchier as to Monsieur de Créquy.

'"Clément was dead – guillotined. Virginie was dead – guillotined."

'When Fléchier had told me thus much, he could not speak for sobbing; and I, myself, could hardly tell how to restrain my tears sufficiently, until I could go to my own room and be at liberty to give way. He asked my leave to bring in his friend Le Fèbvre, who was walking in the square, awaiting a possible summons to tell his story. I heard afterwards a good many details, which filled up the account, and made me feel – which brings me back to the point I started from – how unfit the lower orders are for being trusted indiscriminately with the dangerous powers of education. I have made a long preamble, but now I am coming to the moral of my story.'

My lady was trying to shake off the emotion which she evidently felt in recurring to this sad history of Monsieur de Créquy's death. She came behind me, and arranged my pillows, and then, seeing I had been crying – for, indeed, I was weak-spirited at the time, and a little served to unloose my tears – she stooped down, and kissed my forehead, and said 'Poor child!' almost as if she thanked me for feeling that old grief of hers.

'Being once in France, it was no difficult thing for Clément to get into Paris. The difficulty in those days was to leave, not to enter. He came in dressed as a Norman peasant, in charge of a load of fruit and vegetables, with which one of the Seine barges was freighted. He worked hard with his companions in landing and arranging their produce on the quays; and then, when they dispersed to get their breakfasts at some of the estaminets near the old Marché aux Fleurs, he sauntered up a street which conducted him, by many an odd turn, through the Quartier Latin to a horrid back alley, leading out of the Rue l'Ecole de Médécine; some atrocious place, as I have heard, not far from the shadow of that terrible Abbaye, where so many of the best blood of France awaited their deaths. But here some old man lived on whose fidelity Clément thought that he might rely. I am not sure if he had not been gardener in those very gardens behind the Hôtel Créquy where Clément and Urian used to play together years before. But, whatever the old man's dwelling might be, Clément was only too glad to reach it, you may be sure. He had been kept in Normandy, in all sorts of disguises, for many days after landing in Dieppe, through the difficulty of entering Paris unsuspected by the many ruffians who were always on the look-out for aristocrats.

'The old gardener was, I believe, both faithful and tried, and sheltered Clément in his garret as well as might be. Before he could stir out, it was necessary to procure a fresh disguise; and one more in character with an inhabitant of Paris than that of a Norman carter was procured; and, after waiting in-doors for one or two days, to see if any suspicion was excited, Clément set off to discover Virginie.

'He found her at the old concièrge's dwelling. Madame Babette was the name of this woman, who must have been a less faithful – or rather, perhaps I should say, a more interested – friend to her guest than the old gardener Jacques was to Clément.

'I have seen a miniature of Virginie, which a French lady of quality happened to have in her possession at the time of her flight from Paris, and which she brought with her to England unwittingly; for it belonged to the Count de Créquy, with whom she was slightly acquainted. I should fancy from it, that Virginie was taller and of a more powerful figure for a woman than her cousin Clément was for a man. Her dark-brown hair was arranged in short curls – the way of dressing the hair announced the politics of the individual, in those days, just as patches did in my grandmother's time; and Virginie's hair was not to my taste, or according to my principles; it was too classical. Her large, black eyes looked out at you steadily. One cannot judge of the shape of a nose from a full-face miniature, but the nostrils were clearly cut and largely opened. I do not fancy her nose could have been pretty; but her mouth had a character all its own, and which would, I think, have redeemed a plainer face. It was wide and deep set into the cheeks at the corners; the upper lip was very much arched, and hardly closed over the teeth; so that the whole face looked (from the serious, intent look in the eyes, and the sweet intelligence of the mouth) as if she were listening eagerly to something to which her answer was quite ready, and would come out of those red, opening lips as soon as ever you had done speaking, and you longed to know what she would say.

'Well; this Virginie de Créquy was living with Madame Babette in the concièrgerie of an old French inn, somewhere to the north of Paris, so, far enough from Clément's refuge. The inn had been frequented by farmers from Brittany and such kind of people, in the days when that sort of intercourse went on between Paris and the provinces which had nearly stopped now. Few Bretons came near it now, and the inn had fallen into the hands of Madame Babette's brother, as payment for a bad wine debt of the last proprietor. He put his sister and her child in, to keep it open, as it were, and sent all the people he could to occupy the half-furnished rooms of the house. They paid Babette for their lodging every morning as they went out to breakfast, and returned or not as they chose, at night. Every three days, the wine-merchant or his son came to Madame Babette, and she accounted to them for the money she had received. She and her child occupied the porter's office (in which the lad slept at nights) and a little, miserable bed-room which opened out of it, and received all the light and air that was admitted through the door of communication, which was half glass. Madame Babette must have had a kind of attachment for the De Créquys – her De Créquys, you understand – Virginie's father, the Count; for, at some risk to herself, she had warned both him and his daughter of the danger impending over them. But he, infatuated, would not believe that his dear Human Race could ever do him harm; and, as long as he did not fear, Virginie was not afraid. It was by some ruse, the nature of which I never heard, that Madame Babette induced Virginie to come to her abode at the very hour in which the Count had been recognized in the streets, and hurried off to the Lanterne. It was after Babette had got her there, safe shut up in the little back den, that she told her what had befallen her father. From that day, Virginie had never stirred out of the gates, or crossed the threshold of the porter's lodge. I do not say that Madame Babette was tired of her continual presence, or regretted the impulse which had made her rush to the De

Créquys' well-known house – after being compelled to form one of the mad crowds that saw the Count de Créquy seized and hung – and hurry his daughter out, through alleys and back-ways, until at length she had the orphan safe in her own dark sleeping-room, and could tell her tale of horror: but Madame Babette was poorly paid for her porter's work by her avaricious brother; and it was hard enough to find food for herself and her growing boy; and, though the poor girl ate little enough, I dare say, yet there seemed no end to the burthen that Madame Babette had imposed upon herself: the De Créquys were plundered, ruined, had become an extinct race, all but a lonely, friendless girl, in broken health and spirits; and, though she lent no positive encouragement to his suit, yet, at the time, when Clément reappeared in Paris, Madame Babette was beginning to think that Virginie might do worse than encourage the attentions of Monsieur Morin Fils, her nephew, and the wine-merchant's son. Of course, he and his father had the entrée into the concièrgerie of the hotel that belonged to them, in right of being both proprietors and relations. The son, Morin, had seen Virginie in this manner. He was fully aware that she was far above him in rank, and guessed from her whole aspect that she had lost her natural protectors by the terrible guillotine; but he did not know her exact name or station, nor could he persuade his aunt to tell him. However, he fell head over ears in love with her, whether she were princess or peasant; and, though at first there was something about her which made his passionate love conceal itself with shy, awkward reserve, and then, made it only appear in the guise of deep, respectful devotion; yet, by-and-by – by the same process of reasoning I suppose that his aunt had gone through even before him – Jean Morin began to let Hope oust Despair from his heart. Sometimes he thought – perhaps years hence – that solitary, friendless lady, pent up in squalor, might turn to him as to a friend and comforter – and then – and then. Meanwhile Jean Morin was most attentive to his aunt; whom he had rather slighted before. He would linger over the accounts; would bring her little presents; and, above all, he made a pet and favourite of Pierre, the little cousin who could tell him about all the ways of going on of Mam'selle Cannes, as Virginie was called. Pierre was thoroughly aware of the drift and cause of his cousin's inquiries; and was his ardent partisan, as I have heard, even before Jean Morin had exactly acknowledged his wishes to himself.

'It must have required some patience and much diplomacy, before Clément de Créquy found out the exact place where his cousin was hidden. The old gardener took the cause very much to heart; as, judging from my recollections, I imagine he would have forwarded any fancy, however wild, of Monsieur Clément's. (I will tell you afterwards how I came to know all these particulars so well.)

'After Clément's return, on two succeeding days, from his dangerous search without meeting with any good result, Jacques entreated Monsieur de Créquy to let him take it in hand. He represented that he, as gardener for the space of twenty years and more at the Hôtel de Créquy, had a right to be acquainted with all the successive concièrges at the Count's house; that he should not go among them as a stranger, but as an old friend, anxious to renew pleasant intercourse; and that if the Intendant's story, which he had told Monsieur de Créquy in England, was true, that Mademoiselle was in hiding at the house of a former concièrge, why, something relating to her would surely drop out in the course of conversation. So he persuaded Clément to remain in-doors, while he set off on his round, with no apparent object but to gossip.

'At night he came home – having seen Mademoiselle. He told Clément much of the story relating to Madame Babette that I have told to you. Of course, he had heard nothing of the ambitious hopes of Morin Fils – hardly of his existence, I should think. Madame Babette had received him kindly; although, for some time, she had kept him standing in the carriage gateway outside her door. But, on his complaining of the draught and his rheumatism, she had asked him in: first looking round with some anxiety, to see who was in the room behind her. No one was there when he entered and sat down. But, in a minute or two, a tall, thin young lady, with great, sad eyes, and pale cheeks, came from the inner room, and, seeing him, retired. "It is Mademoiselle Cannes," said Madame Babette, rather unnecessarily; for, if he had not been on the watch for some sign of Mademoiselle de Créquy, he would hardly have noticed the entrance and withdrawal.

'Clément and the good old gardener were always rather perplexed by Madame Babette's evident avoidance of all mention of the De Créquy family. If she were so much interested in one member as to be willing to undergo the pains and penalties of a domiciliary visit, it was strange that she never inquired after the existence of her charge's friends and relations from one who might very probably have heard something of them. They settled that Madame Babette must believe that the Marquise and Clément were dead; and admired her for her reticence in never speaking of Virginie. The truth was, I suspect, that she was so desirous of her nephew's success by this time, that she did not like letting any one into the secret of Virginie's whereabouts who might interfere with their plan. However, it was arranged between Clément and his humble friend, that the former, dressed in the peasant's clothes in which he had entered Paris, but smartened up in one or two particulars, as if, although a countryman, he had money to spare, should go and engage a sleeping-room in the old Breton Inn; where, as I told you, accommodation for the night was to be had. This was accordingly done, without exciting Madame Babette's suspicions, for she was unacquainted with the Normandy accent, and consequently did not perceive the exaggeration of it which Monsieur de Créquy adopted in order to disguise his pure Parisian. But after he had for two nights slept in a queer, dark closet, at the end of one of the numerous short galleries in the Hôtel Duguesclin, and paid his money for such accommodation each morning at the little bureau under the window of the concièrgerie, he found himself no nearer to his object. He stood outside in the gateway: Madame Babette opened a pane in her window, counted out the change, gave polite thanks, and shut the pane with a clack, before he could ever find out what to say that might be the means of opening a conversation. Once in the streets, he was in danger from the bloodthirsty mob, who were ready in those days to hunt to death every one who looked like a gentleman, as an aristocrat: and Clément, depend upon it, looked a gentleman, whatever dress he wore. Yet it was unwise to traverse Paris to his old friend the gardener's grénier, so he had to loiter about, where I hardly know. Only he did leave the Hôtel Duguesclin, and he did not go to old Jacques, and there was not another house in Paris open to him. At the end of two days, he had made out Pierre's existence; and he began to try to make friends with the lad. Pierre was too sharp and shrewd not to suspect something from the confused attempts at friendliness. It was not for nothing that the Norman farmer lounged in the court and doorway, and brought home presents of galette. Pierre accepted the galette, reciprocated the civil speeches, but kept his eyes open. Once, returning home pretty late at night, he surprised the Norman studying the shadows on the blind, which was drawn down when Madame Babette's lamp was lighted. On going in, he found Mademoiselle Cannes with his mother, sitting by the table, and helping in the family mending.

'Pierre was afraid that the Norman had some view upon the money which his mother, as concièrge, collected for her brother. But the money was all safe next evening when his cousin, Monsieur Morin Fils, came to collect it. Madame Babette asked her nephew to sit down, and skilfully barred the passage to the inner door, so that Virginie, had she been ever so much disposed, could not have retreated. She sat silently sewing. All at once the little party were startled by a very sweet tenor voice, just close to the street window, singing one of the airs out of Beaumarchais' operas, which, a few years before, had been popular all over Paris.

But after a few moments of silence, and one or two remarks, the talking went on again. Pierre, however, noticed an increased air of abstraction in Virginie, who, I suppose, was recurring to the last time that she had heard the song, and did not consider, as her cousin had hoped she would have done, what were the words set to the air, which he imagined she would remember, and which would have told her so much. For, only a few years before, Adam's opera of *Richard le Roi* had made the story of the Minstrel Blondel and our English Coeur de Lion familiar to all the opera-going part of the Parisian public, and Clément had bethought him of establishing a communication with Virginie by some such means.

'The next night, about the same hour, the same voice was singing outside the window again. Pierre, who had been irritated by the proceeding the evening before, as it had diverted Virginie's attention from his cousin, who had been doing his utmost to make himself agreeable, rushed out to the door, just as the Norman was ringing the bell to be admitted for the night. Pierre looked up and down the street; no one else was to be seen. The next day, the Norman mollified him somewhat by knocking at the door of the concièrgerie, and begging Monsieur Pierre's acceptance of some knee-buckles, which had taken the country farmer's fancy the day before, as he had been gazing into the shops, but which, being too small for his purpose, he took the liberty of offering to Monsieur Pierre. Pierre, a French boy, inclined to foppery, was charmed, ravished by the beauty of the present and with Monsieur's goodness, and he began to adjust them to his breeches immediately, as well as he could, at least, in his mother's absence. The Norman, whom Pierre kept carefully on the outside of the threshold, stood by, as if amused at the boy's eagerness.

' "Take care," said he, clearly and distinctly; "take care, my little friend, lest you become a fop; and, in that case, some day, years hence, when your heart is devoted to some young lady, she may be inclined to say to you" – here he raised his voice – "No, thank you; when I marry, I marry a man, not a petit-maître; I marry a man, who, whatever his position may be, will add dignity to the human race by his virtues." Farther than that in his quotation Clément dared not go. His sentiments (so much above the apparent occasion) met with applause from Pierre, who liked to contemplate himself in the light of a lover, even though it should be a rejected one, and who hailed the mention of the words "virtues" and "dignity of the human race" as belonging to the cant of a good citizen.

'But Clément was more anxious to know how the invisible lady took his speech. There was no sign at the time. But when he returned at night, he heard a voice, low singing, behind Madame Babette, as she handed him his candle, the very air he had sung without effect for two nights past. As if he had caught it up from her murmuring voice, he sang it loudly and clearly as he crossed the court.

'"Here is our opera-singer!" exclaimed Madame Babette. "Why, the Norman grazier sings like Boupré," naming a favourite singer at the neighbouring theatre.

'Pierre was struck by the remark, and quietly resolved to look after the Norman; but again, I believe, it was more because of his mother's deposit of money than with any thought of Virginie.

'However, the next morning, to the wonder of both mother and son, Mademoiselle Cannes proposed, with much hesitation, to go out and make some little purchase for herself. A month or two ago, this was what Madame Babette had been never weary of urging. But now she was as much surprised as if she had expected Virginie to remain a prisoner in her rooms all the rest of her life. I suppose she had hoped that her first time of quitting it would be when she left it for Monsieur Morin's house as his wife.

'A quick look from Madame Babette towards Pierre was all that was needed to encourage the boy to follow her. He went out cautiously. She was at the end of the street. She looked up and down, as if waiting for some one. No one was there. Back she came, so swiftly that she nearly caught Pierre before he could retreat through the porte-cochère. There he looked out again. The neighbourhood was low and wild, and strange; and some one spoke to Virginie – nay, laid his hand upon her arm – whose dress and aspect (he had emerged out of a side-street) Pierre did not know; but, after a start, and (Pierre could fancy) a little scream, Virginie recognised the stranger, and the two turned up the side street whence the man had come. Pierre stole swiftly to the corner of this street; no one was there: they had disappeared up some of the alleys. Pierre returned home to excite his mother's infinite surprise. But they had hardly done talking, when Virginie returned, with a colour and a radiance in her face, which they had never seen there since her father's death.

Chapter VII

'I have told you that I heard much of this story from a friend of the Intendant of the De Créquys, whom he met with in London. Some years afterwards – the summer before my lord's death – I was travelling with him in Devonshire, and we went to see the French prisoners of war on Dartmoor. We fell into conversation with one of them, whom I found out to be the very Pierre of whom I had heard before, as having been involved in the fatal story of Clément and Virginie, and by him I was told much of their last days, and thus I learnt how to have some sympathy with all those who were concerned in those terrible events; yes, even with the younger Morin himself, on whose behalf Pierre spoke warmly, even after so long a time had elapsed.

'For when the younger Morin called at the porter's lodge, on the evening of the day when Virginie had gone out for the first time after so many months' confinement to the concièrgerie, he was struck with the improvement in her appearance. It seems to have hardly been that he thought her beauty greater; for, in addition to the fact that she was not beautiful, Morin had arrived at that point of being enamoured when it does not signify whether the beloved one is plain or handsome – she has enchanted one pair of eyes, which henceforward see her through their own medium. But Morin noticed the faint increase of colour and light in her countenance. It was as though she had broken through her thick cloud of hopeless sorrow, and was dawning forth into a happier life. And so, whereas during her grief, he had revered and respected it even to a point of silent sympathy, now that she was gladdened, his heart rose on the wings of strengthened hopes. Even in the dreary monotony of this existence in his Aunt Babette's concièrgerie, Time had not failed in his work, and now, perhaps, soon he might humbly strive to help Time. The very next day he returned – on some pretence of business – to the Hôtel Duguesclin, and made his aunt's room, rather than his aunt herself, a present of roses and geraniums tied up in a bouquet with a tricolour ribbon. Virginie was in the room, sitting at the coarse sewing she liked to do for Madame Babette. He saw her eyes brighten at the sight of the flowers: she asked his aunt to let her arrange them; he saw her untie the ribbon, and with a gesture of dislike, throw it on the ground, and give it a kick with her little foot, and even in this girlish manner of insulting his dearest prejudices, he found something to admire.

'As he was coming out, Pierre stopped him. The lad had been trying to arrest his cousin's attention by futile grimaces and signs played off behind Virginie's back; but Monsieur Morin saw nothing but Mademoiselle Cannes. However, Pierre was not to be baffled, and Monsieur Morin found him in waiting just outside the threshold. With his finger on his lips, Pierre walked on tiptoe by his companion's side till they would have been long past sight or hearing of the concièrgerie, even had the inhabitants devoted themselves to the purposes of spying or listening.

'"Chut!" said Pierre, at last. "She goes out walking."

' "Well?" said Monsieur Morin, half curious, half annoyed at being disturbed in the delicious reverie of the future into which he longed to fall.

' "Well! It is not well. It is bad."

' "Why? I do not ask who she is, but I have my ideas. She is an aristocrat. Do the people about here begin to suspect her?"

' "No, no!" said Pierre. "But she goes out walking. She has gone these two mornings. I have watched her. She meets a man – she is friends with him, for she talks to him as eagerly as he does to her – mamma cannot tell who he is."

' "Has my aunt seen him?"

' "No, not so much as a fly's wing of him. I myself have only seen his back. It strikes me like a familiar back, and yet I cannot think who it is. But they separate with sudden darts, like two birds who have been together to feed their young ones. One moment they are in close talk, their heads together chuckotting, the next he has turned up some by-street, and Mademoiselle Cannes is close upon me – has almost caught me."

' "But she did not see you?" inquired Monsieur Morin, in so altered a voice that Pierre gave him one of his quick penetrating looks. He was struck by the way in which his cousin's features – always coarse and commonplace – had become contracted and pinched; struck, too, by the livid look on his sallow complexion. But as if Morin was conscious of the manner in which his face belied his feelings, he made an effort, and smiled, and patted Pierre's head, and thanked him for his intelligence, and gave him a five-franc piece, and bade him go on with his observations of Mademoiselle Cannes' movements, and report all to him.

'Pierre returned home with a light heart, tossing up his five-franc piece as he ran. Just as he was at the concièrgerie door, a great tall man bustled past him, and snatched his money away from him, looking back with a laugh, which added insult to injury. Pierre had no redress; no one had witnessed the impudent theft, and if they had, no one to be seen in the street was strong enough

then see whether he thought it right to act as a spy upon her or not – the one action did not pledge him to the other, nor yet did she make any conditions with her gift – Pierre went off with her ring; and, after repaying himself his five francs, he was enabled to bring Virginie back two more, so well had he managed his affairs. But, although the whole transaction did not leave him bound, in any way, to discover or forward Virginie's wishes, it did leave him pledged, according to his code, to act according to her advantage, and he considered himself the judge of the best course to be pursued to this end. And, moreover, this little kindness attached him to her personally. He began to think how pleasant it would be to have so kind and generous a person for a relation; how easily his troubles might be borne if he had always such a ready helper at hand; how much he should like to make her like him, and come to him for the protection of his masculine power! First of all his duties, as her self-appointed squire, came the necessity of finding out who her strange new acquaintance was. Thus, you see, he arrived at the same end, via supposed duty, that he was previously pledged to via interest. I fancy a good number of us, when any line of action will promote our own interest, can make ourselves believe that reasons exist which compel us to it as a duty.

'In the course of a very few days, Pierre had so circumvented Virginie as to have discovered that her new friend was no other than the Norman farmer in a different dress. This was a great piece of knowledge to impart to Morin. But Pierre was not prepared for the immediate physical effect it had on his cousin. Morin sat suddenly down on one of the seats in the Boulevards – it was there Pierre had met with him accidentally – when he heard who it was that Virginie met. I do not suppose the man had the faintest idea of any relationship or even previous acquaintanceship between Clément and Virginie. If he thought of anything beyond the mere fact presented to him, that his idol was in communication with another, younger, handsomer man than himself, it must have been that the Norman farmer had seen her at the concièrgerie, and had been attracted by her, and, as was but natural, had tried to make her acquaintance, and had succeeded. But, from what Pierre told me, I should not think that even this much thought passed through Morin's mind. He seems to have been a man of rare and concentrated attachments; violent, though restrained and undemonstrative passions; and, above all, a capability of jealousy, of which his dark oriental complexion must have been a type. I could fancy that if he had married Virginie, he would have coined his life-blood for luxuries to make her happy; would have watched over and petted her, at every sacrifice to himself, as long as she would have been content to live for him alone. But, as Pierre expressed it to me: "When I saw what my cousin was, when I learned his nature too late, I perceived that he would have strangled a bird if she whom he loved was attracted by it from him."

'When Pierre had told Morin of his discovery, Morin sat down, as I have said, quite suddenly, as if he had been shot. He found out that the first meeting between the Norman and Virginie was no accidental, isolated circumstance. Pierre was torturing him with his accounts of daily rendezvous: if but for a moment, they were seeing each other every day, sometimes twice a day. And Virginie could speak to this man, though to himself she was so coy and reserved as hardly to utter a sentence. Pierre caught these broken words while his cousin's complexion grew more and more livid, and then purple, as if some great effect were produced on his circulation by the news he had just heard. Pierre was so startled by his cousin's wandering senseless eyes, and otherwise disordered looks, that he rushed into a neighbouring cabaret for a glass of absinthe, which he paid for, as he recollected afterwards, with a portion of Virginie's five francs. By-and-by Morin recovered his natural appearance; but he was gloomy and silent; and all that Pierre could get out of him was, that the Norman farmer should not sleep another night at the Hôtel Duguesclin, giving him such opportunities of passing and repassing by the concièrgerie door.

He was too much absorbed in his own thoughts to repay Pierre the half-franc he had spent on the absinthe, which Pierre perceived, and seems to have noted down in the ledger of his mind as on Virginie's balance of favour.

Altogether, he was so much disappointed at his cousin's mode of receiving intelligence, which the lad thought worth another five-franc piece at least; or, if not paid for in money, to be paid for in open-mouthed confidence and expression of feeling, that he was for a time, so far a partisan of Virginie's − unconscious Virginie − against his cousin, as to feel regret when the Norman returned no more to his night's lodging, and when Virginie's eager watch at the crevice of the closely-drawn blind ended only with a sigh of disappointment. If it had not been for his mother's presence at the time, Pierre thought he should have told her all. But how far was his mother in his cousin's confidence as regarded the dismissal of the Norman?

'In a few days, however, Pierre felt almost sure that they had established some new means of communication. Virginie went out for a short time every day; but, though Pierre followed her as closely as he could without exciting her observation, he was unable to discover what kind of intercourse she held with the Norman. She went, in general, the same short round among the little shops in the neighbourhood; not entering any, but stopping at two or three. Pierre afterwards remembered that she had invariably paused at the nosegays displayed in a certain window, and studied them long; but, then, she stopped and looked at caps, hats, fashions, confectionery (all of the humble kind common in that quarter), so how should he have known that any particular attraction existed among the flowers? Morin came more regularly than ever to his aunt's; but Virginie was apparently unconscious that she was the attraction. She looked healthier and more hopeful than she had done for months, and her manners to all were gentler and not so reserved. Almost as if she wished to manifest her gratitude to Madame Babette for her long continuance of a kindness, the necessity for which was nearly ended, Virginie showed an unusual alacrity in rendering the old woman any little service in her power, and evidently tried to respond to Monsieur Morin's civilities, he being Madame Babette's nephew, with the soft graciousness which must have made one of her principal charms; for all who knew her speak of the fascination of her manners, so winning and attentive to others, while yet her opinions, and often her actions, were of so decided a character. For, as I have said, her beauty was by no means great; yet every man who came near her seems to have fallen into the sphere of her influence. Monsieur Morin was deeper than ever in love with her during these last few days: he was worked up into a state capable of any sacrifice, either of himself or others, so that he might obtain her at last. He sat "devouring her with his eyes" (to use Pierre's expression) whenever she could not see him; but, if she looked towards him, he looked to the ground – anywhere – away from her, and almost stammered in his replies if she addressed any question to him.

'He had been, I should think, ashamed of his extreme agitation on the Boulevards, for Pierre thought that he absolutely shunned him for these few succeeding days. He must have believed that he had driven the Norman (my poor Clément!) off the field, by banishing him from his inn; and thought that the intercourse between him and Virginie, which he had thus interrupted, was of so slight and transient a character as to be quenched by a little difficulty.

'But he appears to have felt that he made but little way, and he awkwardly turned to Pierre for help – not yet confessing his love, though; he only tried to make friends again with the lad after their silent estrangement. And Pierre for some time did not choose to perceive his cousin's advances. He would reply to all the roundabout questions Morin put to him respecting household conversations when he was not present, or household occupations and tone of thought, without mentioning Virginie's name any more than his questioner did. The lad would seem to suppose, that his cousin's strong interest in their domestic ways of going on was all on account of Madame Babette. At last he worked his cousin up to the point of making him a confidant; and then the boy was half frightened at the torrent of vehement words he had unloosed. The lava came down with a greater rush for having been pent up so long. Morin cried out his words in a hoarse, passionate voice, clenched his teeth, his fingers, and seemed almost convulsed, as he spoke out his terrible love for Virginie, which would lead him to kill her sooner than see her another's; and if another stepped in between him and her! – and then he smiled a fierce, triumphant smile, but did not say any more.

'Pierre was, as I said, half-frightened; but also half-admiring. This was really love – a "grande passion," – a really fine, dramatic thing – like the plays they acted at the little theatre yonder. He had a dozen times the sympathy with his cousin now that he had had before, and readily swore by the infernal gods, for they were far too enlightened to believe in one God, or Christianity, or anything of the kind – that he would devote himself, body and soul, to forwarding his cousin's views. Then his cousin took him to a shop, and bought him a smart second-hand watch, on which they scratched the word Fidélité, and thus was the compact sealed. Pierre settled in his own mind, that if he were a woman, he should like to be beloved as Virginie was by his cousin, and that it would be an extremely good thing for her to be the wife of so rich a citizen as Morin Fils – and for Pierre himself, too, for doubtless their gratitude would lead them to give him rings and watches *ad infinitum*.

'A day or two afterwards, Virginie was taken ill. Madame Babette said it was because she had persevered in going out in all weathers, after confining herself to two warm rooms for so long; and very probably this was really the cause, for, from Pierre's account, she must have been suffering from a feverish cold, aggravated, no doubt, by her impatience at Madame Babette's familiar prohibitions of any more walks until she was better. Every day, in spite of her trembling aching limbs, she would fain have arranged her dress for her walk at the usual time; but Madame Babette was fully prepared to put physical obstacles in her way, if she was not obedient in remaining tranquil on the little sofa by the side of the fire. The third day, she called Pierre to her, when his mother was not attending (having, in fact, locked up Mademoiselle Cannes' out-of-door things).

'"See, my child," said Virginie. "Thou must do me a great favour. Go to the gardener's shop in the Rue des Bons-Enfans, and look at the nosegays in the window. I long for pinks; they are my favourite flower. Here are two francs. If thou seest a nosegay of pinks displayed in the window, if it be ever so faded – nay, if thou seest two or three nosegays of pinks, remember, buy them all, and bring them to me, I have so great a desire for the smell." She fell back weak and exhausted. Pierre hurried out. Now was the time; here was the clue to the long inspection of the nosegay in this very shop.

'Sure enough, there was a drooping nosegay of pinks in the window. Pierre went in, and, with all his impatience, he made as good a bargain as he could, urging that the flowers were faded, and good for nothing. At last he purchased them at a very moderate price. And now you will learn the bad consequences of teaching the lower orders anything beyond what is immediately necessary to enable them to earn their daily bread! The silly Count de Créquy – he who had been sent to his bloody rest, by the very canaille of whom he thought so much – he who had made Virginie (indirectly, it is true) reject such a man as her cousin Clément, by inflating her mind with his bubbles of theories – this Count de Créquy had long ago taken a fancy to Pierre, as he saw the bright sharp child playing about his courtyard. Monsieur de Créquy had even begun to educate the boy himself, to try to work out certain opinions of his into practice – but the drudgery of the affair wearied him, and, beside, Babette had left his employment.

Still the Count took a kind of interest in his former pupil; and made some sort of arrangement by which Pierre was to be taught reading and writing, and accounts, and Heaven knows what besides – Latin, I dare say. So Pierre, instead of being an innocent messenger, as he ought to have been – (as Mr Horner's little lad Gregson ought to have been this morning) – could read writing as well as either you or I. So what does he do, on obtaining the nosegay, but examine it well. The stalks of the flowers were tied up with slips of matting in wet moss. Pierre undid the strings, unwrapped the moss, and out fell a piece of wet paper, with the writing all blurred with moisture. It was but a torn piece of writing-paper, apparently, but Pierre's wicked mischievous eyes read what was written on it – written so as to look like a fragment. – "Ready, every and any night at nine. All is prepared. Have no fright. Trust one who, whatever hopes he might once have had, is content now to serve you as a faithful cousin;" and a place was named, which I forget, but which Pierre did not, as it was evidently the rendezvous. After the lad had studied every word, till he could say it off by heart, he placed the paper where he had found it, enveloped it in moss, and tied the whole up again carefully. Virginie's face coloured scarlet as she received it. She kept smelling at it, and trembling: but she did not untie it, although Pierre suggested how much fresher it would be if the stalks were immediately put into water. But once, after his back had been turned for a minute, he saw it untied when he looked round again, and Virginie was blushing, and hiding something in her bosom.

'Pierre was now all impatience to set off and find his cousin. But his mother seemed to want him for small domestic purposes even more than usual; and he had chafed over a multitude of errands connected with the Hôtel before he could set off and search for his cousin at his usual haunts. At last the two met; and Pierre related all the events of the morning to Morin. He said the note off word by word. (That lad this morning had something of the magpie look of Pierre — it made me shudder to see him, and hear him repeat the note by heart.) Then Morin asked him to tell him all over again. Pierre was struck by Morin's heavy sighs as he repeated the story. When he came the second time to the note, Morin tried to write the words down; but either he was not a good, ready scholar, or his fingers trembled too much. Pierre hardly remembered, but, at any rate, the lad had to do it, with his wicked reading and writing. When this was done, Morin sat heavily silent. Pierre would have preferred the expected outburst, for this impenetrable gloom perplexed and baffled him. He had even to speak to his cousin to rouse him; and when he replied, what he said had so little apparent connexion with the subject which Pierre had expected to find uppermost in his mind, that he was half-afraid that his cousin had lost his wits.

'"My Aunt Babette is out of coffee."

'"I am sure I do not know," said Pierre.

'"Yes, she is. I heard her say so. Tell her that a friend of mine has just opened a shop in the Rue Saint Antoine, and that if she will join me there in an hour, I will supply her with a good stock of coffee, just to give my friend encouragement. His name is Antoine Meyer, Number One hundred and Fifty, at the sign of the Cap of Liberty."

'"I could go with you now. I can carry a few pounds of coffee better than my mother," said Pierre, all in good faith. He told me he should never forget the look on his cousin's face, as he turned round, and bade him begone, and give his mother the message without another word. It had evidently sent him home promptly to obey his cousin's command. Morin's message perplexed Madame Babette.

'"How could he know I was out of coffee?" said she. "I am; but I only used the last up this morning. How could Jean know about it?"

'"I am sure I can't tell," said Pierre, who by this time had recovered his usual self-possession. "All I know is, that Monsieur is in a pretty temper, and that if you are not sharp to your time at this Antoine Meyer's you are likely to come in for some of his black looks."

' "Well, it is very kind of him to offer to give me some coffee, to be sure! But how could he know I was out?"

'Pierre hurried his mother off impatiently, for he was certain that the offer of the coffee was only a blind to some hidden purpose on his cousin's part; and he made no doubt that when his mother had been informed of what his cousin's real intention was, he, Pierre, could extract it from her by coaxing or bullying. But he was mistaken. Madame Babette returned home, grave, depressed, silent, and loaded with the best coffee. Some time afterwards he learnt why his cousin had sought for this interview. It was to extract from her, by promises and threats, the real name of Mam'selle Cannes, which would give him a clue to the true appellation of The Faithful Cousin. He concealed this second purpose from his aunt, who had been quite unaware of his jealousy of the Norman farmer, or of his identification of him with any relation of Virginie's. But Madame Babette instinctively shrank from giving him any information: she must have felt that, in the lowering mood in which she found him, his desire for greater knowledge of Virginie's antecedents boded her no good. And yet he made his aunt his confidante – told her what she had only suspected before that he was deeply enamoured of Mam'selle Cannes, and would gladly marry her. He spoke to Madame Babette of his father's hoarded riches; and of the share which he, as partner, had in them at the present time; and of the prospect of the succession to the whole, which he had, as an only child. He told his aunt of the provision for her (Madame Babette's) life, which he would make on the day when he married Mam'selle Cannes. And yet – and yet – Babette saw that in his eye and look which made her more and more reluctant to confide in him. By and by he tried threats. She should leave the concièrgerie, and find employment where she liked. Still silence. Then he grew angry, and swore that he would inform against her at the bureau of the Directory, for harbouring an aristocrat; an aristocrat he knew Mademoiselle was, whatever her real name might be. His aunt should have a domiciliary visit, and see how she liked that. The officers of the Government were the people for finding out secrets. In vain she reminded him that, by so doing, he would expose to imminent danger the lady whom he had professed to love. He told her, with a sullen relapse into silence after his vehement outpouring of passion, never to trouble herself about that. At last he wearied out the old woman, and, frightened alike of herself, and of him, she told him all – that Mam'selle Cannes was Mademoiselle Virginie de Créquy, daughter of the Count of that name. Who was the Count? Younger brother of the Marquis. Where was the Marquis? Dead long ago, leaving a widow and child. A son? (eagerly). Yes, a son. Where was he? Parbleu! how should she know? – for her courage returned a little as the talk went away from the only person of the De Créquy family that she cared about. But, by dint of some small glasses out of a bottle of Antoine Meyer's, she told him more about the De Créquys than she liked afterwards to remember. For the exhilaration of the brandy lasted but a very short time, and she came home, as I have said, depressed, with a presentiment of coming evil. She would not answer Pierre, but cuffed him about in a manner to which the spoilt boy was quite unaccustomed. His cousin's short, angry words, and sudden withdrawal of confidence – his mother's unwonted crossness and fault-finding, all made Virginie's kind, gentle treatment more than ever charming to the lad. He half resolved to tell her how he had been acting as a spy upon her actions, and at whose desire he had done it. But he was afraid of Morin, and of the vengeance which he was sure would fall upon him for any breach of confidence. Towards half-past eight that evening – Pierre, watching, saw Virginie arrange several little things – she was in the inner room, but he sat where he could see her through the glazed partition. His mother sat – apparently sleeping – in the great easy-chair; Virginie moved about softly, for fear of disturbing her. She made up one or two little parcels of the few things she could call her own: one packet she concealed about herself – the others she directed, and left on the shelf. "She is going," thought Pierre, and (as he said in giving me the account) his heart gave a spring, to think that he should never see her again. If either his mother or his cousin had been more kind to him, he might have endeavoured to intercept her; but as it was, he held his breath, and when she came out he pretended to read, scarcely knowing whether he wished her to succeed in the purpose which he was almost sure she entertained, or not. She stopped by him, and passed her hand over his hair. He told me that his eyes filled with tears at this caress. Then she stood for a moment, looking at the sleeping Madame Babette, and stooped down and softly kissed her on the forehead. Pierre dreaded lest his mother should awake (for by this time the wayward, vacillating boy must have been quite on Virginie's side), but the brandy she had drunk made her slumber heavily. Virginie went. Pierre's heart beat fast. He was sure his cousin would try to intercept her; but how, he could not imagine. He longed to run out and see the catastrophe – but he had let the moment slip; he was also afraid of reawakening his mother to her unusual state of anger and violence.

Chapter VIII

'Pierre went on pretending to read, but in reality listening with acute tension of ear to every little sound. His perceptions became so sensitive in this respect that he was incapable of measuring time, every moment had seemed so full of noises, from the beating of his heart up to the roll of the heavy carts in the distance. He wondered whether Virginie would have reached the place of rendezvous, and yet he was unable to compute the passage of with sulky, and yet humble, uncouthness. I dare say he would have given worlds if he might have had that little hand within his arm; but, though she still kept silence, she shuddered up away from him, as you shrink from touching a toad. He had said something to her during that walk, you may be sure, which had made her loathe him. He marked and understood the gesture. He held himself aloof while Pierre gave her all the assistance he could in their slow progress homewards. But Morin accompanied her all the same. He had played too desperate a game to be balked now. He had given information against the çi-devant Marquis de Créquy, as a returned émigré, to be met with at such a time, in such a place. Morin had hoped that all sign of the arrest would have been cleared away before Virginie reached the spot – so swiftly were terrible deeds done in those days. But Clément defended himself desperately: Virginie was punctual to a second; and, though the wounded man was borne off to the Abbaye, amid a crowd of the unsympathizing jeerers who mingled with the armed officials of the Directory, Morin feared lest Virginie had recognized him; and he would have preferred that she should have thought that the "faithful cousin" was faithless, than that she should have seen him in bloody danger on her account. I suppose he fancied that, if Virginie never saw or heard more of him, her imagination would not dwell on his simple disappearance, as it would do if she knew what he was suffering for her sake.

'At any rate, Pierre saw that his cousin was deeply mortified by the whole tenor of his behaviour during their walk home. When they arrived at Madame Babette's, Virginie fell fainting on the floor; her strength had but just sufficed for this exertion of reaching the shelter of the house. Her first sign of restoring consciousness consisted in avoidance of Morin. He had been most assiduous in his efforts to bring her round; quite tender in his way, Pierre said; and this marked, instinctive repugnance to him evidently gave him extreme pain. I suppose Frenchmen are more demonstrative than we are; for Pierre declared that he saw his cousin's eyes fill with tears, as she shrank away from his touch, if he tried to arrange the shawl they had laid under her head like a pillow, or as she shut her eyes when he passed before her. Madame Babette was urgent with her to go and lie down on the bed in the inner room; but it was some time before she was strong enough to rise and do this.

'When Madame Babette returned from arranging the girl comfortably, the three relations sat down in silence; a silence which Pierre thought would never be broken. He wanted his mother to ask his cousin what had happened. But Madame Babette was afraid of her nephew, and thought it more discreet to wait for such crumbs of intelligence as he might think fit to throw to her. But, after she had twice reported Virginie to be asleep, without a word being uttered in reply to her whispers by either of her companions, Morin's powers of self-containment gave way.

' "It is hard!" he said.

' "What is hard?" asked Madame Babette, after she had paused for a time, to enable him to add to, or to finish, his sentence, if he pleased.

' "It is hard for a man to love a woman as I do," he went on. "I did not seek to love her, it came upon me before I was aware – before I had ever thought about it at all, I loved her better than all the world beside. All my life, before I knew her, seems a dull blank. I neither know nor care for what I did before then. And now there are just two lives before me. Either I have her, or I have not. That is all: but that is everything. And what can I do to make her have me? Tell me, aunt," and he caught at Madame Babette's arm, and gave it so sharp a shake, that she half screamed out, Pierre said, and evidently grew alarmed at her nephew's excitement.

' "Hush, Jean!" said she. "There are other women in the world, if this one will not have you."

' "None other for me," he said, sinking back as if hopeless. "I am plain and coarse, not one of the scented darlings of the aristocrats. Say that I am ugly, brutish; I did not make myself so, any more than I made myself love her. It is my fate. But am I to submit to the consequences of my fate without a struggle? Not I. As strong as my love is, so strong is my will. It can be no stronger," continued he, gloomily. "Aunt Babette, you must help me – you must make her love me." He was so fierce here, that Pierre said he did not wonder that his mother was frightened.

'"I, Jean!" she exclaimed. "I make her love you? How can I? Ask me to speak for you to Mademoiselle Didot, or to Mademoiselle Cauchois even, or to such as they, and I'll do it, and welcome. But to Mademoiselle de Créquy, why, you don't know the difference! Those people – the old nobility I mean – why, they don't know a man from a dog, out of their own rank! And no wonder, for the young gentlemen of quality are treated differently to us from their very birth. If she had you to-morrow, you would be miserable. Let me alone for knowing the aristocracy. I have not been a concièrge to a duke and three counts for nothing. I tell you, all your ways are different to her ways."

'"I would change 'my ways,' as you call them."

'"Be reasonable, Jean."

'"No, I will not be reasonable, if by that you mean giving her up. I tell you two lives are before me; one with her, one without her. But the latter will be but a short career for both of us. You said, aunt, that the talk went in the concièrgerie of her father's hôtel, that she would have nothing to do with this cousin whom I put out of the way to-day?"

'"So the servants said. How could I know? All I know is, that he left off coming to our hôtel, and that at one time before then he had never been two days absent."

'"So much the better for him. He suffers now for having come between me and my object – in trying to snatch her away out of my sight. Take you warning, Pierre! I did not like your meddling to-night." And so he went off, leaving Madame Babette rocking herself backwards and forwards, in all the depression of spirits consequent upon the reaction after the brandy, and upon her elegance which I always noticed about his appearance, and which I believed was innate in the wearer – I have no doubt it seemed like the usual apparel of a gentleman. No coarseness of texture, nor clumsiness of cut, could disguise the nobleman of thirty descents, it appeared; for, immediately on arriving at the place of rendezvous, he was recognized by the men placed there on Morin's information to seize him. Jacques, following at a little distance, with a bundle under his arm containing articles of feminine disguise for Virginie, saw four men attempt Clément's arrest – saw him, quick as lightning, draw a sword hitherto concealed in a clumsy stick – saw his agile figure spring to his guard – and saw him defend himself with the rapidity and art of a man skilled in arms. But what good did it do? as Jacques piteously used to ask, Monsieur Fléchier told me. A great blow from a heavy club on the sword-arm of Monsieur de Créquy laid it helpless and immovable by his side. Jacques always thought that that blow came from one of the spectators, who by this time had collected round the scene of the affray. The next instant, his master – his little marquis – was down among the feet of the crowd, and though he was up again before he had received much damage – so active and light was my poor Clément – it was not before the old gardener had hobbled forwards, and, with many an old-fashioned oath and curse, proclaimed himself a partisan of the losing side – a follower of a çi-devant aristocrat. It was quite enough. He received one or two good blows, which were, in fact, aimed at his master; and then, almost before he was aware, he found his arms pinioned behind him with a woman's garter, which one of the viragos in the crowd had made no scruple of pulling off in public, as soon as she heard for what purpose it was wanted. Poor Jacques was stunned and unhappy – his master was out of sight, on before; and the old gardener scarce knew whither they were taking him. His head ached from the blows which had fallen upon it; it was growing dark – June day though it was – and when first he seems to have become exactly aware of what had happened to him, it was when he was turned into one of the larger rooms of the Abbaye, in which all were put who had no other allotted place wherein to sleep. One or two iron lamps hung from the ceiling by chains, giving a dim light for a little circle. Jacques stumbled forwards over a sleeping body lying on the ground. The sleeper wakened up enough to complain; and the apology of the old man in reply caught the ear of his master, who, until this time, could hardly have been aware of the straits and difficulties of his faithful Jacques. And there they sat – against a pillar, the live-long night, holding one another's hands, and each restraining expressions of pain, for fear of adding to the other's distress. That night made them intimate friends, in spite of the difference of age and rank. The disappointed hopes, the acute suffering of the present, the apprehensions of the future, made them seek solace in talking of the past. Monsieur de Créquy and the gardener found themselves disputing with interest in which chimney of the stack the starling used to build – the starling whose nest Clément sent to Urian, you remember – and discussing the merits of different espalier-pears which grew, and may grow still, in the old garden of the Hôtel de Créquy. Towards morning both fell asleep. The old man wakened first. His frame was deadened to suffering, I suppose, for he felt relieved of his pain; but Clément moaned and cried in feverish slumber. His broken arm was beginning to inflame his blood. He was, besides, much injured by some kicks from the crowd as he fell. As the old man looked sadly on the white, baked lips, and the flushed cheeks, contorted with suffering even in his sleep, Clément gave a sharp cry, which disturbed his miserable neighbours, all slumbering around in uneasy attitudes. They bade him with curses be silent; and then turning round, tried again to forget their own misery in sleep. For you see, the bloodthirsty canaille had not been sated with guillotining and hanging all the nobility they could find, but were now informing, right and left, even against each other; and when Clément and Jacques were in the prison, there were few of gentle blood in the place, and fewer still of gentle manners. At the sound of the angry words and threats, Jacques thought it best to awaken his master from his feverish uncomfortable sleep, lest he should provoke more enmity; and, tenderly lifting him up, he tried to adjust his own body, so that it should serve as a rest and a pillow for the younger man. The motion aroused Clément, and he began to talk in a strange, feverish way, of Virginie, too – whose name he would not have breathed in such a place had he been quite himself. But Jacques had as much delicacy of feeling as any lady in the land, although, mind you, he knew neither how to read nor write – and bent his head low down, so that his master might tell him in a whisper what messages he was to take to Mademoiselle de Créquy, in case – Poor Clément, he knew it must come to that! No escape for him now, in Norman disguise or otherwise! Either by gathering fever or guillotine, death was sure of his prey. Well! when that happened, Jacques was to go and find Mademoiselle de Créquy, and tell her that her cousin loved her at the last as he had loved her at the first; but that she should never have heard another word of his attachment from his living lips; that he knew he was not good enough for her, his queen; and that no thought of earning her love by his devotion had prompted his return to France, only that, if possible, he might have the great privilege of serving her whom he loved. And then he went off into rambling talk about petit-maîtres, and such kind of expressions, said Jacques to Fléchier, the Intendant, little knowing what a clue that one word gave to much of the poor lad's suffering.

'The summer morning came slowly on in that dark prison, and when Jacques could look round – his master was now sleeping on his shoulder, still the uneasy starting sleep of fever – he saw that there were many women among the prisoners. (I have heard some of those who have escaped from the prisons say, that the look of despair and agony that came into the faces of the prisoners on first wakening, as the sense of their situation grew upon them, was what lasted the longest in the memory of the survivors. This look, they said, passed away from the women's faces sooner than it did from those of the men.)

'Poor old Jacques kept falling asleep, and plucking himself up again for fear lest, if he did not attend to his master, some harm might come to the swollen helpless arm. Yet his weariness grew upon him in spite of all his efforts, and at last he felt as if he must give way to the irresistible desire, if only for five minutes. But just then there was a bustle at the door. Jacques opened his eyes wide to look.

'"The gaoler is early with breakfast," said some one, lazily.

'"It is the darkness of this accursed place that makes us think it early," said another.

'All this time a parley was going on at the door. Some one came in; not the gaoler – a woman. The door was shut to and locked behind her. She only advanced a step or two; for it was too sudden a change, out of the light into that dark shadow, for any one to see clearly for the first few minutes. Jacques had his eyes fairly open now; and was wide awake. It was Mademoiselle de Créquy, looking bright, clear, and resolute. The faithful heart of the old man read that look like an open page. Her cousin should not die there on her behalf, without at least the comfort of her sweet presence.

'"Here he is," he whispered, as her gown would have touched him in passing, without her perceiving him, in the heavy obscurity of the place.

'"The good God bless you, my friend!" she murmured, as she saw the attitude of the old man, propped against a pillar, and holding Clément in his arms, as if the young man had been a helpless baby, while one of the poor gardener's hands supported the broken limb in the easiest position. Virginie sat down by the old man, and held out her arms. Softly she moved Clément's head to her own shoulder; softly she transferred the task of holding the arm to herself. Clément lay on the floor, but she supported him, and Jacques was at liberty to arise and stretch and shake his stiff weary old body. He then sat down at a little distance, and watched the pair until he fell asleep. Clément had muttered "Virginie," as they half roused him by their movements out of his stupor; but Jacques thought he was only dreaming; nor did he seem fully awake when once his eyes opened, and he looked full at Virginie's face bending over him, and growing crimson under his gaze, though she never stirred, for fear of hurting him if she moved. Clément looked in silence, until his heavy eyelids came slowly down, and he fell into his oppressive slumber again. Either he did not recognize her, or she came in too completely as a part of his sleeping visions for him to be disturbed by her appearance there.

'When Jacques awoke it was full daylight – at least as full as it would ever be in that place. His breakfast – the gaol-allowance of bread and vin ordinaire – was by his side. He must have slept soundly. He looked for his master. He and Virginie had recognized each other now – hearts, as well as appearance. They were smiling into each other's faces, as if that dull vaulted room in the grim Abbaye were the sunny gardens of Versailles, with music and festivity all abroad. Apparently they had much to say to each other; for whispered questions and answers never ceased.

'Virginie had made a sling for the poor broken arm; nay, she had obtained two splinters of wood in some way, and one of their fellow-prisoners – having, it appeared, some knowledge of surgery – had set it. Jacques felt more desponding by far than they did, for he was suffering from the night he had passed, which told upon his aged frame; while they must have heard some good news, as it seemed to him, so bright and happy did they look. Yet Clément was still in bodily pain and suffering, and Virginie, by her own act and deed, was a prisoner in that dreadful Abbaye, whence the only issue was the guillotine. But they were together: they loved: they understood each other at length.

'When Virginie saw that Jacques was awake, and languidly munching his breakfast, she rose from the wooden stool on which she was sitting, and went to him, holding out both hands, and refusing to allow him to rise, while she thanked him with pretty eagerness for all his kindness to Monsieur. Monsieur himself came towards him – following Virginie – but with tottering steps, as if his head was weak and dizzy, to thank the poor old man, who, now on his feet, stood between them, ready to cry while they gave him credit for faithful actions which he felt to have been almost involuntary on his part – for loyalty was like an instinct in the good old days, before your educational cant had come up. And so two days went on. The only event was the morning call for the victims, a certain number of whom were summoned to trial every day. And to be tried was to be condemned. Every one of the prisoners became grave, as the hour for their summons approached. Most of the victims went to their doom with uncomplaining resignation, and for awhile after their departure there was comparative silence in the prison. But, by and by – so said Jacques – the conversation or amusements began again. Human nature cannot stand the perpetual pressure of such keen anxiety, without an effort to relieve itself by thinking of something else. Jacques said that Monsieur and Mademoiselle were for ever talking together of the past days – it was "Do you remember this?" or, "Do you remember that?" perpetually. He sometimes thought they forgot where they were, and what was before them. But Jacques did not, and every day he trembled more and more as the list was called over.

'The third morning of their incarceration, the gaoler brought in a man whom Jacques did not recognize, and therefore did not at once observe; for he was waiting, as in duty bound, upon his master and his sweet young lady (as he always called her in repeating the story). He thought that the new introduction was some friend of the gaoler, as the two seemed well acquainted, and the latter stayed a few minutes talking with his visitor before leaving him in the prison. So Jacques was surprised when, after a short time had elapsed, he looked round, and saw the fierce stare with which the stranger was regarding Monsieur and

Mademoiselle de Créquy, as the pair sat at breakfast – the said breakfast being laid as well as Jacques knew how, on a bench fastened into the prison wall – Virginie sitting on her low stool, and Clément half lying on the ground by her side, and submitting gladly to be fed by her pretty white fingers; for it was one of her fancies, Jacques said, to do all she could for him, in consideration of his broken arm. And, indeed, Clément was wasting away daily; for he had received other injuries, internal and more serious than that to his arm, during the mêlée which had ended in his capture. The stranger made Jacques conscious of his presence by a sigh, which was almost a groan. All three prisoners looked round at the sound. Clément's face expressed little but scornful indifference; but Virginie's face froze into stony hate. Jacques said he never saw such a look, and hoped that he never should again. Yet after that first revelation of feeling, her look was steady and fixed in another direction to that in which the stranger stood – still motionless – still watching. He came a step nearer at last.

'"Mademoiselle," he said. Not the quivering of an eyelash showed that she heard him. "Mademoiselle!" he said again, with an intensity of beseeching that made Jacques – not knowing who he was – almost pity him, when he saw his young lady's obdurate face.

'There was perfect silence for a space of time which Jacques could not measure. Then again the voice, hesitatingly, saying, "Monsieur!" Clément could not hold the same icy countenance as Virginie; he turned his head with an impatient gesture of disgust; but even that emboldened the man.

'"Monsieur, do ask Mademoiselle to listen to me – just two words!"

'"Mademoiselle de Créquy only listens to whom she chooses." Very haughtily my Clément would say that, I am sure.

'"But, Mademoiselle," – lowering his voice, and coming a step or two nearer. Virginie must have felt his approach, though she did not see it; for she drew herself a little on one side, so as to put as much space as possible between him and her. "Mademoiselle, it is not too late. I can save you; but to-morrow your name is down on the list. I can save you, if you will listen."

'Still no word or sign. Jacques did not understand the affair. Why was she so obdurate to one who might be ready to include Clément in the proposal, as far as Jacques knew?

'The man withdrew a little, but did not offer to leave the prison. He never took his eyes off Virginie; he seemed to be suffering from some acute and terrible pain as he watched her.

'Jacques cleared away the breakfast-things as well as he could. Purposely, as I suspect, he passed near the man.

' "Hist!" said the stranger. "You are Jacques, the gardener, arrested for assisting an aristocrat. I know the gaoler. You shall escape, if you will. Only take this message from me to Mademoiselle. You heard. She will not listen to me: I did not want her to come here. I never knew she was here, and she will die to-morrow. They will put her beautiful round throat under the guillotine. Tell her, good old man, tell her how sweet life is; and how I can save her; and how I will not ask for more than just to see her from time to time. She is so young; and death is annihilation, you know. Why does she hate me so? I want to save her; I have done her no harm. Good old man, tell her how terrible death is; and that she will die to-morrow, unless she listens to me."

'Jacques saw no harm in repeating this message. Clément listened in silence, watching Virginie with an air of infinite tenderness.

' "Will you not try him, my cherished one?" he said. "Towards you he may mean well" (which makes me think that Virginie had never repeated to Clément the conversation which she had overheard that last night at Madame Babette's); "you would be in no worse a situation than you were before!"

' "No worse, Clément! and I should have known what you were, and have lost you. My Clément!" said she, reproachfully.

' "Ask him," said she, turning to Jacques, suddenly, "if he can save Monsieur de Créquy as well – if he can? – O Clément, we might escape to England; we are but young." And she hid her face on his shoulder.

'Jacques returned to the stranger, and asked him Virginie's question. His eyes were fixed on the cousins; he was very pale, and the twitchings or contortions, which must have been involuntary whenever he was agitated, convulsed his whole body.

'He made a long pause. "I will save mademoiselle and monsieur, if she will go straight from prison to the mairie, and be my wife."

' "Your wife!" Jacques could not help exclaiming. "That she will never be – never!"

' "Ask her!" said Morin, hoarsely.

'But almost before Jacques thought he could have fairly uttered the words, Clément caught their meaning.

' "Begone!" said he; "not one word more." Virginie touched the old man as he was moving away. ' "Tell him he does not know how he makes me welcome Death." And smiling, as if triumphant, she turned again to Clément.

'The stranger did not speak as Jacques gave him the meaning, not the words, of their replies. He was going away, but stopped. A minute or two afterwards, he beckoned to Jacques. The old gardener seems to have thought it undesirable to throw away even the chance of assistance from such a man as this, for he went forwards to speak to him.

' "Listen! I have influence with the gaoler. He shall let thee pass out with the victims to-morrow. No one will notice it, or miss thee – They will be led to trial – even at the last moment, I will save her, if she sends me word she relents. Speak to her, as the time draws on. Life is very sweet – tell her how sweet. Speak to him; he will do more with her than thou canst. Let him urge her to live. Even at the last, I will be at the Palais de Justice – at the Grève. I have followers – I have interest. Come among the crowd that follow the victims – I shall see thee. It will be no worse for him, if she escapes."

' "Save my master, and I will do all," said Jacques.

' "Only on my one condition," said Morin, doggedly; and Jacques was hopeless of that condition ever being fulfilled. But he did not see why his own life might not be saved. By remaining in prison until the next day, he should have rendered every service in his power to his master and the young lady. He, poor fellow, shrank from death; and he agreed with Morin to escape, if he could, by the means Morin suggested, and to bring him word if Mademoiselle de Créquy relented. (Jacques had no expectation that she would; but I fancy he did not think it necessary to tell Morin of this conviction of his.) This bargaining with so base a man for so slight a thing as life, was the only flaw that I heard of in the old gardener's behaviour. Of course, the mere reopening of the subject was enough to stir Virginie to displeasure. Clément urged her, it is true; but the light he had gained upon Morin's motions, made him rather try to set the case before her in as fair a manner as possible than use any persuasive arguments. And, even as it was, what he said on the subject made Virginie shed tears – the first that had fallen from her since she entered the prison. So, they were summoned and went together, at the fatal call of the muster-roll of victims the next morning. He, feeble from his wounds and his injured health; she, calm and serene, only petitioning to be allowed to walk next to him, in order that she might hold him up when he turned faint and giddy from his extreme suffering.

'Together they stood at the bar; together they were condemned. As the words of judgement were pronounced, Virginie turned to Clément, and embraced him with passionate fondness. Then, making him lean on her, they marched out towards the Place de la Grève.

'Jacques was free now. He had told Morin how fruitless his efforts at persuasion had been; and, scarcely caring to note the effect of his information upon the man, he had devoted himself to watching Monsieur and Mademoiselle de Créquy. And now he followed them to the Place de la Grève. He saw them mount the platform; saw them kneel down together till plucked up by the impatient officials; could see that she was urging some request to the executioner; the end of which seemed to be, that Clément advanced first to the guillotine, was executed (and just at this moment there was a stir among the crowd, as of a man pressing forward towards the scaffold). Then she, standing with her face to the guillotine, slowly made the sign of the cross, and knelt down.

'Jacques covered his eyes, blinded with tears. The report of a pistol made him look up. She was gone – another victim in her place – and where there had been the little stir in the crowd not five minutes before, some men were carrying off a dead body. A man had shot himself, they said. Pierre told me who that man was.'

Chapter IX

After a pause, I ventured to ask what became of Madame de Créquy, Clément's mother.

'She never made any inquiry about him again,' said my lady. 'She must have known that he was dead; though how, we never could tell. Medlicott remembered afterwards that it was about, if not on – Medlicott to this day declares that it was on the very Monday, June the nineteenth, when her son was executed, that Madame de Créquy left off her rouge, and took to her bed, as one bereaved and hopeless. It certainly was about that time; and Medlicott – who was deeply impressed by that dream of Madame de Créquy's (the relation of which I told you had had such an effect on my lord), in which she had seen the figure of Virginie – as the only light object amid much surrounding darkness as of night, smiling and beckoning Clément on – on – till at length the bright phantom stopped, motionless, and Madame de Créquy's eyes began to penetrate the murky darkness, and to see closing

around her the gloomy dripping walls which she had once seen
and never forgotten – the walls of the vault of the chapel of the
De Créquys in Saint Germain l'Auxerrois; and there the two last
of the Créquys laid them down among their forefathers, and
Madame de Créquy had wakened to the sound of the great door,
which led to the open air, being locked upon her – I say
Medlicott, who was predisposed by this dream to look out for the
supernatural, always declared that Madame de Créquy was made
conscious, in some mysterious way, of her son's death, on the very
day and hour when it occurred, and that after that she had no
more anxiety, but was only conscious of a kind of stupefying
despair.'

'And what became of her, my lady?' asked I, repeating my
question.

'What could become of her?' replied Lady Ludlow. 'She never
could be induced to rise again, though she lived more than a year
after her son's departure. She kept her bed; her room darkened,
her face turned towards the wall, whenever any one besides
Medlicott was in the room. She hardly ever spoke, and would
have died of starvation but for Medlicott's tender care, in putting
a morsel to her lips every now and then, feeding her, in fact, just
as an old bird feeds her young ones. In the height of summer my
lord and I left London. We would fain have taken her with us into
Scotland, but the doctor (we had the old doctor from Leicester
Square) forbade her removal; and this time he gave such good
reasons against it that I acquiesced. Medlicott and a maid were left
with her. Every care was taken of her. She survived till our return.
Indeed, I thought she was in much the same state as I had left her
in, when I came back to London. But Medlicott spoke of her as
much weaker; and one morning, on awakening, they told me she
was dead. I sent for Medlicott, who was in sad distress, she had
become so fond of her charge. She said that, about two o'clock,
she had been awakened by unusual restlessness on Madame de
Créquy's part; that she had gone to her bedside, and found the

poor lady feebly but perpetually moving her wasted arm up and down – and saying to herself in a wailing voice: "I did not bless him when he left me – I did not bless him when he left me!" Medlicott gave her a spoonful or two of jelly, and sat by her, stroking her hand, and soothing her till she seemed to fall asleep. But in the morning she was dead.'

'It is a sad story, your ladyship,' said I, after a while.

'Yes, it is. People seldom arrive at my age without having watched the beginning, middle, and end of many lives and many fortunes. We do not talk about them, perhaps; for they are often so sacred to us, from having touched into the very quick of our own hearts, as it were, or into those of others who are dead and gone, and veiled over from human sight, that we cannot tell the tale as if it was a mere story. But young people should remember that we have had this solemn experience of life, on which to base our opinions and form our judgements, so that they are not mere untried theories. I am not alluding to Mr Horner just now, for he is nearly as old as I am – within ten years, I daresay – but I am thinking of Mr Gray, with his endless plans for some new thing – schools, education, Sabbaths, and what not. Now he has not seen what all this leads to.'

'It is a pity he has not heard your ladyship tell the story of poor Monsieur de Créquy.'

'Not at all a pity, my dear. A young man like him, who, both by position and age, must have had his experience confined to a very narrow circle, ought not to set up his opinion against mine; he ought not to require reasons from me, nor to need such explanation of my arguments (if I condescend to argue), as going into relation of the circumstances on which my arguments are based in my own mind, would be.'

'But, my lady, it might convince him,' I said, with perhaps injudicious perseverance.

'And why should he be convinced?' she asked, with gentle inquiry in her tone. 'He has only to acquiesce. Though he is appointed by Mr Croxton, I am the lady of the manor, as he must know. But it is with Mr Horner that I must have to do about this unfortunate lad Gregson. I am afraid there will be no method of making him forget his unlucky knowledge. His poor brains will be intoxicated with the sense of his powers, without any counterbalancing principles to guide him. Poor fellow! I am quite afraid it will end in his being hanged!'

The next day Mr Horner came to apologize and explain. He was evidently – as I could tell from his voice, as he spoke to my lady in the next room – extremely annoyed at her ladyship's discovery of the education he had been giving to this boy. My lady spoke with great authority, and with reasonable grounds of complaint. Mr Horner was well acquainted with her thoughts on the subject, and had acted in defiance of her wishes. He acknowledged as much, and should on no account have done it, in any other instance, without her leave.

'Which I could never have granted you,' said my lady.

But this boy had extraordinary capabilities; would, in fact, have taught himself much that was bad, if he had not been rescued, and another direction given to his powers. And in all Mr Horner had done, he had had her ladyship's service in view. The business was getting almost beyond his power, so many letters and so much account-keeping was required by the complicated state in which things were.

Lady Ludlow felt what was coming – a reference to the mortgage for the benefit of my lord's Scottish estates, which, she was perfectly aware, Mr Horner considered as having been a most unwise proceeding – and she hastened to observe:

'All this may be very true, Mr Horner, and I am sure I should be the last person to wish you to overwork or distress yourself; but of that we will talk another time. What I am now anxious to remedy is, if possible, the state of this poor little Gregson's mind. Would not hard work in the fields be a wholesome and excellent way of enabling him to forget?'

'I was in hopes, my lady, that you would have permitted me to bring him up to act as a kind of clerk,' said Mr Horner, jerking out his project abruptly.

'A what?' asked my lady, in infinite surprise.

'A kind of – of assistant, in the way of copying letters and doing up accounts. He is already an excellent penman and very quick at figures.'

'Mr Horner,' said my lady, with dignity, 'the son of a poacher and vagabond ought never to have been able to copy letters relating to the Hanbury estates; and, at any rate, he shall not. I wonder how it is that, knowing the use he has made of his power of reading a letter, you should venture to propose such an employment for him as would require his being in your confidence, and you the trusted agent of this family. Why, every secret (and every ancient and honourable family has its secrets, as you know, Mr Horner!) would be learnt off by heart, and repeated to the first comer!'

'I should have hoped to have trained him, my lady, to understand the rules of discretion.'

'Trained! Train a barn-door fowl to be a pheasant, Mr Horner! That would be the easier task. But you did right to speak of discretion rather than honour. Discretion looks to the consequences of actions – honour looks to the action itself, and is an instinct rather than a virtue. After all, it is possible, you might have trained him to be discreet.'

Mr Horner was silent. My lady was softened by his not replying, and began, as she always did in such cases, to fear lest she had been too harsh. I could tell that by her voice and by her next speech, as well as if I had seen her face.

'But I am sorry you are feeling the pressure of the affairs; I am quite aware that I have entailed much additional trouble upon you by some of my measures; I must try and provide you with some suitable assistance. Copying letters and doing up accounts, I think you said?'

Mr Horner had certainly had a distant idea of turning the little boy, in process of time, into a clerk; but he had rather urged this possibility of future usefulness beyond what he had at first intended, in speaking of it to my lady as a palliation of his offence, and he certainly was very much inclined to retract his statement that the letter-writing, or any other business, had increased, or that he was in the slightest want of help of any kind, when my lady, after a pause of consideration, suddenly said:

'I have it. Miss Galindo will, I am sure, be glad to assist you. I will speak to her myself. The payment we should make to a clerk would be of real service to her!'

I could hardly help echoing Mr Horner's tone of surprise as he said –

'Miss Galindo!'

For, you must be told who Miss Galindo was; at least, told as much as I know. Miss Galindo had lived in the village for many years, keeping house on the smallest possible means, yet always managing to maintain a servant. And this servant was invariably chosen because she had some infirmity that made her undesirable to every one else. I believe Miss Galindo had had lame and blind and hump-backed maids. She had even at one time taken in a girl hopelessly gone in consumption, because if not she would have had to go to the workhouse, and not have had enough to eat. Of course the poor creature could not perform a single duty usually required of a servant, and Miss Galindo herself was both servant and nurse.

Her present maid was scarcely four feet high, and bore a terrible character for ill-temper. Nobody but Miss Galindo would have kept her; but, as it was, mistress and servant squabbled perpetually, and were, at heart, the best of friends. For it was one of Miss Galindo's peculiarities to do all manner of kind and self-denying actions, and to say all manner of provoking things. Lame, blind, deformed, and dwarf, all came in for scoldings without number: it was only the consumptive girl that never had heard a sharp word.

I don't think any of her servants liked her the worse for her peppery temper, and passionate odd ways, for they knew her real and beautiful kindness of heart; and, besides, she had so great a turn for humour, that very often her speeches amused as much or more than they irritated; and, on the other side, a piece of witty impudence from her servant would occasionally tickle her so much and so suddenly, that she would burst out laughing in the middle of her passion.

But the talk about Miss Galindo's choice and management of her servants was confined to village gossip, and had never reached my Lady Ludlow's ears, though doubtless Mr Horner was well acquainted with it. What my lady knew of her amounted to this. It was the custom in those days for the wealthy ladies of the county to set on foot a repository, as it was called, in the assize-town. The ostensible manager of this repository was generally a decayed gentlewoman, a clergyman's widow, or so forth. She was, however, controlled by a committee of ladies; and paid by them in proportion to the amount of goods she sold; and these goods were the small manufactures of ladies of little or no fortune, whose names, if they chose it, were only signified by initials.

Poor water-colour drawings, in indigo and Indian ink; screens, ornamented with moss and dried leaves; paintings on velvet, and such faintly ornamental works were displayed on one side of the shop. It was always reckoned a mark of characteristic gentility in the repository, to have only common heavy-framed sash-windows, which admitted very little light, so I never was quite certain of the merit of these Works of Art, as they were entitled. But, on the other side, where the Useful Work placard was put up, there was a great variety of articles, of whose unusual excellence every one might judge. Such fine sewing, and stitching, and button-holing! Such bundles of soft delicate knitted stockings and socks; and, above all, in Lady Ludlow's eyes, such hanks of the finest spun flaxen thread!

And the most delicate dainty work of all was done by Miss

Galindo, as Lady Ludlow very well knew. Yet, for all their fine sewing, it sometimes happened that Miss Galindo's patterns were of an old-fashioned kind; and the dozen night-caps, may-be, on the materials for which she had expended bona-fide money, and on the making-up, no little time and eyesight, would lie for months in a yellow neglected heap; and at such times, it was said, Miss Galindo was more amusing than usual, more full of dry drollery and humour; just as at the times when an order came in to X (the initial she had chosen) for a stock of well-paying things, she sat and stormed at her servant as she stitched away. She herself explained her practice in this way: –

'When everything goes wrong, one would give up breathing if one could not lighten one's heart by a joke. But when I've to sit still from morning till night, I must have something to stir my blood, or I should go off into an apoplexy, so I set to, and quarrel with Sally.'

Such were Miss Galindo's means and manner of living in her own house. Out of doors, and in the village, she was not popular, although she would have been sorely missed had she left the place. But she asked too many home questions (not to say impertinent) respecting the domestic economies (for even the very poor like to spend their bit of money their own way), and would open cupboards to find out hidden extravagances, and question closely respecting the weekly amount of butter, till one day she met with what would have been a rebuff to any other person, but which she rather enjoyed than otherwise.

She was going into a cottage, and in the doorway met the good woman chasing out a duck, and apparently unconscious of her visitor.

'Get out, Miss Galindo!' she cried, addressing the duck. 'Get out! O, I ask your pardon,' she continued, as if seeing the lady for the first time. 'It's only that weary duck that will come in. Get out, Miss Gal – ' (to the duck).

'And so you call it after me, do you?' inquired her visitor.

'O, yes, ma'am, my master would have it so, for he said, sure enough the unlucky bird was always poking herself where she was not wanted.'

'Ha, ha! very good! And so your master is a wit, is he? Well! tell him to come up and speak to me to-night about my parlour chimney, for there is no one like him for chimney doctoring.'

And the master went up, and was so won over by Miss Galindo's merry ways, and sharp insight into the mysteries of his various kinds of business (he was a mason, chimney-sweeper, and ratcatcher), that he came home and abused his wife the next time she called the duck the name by which he himself had christened her.

But odd as Miss Galindo was in general, she could be as well-bred a lady as any one when she chose. And choose she always did when my Lady Ludlow was by. Indeed, I don't know the man, woman, or child, that did not instinctively turn out its best side to her ladyship. So she had no notion of the qualities which, I am sure, made Mr Horner think that Miss Galindo would be most unmanageable as a clerk, and heartily wish that the idea had never come into my lady's head. But there it was; and he had annoyed her ladyship already more than he liked to-day, so he could not directly contradict her, but only urge difficulties which he hoped might prove insuperable. But every one of them Lady Ludlow knocked down. Letters to copy? Doubtless. Miss Galindo could come up to the Hall; she should have a room to herself; she wrote a beautiful hand; and writing would save her eyesight. 'Capability with regard to accounts?' My lady would answer for that too; and for more than Mr Horner seemed to think it necessary to inquire about. Miss Galindo was by birth and breeding a lady of the strictest honour, and would, if possible, forget the substance of any letters that passed through her hands; at any rate, no one would ever hear of them again from her. 'Remuneration?' Oh! as for that, Lady Ludlow would herself take care that it was managed in the most delicate manner possible. She would send to invite Miss

Galindo to tea at the Hall that very afternoon, if Mr Horner would only give her ladyship the slightest idea of the average length of time that my lady was to request Miss Galindo to sacrifice to her daily. 'Three hours! Very well.' Mr Horner looked very grave as he passed the windows of the room where I lay. I don't think he liked the idea of Miss Galindo as a clerk.

Lady Ludlow's invitations were like royal commands. Indeed, the village was too quiet to allow the inhabitants to have many evening engagements of any kind. Now and then, Mr and Mrs Horner gave a tea and supper to the principal tenants and their wives, to which the clergyman was invited, and Miss Galindo, Mrs Medlicott, and one or two other spinsters and widows. The glory of the supper-table on these occasions was invariably furnished by her ladyship: it was a cold roasted peacock, with his tail stuck out as if in life. Mrs Medlicott would take up the whole morning arranging the feathers in the proper semicircle, and was always pleased with the wonder and admiration it excited. It was considered a due reward and fitting compliment to her exertions that Mr Horner always took her in to supper, and placed her opposite to the magnificent dish, at which she sweetly smiled all the time they were at table. But since Mrs Horner had had the paralytic stroke these parties had been given up; and Miss Galindo wrote a note to Lady Ludlow in reply to her invitation, saying that she was entirely disengaged, and would have great pleasure in doing herself the honour of waiting upon her ladyship.

Whoever visited my lady took their meals with her, sitting on the dais, in the presence of all my former companions. So I did not see Miss Galindo until some time after tea; as the young gentlewomen had had to bring her their sewing and spinning, to hear the remarks of so competent a judge. At length her ladyship brought her visitor into the room where I lay – it was one of my bad days, I remember – in order to have her little bit of private conversation. Miss Galindo was dressed in her best gown, I am sure, but I had never seen anything like it except in a picture, it was so old-fashioned. She wore a white muslin apron, delicately embroidered, and put on a little crookedly, in order, as she told us, even Lady Ludlow, before the evening was over, to conceal a spot whence the colour had been discharged by a lemon-stain. This crookedness had an odd effect, especially when I saw that it was intentional; indeed, she was so anxious about her apron's right adjustment in the wrong place, that she told us straight out why she wore it so, and asked her ladyship if the spot was properly hidden, at the same time lifting up her apron and showing her how large it was.

'When my father was alive, I always took his right arm, so, and used to remove any spotted or discoloured breadths to the left side, if it was a walking-dress. That's the convenience of a gentleman. But widows and spinsters must do what they can. Ah, my dear (to me)! when you are reckoning up the blessings in your lot – though you may think it a hard one in some respects – don't forget how little your stockings want darning, as you are obliged to lie down so much! I would rather knit two pairs of stockings than darn one, any day.'

'Have you been doing any of your beautiful knitting lately?' asked my lady, who had now arranged Miss Galindo in the pleasantest chair, and taken her own little wicker-work one, and, having her work in her hands, was ready to try and open the subject.

'No, and alas! your ladyship. It is partly the hot weather's fault, for people seem to forget that winter must come; and partly, I suppose, that every one is stocked who has the money to pay four-and-sixpence a pair for stockings.'

'Then may I ask if you have any time in your active days at liberty?' said my lady, drawing a little nearer to her proposal, which I fancy she found it a little awkward to make.

'Why, the village keeps me busy, your ladyship, when I have neither knitting or sewing to do. You know I took X. for my letter at the repository, because it stands for Xantippe, who was a great scold in old times, as I have learnt. But I'm sure I don't know how the world would get on without scolding, your ladyship. It would go to sleep, and the sun would stand still.'

'I don't think I could bear to scold, Miss Galindo,' said her ladyship, smiling.

'No! because your ladyship has people to do it for you. Begging your pardon, my lady, it seems to me the generality of people may be divided into saints, scolds, and sinners. Now, your ladyship is a saint, because you have a sweet and holy nature, in the first place; and have people to do your anger and vexation for you, in the second place. And Jonathan Walker is a sinner, because he is sent to prison. But here am I, half way, having but a poor kind of disposition at best, and yet hating sin, and all that leads to it, such as wasting and extravagance, and gossiping – and yet all this lies right under my nose in the village, and I am not saint enough to be vexed at it; and so I scold. And though I had rather be a saint, yet I think I do good in my way.'

'No doubt you do, dear Miss Galindo,' said Lady Ludlow. 'But I am sorry to hear that there is so much that is bad going on in the village – very sorry.'

'O, your ladyship! then I am sorry I brought it out. It was only by way of saying, that when I have no particular work to do at home, I take a turn abroad, and set my neighbours to rights, just by way of steering clear of Satan.

> For Satan finds some mischief still
> For idle hands to do,

you know, my lady.'

There was no leading into the subject by delicate degrees, for Miss Galindo was evidently so fond of talking, that, if asked a question, she made her answer so long, that before she came to an end of it, she had wandered far away from the original starting-point. So Lady Ludlow plunged at once into what she had to say.

'Miss Galindo, I have a great favour to ask of you.'

'My lady, I wish I could tell you what a pleasure it is to hear you say so,' replied Miss Galindo, almost with tears in her eyes; so glad were we all to do anything for her ladyship, which could be called a free service and not merely a duty.

'It is this. Mr Horner tells me that the business-letters, relating to the estate, are multiplying so much that he finds it impossible to copy them all himself, and I therefore require the services of some confidential and discreet person to copy these letters, and occasionally to go through certain accounts. Now, there is a very pleasant little sitting-room very near to Mr Horner's office (you know Mr Horner's office? on the other side of the stone hall?), and if I could prevail upon you to come here to breakfast and afterwards sit there for three hours every morning, Mr Horner should bring or send you the papers – '

Lady Ludlow stopped. Miss Galindo's countenance had fallen. There was some great obstacle in her mind to her wish for obliging Lady Ludlow.

'What would Sally do?' she asked at length. Lady Ludlow had not a notion who Sally was. Nor if she had had a notion, would she have had a conception of the perplexities that poured into Miss Galindo's mind, at the idea of leaving her rough forgetful dwarf without the perpetual monitorship of her mistress. Lady Ludlow, accustomed to a household where everything went on noiselessly, perfectly, and by clock-work, conducted by a number of highly-paid, well-chosen, and accomplished servants, had not a conception of the nature of the rough material from which her servants came. Besides, in her establishment, so that the result was good, no one inquired if the small economies had been observed in the production. Whereas every penny – every halfpenny, was of consequence to Miss Galindo; and visions of squandered drops of milk and wasted crusts of bread filled her mind with dismay. But she swallowed all her apprehensions down, out of her regard for Lady Ludlow, and desire to be of service to her. No one knows how great a trial it was to her when she thought of Sally, unchecked and unscolded for three hours every morning. But all she said was:

'"Sally, go to the Deuce." I beg your pardon, my lady, if I was talking to myself; it's a habit I have got into of keeping my tongue in practice, and I am not quite aware when I do it. Three hours every morning! I shall be only too proud to do what I can for your ladyship; and I hope Mr Horner will not be too impatient with me at first. You know, perhaps, that I was nearly being an authoress once, and that seems as if I was destined to "employ my time in writing."'

'No, indeed; we must return to the subject of the clerkship afterwards, if you please. An authoress, Miss Galindo! You surprise me!'

'But, indeed, I was. All was quite ready. Doctor Burney used to teach me music: not that I ever could learn, but it was a fancy of my poor father's. And his daughter wrote a book, and they said she was but a very young lady, and nothing but a music-master's daughter; so why should not I try?'

'Well?'

'Well! I got paper and half-a-hundred good pens, a bottle of ink, all ready – '

'And then – '

'O, it ended in my having nothing to say, when I sat down to write. But sometimes, when I get hold of a book, I wonder why I let such a poor reason stop me. It does not others.'

'But I think it was very well it did, Miss Galindo,' said her ladyship. 'I am extremely against women usurping men's employments, as they are very apt to do. But perhaps, after all, the notion of writing a book improved your hand. It is one of the most legible I ever saw.'

'I despise z's without tails,' said Miss Galindo, with a good deal of gratified pride at my lady's praise. Presently, my lady took her to look at a curious old cabinet, which Lord Ludlow had picked up at the Hague; and while they were out of the room on this errand, I suppose the question of remuneration was settled, for I heard no more of it.

When they came back, they were talking of Mr Gray. Miss Galindo was unsparing in her expressions of opinion about him: going much farther than my lady – in her language, at least.

'A little blushing man like him, who can't say bo to a goose without hesitating and colouring, to come to this village – which is as good a village as ever lived – and cry us down for a set of sinners, as if we had all committed murder and that other thing! – I have no patience with him, my lady. And then, how is he to help us to heaven, by teaching us our a b, ab – b a, ba? And yet, by all accounts, that's to save poor children's souls. O, I knew your ladyship would agree with me. I am sure my mother was as good a creature as ever breathed the blessed air; and if she's not gone to heaven, I don't want to go there; and she could not spell a letter decently. And does Mr Gray think God took note of that?'

'I was sure you would agree with me, Miss Galindo,' said my lady. 'You and I can remember how this talk about education – Rousseau, and his writings – stirred up the French people to their Reign of Terror, and all those bloody scenes.'

'I'm afraid that Rousseau and Mr Gray are birds of a feather,' replied Miss Galindo, shaking her head. 'And yet there is some good in the young man, too. He sat up all night with Billy Davis, when his wife was fairly worn out with nursing him.'

'Did he, indeed!' said my lady, her face lighting up, as it always did when she heard of any kind or generous action, no matter who performed it. 'What a pity he is bitten with these new revolutionary ideas, and is so much for disturbing the established order of society!'

When Miss Galindo went, she left so favourable an impression of her visit on my lady, that she said to me with a pleased smile:

'I think I have provided Mr Horner with a far better clerk than he would have made of that lad Gregson in twenty years. And I will send the lad to my lord's grieve, in Scotland, that he may be kept out of harm's way.'

But something happened to the lad before this purpose could be accomplished.

Chapter X

The next morning, Miss Galindo made her appearance, and, by some mistake, unusual in my lady's well-trained servants, was shown into the room where I was trying to walk; for a certain amount of exercise was prescribed for me, painful although the exertion had become.

She brought a little basket along with her; and while the footman was gone to inquire my lady's wishes (for I don't think that Lady Ludlow expected Miss Galindo so soon to assume her clerkship; nor, indeed, had Mr Horner any work of any kind ready for his new assistant to do), she launched out into conversation with me.

'It was a sudden summons, my dear! However, as I have often said to myself, ever since an occasion long ago, if Lady Ludlow ever honours me by asking for my right hand, I'll cut it off, and wrap the stump up so tidily she shall never find out it bleeds. But, if I had had a little more time, I could have mended my pens better. You see, I have had to sit up pretty late to get these sleeves made' – and she took out of her basket a pair of brown-holland over-sleeves, very much such as a grocer's apprentice wears – 'and I had only time to make seven or eight pens, out of some quills Farmer Thomson gave me last autumn. As for ink, I'm thankful to say, that's always ready; an ounce of steel filings, an ounce of nut-gall, and a pint of water (tea, if you're extravagant, which, thank Heaven! I'm not), put all in a bottle, and hang it up behind the house door, so that the whole gets a good shaking every time you slam it to – and even if you are in a passion and bang it, as Sally and I often do, it is all the better for it – and there's my ink ready for use; ready to write my lady's will with, if need be.'

'O, Miss Galindo!' said I, 'don't talk so; my lady's will! and she not dead yet.'

'And if she were, what would be the use of talking of making her will! Now, if you were Sally, I should say, "Answer me that, you goose!" But, as you're a relation of my lady's, I must be civil, and only say, "I can't think how you can talk so like a fool!" To be sure, poor thing, you're lame!'

I do not know how long she would have gone on; but my lady came in, and I, released from my duty of entertaining Miss Galindo, made my limping way into the next room. To tell the truth, I was rather afraid of Miss Galindo's tongue, for I never knew what she would say next.

After a while my lady came, and began to look in the bureau for something; and as she looked she said:

'I think Mr Horner must have made some mistake, when he said he had so much work that he almost required a clerk, for this morning he cannot find anything for Miss Galindo to do; and there she is, sitting with her pen behind her ear, waiting for something to write. I am come to find her my mother's letters, for I should like to have a fair copy made of them. O, here they are! don't trouble yourself, my dear child.'

When my lady returned again, she sat down and began to talk of Mr Gray.

'Miss Galindo says she saw him going to hold a prayer-meeting in a cottage. Now, that really makes me unhappy, it is so like what Mr Wesley used to do in my younger days; and since then we have had rebellion in the American colonies and the French Revolution. You may depend upon it, my dear, making religion and education common – vulgarizing them, as it were – is a bad thing for a nation. A man who hears prayers read in the cottage where he has just supped on bread and bacon, forgets the respect due to a church: he begins to think that one place is as good as another, and, by and by, that one person is as good as another; and after that, I always find that people begin to talk of their rights, instead of thinking of their duties. I wish Mr Gray had been more tractable, and had left well alone. What do you think I heard this morning? Why, that the Home Hill estate, which niches into the Hanbury property, was bought by a Baptist baker from Birmingham!'

'A Baptist baker!' I exclaimed. I had never seen a Dissenter, to my knowledge; but, having always heard them spoken of with horror, I looked upon them almost as if they were rhinoceroses. I wanted to see a live Dissenter, I believe, and yet I wished it were over. I was almost surprised when I heard that any of them were engaged in such peaceful occupations as baking.

'Yes! so Mr Horner tells me. A Mr Lambe, I believe. But, at any rate, he is a Baptist, and has been in trade. What with his schismatism and Mr Gray's methodism, I am afraid all the primitive character of this place will vanish.'

From what I could hear, Mr Gray seemed to be taking his own way; at any rate, more than he had done when he first came to the village, when his natural timidity had made him defer to my lady, and seek her consent and sanction before embarking in any new plan. But newness was a quality Lady Ludlow especially disliked. Even in the fashions of dress and furniture, she clung to the old, to the modes which had prevailed when she was young; and, though she had a deep personal regard for Queen Charlotte (to whom, as I have already said, she had been maid-of-honour), yet there was a tinge of Jacobitism about her, such as made her extremely dislike to hear Prince Charles Edward called the Young Pretender, as many loyal people did in those days, and made her fond of telling of the thorn-tree in my lord's park in Scotland, which had been planted by bonny Queen Mary herself, and before which every guest in the Castle of Monkshaven was expected to stand bare-headed, out of respect to the memory and misfortunes of the royal planter.

We might play at cards, if we so chose, on a Sunday; at least, I suppose we might, for my lady and Mr Mountford used to do so often when I first went. But we must neither play cards, nor read, nor sew, on the fifth of November and on the thirtieth of January, but must go to church, and meditate all the rest of the day – and very hard work meditating was. I would far rather have scoured a room. That was the reason, I suppose, why a passive life was seen to be better discipline for me than an active one.

But I am wandering away from my lady, and her dislike to all innovation. Now, it seemed to me, as far as I heard, that Mr Gray was full of nothing but new things, and that what he first did was to attack all our established institutions, both in the village and the parish, and also in the nation. To be sure, I heard of his ways of going on principally from Miss Galindo, who was apt to speak more strongly than accurately.

'There he goes,' she said, 'clucking up the children just like an old hen, and trying to teach them about their salvation and their souls, and I don't know what – things that it is just blasphemy to speak about out of church. And he potters old people about reading their Bibles. I am sure I don't want to speak disrespectfully about the Holy Scriptures, but I found old Job Horton busy reading his Bible yesterday. Says I, "What are you reading, and where did you get it, and who gave it you?" So he made answer, "That he was reading Susannah and the Elders, for that he had read Bel and the Dragon till he could pretty near say it off by heart, and they were two as pretty stories as ever he had read, and that it was a caution to him what bad old chaps there were in the world." Now, as Job is bed-ridden, I don't think he is likely to meet with the Elders, and I say that I think repeating his Creed, the Commandments, and the Lord's Prayer, and, maybe, throwing in a verse of the Psalms, if he wanted a bit of a change, would have done him far more good than his pretty stories, as he called them. And what's the next thing our young parson does? Why, he tries to make us all feel pitiful for the black slaves, and leaves little pictures of negroes about, with the question printed below, "Am I not a man and a brother?" just as if I was to be hail-fellow-well-met with every negro footman. They do say he takes no sugar in his tea, because he thinks he sees spots of blood in it. Now I call that superstition.'

The next day it was a still worse story.

'Well, my dear! and how are you? My lady sent me in to sit a bit with you, while Mr Horner looks out some papers for me to copy. Between ourselves, Mr Steward Horner does not like having me for a clerk. It is all very well he does not; for, if he were decently civil to me, I might want a chaperone, you know, now poor Mrs Horner is dead.' This was one of Miss Galindo's grim jokes. 'As it is, I try to make him forget I'm a woman. I do everything as shipshape as a masculine man-clerk. I see he can't find a fault – writing good, spelling correct, sums all right. And then he squints up at me with the tail of his eye, and looks glummer than ever, just because I'm a woman – as if I could help that. I have gone good lengths to set his mind at ease. I have stuck my pen behind my ear, I have made him a bow instead of a curtsy, I have whistled – not a tune, I can't pipe up that – nay, if you won't tell my lady, I don't mind telling you that I have said "Confound it!" and "Zounds!" I can't get any farther. For all that, Mr Horner won't forget I am a lady, and so I am not half the use I might be, and if it were not to please my Lady Ludlow, Mr Horner and his books might go hang (see how natural that came out!). And there is an order for a dozen nightcaps for a bride, and I am so afraid I shan't have time to do them. Worst of all, there's Mr Gray taking advantage of my absence to seduce Sally!'

'To seduce Sally! Mr Gray!'

'Pooh, pooh, child! There's many a kind of seduction. Mr Gray is seducing Sally to want to go to church. There has he been twice at my house, while I have been away in the mornings, talking to Sally about the state of her soul and that sort of thing. But when I found the meat all roasted to a cinder, I said, "Come, Sally, let's have no more praying when beef is down at the fire. Pray at six o'clock in the morning and nine at night, and I won't hinder you." So she sauced me, and said something about Martha and Mary, implying that, because she had let the beef get so overdone that I declare I could hardly find a bit fit for Nancy Pole's sick grandchild, she had chosen the better part. I was very much put about, I own, and perhaps you'll be shocked at what I said – indeed, I don't know if it was right myself – but I told her I had a soul as well as she, and if it was to be saved by my sitting still and thinking about salvation and never doing my duty, I thought I had as good a right as she had to be Mary, and save my soul. So, that afternoon, I sat quite still, and it was really a comfort, for I am often too busy, I know, to pray as I ought. There is first one person wanting me, and then another, and the house and the food and the neighbours to see after. So, when tea-time comes, there enters my maid with her hump on her back, and her soul to be saved. "Please, ma'am, did you order the pound of butter?" – "No, Sally," I said, shaking my head, "this morning I did not go round by Hale's farm, and this afternoon I have been employed in spiritual things."

'Now, our Sally likes tea and bread-and-butter above everything, and dry bread was not to her taste.

' "I'm thankful," said the impudent hussy, "that you have taken a turn towards godliness. It will be my prayers, I trust, that's given it you."

'I was determined not to give her an opening towards the carnal subject of butter, so she lingered still, longing to ask leave to run for it. But I gave her none, and munched my dry bread myself, thinking what a famous cake I could make for little Ben Pole with the bit of butter we were saving; and when Sally had had her butterless tea, and was in none of the best of tempers because Martha had not bethought herself of the butter, I just quietly said:

' "Now, Sally, to-morrow we'll try to hash that beef well, and to remember the butter, and to work out our salvation all at the same time, for I don't see why it can't all be done, as God has set us to do it all." But I heard her at it again about Mary and Martha, and I have no doubt that Mr Gray will teach her to consider me a lost sheep.'

I had heard so many little speeches about Mr Gray from one person or another, all speaking against him, as a mischief-maker, a setter-up of new doctrines, and of a fanciful standard of life (and you may be sure that, where Lady Ludlow led, Mrs Medlicott and Adams were certain to follow, each in their different ways showing the influence my lady had over them), that I believe I had grown to consider him as a very instrument of evil, and to expect to perceive in his face marks of his presumption, and arrogance, and impertinent interference. It was now many weeks since I had seen him, and when he was one morning shown into the blue drawing-room (into which I had been removed for a change), I was quite surprised to see how innocent and awkward a young man he appeared, confused even more than I was at our unexpected tête-à-tête. He looked thinner, his eyes more eager, his expression more anxious, and his colour came and went more than it had done when I had seen him last. I tried to make a little conversation, as I was, to my own surprise, more at my ease than he was; but his thoughts were evidently too much preoccupied for him to do more than answer me with monosyllables.

Presently my lady came in. Mr Gray twitched and coloured more than ever; but plunged into the middle of his subject at once.

'My lady, I cannot answer it to my conscience, if I allow the children of this village to go on any longer the little heathens that they are. I must do something to alter their condition. I am quite aware that your ladyship disapproves of many of the plans which have suggested themselves to me; but nevertheless I must do something, and I am come now to your ladyship to ask respectfully, but firmly, what you would advise me to do.'

His eyes were dilated, and I could almost have said they were full of tears with his eagerness. But I am sure it is a bad plan to remind people of decided opinions which they have once expressed, if you wish them to modify those opinions. Now, Mr Gray had done this with my lady; and though I do not mean to say she was obstinate, yet she was not one to retract.

She was silent for a moment or two before she replied.

'You ask me to suggest a remedy for an evil of the existence of which I am not conscious,' was her answer – very coldly, very gently given. 'In Mr Mountford's time I heard no such complaints: whenever I see the village children (and they are not unfrequent visitors at this house, on one pretext or another), they are well and decently behaved.'

'Oh, madam, you cannot judge,' he broke in. 'They are trained to respect you in word and deed; you are the highest they ever look up to; they have no notion of a higher.'

'Nay, Mr Gray,' said my lady, smiling, 'they are as loyally disposed as any children can be. They come up here every fourth of June, and drink his Majesty's health, and have buns, and (as Margaret Dawson can testify) they take a great and respectful interest in all the pictures I can show them of the Royal family.'

'But, madam, I think of something higher than any earthly dignities.'

My lady coloured at the mistake she had made; for she herself was truly pious. Yet when she resumed the subject, it seemed to me as if her tone was a little sharper than before.

'Such want of reverence is, I should say, the clergyman's fault. You must excuse me, Mr Gray, if I speak plainly.'

'My lady, I want plain-speaking. I myself am not accustomed to those ceremonies and forms which are, I suppose, the etiquette in your ladyship's rank of life, and which seem to hedge you in from any power of mine to touch you. Among those with whom I have passed my life hitherto, it has been the custom to speak plainly out what we have felt earnestly. So, instead of needing any apology from your ladyship for straightforward speaking, I will meet what you say at once, and admit that it is the clergyman's fault, in a great measure, when the children of his parish swear, and curse, and are brutal, and ignorant of all saving grace; nay, some of them of the very name of God. And because this guilt of mine, as the clergyman of this parish, lies heavy on my soul, and every day leads but from bad to worse, till I am utterly bewildered how to do good to children who escape from me as if I were a monster, and who are growing up to be men fit for and capable of any crime, but those requiring wit or sense, I come to you, who seem to me all-powerful, as far as material power goes – for your ladyship only knows the surface of things, and barely that, that pass in your village – to help me with advice, and such outward help as you can give.'

Mr Gray had stood up and sat down once or twice while he had been speaking, in an agitated, nervous kind of way, and now he was interrupted by a violent fit of coughing, after which he trembled all over.

My lady rang for a glass of water, and looked much distressed.

'Mr Gray,' said she, 'I am sure you are not well; and that makes you exaggerate childish faults into positive evils. It is always the case with us when we are not strong in health. I hear of you exerting yourself in every direction: you over-work yourself, and the consequence is, that you imagine us all worse people than we are.'

And my lady smiled very kindly and pleasantly at him, as he sat, a little panting, a little flushed, trying to recover his breath. I am sure that now they were brought face to face, she had quite forgotten all the offence she had taken at his doings when she heard of them from others; and, indeed, it was enough to soften any one's heart to see that young, almost boyish face, looking in such anxiety and distress.

'O, my lady, what shall I do?' he asked, as soon as he could recover breath, and with such an air of humility that I am sure no one who had seen it could have ever thought him conceited again. 'The evil of this world is too strong for me. I can do so little. It is all in vain. It was only to-day – ' And again the cough and agitation returned.

'My dear Mr Gray,' said my lady (the day before, I could never have believed she could have called him My dear), 'you must take the advice of an old woman about yourself. You are not fit to do anything just now but attend to your own health: rest, and see a doctor (but, indeed, I will take care of that), and when you are pretty strong again, you will find that you have been magnifying evils to yourself.'

'But, my lady, I cannot rest. The evils do exist, and the burden of their continuance lies on my shoulders. I have no place to gather the children together in, that I may teach them the things necessary to salvation. The rooms in my own house are too small; but I have tried them. I have money of my own; and, as your ladyship knows, I tried to get a piece of leasehold property on which to build a school-house at my own expense. Your ladyship's lawyer comes forward, at your instructions, to enforce some old feudal right, by which no building is allowed on leasehold property without the sanction of the lady of the manor. It may be all very true; but it was a cruel thing to do – that is, if your ladyship had known (which I am sure you do not) the real moral and spiritual state of my poor parishioners. And now I come to you to know what I am to do. Rest! I cannot rest, while children whom I could possibly save are being left in their ignorance, their blasphemy, their uncleanness, their cruelty. It is known through the village that your ladyship disapproves of my efforts, and opposes all my plans. If you think them wrong, foolish, ill-digested (I have been a student, living in a college, and eschewing all society but that of pious men, until now: I may not judge for the best, in my ignorance of this sinful human nature), tell me of better plans and wiser projects for accomplishing my end; but do not bid me rest, with Satan compassing me round, and stealing souls away.'

'Mr Gray,' said my lady, 'there may be some truth in what you have said. I do not deny it, though I think, in your present state of indisposition and excitement, you exaggerate it much. I believe – nay, the experience of a pretty long life has convinced me – that education is a bad thing, if given indiscriminately. It unfits the lower orders for their duties, the duties to which they are called by God, of submission to those placed in authority over them, of contentment with that state of life to which it has pleased God to call them, and of ordering themselves lowly and reverently to all their betters. I have made this conviction of mine tolerably evident to you; and have expressed distinctly my disapprobation of some of your ideas. You may imagine, then, that I was not well pleased when I found that you had taken a rood or more of Farmer Hale's land, and were laying the foundations of a school-house. You had done this without asking for my permission, which, as Farmer Hale's liege lady, ought to have been obtained legally, as well as asked for out of courtesy. I put a stop to what I believed to be calculated to do harm to a village, to a population in which, to say the least of it, I may be supposed to take as much interest as you can do. How can reading and writing, and the multiplication-table (if you choose to go so far), prevent blasphemy, and uncleanness and cruelty? Really, Mr Gray, I hardly like to express myself so strongly on the subject in your present state of health, as I should do at any other time. It seems to me that books do little; character much; and character is not formed from books.'

'I do not think of character: I think of souls. I must get some hold upon these children, or what will become of them in the next world? I must be found to have some power beyond what they have, and which they are rendered capable of appreciating, before they will listen to me. At present, physical force is all they look up to; and I have none.'

'Nay, Mr Gray, by your own admission, they look up to me.'

'They would not do anything your ladyship disliked if it was likely to come to your knowledge; but if they could conceal it from you, the knowledge of your dislike to a particular line of conduct would never make them cease from pursuing it.'

'Mr Gray' – surprise in her air, and some little indignation – 'they and their fathers have lived on the Hanbury lands for generations!'

'I cannot help it, madam. I am telling you the truth, whether you believe me or not.' There was a pause; my lady looking perplexed, and somewhat ruffled; Mr Gray as though hopeless and wearied out. 'Then, my lady,' said he, at last, rising as he spoke, 'you can suggest nothing to ameliorate the state of things which, I do assure you, does exist on your lands, and among your tenants. Surely, you will not object to my using Farmer Hale's great barn every Sabbath? He will allow me the use of it, if your ladyship will grant your permission.'

'You are not fit for any extra work at present' (and indeed he had been coughing very much all through the conversation). 'Give me time to consider of it. Tell me what you wish to teach. You will be able to take care of your health and grow stronger while I consider. It shall not be the worse for you, if you leave it in my hands for a time.'

My lady spoke very kindly; but he was in too excited a state to recognize the kindness, while the idea of delay was evidently a sore irritation. I heard him say: 'And I have so little time in which to do my work. Lord! lay not this sin to my charge.'

But my lady was speaking to the old butler, for whom, at her sign, I had rung the bell some little time before. Now she turned round.

'Mr Gray, I find I have some bottles of Malmsey, of the vintage of seventeen hundred and seventy-eight, yet left. Malmsey, as perhaps you know, used to be considered a specific for coughs arising from weakness. You must permit me to send you half-a-dozen bottles, and, depend upon it, you will take a more cheerful view of life and its duties before you have finished them, especially if you will be so kind as to see Doctor Trevor, who is coming to see me in the course of the week. By the time you are strong enough to work, I will try and find some means of preventing the

420

children from using such bad language, and otherwise annoying you.'

'My lady, it is the sin, and not the annoyance. I wish I could make you understand.' He spoke with some impatience; poor fellow, he was too weak, exhausted, and nervous. 'I am perfectly well; I can set to work to-morrow; I will do anything not to be oppressed with the thought of how little I am doing. I do not want your wine. Liberty to act in the manner I think right, will do me far more good. But it is of no use. It is pre-ordained that I am to be nothing but a cumberer of the ground. I beg your ladyship's pardon for this call.'

He stood up, and then turned dizzy. My lady looked on, deeply hurt, and not a little offended. He held out his hand to her, and I could see that she had a little hesitation before she took it. He then saw me, I almost think, for the first time; and put out his hand once more, drew it back, as if undecided, put it out again, and finally took hold of mine for an instant in his damp, listless hand, and was gone.

Lady Ludlow was dissatisfied with both him and herself, I was sure. Indeed, I was dissatisfied with the result of the interview myself. But my lady was not one to speak out her feelings on the subject; nor was I one to forget myself, and begin on a topic which she did not begin. She came to me, and was very tender with me; so tender, that that, and the thoughts of Mr Gray's sick, hopeless, disappointed look, nearly made me cry.

'You are tired, little one,' said my lady. 'Go and lie down in my room, and hear what Medlicott and I can decide upon in the way of strengthening dainties for that poor young man, who is killing himself with his over-sensitive conscientiousness.'

'O, my lady!' said I, and then I stopped.

'Well. What?' asked she.

'If you would but let him have Farmer Hale's barn at once, it would do him more good than all.'

'Pooh, pooh, child!' though I don't think she was displeased, 'he is not fit for more work just now. I shall go and write for Doctor Trevor.'

And, for the next half-hour, we did nothing but arrange physical comforts and cures for poor Mr Gray. At the end of the time, Mrs Medlicott said:

'Has your ladyship heard that Harry Gregson has fallen from a tree, and broken his thigh-bone, and is like to be a cripple for life?'

'Harry Gregson! That black-eyed lad who read my letter? It all comes from over-education!'

Chapter XI

But I don't see how my lady could think it was over-education that made Harry Gregson break his thigh, for the manner in which he met with the accident was this: –

Mr Horner, who had fallen sadly out of health since his wife's death, had attached himself greatly to Harry Gregson. Now, Mr Horner had a cold manner to every one, and never spoke more than was necessary, at the best of times. And, latterly, it had not been the best of times with him. I dare say, he had had some causes for anxiety (of which I knew nothing) about my lady's affairs; and he was evidently annoyed by my lady's whim (as he once inadvertently called it) of placing Miss Galindo under him in the position of a clerk. Yet he had always been friends, in his quiet way, with Miss Galindo, and she devoted herself to her new occupation with diligence and punctuality, although more than once she had moaned to me over the orders for needlework which had been sent to her, and which, owing to her occupation in the service of Lady Ludlow, she had been unable to fulfil.

The only living creature to whom the staid Mr Horner could be said to be attached, was Harry Gregson. To my lady he was a faithful and devoted servant, looking keenly after her interests, and anxious to forward them at any cost of trouble to himself. But the more shrewd Mr Horner was, the more probability was there of his being annoyed at certain peculiarities of opinion which my lady held with a quiet, gentle pertinacity; against which no arguments, based on mere worldly and business calculations, made any way. This frequent opposition to views which Mr Horner entertained, although it did not interfere with the sincere respect which the lady and the steward felt for each other, yet prevented any warmer feeling of affection from coming in. It seems strange to say it, but I must repeat it – the only person for whom, since his wife's death, Mr Horner seemed to feel any love, was the little imp Harry Gregson, with his bright, watchful eyes, his tangled hair hanging right down to his eyebrows, for all the world like a Skye terrier. This lad, half gipsy and whole poacher, as many people esteemed him, hung about the silent, respectable, staid Mr Horner, and followed his steps with something of the affectionate fidelity of the dog which he resembled. I suspect, this demonstration of attachment to his person on Harry Gregson's part was what won Mr Horner's regard. In the first instance, the steward had only chosen the lad out as the cleverest instrument he could find for his purpose; and I don't mean to say that, if Harry had not been almost as shrewd as Mr Horner himself was, both by original disposition and subsequent experience, the steward would have taken to him as he did, let the lad have shown ever so much affection for him.

But even to Harry Mr Horner was silent. Still, it was pleasant to find himself in many ways so readily understood; to perceive that the crumbs of knowledge he let fall were picked up by his little follower, and hoarded like gold; that here was one to hate the persons and things whom Mr Horner coldly disliked, and to reverence and admire all those for whom he had any regard. Mr Horner had never had a child, and unconsciously, I suppose, something of the paternal feeling had begun to develop itself in him towards Harry Gregson. I heard one or two things from different people, which have always made me fancy that Mr Horner secretly and almost unconsciously hoped that Harry Gregson might be trained so as to be first his clerk, and next his assistant, and finally his successor in his stewardship to the Hanbury estates.

Harry's disgrace with my lady, in consequence of his reading the letter, was a deeper blow to Mr Horner than his quiet manner would ever have led any one to suppose, or than Lady Ludlow ever dreamed of inflicting, I am sure.

Probably Harry had a short, stern rebuke from Mr Horner at the time, for his manner was always hard even to those he cared for the most. But Harry's love was not to be daunted or quelled by a few sharp words. I dare say, from what I heard of them afterwards, that Harry accompanied Mr Horner in his walk over the farm the very day of the rebuke; his presence apparently unnoticed by the agent, by whom his absence would have been painfully felt nevertheless. That was the way of it, as I have been told. Mr Horner never bade Harry go with him; never thanked him for going, or being at his heels ready to run on any errands, straight as the crow flies to his point, and back to heel in as short a time as possible. Yet, if Harry were away, Mr Horner never inquired the reason from any of the men who might be supposed to know whether he was detained by his father, or otherwise engaged; he never asked Harry himself where he had been. But Miss Galindo said that those labourers who knew Mr Horner well, told her that he was always more quick-eyed to shortcomings, more savage-like in fault-finding, on those days when the lad was absent.

Miss Galindo, indeed, was my great authority for most of the village news which I heard. She it was who gave me the particulars of poor Harry's accident.

'You see, my dear,' she said, 'the little poacher has taken some unaccountable fancy to my master.' (This was the name by which Miss Galindo always spoke of Mr Horner to me, ever since she had been, as she called it, appointed his clerk.)

'Now, if I had twenty hearts to lose, I never could spare a bit of one of them for that good, grey, square, severe man. But different people have different tastes, and here is that little imp of a gipsy-tinker ready to turn slave for my master; and, odd enough, my master – who, I should have said beforehand, would have made short work of imp, and imp's family, and have sent Hall, the Bang-beggar, after them in no time – my master, as they tell me, is in his way quite fond of the lad, and if he could, without vexing my lady too much, he would have made him what the folks here call a Latiner. However, last night, it seems that there was a letter of some importance forgotten (I can't tell you what it was about, my dear, though I know perfectly well, but *"service oblige,"* as well as "noblesse," and you must take my word for it that it was important, and one that I am surprised my master could forget), till too late for the post. (The poor, good, orderly man is not what he was before his wife's death.) Well, it seems that he was sore annoyed by his forgetfulness, and well he might be. And it was all the more vexatious, as he had no one to blame but himself. As for that matter, I always scold somebody else when I'm in fault; but I suppose my master would never think of doing that, else it's a mighty relief. However, he could eat no tea, and was altogether put out and gloomy. And the little faithful imp-lad, perceiving all this, I suppose, got up like a page in an old ballad, and said he would run for his life across country to Comberford, and see if he could not get there before the bags were made up. So my master gave him the letter, and nothing more was heard of the poor fellow till this morning, for the father thought his son was sleeping in Mr Horner's barn, as he does occasionally, it seems, and my master, as was very natural, that he had gone to his father's.'

'And he had fallen down the old stone quarry, had he not?'

'Yes, sure enough. Mr Gray had been up here fretting my lady with some of his new-fangled schemes, and because the young man could not have it all his own way, from what I understand, he was put out, and thought he would go home by the back lane, instead of through the village, where the folks would notice if the parson looked glum. But, however, it was a mercy, and I don't mind saying so, aye, and meaning it too, though it may be like Methodism, for, as Mr Gray walked by the quarry, he heard a groan, and at first he thought it was a lamb fallen down; and he stood still, and then he heard it again; and then, I suppose, he looked down and saw Harry. So he let himself down by the boughs of the trees to the ledge where Harry lay half-dead, and with his poor thigh broken. There he had lain ever since the night before: he had been returning to tell the master that he had safely posted the letter, and the first words he said, when they recovered him from the exhausted state he was in, were' (Miss Galindo tried hard not to whimper, as she said it), ' "It was in time, sir. I see'd it put in the bag with my own eyes."'

'But where is he?' asked I. 'How did Mr Gray get him out?'

'Aye! there it is, you see. Why, the old gentleman (I daren't say Devil in Lady Ludlow's house) is not so black as he is painted; and Mr Gray must have a deal of good in him, as I say at times; and then at others, when he has gone against me, I can't bear him, and think hanging too good for him. But he lifted the poor lad, as if he had been a baby, I suppose, and carried him up the great ledges that were formerly used for steps; and laid him soft and easy on the wayside grass, and ran home and got help and a door, and had him carried to his house, and laid on his bed; and then somehow, for the first time either he or any one else perceived it, he himself was all over blood – his own blood – he had broken a blood-vessel; and there he lies in the little dressing-room, as white and as still as if he were dead; and the little imp in Mr Gray's own bed, sound asleep, now his leg is set, just as if linen sheets and a feather bed were his native element, as one may say. Really, now he is doing so well, I've no patience with him, lying there where Mr Gray ought to be. It is just what my lady always prophesied would come to pass, if there was any confusion of ranks.'

'Poor Mr Gray!' said I, thinking of his flushed face, and his feverish, restless ways, when he had been calling on my lady not an hour before his exertions on Harry's behalf. And I told Miss Galindo how ill I had thought him.

'Yes,' said she. 'And that was the reason my lady had sent for Doctor Trevor. Well, it has fallen out admirably, for he looked well after that old donkey of a Prince, and saw that he made no blunders.'

Now 'that old donkey of a Prince' meant the village surgeon, Mr Prince, between whom and Miss Galindo there was war to the knife, as they often met in the cottages, when there was illness, and she had her queer, odd recipes, which he, with his grand pharmacopoeia, held in infinite contempt, and the consequence of their squabbling had been, not long before this very time, that he had established a kind of rule, that into whatever sick-room Miss Galindo was admitted, there he refused to visit. But Miss Galindo's prescriptions and visits cost nothing, and were often backed by kitchen-physic; so, though it was true that she never came but she scolded about something or other, she was generally preferred as medical attendant to Mr Prince.

'Yes, the old donkey is obliged to tolerate me, and be civil to me; for, you see, I got there first, and had possession, as it were, and yet my lord the donkey likes the credit of attending the parson, and being in consultation with so grand a county-town doctor as Doctor Trevor. And Doctor Trevor is an old friend of mine' (she sighed a little, some time I may tell you why), 'and treats me with infinite bowing and respect; so the donkey, not to be out of medical fashion, bows too, though it is sadly against the grain: and he pulled a face as if he had heard a slate-pencil gritting against a slate, when I told Doctor Trevor I meant to sit up with the two lads, for I call Mr Gray little more than a lad, and a pretty conceited one, too, at times.'

'But why should you sit up, Miss Galindo? It will tire you sadly.'

'Not it. You see, there is Gregson's mother to keep quiet; for she sits by her lad, fretting and sobbing, so that I'm afraid of her disturbing Mr Gray; and there's Mr Gray to keep quiet, for Doctor Trevor says his life depends on it; and there is medicine to be given to the one, and bandages to be attended to for the other; and the wild horde of gipsy brothers and sisters to be turned out, and the father to be held in from showing too much gratitude to Mr Gray, who can't bear it – and who is to do it all but me? The only servant is old lame Betty, who once lived with me, and *would* leave me because she said I was always bothering – (there was a good deal of truth in what she said, I grant, but she need not have said it; a good deal of truth is best let alone at the bottom of the well), and what can she do – deaf as ever she can be, too?'

So Miss Galindo went her ways; but not the less was she at her post in the morning; a little crosser and more silent than usual; but the first was not to be wondered at, and the last was rather a blessing.

Lady Ludlow had been extremely anxious both about Mr Gray and Harry Gregson. Kind and thoughtful in any case of illness and accident, she always was; but somehow, in this, the feeling that she was not quite – what shall I call it? – 'friends' seems hardly the right word to use, as to the possible feeling between the Countess Ludlow and the little vagabond messenger, who had only once been in her presence – that she had hardly parted from either as she could have wished to do, had death been near, made her more than usually anxious. Doctor Trevor was not to spare obtaining the best medical advice the county could afford; whatever he ordered in the way of diet, was to be prepared under Mrs Medlicott's own eye, and sent down from the Hall to the Parsonage. As Mr Horner had given somewhat similar directions, in the case of Harry Gregson at least, there was rather a multiplicity of counsellors and dainties, than any lack of them. And, the second night, Mr Horner insisted on taking the superintendence of the nursing himself, and sat and snored by Harry's bedside, while the poor, exhausted mother lay by her child – thinking that she watched him, but in reality fast asleep, as Miss Galindo told us; for, distrusting any one's powers of watching and nursing but her own, she had stolen across the quiet village street in cloak and dressing-gown, and found Mr Gray in vain trying to reach the cup of barley-water which Mr Horner had placed just beyond his reach.

In consequence of Mr Gray's illness, we had to have a strange curate to do duty; a man who dropped his h's, and hurried through the service, and yet had time enough to stand in my lady's way, bowing to her as she came out of church, and so subservient in manner, that I believe that sooner than remain unnoticed by a countess, he would have preferred being scolded, or even cuffed. Now I found out, that great as was my lady's liking and approval of respect, nay, even reverence, being paid to her as a person of quality – a sort of tribute to her Order, which she had no individual right to remit, or, indeed, not to exact – yet she, being personally simple, sincere, and holding herself in low esteem, could not endure anything like the servility of Mr Crosse, the temporary curate. She grew absolutely to loathe his perpetual smiling and bowing; his instant agreement with the slightest opinion she uttered; his veering round as she blew the wind. I have often said that my lady did not talk much, as she might have done had she lived among her equals. But we all loved her so much, that we had learnt to interpret all her little ways pretty truly; and I knew what particular turns of her head, and contractions of her delicate fingers meant, as well as if she had expressed herself in words. I began to suspect that my lady would be very thankful to have Mr Gray about again, and doing his duty even with a con-scientiousness that might amount to worrying himself, and fidgeting others; and although Mr Gray might hold her opinions in as little esteem as those of any simple gentlewoman, she was too sensible not to feel how much flavour there was in his conversation, compared to that of Mr Crosse, who was only her tasteless echo.

As for Miss Galindo, she was utterly and entirely a partisan of Mr Gray's, almost ever since she had begun to nurse him during his illness.

'You know, I never set up for reasonableness, my lady. So I don't pretend to say, as I might do if I were a sensible woman and all that – that I am convinced by Mr Gray's arguments of this thing or t'other. For one thing, you see, poor fellow! he has never been able to argue, or hardly indeed to speak, for Doctor Trevor has been very peremptory. So there's been no scope for arguing! But what I mean is this: – When I see a sick man thinking always of others, and never of himself; patient, humble – a trifle too much at times, for I've caught him praying to be forgiven for having neglected his work as a parish priest' (Miss Galindo was making horrible faces, to keep back tears, squeezing up her eyes in a way which would have amused me at any other time, but when she was speaking of Mr Gray); 'when I see a downright good, religious man, I'm apt to think he's got hold of the right clue, and that I can do no better than hold on by the tails of his coat and shut my eyes, if we've got to go over doubtful places on our road to Heaven. So, my lady, you must excuse me, if, when he gets about again, he is all agog about a Sunday-school, for if he is, I shall be agog too, and perhaps twice as bad as him, for, you see, I've a strong constitution compared to his, and strong ways of speaking and acting. And I tell your ladyship this now, because I think from your rank – and still more, if I may say so, for all your kindness to me long ago, down to this very day – you've a right to be first told of anything about me. Change of opinion I can't exactly call it, for I don't see the good of schools and teaching ABC, any more than I did before, only Mr Gray does, so I'm to shut my eyes, and leap over the ditch to the side of education. I've told Sally already, that if she does not mind her work, but stands gossiping with Nelly Mather, I'll teach her her lessons; and I've never caught her with old Nelly since.'

I think Miss Galindo's desertion to Mr Gray's opinions in this matter hurt my lady just a little bit; but she only said:

'Of course, if the parishioners wish for it, Mr Gray must have his Sunday-school. I shall, in that case, withdraw my opposition. I am sorry I cannot change my opinions as easily as you.'

My lady made herself smile as she said this. Miss Galindo saw it was an effort to do so. She thought a minute before she spoke again.

'Your ladyship has not seen Mr Gray as intimately as I have done. That's one thing. But, as for the parishioners, they will follow your ladyship's lead in everything; so there is no chance of their wishing for a Sunday-school.'

'I have never done anything to make them follow my lead, as you call it, Miss Galindo,' said my lady, gravely.

'Yes, you have,' replied Miss Galindo, bluntly. And then, correcting herself, she said, 'Begging your ladyship's pardon, you have. Your ancestors have lived here time out of mind, and have owned the land on which their forefathers have lived ever since there were forefathers. You yourself were born amongst them, and have been like a little queen to them ever since, I might say, and they've never known your ladyship do anything but what was kind and gentle; but I'll leave fine speeches about your ladyship to Mr Crosse. Only you, my lady, lead the thoughts of the parish; and save some of them a world of trouble, for they could never tell what was right if they had to think for themselves. It's all quite right that they should be guided by you, my lady – if only you would agree with Mr Gray.'

'Well,' said my lady, 'I told him only the last day that he was here, that I would think about it. I do believe I could make up my mind on certain subjects better if I were left alone, than while being constantly talked to about them.'

My lady said this in her usual soft tones; but the words had a tinge of impatience about them; indeed, she was more ruffled than I had often seen her; but, checking herself in an instant, she said:

'You don't know how Mr Horner drags in this subject of

education apropos of everything. Not that he says much about it at any time: it is not his way. But he cannot let the thing alone.'

'I know why, my lady,' said Miss Galindo. 'That poor lad, Harry Gregson, will never be able to earn his livelihood in any active way, but will be lame for life. Now, Mr Horner thinks more of Harry than of any one else in the world – except, perhaps, your ladyship.' Was it not a pretty companionship for my lady? 'And he has schemes of his own for teaching Harry; and if Mr Gray could but have his school, Mr Horner and he think Harry might be schoolmaster, as your ladyship would not like to have him coming to you as steward's clerk. I wish your ladyship would fall into this plan; Mr Gray has it so at heart.'

Miss Galindo looked wistfully at my lady, as she said this. But my lady only said, drily, and rising at the same time, as if to end the conversation:

'So! Mr Horner and Mr Gray seem to have gone a long way in advance of my consent to their plans.'

'There!' exclaimed Miss Galindo, as my lady left the room, with an apology for going away; 'I have gone and done mischief with my long, stupid tongue. To be sure, people plan a long way ahead of to-day; more especially when one is a sick man, lying all through the weary day on a sofa.'

'My lady will soon get over her annoyance,' said I, as it were apologetically. I only stopped Miss Galindo's self-reproaches to draw down her wrath upon myself.

'And has not she a right to be annoyed with me, if she likes, and to keep annoyed as long as she likes? Am I complaining of her, that you need tell me that? Let me tell you, I have known my lady these thirty years; and if she were to take me by the shoulders, and turn me out of the house, I should only love her the more. So don't you think to come between us with any little mincing, peace-making speeches. I have been a mischief-making parrot, and I like her the better for being vexed with me. So good-bye to you, Miss; and wait till you know Lady Ludlow as well as I do, before

the county; and the tale was yet told in the village of how Gregson the father came back from the trial in a state of wild rage, striding through the place, and uttering oaths of vengeance to himself, his great black eyes gleaming out of his matted hair, and his arms working by his side, and now and then tossed up in his impotent despair. As I heard the account, his wife followed him, child-laden and weeping. After this, they had vanished from the country for a time, leaving their mud hovel locked up, and the door-key, as the neighbours said, buried in a hedge-bank. The Gregsons had reappeared much about the same time that Mr Gray came to Hanbury. He had either never heard of their evil character, or considered that it gave them all the more claims upon his Christian care; and the end of it was, that this rough, untamed, strong giant of a heathen was loyal slave to the weak, hectic, nervous, self-distrustful parson. Gregson had also a kind of grumbling respect for Mr Horner: he did not quite like the steward's monopoly of his Harry: the mother submitted to that with a better grace, swallowing down her maternal jealousy in the prospect of her child's advancement to a better and more respectable position than that in which his parents had struggled through life. But Mr Horner, the steward, and Gregson, the poacher and squatter, had come into disagreeable contact too often in former days for them to be perfectly cordial at any future time. Even now, when there was no immediate cause for anything but gratitude for his child's sake on Gregson's part, he would skulk out of Mr Horner's way, if he saw him coming; and it took all Mr Horner's natural reserve and acquired self-restraint to keep him from occasionally holding up his father's life as a warning to Harry. Now Gregson had nothing of this desire for avoidance with regard to Mr Gray. The poacher had a feeling of physical protection towards the parson; while the latter had shown the moral courage, without which Gregson would never have respected him, in coming right down upon him more than once in the exercise of unlawful pursuits, and simply and boldly telling him he was doing wrong, with such a quiet reliance upon Gregson's better feeling, at the same time, that the strong poacher could not have lifted a finger against Mr Gray, though it had been to save himself from being apprehended and taken to the lock-ups the very next hour. He had rather listened to the parson's bold words with an approving smile, much as Mr Gulliver might have hearkened to a lecture from a Lilliputian. But when brave words passed into kind deeds, Gregson's heart mutely acknowledged its master and keeper. And the beauty of it all was, that Mr Gray knew nothing of the good work he had done, or recognized himself as the instrument which God had employed. He thanked God, it is true, fervently and often, that the work was done; and loved the wild man for his rough gratitude; but it never occurred to the poor young clergyman, lying on his sick-bed, and praying, as Miss Galindo had told us he did, to be forgiven for his unprofitable life, to think of Gregson's reclaimed soul as anything with which he had had to do. It was now more than three months since Mr Gray had been at Hanbury Court. During all that time, he had been confined to his house, if not to his sick-bed, and he and my lady had never met since their last discussion and difference about Farmer Hale's barn.

This was not my dear lady's fault; no one could have been more attentive in every way to the slightest possible want of either of the invalids, especially of Mr Gray. And she would have gone to see him at his own house, as she sent him word, but that her foot had slipped upon the polished oak staircase, and her ankle had been sprained.

So we had never seen Mr Gray since his illness, when one November day he was announced as wishing to speak to my lady. She was sitting in her room – the room in which I lay now pretty constantly – and I remember she looked startled, when word was brought to her of Mr Gray's being at the Hall.

She could not go to him, she was too lame for that, so she bade him be shown into where she sat.

'Such a day for him to go out!' she exclaimed, looking at the fog which had crept up to the windows, and was sapping the little remaining life in the brilliant Virginian creeper leaves that draperied the house on the terrace side.

He came in white, trembling, his large eyes wild and dilated. He hastened up to Lady Ludlow's chair, and, to my surprise, took one of her hands and kissed it, without speaking, yet shaking all over.

'Mr Gray!' said she, quickly, with sharp, tremulous apprehension of some unknown evil. 'What is it? There is something unusual about you.'

'Something unusual has occurred,' replied he, forcing his words to be calm, as with a great effort. 'A gentleman came to my house, not half-an-hour ago – a Mr Howard. He came straight from Vienna.'

'My son!' said my dear lady, stretching out her arms in dumb questioning attitude.

'The Lord gave and the Lord taketh away. Blessed be the name of the Lord.'

But my poor lady could not echo the words. He was the last remaining child. And once she had been the joyful mother of nine.

Chapter XII

I am ashamed to say what feeling became strongest in my mind about this time. Next to the sympathy we all of us felt for my dear lady in her deep sorrow, I mean. For that was greater and stronger than anything else, however contradictory you may think it, when you hear all.

It might arise from my being so far from well at the time, which produced a diseased mind in a diseased body; but I was absolutely jealous for my father's memory, when I saw how many signs of grief there were for my lord's death, he having done next to nothing for the village and parish, which now changed, as it were, its daily course of life, because his lordship died in a far-off city. My father had spent the best years of his manhood in labouring hard, body and soul, for the people amongst whom he lived. His family, of course, claimed the first place in his heart; he would have been good for little, even in the way of benevolence, if they had not. But close after them he cared for his parishioners and neighbours. And yet, when he died, though the church-bells tolled, and smote upon our hearts with hard, fresh pain at every beat, the sounds of every-day life still went on, close pressing around us – carts and carriages, street-cries, distant barrel-organs (the kindly neighbours kept them out of our street): life, active, noisy life, pressed on our acute consciousness of Death, and jarred upon it as on a quick nerve.

And when we went to church – my father's own church – though the pulpit-cushions were black, and many of the congregation had put on some humble sign of mourning, yet it did not alter the whole material aspect of the place. And yet what was Lord Ludlow's relation to Hanbury, compared to my father's work and place in—?

O! it was very wicked in me! I think if I had seen my lady – if I had dared to ask to go to her, I should not have felt so miserable, so discontented. But she sat in her own room, hung with black, all, even over the shutters. She saw no light but that which was artificial – candles, lamps, and the like – for more than a month. Only Adams went near her. Mr Gray was not admitted, though he called daily. Even Mrs Medlicott did not see her for near a fortnight. The sight of my lady's griefs, or rather the recollection of it, made Mrs Medlicott talk far more than was her wont. She told us, with many tears, and much gesticulation, even speaking German at times, when her English would not flow, that my lady sat there, a white figure in the middle of the darkened room; a shaded lamp near her, the light of which fell on an open Bible – the great family Bible. It was not opened at any chapter, or consoling verse; but at the page whereon were registered the births of her nine children. Five had died in infancy – sacrificed to the cruel system which forbade the mother to suckle her babies. Four had lived longer; Urian had been the first to die, Ughtred-Mortimar, Earl Ludlow, the last.

My lady did not cry, Mrs Medlicott said. She was quite composed; very still, very silent. She put aside everything that savoured of mere business; sent people to Mr Horner for that. But she was proudly alive to every possible form which might do honour to the last of her race.

In those days, expresses were slow things, and forms still slower. Before my lady's directions could reach Vienna, my lord was buried. There was some talk (so Mrs Medlicott said) about taking the body up, and bringing him to Hanbury. But his executors – connexions on the Ludlow side – demurred to this. If he were removed to England, he must be carried on to Scotland, and interred with his Monkshaven forefathers. My lady, deeply hurt, withdrew from the discussion before it degenerated to an unseemly contest. But all the more, for this understood mortification of my lady's, did the whole village and estate of Hanbury assume every outward sign of mourning. The church-bells tolled morning and evening. The church itself was draped in black inside. Hatchments were placed everywhere, where hatchments could be put. All the tenantry spoke in hushed voices for more than a week, scarcely daring to observe that all flesh, even that of an Earl Ludlow, and the last of the Hanburys, was but grass after all. The very Fighting Lion closed its front door, front shutters it had none, and those who needed drink stole in at the back, and were silent and maudlin over their cups, instead of riotous and noisy. Miss Galindo's eyes were swollen up with crying, and she told me, with a fresh burst of tears, that even hump-backed Sally had been found sobbing over her Bible, and using a pocket-handkerchief for the first time in her life; her aprons having hitherto stood her in the necessary stead, but not being sufficiently in accordance with etiquette to be used when mourning over an earl's premature decease.

If it was in this way out of the Hall, 'you might work it by the rule of three,' as Miss Galindo used to say, and judge what it was in the Hall. We none of us spoke but in a whisper: we tried not to eat; and indeed the shock had been so really great, and we did really care so much for my lady, that for some days we had but little appetite. But after that, I fear our sympathy grew weaker, while our flesh grew stronger. But we still spoke low, and our hearts ached whenever we thought of my lady sitting there alone in the darkened room, with the light ever falling on that one solemn page.

We wished, O how I wished that she would see Mr Gray! But Adams said, she thought my lady ought to have a bishop come to see her. Still no one had authority enough to send for one.

Mr Horner all this time was suffering as much as any one. He was too faithful a servant of the great Hanbury family, though now the family had dwindled down to a fragile old lady, not to mourn acutely over its probable extinction. He had, besides, a deeper sympathy and reverence with, and for, my lady in all things, than probably he ever cared to show, for his manners were always measured and cold. He suffered from sorrow. He also suffered from wrong. My lord's executors kept writing to him continually. My lady refused to listen to mere business, saying she intrusted all to him. But the 'all' was more complicated than I ever thoroughly understood. As far as I comprehended the case, it was something of this kind: – There had been a mortgage raised on my lady's property of Hanbury, to enable my lord, her husband, to spend money in cultivating his Scotch estates, after some new fashion that required capital. As long as my lord, her son, lived, who was to succeed to both the estates after her death, this did not signify; so she had said and felt; and she had refused to take any steps to secure the repayment of capital, or even the payment of the interest of the mortgage from the possible representatives and possessors of the Scotch estates, to the possible owner of the Hanbury property; saying it ill became her to calculate on the contingency of her son's death.

But he had died, childless, unmarried. The heir of the Monkshaven property was an Edinburgh advocate, a far-away kinsman of my lord's: the Hanbury property, at my lady's death, would go to the descendants of a third son of the Squire Hanbury in the days of Queen Anne.

This complication of affairs was most grievous to Mr Horner. He had always been opposed to the mortgage; had hated the payment of the interest, as obliging my lady to practise certain economies which, though she took care to make them as personal as possible, he disliked as derogatory to the family. Poor Mr Horner! He was so cold and hard in his manner, so curt and decisive in his speech, that I don't think we any of us did him justice. Miss Galindo was almost the first, at this time, to speak a kind word of him, or to take thought of him at all, any farther than to get out of his way when we saw him approaching.

'I don't think Mr Horner is well,' she said one day, about three weeks after we had heard of my lord's death. 'He sits resting his head on his hand, and hardly hears me when I speak to him.'

But I thought no more of it, as Miss Galindo did not name it again. My lady came amongst us once more. From elderly she had become old; a little, frail, old lady, in heavy black drapery, never speaking about nor alluding to her great sorrow; quieter, gentler, paler than ever before; and her eyes dim with much weeping, never witnessed by mortal.

She had seen Mr Gray at the expiration of the month of deep retirement. But I do not think that even to him she had said one word of her own particular individual sorrow. All mention of it seemed buried deep for evermore. One day, Mr Horner sent word that he was too much indisposed to attend to his usual business at the Hall; but he wrote down some directions and requests to Miss Galindo, saying that he would be at his office early the next morning. The next morning he was dead!

Miss Galindo told my lady. Miss Galindo herself cried plentifully, but my lady, although very much distressed, could not cry. It seemed a physical impossibility, as if she had shed all the tears in her power. Moreover, I almost think her wonder was far greater that she herself lived than that Mr Horner died. It was almost natural that so faithful a servant should break his heart, when the family he belonged to lost their stay, their heir and their last hope.

Yes! Mr Horner was a faithful servant. I do not think there are many so faithful now; but, perhaps, that is an old woman's fancy of mine. When his will came to be examined, it was discovered that, soon after Harry Gregson's accident, Mr Horner had left the few thousands (three, I think) of which he was possessed, in trust for Harry's benefit, desiring his executors to see that the lad was well educated in certain things, for which Mr Horner had thought that he had shown especial aptitude; and there was a kind of implied apology to my lady in one sentence, where he stated that Harry's lameness would prevent his being ever able to gain his living by the exercise of any mere bodily faculties, 'as had been wished by a lady whose wishes' he, the testator, 'was bound to regard.'

But there was a codicil to the will, dated since Lord Ludlow's death – feebly written by Mr Horner himself, as if in preparation only for some more formal manner of bequest; or, perhaps, only as a mere temporary arrangement till he could see a lawyer, and have a fresh will made. In this he revoked his previous bequest to Harry Gregson. He only left two hundred pounds to Mr Gray to be used, as that gentleman thought best, for Harry Gregson's benefit. With this one exception, he bequeathed all the rest of his savings to my lady, with a hope that they might form a nest-egg, as it were, towards the paying off of the mortgage which had been such a grief to him during his life. I may not repeat all this in lawyer's phrase; I heard it through Miss Galindo, and she might make mistakes. Though, indeed, she was very clear-headed, and soon earned the respect of Mr Smithson, my lady's lawyer from Warwick. Mr Smithson knew Miss Galindo a little before, both personally and by reputation; but I don't think he was prepared to find her installed as steward's clerk, and, at first, he was inclined to treat her, in this capacity, with polite contempt. But Miss Galindo was both a lady and a spirited, sensible woman, and she could put aside her self-indulgence in eccentricity of speech and manner whenever she chose. Nay more; she was usually so talkative, that if she had not been amusing and warm-hearted, one might have thought her wearisome occasionally. But, to meet Mr Smithson, she came out daily in her Sunday gown; she said no more than was required in answer to his questions; her books and papers were in thorough order, and methodically kept; her statements of matters-of-fact accurate, and to be relied on. She was amusingly conscious of her victory over his contempt of a woman-clerk and his preconceived opinion of her unpractical eccentricity.

'Let me alone,' said she, one day when she came in to sit awhile with me. 'That man is a good man – a sensible man – and, I have no doubt, he is a good lawyer; but he can't fathom women yet. I make no doubt he'll go back to Warwick, and never give credit again to those people who made him think me half-cracked to begin with. O, my dear, he did! He showed it twenty times worse than my poor dear master ever did. It was a form to be gone through to please my lady, and, for her sake, he would hear my statements and see my books. It was keeping a woman out of harm's way, at any rate, to let her fancy herself useful. I read the man. And, I am thankful to say, he cannot read me. At least, only one side of me. When I see an end to be gained, I can behave myself accordingly. Here was a man who thought that a woman in a black silk gown was a respectable, orderly kind of person; and I was a woman in a black silk gown. He believed that a woman could not write straight lines, and required a man to tell her that two and two made four. I was not above ruling my books, and had Cocker a little more at my fingers' ends than he had. But my greatest triumph has been holding my tongue. He would have thought nothing of my books, or my sums, or my black silk gown, if I had spoken unasked. So I have buried more sense in my bosom these ten days than ever I have uttered in the whole course of my life before. I have been so curt, so abrupt, so abominably dull, that I'll answer for it he thinks me worthy to be a man. But I must go back to him, my dear, so good-bye to conversation and you.'

But though Mr Smithson might be satisfied with Miss Galindo, I am afraid she was the only part of the affair with which he was content. Everything else went wrong. I could not say who told me so – but the conviction of this seemed to pervade the house, I never knew how much we had all looked up to the silent, gruff Mr Horner for decisions, until he was gone. My lady herself was a pretty good woman of business, as women of business go. Her father, seeing that she would be the heiress of the Hanbury property, had given her a training which was thought unusual in those days, and she liked to feel herself queen regnant, and to have to decide in all cases between herself and her tenantry. But, perhaps, Mr Horner would have done it more wisely; not but what she always attended to him at last. She would begin by saying, pretty clearly and promptly, what she would have done, and what she would not have done. If Mr Horner approved of it, he bowed, and set about obeying her directly; if he disapproved of it, he bowed, and lingered so long before he obeyed her, that she forced his opinion out of him with her 'Well, Mr Horner! and what have you to say against it?' For she always understood his silence as well as if he had spoken. But the estate was pressed for ready money, and Mr Horner had grown gloomy and languid since the death of his wife, and even his own personal affairs were not in the order in which they had been a year or two before, for his old clerk had gradually become superannuated, or, at any rate, unable by the superfluity of his own energy and wit to supply the spirit that was wanting in Mr Horner.

Day after day Mr Smithson seemed to grow more fidgety, more annoyed at the state of affairs. Like every one else employed by Lady Ludlow, as far as I could learn, he had an hereditary tie to the

Hanbury family. As long as the Smithsons had been lawyers, they had been lawyers to the Hanburys; always coming in on all great family occasions, and better able to understand the characters, and connect the links of what had once been a large and scattered family, than any individual thereof had ever been.

As long as a man was at the head of the Hanburys, the lawyers had simply acted as servants, and had only given their advice when it was required. But they had assumed a different position on the memorable occasion of the mortgage: they had remonstrated against it. My lady had resented this remonstrance, and a slight unspoken coolness had existed between her and the father of this Mr Smithson ever since.

I was very sorry for my lady. Mr Smithson was inclined to blame Mr Horner for the disorderly state in which he found some of the outlying farms, and for the deficiencies in the annual payment of rents. Mr Smithson had too much good feeling to put this blame into words; but my lady's quick instinct led her to reply to a thought, the existence of which she perceived; and she quietly told the truth, and explained how she had interfered repeatedly to prevent Mr Horner from taking certain desirable steps, which were discordant to her hereditary sense of right and wrong between landlord and tenant. She also spoke of the want of ready money as a misfortune that could be remedied, by more economical personal expenditure on her own part; by which individual saving, it was possible that a reduction of fifty pounds a year might have been accomplished. But as soon as Mr Smithson touched on larger economies, such as either affected the welfare of others, or the honour and standing of the great House of Hanbury, she was inflexible. Her establishment consisted of somewhere about forty servants, of whom nearly as many as twenty were unable to perform their work properly, and yet would have been hurt if they had been dismissed; so they had the credit of fulfilling duties, while my lady paid and kept their substitutes. Mr Smithson made a calculation, and would have saved some hundreds a year by pensioning off these old servants. But my lady would not hear of it. Then, again, I know privately that he urged her to allow some of us to return to our homes. Bitterly we should have regretted the separation from Lady Ludlow; but we would have gone back gladly, had we known at the time that her circumstances required it: but she would not listen to the proposal for a moment.

'If I cannot act justly towards every one, I will give up a plan which has been a source of much satisfaction; at least, I will not carry it out to such an extent in future. But to these young ladies, who do me the favour to live with me at present, I stand pledged. I cannot go back from my word, Mr Smithson. We had better talk no more of this.'

As she spoke, she entered the room where I lay. She and Mr Smithson were coming for some papers contained in the bureau. They did not know I was there, and Mr Smithson started a little when he saw me, as he must have been aware that I had overheard something. But my lady did not change a muscle of her face. All the world might overhear her kind, just, pure sayings, and she had no fear of their misconstruction. She came up to me, and kissed me on the forehead, and then went to search for the required papers.

'I rode over the Conington farms yesterday, my lady. I must say I was quite grieved to see the condition they are in; all the land that is not waste is utterly exhausted with working successive white crops. Not a pinch of manure laid on the ground for years. I must say that a greater contrast could never have been presented than that between Harding's farm and the next fields – fences in perfect order, rotation crops, sheep eating down the turnips on the waste lands – everything that could be desired.'

'Whose farm is that?' asked my lady.

'Why, I am sorry to say, it was on none of your ladyship's that I saw such good methods adopted. I hoped it was, I stopped my horse to inquire. A queer-looking man, sitting on his horse like a

445

tailor, watching his men with a couple of the sharpest eyes I ever saw, and dropping his h's at every word, answered my question, and told me it was his. I could not go on asking him who he was; but I fell into conversation with him, and I gathered that he had earned some money in trade in Birmingham, and had bought the estate (five hundred acres, I think he said), on which he was born, and now was setting himself to cultivate it in downright earnest, going to Holkham and Woburn, and half the country over, to get himself up on the subject.'

'It would be Brooke, that dissenting baker from Birmingham,' said my lady in her most icy tone. 'Mr Smithson, I am sorry I have been detaining you so long, but I think these are the letters you wished to see.'

If her ladyship thought by this speech to quench Mr Smithson she was mistaken. Mr Smithson just looked at the letters, and went on with the old subject.

'Now, my lady, it struck me that if you had such a man to take poor Horner's place, he would work the rents and the land round most satisfactorily. I should not despair of inducing this very man to undertake the work. I should not mind speaking to him myself on the subject, for we got capital friends over a snack of luncheon that he asked me to share with him.'

Lady Ludlow fixed her eyes on Mr Smithson as he spoke, and never took them off his face until he had ended. She was silent a minute before she answered.

'You are very good, Mr Smithson, but I need not trouble you with any such arrangements. I am going to write this afternoon to Captain James, a friend of one of my sons, who has, I hear, been severely wounded at Trafalgar, to request him to honour me by accepting Mr Horner's situation.'

'A Captain James! A captain in the navy! going to manage your ladyship's estate!'

'If he will be so kind. I shall esteem it a condescension on his part; but I hear that he will have to resign his profession, his state of health is so bad, and a country life is especially prescribed for him. I am in some hopes of tempting him here, as I learn he has but little to depend on if he gives up his profession.'

'A Captain James! an invalid captain!'

'You think I am asking too great a favour,' continued my lady. (I never could tell how far it was simplicity, or how far a kind of innocent malice, that made her misinterpret Mr Smithson's words and looks as she did.) 'But he is not a post-captain, only a commander, and his pension will be but small. I may be able, by offering him country air and a healthy occupation, to restore him to health.'

'Occupation! My lady, may I ask how a sailor is to manage land? Why, your tenants will laugh him to scorn.'

'My tenants, I trust, will not behave so ill as to laugh at any one I choose to set over them. Captain James has had experience in managing men. He has remarkable practical talents, and great common sense, as I hear from every one. But, whatever he may be, the affair rests between him and myself. I can only say I shall esteem myself fortunate if he comes.'

There was no more to be said, after my lady spoke in this manner. I had heard her mention Captain James before, as a middy who had been very kind to her son Urian. I thought I remembered then, that she had mentioned that his family circumstances were not very prosperous. But, I confess, that little as I knew of the management of land, I quite sided with Mr Smithson. He, silently prohibited from again speaking to my lady on the subject, opened his mind to Miss Galindo, from whom I was pretty sure to hear all the opinions and news of the household and village. She had taken a great fancy to me, because she said I talked so agreeably. I believe it was because I listened so well.

'Well, have you heard the news,' she began, 'about this Captain James? A sailor – with a wooden leg, I have no doubt. What would the poor, dear, deceased master have said to it, if he had known who was to be his successor? My dear, I have often

447

thought of the postman's bringing me a letter as one of the pleasures I shall miss in heaven. But, really, I think Mr Horner may be thankful he has got out of the reach of news; or else he would hear of Mr Smithson's having made up to the Birmingham baker, and of this one-legged Captain, coming to dot-and-go-one over the estate. I suppose he will look after the labourers through a spy-glass. I only hope he won't stick in the mud with his wooden leg; for I, for one, won't help him out. Yes, I would,' said she, correcting herself; 'I would, for my lady's sake.'

'But are you sure he has a wooden leg?' asked I. 'I heard Lady Ludlow tell Mr Smithson about him, and she only spoke of him as wounded.'

'Well, sailors are almost always wounded in the leg. Look at Greenwich Hospital! I should say there were twenty one-legged pensioners to one without an arm there. But say he has got half-a-dozen legs, what is he to do with managing land? I shall think him very impudent if he comes, taking advantage of my lady's kind heart.'

However, come he did. In a month from that time, the carriage was sent to meet Captain James; just as three years before it had been sent to meet me. His coming had been so much talked about that we were all as curious as possible to see him, and to know how so unusual an experiment, as it seemed to us, would answer. But, before I tell you anything about our new agent, I must speak of something quite as interesting, and I really think quite as important. And this was my lady's making friends with Harry Gregson. I do believe she did it for Mr Horner's sake; but, of course, I can only conjecture why my lady did anything. But I heard one day, from Mary Legard, that my lady had sent for Harry to come and see her, if he was well enough to walk so far; and the next day he was shown into the room he had been in once before under such unlucky circumstances.

The lad looked pale enough, as he stood propping himself up on his crutch, and the instant my lady saw him, she bade John

Footman place a stool for him to sit down upon while she spoke to him. It might be his paleness that gave his whole face a more refined and gentle look; but I suspect it was that the boy was apt to take impressions, and that Mr Horner's grave, dignified ways, and Mr Gray's tender and quiet manners, had altered him; and then the thoughts of illness and death seem to turn many of us into gentlemen, and gentlewomen, as long as such thoughts are in our minds. We cannot speak loudly or angrily at such times; we are not apt to be eager about mere worldly things, for our very awe at our quickened sense of the nearness of the invisible world, makes us calm and serene about the petty trifles of to-day. At least, I know that was the explanation Mr Gray once gave me of what we all thought the great improvement in Harry Gregson's way of behaving.

My lady hesitated so long about what she had best say, that Harry grew a little frightened at her silence. A few months ago it would have surprised me more than it did now; but since my lord her son's death, she had seemed altered in many ways – more uncertain and distrustful of herself, as it were.

At last she said, and I think the tears were in her eyes: 'My poor little fellow, you have had a narrow escape with your life since I saw you last.'

To this there was nothing to be said but 'Yes;' and again there was silence.

'And you have lost a good, kind friend, in Mr Horner.'

The boy's lips worked, and I think he said, 'Please, don't.' But I can't be sure; at any rate, my lady went on:

'And so have I – a good, kind friend, he was to both of us; and to you he wished to show his kindness in even a more generous way than he has done. Mr Gray has told you about his legacy to you, has he not?'

There was no sign of eager joy on the lad's face, as if he realised the power and pleasure of having what to him must have seemed like a fortune.

'Mr Gray said as how he had left me a matter of money.'

'Yes, he has left you two hundred pounds.'

'But I would rather have had him alive, my lady,' he burst out, sobbing as if his heart would break.

'My lad, I believe you. We would rather have had our dead alive, would we not? and there is nothing in money that can comfort us for their loss. But you know – Mr Gray has told you – who has appointed us all our times to die. Mr Horner was a good, just man; and has done well and kindly, both by me and you. You perhaps do not know' (and now I understood what my lady had been making up her mind to say to Harry, all the time she was hesitating how to begin) 'that Mr Horner, at one time, meant to leave you a great deal more; probably all he had, with the exception of a legacy to his old clerk, Morrison. But he knew that this estate – on which my forefathers had lived for six hundred years – was in debt, and that I had no immediate chance of paying off this debt; and yet he felt that it was a very sad thing for an old property like this to belong in part to those other men, who had lent the money. You understand me, I think, my little man?' said she, questioning Harry's face.

He had left off crying, and was trying to understand, with all his might and main; and I think he had got a pretty good general idea of the state of affairs; though probably he was puzzled by the term 'the estate being in debt.' But he was sufficiently interested to want my lady to go on; and he nodded his head at her, to signify this to her.

'So Mr Horner took the money which he once meant to be yours, and has left the greater part of it to me, with the intention of helping me to pay off this debt I have told you about. It will go a long way, and I shall try hard to save the rest, and then I shall die happy in leaving the land free from debt.' She paused. 'But I shall not die happy in thinking of you. I do not know if having money, or even having a great estate and much honour, is a good thing for any of us. But God sees fit that some of us should be called to this condition, and it is our duty then to stand by our posts, like brave soldiers. Now, Mr Horner intended you to have this money first. I shall only call it borrowing it from you, Harry Gregson, if I take it and use it to pay off the debt. I shall pay Mr Gray interest on this money, because he is to stand as your guardian, as it were, till you come of age; and he must fix what ought to be done with it, so as to fit you for spending the principal rightly when the estate can repay it you. I suppose, now, it will be right for you to be educated. That will be another snare that will come with your money. But have courage, Harry. Both education and money may be used rightly, if we only pray against the temptations they bring with them.'

Harry could make no answer, though I am sure he understood it all. My lady wanted to get him to talk to her a little, by way of becoming acquainted with what was passing in his mind; and she asked him what he would like to have done with his money, if he could have part of it now? To such a simple question, involving no talk about feelings, his answer came readily enough.

'Build a cottage for father, with stairs in it, and give Mr Gray a school-house. O, father does so want Mr Gray for to have his wish! Father saw all the stones lying quarried and hewn on Farmer Hale's land; Mr Gray had paid for them all himself. And father said he would work night and day, and little Tommy should carry mortar, if the parson would let him, sooner than that he should be fretted and frabbed as he was, with no one giving him a helping hand or a kind word.'

Harry knew nothing of my lady's part in the affair; that was very clear. My lady kept silence.

'If I might have a piece of my money, I would buy land from Mr Brooke: he has got a bit to sell just at the corner of Hendon Lane, and I would give it to Mr Gray; and, perhaps, if your ladyship thinks I may be learned again, I might grow up into the schoolmaster.'

'You are a good boy,' said my lady. 'But there are more things to be thought of, in carrying out such a plan, than you are aware of. However, it shall be tried.'

'The school, my lady?' I exclaimed, almost thinking she did not know what she was saying.

'Yes, the school. For Mr Horner's sake, for Mr Gray's sake, and last, not least, for this lad's sake, I will give the new plan a trial. Ask Mr Gray to come up to me this afternoon about the land he wants. He need not go to a Dissenter for it. And tell your father he shall have a good share in the building of it, and Tommy shall carry the mortar.'

'And I may be schoolmaster?' asked Harry, eagerly.

'We'll see about that,' said my lady, amused. 'It will be some time before that plan comes to pass, my little fellow.'

And now to return to Captain James. My first account of him was from Miss Galindo.

'He's not above thirty; and I must just pack up my pens and my paper, and be off; for it would be the height of impropriety for me to be staying here as his clerk. It was all very well in the old master's days. But here am I, not fifty till next May, and this young, unmarried man, who is not even a widower! O, there would be no end of gossip. Besides, he looks as askance at me as I do at him. My black silk gown had no effect. He's afraid I shall marry him. But I won't; he may feel himself quite safe from that. And Mr Smithson has been recommending a clerk to my lady. She would far rather keep me on; but I can't stop. I really could not think it proper.'

'What sort of a looking man is he?'

'O, nothing particular. Short, and brown, and sunburnt. I did not think it became me to look at him. Well, now for the nightcaps. I should have grudged any one else doing them, for I have got such a pretty pattern!'

But, when it came to Miss Galindo's leaving, there was a great misunderstanding between her and my lady. Miss Galindo had imagined that my lady had asked her as a favour to copy the letters, and enter the accounts, and had agreed to do the work without a notion of being paid for so doing. She had, now and then, grieved over a very profitable order for needlework passing out of her hands on account of her not having time to do it, because of her occupation at the Hall; but she had never hinted this to my lady, but gone on cheerfully at her writing as long as her clerkship was required. My lady was annoyed that she had not made her intention of paying Miss Galindo more clear, in the first conversation she had had with her; but I suppose that she had been too delicate to be very explicit with regard to money matters; and now Miss Galindo was quite hurt at my lady's wanting to pay her for what she had done in such right-down good-will.

'No,' Miss Galindo said; 'my own dear lady, you may be as angry with me as you like, but don't offer me money. Think of six-and-twenty years ago, and poor Arthur, and as you were to me then! Besides, I wanted money – I don't disguise it – for a particular purpose; and when I found that (God bless you for asking me!) I could do you a service, I turned it over in my mind, and I gave up one plan and took up another, and it's all settled now. Bessy is to leave school and come and live with me. Don't, please, offer me money again. You don't know how glad I have been to do anything for you. Have not I, Margaret Dawson? Did you not hear me say, one day, I would cut off my hand for my lady; for am I a stock or a stone, that I should forget kindness? O, I have been so glad to work for you. And now Bessy is coming here; and no one knows anything about her – as if she had done anything wrong, poor child!'

'Dear Miss Galindo,' replied my lady, 'I will never ask you to take money again. Only I thought it was quite understood between us. And, you know, you have taken money for a set of morning wrappers, before now.'

'Yes, my lady; but that was not confidential. Now I was so proud to have something to do for you confidentially.'

'But who is Bessy?' asked my lady. 'I do not understand who

she is, or why she is to come and live with you. Dear Miss Galindo, you must honour me by being confidential with me in your turn!'

Chapter XIII

I had always understood that Miss Galindo had once been in much better circumstances, but I had never liked to ask any questions respecting her. But about this time many things came out respecting her former life, which I will try and arrange; not, however, in the order in which I heard them, but rather as they occurred.

Miss Galindo was the daughter of a clergyman in Westmoreland. Her father was the younger brother of a baronet, his ancestor having been one of those of James the First's creation. This baronet-uncle of Miss Galindo was one of the queer, out-of-the-way people who were bred at that time, and in that northern district of England. I never heard much of him from any one, besides this one great fact: that he had early disappeared from his family, which indeed only consisted of a brother and sister who died unmarried, and lived no one knew where – somewhere on the Continent, it was supposed, for he had never returned from the grand tour which he had been sent to make, according to the general fashion of the day, as soon as he left Oxford. He corresponded occasionally with his brother the clergyman; but the letters passed through a banker's hands; the banker being pledged to secrecy, and, as he told Mr Galindo, having the penalty, if he broke his pledge, of losing the whole profitable business, and of having the management of the baronet's affairs taken out of his hands, without any advantage accruing to the inquirer, for Sir Lawrence had told Messrs Graham that, in case his place of residence was revealed by them, not only would he cease to bank with them, but instantly take measures to baffle any future inquiries as to his whereabouts, by removing to some distant country.

Sir Lawrence paid a certain sum of money to his brother's account every year; but the time of this payment varied, and it was sometimes eighteen or nineteen months between the deposits; then, again, it would not be above a quarter of the time, showing that he intended it to be annual, but, as this intention was never expressed in words, it was impossible to rely upon it, and a great deal of this money was swallowed up by the necessity Mr Galindo felt himself under of living in the large, old, rambling family mansion, which had been one of Sir Lawrence's rarely expressed desires. Mr and Mrs Galindo often planned to live upon their own small fortune and the income derived from the living (a vicarage, of which the great tithes went to Sir Lawrence as lay impropriator), so as to put by the payments made by the baronet, for the benefit of Laurentia – our Miss Galindo. But I suppose they found it difficult to live economically in a large house, even though they had it rent free. They had to keep up with hereditary neighbours and friends, and could hardly help doing it in the hereditary manner.

One of these neighbours, a Mr Gibson, had a son a few years older than Laurentia. The families were sufficiently intimate for the young people to see a good deal of each other: and I was told that this young Mr Mark Gibson was an unusually prepossessing man (he seemed to have impressed every one who spoke of him to me as being a handsome, manly, kind-hearted fellow), just what a girl would be sure to find most agreeable. The parents either forgot that their children were growing up to man's and woman's estate, or thought that the intimacy and probable attachment would be no bad thing, even if it did lead to a marriage. Still, nothing was ever said by young Gibson till later on, when it was too late, as it turned out. He went to and from Oxford; he shot and fished with Mr Galindo, or came to the Mere to skate in winter-time; was asked to accompany Mr Galindo to the Hall, as the latter returned to the quiet dinner with his wife and daughter; and so, and so, it went on, nobody much knew how, until one day, when Mr Galindo received a formal letter from his brother's bankers, announcing Sir Lawrence's death, of malaria fever, at Albano, and congratulating Sir Hubert on his accession to the estates and the baronetcy. 'The king is dead – Long live the king!' as I have since heard that the French express it.

Sir Hubert and his wife were greatly surprised. Sir Lawrence was but two years older than his brother; and they had never heard of any illness till they heard of his death. They were sorry; very much shocked; but still a little elated at the succession to the baronetcy and estates. The London bankers had managed everything well. There was a large sum of ready money in their hands, at Sir Hubert's service, until he should touch his rents, the rent-roll being eight thousand a-year. And only Laurentia to inherit it all! Her mother, a poor clergyman's daughter, began to plan all sorts of fine marriages for her; nor was her father much behind his wife in his ambition. They took her up to London, when they went to buy new carriages, and dresses, and furniture. And it was then and there she made my lady's acquaintance. How it was that they came to take a fancy to each other, I cannot say. My lady was of the old nobility – grand, composed, gentle, and stately in her ways. Miss Galindo must always have been hurried in her manner, and her energy must have shown itself in inquisitiveness and oddness even in her youth. But I don't pretend to account for things: I only narrate them. And the fact was this: – that the elegant, fastidious Countess was attracted to the country girl, who on her part almost worshipped my lady. My lady's notice of their daughter made her parents think, I suppose, that there was no match that she might not command; she, the heiress of eight thousand a-year, and visiting about among earls and dukes. So when they came back to their old Westmoreland Hall, and Mark Gibson rode over to offer his hand and his heart, and prospective estate of nine hundred a-year to his old companion and playfellow, Laurentia, Sir Hubert and Lady Galindo made very short work of it. They refused him plumply themselves; and when he begged to be allowed to speak to Laurentia, they found some excuse for refusing him the opportunity of so doing, until they had talked to her themselves, and brought up every argument and fact in their power to convince her – a plain girl, and conscious of her plainness – that Mr Mark Gibson had never thought of her in the way of marriage till after her father's accession to his fortune; and that it was the estate – not the young lady – that he was in love with. I suppose it will never be known in this world how far this supposition of theirs was true. My Lady Ludlow had always spoken as if it was; but perhaps events, which came to her knowledge about this time, altered her opinion. At any rate, the end of it was, Laurentia refused Mark, and almost broke her heart in doing so. He discovered the suspicions of Sir Hubert and Lady Galindo, and that they had persuaded their daughter to share in them. So he flung off with high words, saying that they did not know a true heart when they met with one; and that, although he had never offered till after Sir Lawrence's death, yet that his father knew all along that he had been attached to Laurentia, only that he, being the eldest of five children, and having as yet no profession, had had to conceal, rather than to express, an attachment, which, in those days, he had believed was reciprocated. He had always meant to study for the bar, and the end of all he had hoped for had been to earn a moderate income, which he might ask Laurentia to share. This, or something like it, was what he said. But his reference to his father cut two ways. Old Mr Gibson was known to be very keen about money. It was just as likely that he would urge Mark to make love to the heiress, now she was an heiress, as that he would have restrained him previously, as Mark said he had done. When this was repeated to Mark, he became proudly reserved, or sullen, and said that Laurentia, at any rate, might have known him better. He left the country, and went up to London to study law soon afterwards; and Sir Hubert and Lady Galindo thought they were well rid of him. But Laurentia never ceased reproaching herself, and never did to her dying day, as I believe. The words, 'She might have known me better,' told to her by some kind friend or other, rankled in her mind, and were never forgotten. Her father and mother took her up to London the next year; but she did not care to visit – dreaded going out even for a drive, lest she should see Mark Gibson's reproachful eyes – pined and lost her health. Lady Ludlow saw this change with regret, and was told the cause by Lady Galindo, who, of course, gave her own version of Mark's conduct and motives. My lady never spoke to Miss Galindo about it, but tried constantly to interest and please her. It was at this time that my lady told Miss Galindo so much about her own early life, and about Hanbury, that Miss Galindo resolved, if ever she could, she would go and see the old place which her friend loved so well. The end of it all was, that she came to live there, as we know.

But a great change was to come first. Before Sir Hubert and Lady Galindo had left London on this, their second visit, they had a letter from the lawyer, whom they employed, saying that Sir Lawrence had left an heir, his legitimate child by an Italian woman of low rank; at least, legal claims to the title and property had been sent into him on the boy's behalf. Sir Lawrence had always been a man of adventurous and artistic, rather than of luxurious tastes; and it was supposed, when all came to be proved at the trial, that he was captivated by the free, beautiful life they lead in Italy, and had married this Neapolitan fisherman's daughter, who had people about her shrewd enough to see that the ceremony was legally performed. She and her husband had wandered about the shores of the Mediterranean for years, leading a happy, careless, irresponsible life, unencumbered by any duties except those connected with a rather numerous family. It was enough for her that they never wanted money, and that her husband's love was always continued to her. She hated the name of England – wicked, cold, heretic England – and avoided the mention of any subjects connected with her husband's early life. So that, when he died at Albano, she was almost roused out of her vehement grief to anger with the Italian doctor, who declared that he must write to a certain address to announce the death of Lawrence Galindo. For some time, she feared lest English barbarians might come down upon her, making a claim to the children. She hid herself and them in the Abruzzi, living upon the sale of what furniture and jewels Sir Lawrence had died possessed of. When these failed, she returned to Naples, which she had not visited since her marriage. Her father was dead; but her brother inherited some of his keenness. He interested the priests, who made inquiries and found that the Galindo succession was worth securing to an heir of the true faith. They stirred about it, obtained advice at the English Embassy; and hence that letter to the lawyers, calling upon Sir Hubert to relinquish title and property, and to refund what money he had expended. He was vehement in his opposition to this claim. He could not bear to think of his brother having married a foreigner – a papist, a fisherman's daughter; nay, of his having become a papist himself. He was in despair at the thought of his ancestral property going to the issue of such a marriage. He fought tooth and nail, making enemies of his relations, and losing almost all his own private property; for he would go on against the lawyer's advice, long after every one was convinced except himself and his wife. At last he was conquered. He gave up his living in gloomy despair. He would have changed his name if he could, so desirous was he to obliterate all tie between himself and the mongrel papist baronet and his Italian mother, and all the succession of children and nurses who came to take possession of the Hall soon after Mr Hubert Galindo's departure, stayed there one winter, and then flitted back to Naples with gladness and delight. Mr and Mrs Hubert Galindo lived in London. He had obtained a curacy somewhere in the city. They would have been thankful now if Mr Mark Gibson had renewed his offer. No one could accuse him of mercenary motives if he had done so. Because he did not come forward, as they wished, they brought his silence up as a justification of what they had previously attributed to him. I don't know what Miss Galindo thought herself; but Lady Ludlow has told me how she shrank from hearing her parents abuse him. Lady Ludlow supposed that he was aware that they were living in London. His father must have known the fact, and it was curious if he had never named it to his son. Besides, the name was very uncommon; and it was unlikely that it should never come across him, in the advertisements of charity sermons which the new and rather eloquent curate of Saint Mark's East was asked to preach. All this time Lady Ludlow never lost sight of them, for Miss Galindo's sake. And when the father and mother died, it was my lady who upheld Miss Galindo in her determination not to apply for any provision to her cousin, the Italian baronet, but rather to live upon the hundred a-year which had been settled on her mother and the children of his son Hubert's marriage by the old grandfather, Sir Lawrence.

Mr Mark Gibson had risen to some eminence as a barrister on the Northern Circuit; but had died unmarried in the lifetime of his father, a victim (so people said) to intemperance. Doctor Trevor, the physician who had been called in to Mr Gray and Harry Gregson, had married a sister of his. And that was all my lady knew about the Gibson family. But who was Bessy?

That mystery and secret came out, too, in process of time. Miss Galindo had been to Warwick, some years before I arrived at Hanbury, on some kind of business or shopping, which can only be transacted in a county town. There was an old Westmoreland connexion between her and Mrs Trevor, though I believe the latter was too young to have been made aware of her brother's offer to Miss Galindo at the time when it took place; and such affairs, if they are unsuccessful, are seldom spoken about in the gentleman's family afterwards. But the Gibsons and Galindos had been county neighbours too long for the connexion not to be kept up between two members settled far away from their early homes. Miss Galindo always desired her parcels to be sent to Doctor Trevor's, when she went to Warwick for shopping purposes. If she were going any journey, and the coach did not come through Warwick as soon as she arrived (in my lady's coach or otherwise) from Hanbury, she went to Doctor Trevor's to wait. She was as much expected to sit down to the household meals as if she had been one of the family; and in after years it was Mrs Trevor who managed her repository business for her.

So, on the day I spoke of, she had gone to Doctor Trevor's to rest, and possibly to dine. The post, in those times, came in at all hours of the morning; and Doctor Trevor's letters had not arrived until after his departure on his morning round. Miss Galindo was sitting down to dinner with Mrs Trevor and her seven children, when the Doctor came in. He was flurried and uncomfortable, and hurried the children away as soon as he decently could. Then (rather feeling Miss Galindo's presence an advantage, both as a present restraint on the violence of his wife's grief, and as a consoler when he was absent on his afternoon round), he told Mrs Trevor of her brother's death. He had been taken ill on circuit, and had hurried back to his chambers in London, only to die. She cried terribly; but Doctor Trevor said afterwards, he never noticed that Miss Galindo cared much about it one way or another. She helped him to soothe his wife, promised to stay with her all the afternoon instead of returning to Hanbury, and afterwards offered to remain with her while the Doctor went to attend the funeral. When they heard of the old love-story between the dead man and Miss Galindo – brought up by mutual friends in Westmoreland, in the review which we are all inclined to take of the events of a man's life when he comes to die – they tried to remember Miss Galindo's speeches and ways of going on during this visit. She was a little pale, a little silent; her eyes were sometimes swollen, and her nose red; but she was at an age when such appearances are generally attributed to a bad cold in the head, rather than to any more sentimental reason. They felt towards her as towards an old friend, a kindly, useful, eccentric old maid. She did not expect more, or wish them to remember that she might once have had other hopes, and more youthful feelings. Doctor Trevor thanked her very warmly for staying with his wife, when he returned home from London (where the funeral had taken place). He begged Miss Galindo to stay with them, when the children were gone to bed, and she was preparing to leave the husband and wife by themselves. He told her and his wife many particulars – then paused – then went on –

'And Mark has left a child – a little girl – '

'But he never was married,' exclaimed Mrs Trevor.

'A little girl,' continued her husband, 'whose mother, I conclude, is dead. At any rate, the child was in possession of his chambers; she and an old nurse, who seemed to have the charge of everything, and has cheated poor Mark, I should fancy, not a little.'

'But the child!' asked Mrs Trevor, still almost breathless with astonishment. 'How do you know it is his?'

'The nurse told me it was, with great appearance of indignation at my doubting it. I asked the little thing her name, and all I could get was "Bessy!" and a cry of "Me wants papa!" The nurse said the mother was dead, and she knew no more about it than that Mr Gibson had engaged her to take care of the little girl, calling it his child. One or two of his lawyer friends, whom I met with at the funeral, told me they were aware of the existence of the child.'

'What is to be done with her?' asked Mrs Trevor.

'Nay, I don't know,' replied he. 'Mark has hardly left assets enough to pay his debts, and your father is not inclined to come forward.'

That night, as Doctor Trevor sat in his study, after his wife had gone to bed, Miss Galindo knocked at his door. She and he had a long conversation. The result was that he accompanied Miss Galindo up to town the next day; that they took possession of the little Bessy, and she was brought down, and placed at nurse at a farm in the country near Warwick, Miss Galindo undertaking to pay one-half the expense, and to furnish her with clothes, and Dr Trevor undertaking that the remaining half should be furnished by the Gibson family, or by himself in their default.

Miss Galindo was not fond of children, and I daresay she dreaded taking this child to live with her for more reasons than one. My Lady Ludlow could not endure any mention of illegitimate children. It was a principle of hers that society ought to ignore them. And I believe Miss Galindo had always agreed with her until now, when the thing came home to her womanly heart. Still she shrank from having this child of some strange woman under her roof. She went over to see it from time to time; she worked at its clothes long after every one thought she was in bed; and, when the time came for Bessy to be sent to school, Miss Galindo laboured away more diligently than ever, in order to pay the increased expense. For the Gibson family had, at first, paid their part of the compact, but with unwillingness and grudging hearts; then they had left it off altogether, and it fell hard on Doctor Trevor with his twelve children; and, latterly, Miss Galindo had taken upon herself almost all the burden. One can hardly live and labour, and plan and make sacrifices, for any human creature, without learning to love it. And Bessy loved Miss Galindo, too, for all the poor girl's scanty pleasures came from her, and Miss Galindo had always a kind word, and, latterly, many a kind caress, for Mark Gibson's child; whereas, if she went to Doctor Trevor's for her holiday, she was overlooked and neglected in that bustling family, who seemed to think that if she had comfortable board and lodging under their roof, it was enough.

I am sure, now, that Miss Galindo had often longed to have Bessy to live with her; but, as long as she could pay for her being at school, she did not like to take so bold a step as bringing her home, knowing what the effect of the consequent explanation would be on my lady. And as the girl was now more than seventeen, and past the age when young ladies are usually kept at school, and as there was no great demand for governesses in those days, and as Bessy had never been taught any trade by which to earn her own living, why, I don't exactly see what could have been done but for Miss Galindo to bring her to her own home in Hanbury. For, although the child had grown up lately, in a kind of unexpected manner, into a young woman, Miss Galindo might have kept her at school for a year longer, if she could have afforded it; but this was impossible when she became Mr Horner's clerk, and relinquished all the payment of her repository work; and perhaps, after all, she was not sorry to be compelled to take the step she was longing for. At any rate, Bessy came to live with Miss Galindo in a very few weeks from the time when Captain James set Miss Galindo free to superintend her own domestic economy again.

For a long time, I knew nothing about this new inhabitant of Hanbury. My lady never mentioned her in any way. This was in accordance with Lady Ludlow's well-known principles. She neither saw nor heard, nor was in any way cognisant of the existence of those who had no legal right to exist at all. If Miss Galindo had hoped to have an exception made in Bessy's favour, she was mistaken. My lady sent a note inviting Miss Galindo herself to tea one evening, about a month after Bessy came; but Miss Galindo 'had a cold and could not come.' The next time she was invited, she 'had an engagement at home' – a step nearer to the absolute truth. And the third time, she 'had a young friend staying with her whom she was unable to leave.' My lady accepted every excuse as bona fide, and took no further notice. I missed Miss Galindo very much; we all did; for, in the days when she was clerk, she was sure to come in and find the opportunity of saying something amusing to some of us before she went away. And I, as an invalid, or perhaps from natural tendency, was particularly fond of little bits of village gossip. There was no Mr Horner – he even had come in, now and then, with formal, stately pieces of intelligence – and there was no Miss Galindo, in these days. I missed her much. And so did my lady, I am sure. Behind all her quiet, sedate manner, I am certain her heart ached sometimes for a few words from Miss Galindo, who seemed to have absented herself altogether from the Hall now Bessy was come.

Captain James might be very sensible, and all that; but not even my lady could call him a substitute for the old familiar friends. He was a thorough sailor, as sailors were in those days – swore a good deal, drank a good deal (without its ever affecting him in the least), and was very prompt and kind-hearted in all his actions; but he was not accustomed to women, as my lady once said, and would judge in all things for himself. My lady had expected, I think, to find some one who would take his notions on the management of her estate from her ladyship's own self; but he spoke as if he were responsible for the good management of the whole, and must, consequently, be allowed full liberty of action. He had been too long in command over men at sea to like to be directed by a woman in anything he undertook, even though that woman was my lady. I suppose this was the common-sense my lady spoke of; but when common-sense goes against us, I don't think we value it quite so much as we ought to do.

Lady Ludlow was proud of her personal superintendence of her own estate. She liked to tell us how her father used to take her with him in his rides, and bid her observe this and that, and on no account to allow such and such things to be done. But I have heard that the first time she told all this to Captain James, he told her point-blank that he had heard from Mr Smithson that the farms were much neglected and the rents sadly behind-hand, and that he meant to set to in good earnest and study agriculture, and see how he could remedy the state of things. My lady would, I am sure, be greatly surprised, but what could she do? Here was the very man she had chosen herself, setting to with all his energy to conquer the defect of ignorance, which was all that those who had presumed to offer her ladyship advice had ever had to say against him. Captain James read Arthur Young's 'Tours' in all his spare time, as long as he was an invalid; and shook his head at my lady's accounts as to how the land had been cropped or left fallow from time immemorial. Then he set to, and tried too many new experiments at once. My lady looked on in dignified silence; but all the farmers and tenants were in an uproar, and prophesied a hundred failures. Perhaps fifty did occur; they were only half as many as Lady Ludlow had feared; but they were twice as many, four, eight times as many as the captain had anticipated. His openly-expressed disappointment made him popular again. The rough country people could not have understood silent and dignified regret at the failure of his plans; but they sympathised with a man who swore at his ill success – sympathised, even while they chuckled over his discomfiture. Mr Brooke, the retired tradesman, did not cease blaming him for not succeeding, and for swearing. 'But what could you expect from a sailor?' Mr Brooke asked, even in my lady's hearing; though he might have known Captain James was my lady's own personal choice, from the old friendship Mr Urian had always shown for him. I think it was this speech of the Birmingham baker's that made my lady determine to stand by Captain James, and encourage him to try again. For she would not allow that her choice had been an unwise one, at the bidding (as it were) of a Dissenting tradesman; the only person in the neighbourhood, too, who had flaunted about in coloured clothes, when all the world was in mourning for my lady's only son.

Captain James would have thrown the agency up at once, if my lady had not felt herself bound to justify the wisdom of her choice, by urging him to stay. He was much touched by her confidence in him, and swore a great oath, that the next year he would make the land such as it had never been before for produce. It was not my lady's way to repeat anything she had heard, especially to another person's disadvantage. So I don't think she ever told Captain James of Mr Brooke's speech about a sailor's being likely to mismanage the property; and the captain was too anxious to succeed in this, the second year of his trial, to be above going to the flourishing, shrewd Mr Brooke, and asking for his advice as to the best method of working the estate. I dare say, if Miss Galindo had been as intimate as formerly at the Hall, we should all of us have heard of this new acquaintance of the agent's long before we did. As it was, I am sure my lady never dreamed that the captain, who held opinions that were even more Church and King than her own, could ever have made friends with a Baptist baker from Birmingham, even to serve her ladyship's own interests in the most loyal manner.

We heard of it first from Mr Gray, who came now often to see my lady, for neither he nor she could forget the solemn tie which the fact of his being the person to acquaint her with my lord's death had created between them. For true and holy words spoken at that time, though having no reference to aught below the solemn subjects of life and death, had made her withdraw her opposition to Mr Gray's wish about establishing a village school. She had sighed a little, it is true, and was even yet more apprehensive than hopeful as to the result; but, almost as if as a memorial to my lord, she had allowed a kind of rough school-house to be built on the green, just by the church; and had gently used the power she undoubtedly had, in expressing her strong wish that the boys might only be taught to read and write, and the first four rules of arithmetic; while the girls were only to learn to read, and to add up in their heads, and the rest of the time to work at mending their own clothes, knitting stockings, and spinning. My lady presented the school with more spinning-wheels than there were girls, and requested that there might be a rule that they should have spun so many hanks of flax, and knitted so many pairs of stockings, before they ever were taught to read at all. After all, it was but making the best of a bad job with my poor lady – but life was not what it had been to her. I remember well the day that Mr Gray pulled some delicately fine yarn (and I was a good judge of those things) out of his pocket, and laid it and a capital pair of knitted stockings before my lady, as the first-fruits, so to say, of his school. I recollect seeing her put on her spectacles, and carefully examine both productions. Then she passed them to me.

'This is well, Mr Gray. I am much pleased. You are fortunate in your schoolmistress. She has had both proper knowledge of womanly things and much patience. Who is she? One out of our village?'

'My lady,' said Mr Gray, stammering and colouring in his old fashion, 'Miss Bessy is so very kind as to teach all those sorts of things – Miss Bessy, and Miss Galindo, sometimes.'

My lady looked at him over her spectacles: but she only repeated the words 'Miss Bessy,' and paused, as if trying to remember who such a person could be; and he, if he had then intended to say more, was quelled by her manner, and dropped the subject. He went on to say that he had thought it his duty to decline the subscription to his school offered by Mr Brooke, because he was a Dissenter; that he (Mr Gray) feared that Captain James, through whom Mr Brooke's offer of money had been made, was offended at his refusing to accept it from a man who held heterodox opinions; nay, whom Mr Gray suspected of being infected by Dodwell's heresy.

'I think there must be some mistake,' said my lady, 'or I have misunderstood you. Captain James would never be sufficiently with a schismatic to be employed by that man Brooke in distributing his charities. I should have doubted, until now, if Captain James knew him.'

'Indeed, my lady, he not only knows him, but is intimate with him, I regret to say. I have repeatedly seen the captain and Mr Brooke walking together; going through the fields together; and people do say – '

My lady looked up in interrogation at Mr Gray's pause.

'I disapprove of gossip, and it may be untrue; but people do say that Captain James is very attentive to Miss Brooke.'

'Impossible!' said my lady, indignantly. 'Captain James is a loyal and religious man. I beg your pardon, Mr Gray, but it is impossible.'

Chapter XIV

Like many other things which have been declared to be impossible, this report of Captain James being attentive to Miss Brooke turned out to be very true.

The mere idea of her agent being on the slightest possible terms of acquaintance with the Dissenter, the tradesman, the Birmingham democrat, who had come to settle in our good, orthodox, aristocratic, and agricultural Hanbury, made my lady very uneasy. Miss Galindo's misdemeanour in having taken Miss Bessy to live with her, faded into a mistake, a mere error of judgement, in comparison with Captain James's intimacy at Yeast House, as the Brookes called their ugly square-built farm. My lady talked herself quite into complacency with Miss Galindo, and even Miss Bessy was named by her, the first time I had ever been aware that my lady recognized her existence; but – I recollect it was a long rainy afternoon, and I sat with her ladyship, and we had time and opportunity for a long uninterrupted talk – whenever we had been silent for a little while she began again, with something like a wonder how it was that Captain James could ever have commenced an acquaintance with 'that man Brooke.' My lady recapitulated all the times she could remember, that anything had occurred, or been said by Captain James which she could now understand as throwing light upon the subject.

'He said once that he was anxious to bring in the Norfolk system of cropping, and spoke a good deal about Mr Coke of Holkham (who, by the way, was no more a Coke than I am – collateral in the female line – which counts for little or nothing among the great old commoners' families of pure blood), and his new ways of cultivation; of course new men bring in new ways, but it does not follow that either are better than the old ways. However, Captain James has been very anxious to try turnips and bone manure, and he really is a man of such good sense and energy, and was so sorry last year about the failure, that I consented; and now I begin to see my error. I have always heard that town bakers adulterate their flour with bone-dust; and, of course, Captain James would be aware of this, and go to Brooke to inquire where the article was to be purchased.'

My lady always ignored the fact which had sometimes, I suspect, been brought under her very eyes during her drives, that Mr Brooke's few fields were in a state of far higher cultivation than her own; so she could not, of course, perceive that there was any wisdom to be gained from asking the advice of the tradesman turned farmer.

But by-and-by this fact of her agent's intimacy with the person whom in the whole world she most disliked (with that sort of dislike in which a large amount of uncomfortableness is combined – the dislike which conscientious people sometimes feel to another without knowing why, and yet which they cannot indulge in with comfort to themselves without having a moral reason why), came before my lady in many shapes. For, indeed, I am sure that Captain James was not a man to conceal or be ashamed of one of his actions. I cannot fancy his ever lowering his strong loud clear voice, or having a confidential conversation with any one. When his crops had failed, all the village had known it. He complained, he regretted, he was angry, or owned himself a — fool, all down the village street; and the consequence was that, although he was a far more passionate man than Mr Horner, all the tenants liked him far better. People, in general, take a kindlier interest in any one, the workings of whose mind and heart they can watch and understand, than in a man who only lets you know what he has been thinking about and feeling, by what he does. But Harry

Gregson was faithful to the memory of Mr Horner. Miss Galindo has told me that she used to watch him hobble out of the way of Captain James, as if to accept his notice, however good-naturedly given, would have been a kind of treachery to his former benefactor. But Gregson (the father) and the new agent rather took to each other; and one day, much to my surprise, I heard that the 'poaching, tinkering vagabond,' as people used to call Gregson when I first had come to live at Hanbury, had been appointed gamekeeper; Mr Gray standing godfather, as it were, to his trustworthiness, if he were trusted with anything; which I thought at the time was rather an experiment, only it answered, as many of Mr Gray's deeds of daring did. It was curious how he was growing to be a kind of autocrat in the village; and how unconscious he was of it. He was as shy and awkward and nervous as ever in any affair that was not of some moral consequence to him. But as soon as he was convinced that a thing was right, he 'shut his eyes and ran and butted at it like a ram,' as Captain James once expressed it, in talking over something Mr Gray had done. People in the village said, 'they never knew what the parson would be at next;' or they might have said, 'where his reverence would next turn up.' For I have heard of his marching right into the middle of a set of poachers, gathered together for some desperate midnight enterprise, or walking into a public-house that lay just beyond the bounds of my lady's estate, and in that extra-parochial piece of ground I named long ago, and which was considered the rendezvous of all the ne'er-do-well characters for miles round, and where a parson and a constable were held in much the same kind of esteem as unwelcome visitors. And yet Mr Gray had his long fits of depression, in which he felt as if he were doing nothing, making no way in his work, useless and unprofitable, and better out of the world than in it. In comparison with the work he had set himself to do, what he did seemed to be nothing. I suppose it was constitutional, those attacks of lowness of spirits which he had about this time; perhaps a part of the nervousness which made him always so awkward when he came to the Hall. Even Mrs Medlicott, who almost worshipped the ground he trod on, as the saying is, owned that Mr Gray never entered one of my lady's rooms without knocking down something, and too often breaking it. He would much sooner have faced a desperate poacher than a young lady any day. At least so we thought.

I do not know how it was that it came to pass that my lady became reconciled to Miss Galindo about this time. Whether it was that her ladyship was weary of the unspoken coolness with her old friend; or that the specimens of delicate sewing and fine spinning at the school had mollified her towards Miss Bessy; but I was surprised to learn one day that Miss Galindo and her young friend were coming that very evening to tea at the Hall. This information was given me by Mrs Medlicott, as a message from my lady, who further went on to desire that certain little preparations should be made in her own private sitting-room, in which the greater part of my days were spent. From the nature of these preparations, I became quite aware that my lady intended to do honour to her expected visitors. Indeed, Lady Ludlow never forgave by halves, as I have known some people do. Whoever was coming as a visitor to my lady, peeress, or poor nameless girl, there was a certain amount of preparation required, in order to do them fitting honour. I do not mean to say that the preparation was of the same degree of importance in each case. I dare say, if a peeress had come to visit us at the Hall, the covers would have been taken off the furniture in the white drawing-room (they never were uncovered all the time I stayed at the Hall), because my lady would wish to offer her the ornaments and luxuries which this grand visitor (who never came – I wish she had! I did so want to see that furniture uncovered!) was accustomed to at home, and to present them to her in the best order in which my lady could. The same rule, modified, held good with Miss Galindo. Certain things, in which my lady knew she took an interest, were laid out ready for her to examine on this very day; and, what was more, great books of prints were laid out, such as I remembered my lady had had brought forth to beguile my own early days of illness – Mr Hogarth's works, and the like – which I was sure were put out for Miss Bessy.

No one knows how curious I was to see this mysterious Miss Bessy – twenty times more mysterious, of course, for want of her surname. And then again (to try and account for my great curiosity, of which in recollection I am more than half ashamed), I had been leading the quiet monotonous life of a crippled invalid for many years – shut up from any sight of new faces; and this was to be the face of one whom I had thought about so much and so long – Oh! I think I might be excused.

Of course, they drank tea in the great hall, with the four young gentlewomen, who, with myself, formed the small bevy now under her ladyship's charge. Of those who were at Hanbury when first I came, none remained; all were married, or gone once more to live at some home which could be called their own, whether the ostensible head were father or brother. I myself was not without some hopes of a similar kind. My brother Harry was now a curate in Westmoreland, and wanted me to go and live with him, as eventually I did for a time. But that is neither here nor there at present. What I am talking about is Miss Bessy.

After a reasonable time had elapsed, occupied as I well knew by the meal in the great hall – the measured, yet agreeable conversation afterwards – and a certain promenade around the hall, and through the drawing-rooms, with pauses before different pictures, the history or subject of each of which was invariably told by my lady to every new visitor – a sort of giving them the freedom of the old family-seat, by describing the kind and nature of the great progenitors who had lived there before the narrator – I heard the steps approaching my lady's room where I lay. I think I was in such a state of nervous expectation, that if I could have moved easily, I should have got up and run away. And yet I need not have been, for Miss Galindo was not in the least altered (her nose a little redder, to be sure, but then that might only have had a temporary cause in the private crying I know she would have had before coming to see her dear Lady Ludlow once again). But I could almost have pushed Miss Galindo away, as she intercepted me in my view of the mysterious Miss Bessy.

Miss Bessy was, as I knew, only about eighteen, but she looked older. Dark hair, dark eyes, a tall, firm figure, a good, sensible face; with a serene expression, not in the least disturbed by what I had been thinking must be such awful circumstances as a first introduction to my lady, who had so disapproved of her very existence: those are the clearest impressions I remember of my first interview with Miss Bessy. She seemed to observe us all, in her quiet manner, quite as much as I did her; but she spoke very little; occupied herself, indeed, as my lady had planned, with looking over the great books of engravings. I think I must have (foolishly) intended to make her feel at her ease, by my patronage; but she was seated far away from my sofa, in order to command the light, and really seemed so unconcerned at her unwonted circumstances, that she did not need my countenance or kindness. One thing I did like – her watchful look at Miss Galindo from time to time: it showed that her thoughts and sympathy were ever at Miss Galindo's service, as indeed they well might be. When Miss Bessy spoke, her voice was full and clear, and what she said, to the purpose, though there was a slight provincial accent in her way of speaking. After a while, my lady set us two to play at chess, a game which I had lately learnt at Mr Gray's suggestion. Still we did not talk much together, though we were becoming attracted towards each other, I fancy.

'You will play well,' said she. 'You have only learnt about six months, have you? And yet you can nearly beat me, who have been at it as many years.'

'I began to learn last November. I remember Mr Gray's bringing me "Philidor on Chess," one very foggy, dismal day.'

What made her look up so suddenly, with bright inquiry in her eyes? What made her silent for a moment, as if in thought, and then go on with something, I know not what, in quite an altered tone?

My lady and Miss Galindo went on talking, while I sat thinking. I heard Captain James's name mentioned pretty frequently; and at last my lady put down her work, and said, almost with tears in her eyes:

'I could not – I cannot believe it. He must be aware she is a schismatic; a baker's daughter; and he is a gentleman by virtue and feeling, as well as by his profession, though his manners may be at times a little rough. My dear Miss Galindo, what will this world come to?'

Miss Galindo might possibly be aware of her own share in bringing the world to the pass which now dismayed my lady – for, of course, though all was now over and forgiven, yet Miss Bessy's being received into a respectable maiden lady's house, was one of the portents as to the world's future which alarmed her ladyship; and Miss Galindo knew this – but, at any rate, she had too lately been forgiven herself not to plead for mercy for the next offender against my lady's delicate sense of fitness and propriety – so she replied:

'Indeed, my lady, I have long left off trying to conjecture what makes Jack fancy Gill, or Gill Jack. It's best to sit down quiet under the belief that marriages are made for us, somewhere out of this world, and out of the range of this world's reasons and laws. I'm not so sure that I should settle it down that they were made in Heaven; t'other place seems to me as likely a workshop; but, at any rate, I've given up troubling my head as to why they take place. Captain James is a gentleman; I make no doubt of that ever since I saw him stop to pick up old Goody Blake (when she tumbled down on the slide last winter) and then swear at a little lad who was laughing at her, and cuff him till he tumbled down crying; but we must have bread somehow, and though I like it better baked at home in a good sweet brick oven, yet, as some folks never can get it to rise, I don't see why a man may not be a baker. You see, my lady, I look upon baking as a simple trade, and as such lawful. There is no machine comes in to take away a man's or woman's power of earning their living, like the spinning-jenny (the old busybody that she is), to knock up all our good old women's livelihood, and send them to their graves before their time. There's an invention of the enemy, if you will!'

'That's very true!' said my lady, shaking her head.

'But baking bread is wholesome, straightforward elbow-work. They have not got to inventing any contrivance for that yet, thank Heaven! It does not seem to me natural, nor according to Scripture, that iron and steel (whose brows can't sweat) should be made to do man's work. And so I say, all those trades where iron and steel do the work ordained to man at the Fall, are unlawful, and I never stand up for them. But say this baker Brooke did knead his bread, and make it rise, and then that people, who had, perhaps, no good ovens, came to him, and bought his good light bread, and in this manner he turned an honest penny, and got rich; why, all I say, my lady, is this – I dare say he would have been born a Hanbury, or a lord, if he could; and if he was not, it is no fault of his, that I can see, that he made good bread (being a baker by trade), and got money, and bought his land. It was his misfortune, not his fault, that he was not a person of quality by birth.'

'That's very true,' said my lady, after a moment's pause for consideration. 'But, although he was a baker, he might have been a Churchman. Even your eloquence, Miss Galindo, shan't convince me that that is not his own fault.'

'I don't see even that, begging your pardon, my lady,' said Miss Galindo, emboldened by the first success of her eloquence. 'When a Baptist is a baby, if I understand their creed aright, he is not baptized; and, consequently, he can have no godfathers and godmothers to do anything for him in his baptism; you agree to that, my lady?'

My lady would rather have known what her acquiescence would lead to, before acknowledging that she could not dissent from this first proposition; still she gave her tacit agreement by bowing her head.

'And, you know, our godfathers and godmothers are expected to promise and vow three things in our name, when we are little babies, and can do nothing but squall for ourselves. It is a great privilege, but don't let us be hard upon those who have not had the chance of godfathers and godmothers. Some people, we know, are born with silver spoons – that's to say, a godfather to give one things, and teach one one's catechism, and see that we're confirmed into good church-going Christians – and others with wooden ladles in their mouths. These poor last folks must just be content to be godfatherless orphans, and Dissenters, all their lives; and if they are tradespeople into the bargain, so much the worse for them; but let us be humble Christians, my dear lady, and not hold our heads too high because we were born orthodox quality.'

'You go on too fast, Miss Galindo! I can't follow you. Besides, I do believe dissent to be an invention of the Devil's. Why can't they believe as we do? It's very wrong. Besides, it's schism and heresy, and, you know, the Bible says that's as bad as witchcraft.'

My lady was not convinced, as I could see. After Miss Galindo had gone, she sent Mrs Medlicott for certain books out of the great old library upstairs, and had them made up into a parcel under her own eye.

'If Captain James comes to-morrow, I will speak to him about these Brookes. I have not hitherto liked to speak to him, because I did not wish to hurt him, by supposing there could be any truth in the reports about his intimacy with them. But now I will try and do my duty by him and them. Surely, this great body of divinity will bring them back to the true church.'

I could not tell, for though my lady read me over the titles, I was not any the wiser as to their contents. Besides, I was much more anxious to consult my lady as to my own change of place. I showed her the letter I had that day received from Harry; and we once more talked over the expediency of my going to live with him, and trying what entire change of air would do to re-establish my failing health. I could say anything to my lady, she was so sure to understand me rightly. For one thing, she never thought of herself, so I had no fear of hurting her by stating the truth. I told her how happy my years had been while passed under her roof; but that now I had begun to wonder whether I had not duties elsewhere, in making a home for Harry – and whether the fulfilment of these duties, quiet ones they must needs be in the case of such a cripple as myself, would not prevent my sinking into the querulous habit of thinking and talking into which I found myself occasionally falling. Add to which, there was the prospect of benefit from the more bracing air of the north.

It was then settled that my departure from Hanbury, my happy home for so long, was to take place before many weeks had passed. And as, when one period of life is about to be shut up for ever, we are sure to look back upon it with fond regret, so I, happy enough in my future prospects, could not avoid recurring to all the days of my life in the Hall, from the time when I came to it, a shy, awkward girl, scarcely past childhood, to now, when a grown woman – past childhood – almost, from the very character of my illness, past youth – I was looking forward to leaving my lady's house (as a residence) for ever. As it has turned out, I never saw either her or it again. Like a piece of sea-wreck, I have drifted away from those days: quiet, happy, eventless days, very happy to remember!

I thought of good, jovial Mr Mountford – and his regrets that he might not keep a pack, 'a very small pack,' of harriers, and his merry ways, and his love of good eating; of the first coming of Mr Gray, and my lady's attempt to quench his sermons, when they tended to enforce any duty connected with education. And now we had an absolute school-house in the village; and since Miss Bessy's drinking tea at the Hall, my lady had been twice inside it, to give directions about some fine yarn she was having spun for table-napery. And her ladyship had so outgrown her old custom of dispensing with sermon or discourse, that even during the temporary preaching of Mr Crosse, she had never had recourse to it, though I believe she would have had all the congregation on her side if she had.

And Mr Horner was dead, and Captain James reigned in his stead. Good, steady, severe, silent Mr Horner! with his clock-like regularity, and his snuff-coloured clothes, and silver buckles! I have often wondered which one misses most when they are dead and gone – the bright creatures full of life, who are hither and thither and everywhere, so that no one can reckon upon their coming and going, with whom stillness and the long quiet of the grave seems utterly irreconcilable, so full are they of vivid motion and passion – or the slow, serious people, whose movements – nay, whose very words, seem to go by clock-work; who never appear much to affect the course of our life while they are with us, but whose methodical ways show themselves, when they are gone, to have been intertwined with our very roots of daily existence. I think I miss these last the most, although I may have loved the former best. Captain James never was to me what Mr Horner was, though the latter had hardly changed a dozen words with me at the day of his death. Then Miss Galindo! I remembered the time, as if it had been only yesterday, when she was but a name – and a very odd one – to me; then she was a queer, abrupt, disagreeable, busy old maid. Now I loved her dearly, and I found out that I was almost jealous of Miss Bessy.

Mr Gray I never thought of with love; the feeling was almost reverence with which I looked upon him. I have not wished to speak much of myself, or else I could have told you how much he had been to me during these long, weary years of illness. But he was almost as much to every one, rich and poor, from my lady down to Miss Galindo's Sally.

The village, too, had a different look about it. I am sure I could not tell you what caused the change; but there were no more lounging young men to form a group at the cross-road, at a time of day when young men ought to be at work. I don't say this was all Mr Gray's doing, for there really was so much to do in the fields that there was but little time for lounging now-a-days. And the children were hushed up in school, and better behaved out of it, too, than in the days when I used to be able to go my lady's errands in the village. I went so little about now, that I am sure I can't tell who Miss Galindo found to scold; and yet she looked so well and so happy that I think she must have had her accustomed portion of that wholesome exercise.

Before I left Hanbury, the rumour that Captain James was going to marry Miss Brooke, Baker Brooke's eldest daughter, who had only a sister to share his property with her, was confirmed. He himself announced it to my lady; nay, more, with a courage, gained, I suppose, in his former profession, where, as I have heard, he had led his ship into many a post of danger, he asked her ladyship, the Countess Ludlow, if he might bring his bride-elect (the Baptist baker's daughter!) and present her to my lady!

I am glad I was not present when he made this request; I should have felt so much ashamed for him, and I could not have helped being anxious till I heard my lady's answer, if I had been there. Of course she acceded; but I can fancy the grave surprise of her look. I wonder if Captain James noticed it.

I hardly dared ask my lady, after the interview had taken place, what she thought of the bride-elect; but I hinted my curiosity, and she told me, that if the young person had applied to Mrs Medlicott for the situation of cook, and Mrs Medlicott had engaged her, she thought that it would have been a very suitable arrangement. I understood from this how little she thought a marriage with Captain James, R.N., suitable.

About a year after I left Hanbury, I received a letter from Miss Galindo; I think I can find it. – Yes, this is it.

'Hanbury, May 4, 1811

'DEAR MARGARET,

'You ask for news of us all. Don't you know there is no news in Hanbury? Did you ever hear of an event here? Now, if you have answered "Yes" in your own mind to these questions, you have fallen into my trap, and never were more mistaken in your life. Hanbury is full of news; and we have more events on our hands than we know what to do with. I will take them in the order of the newspapers – births, deaths, and marriages. In the matter of births, Jenny Lucas has had twins not a week ago. Sadly too much of a good thing, you'll say. Very true: but then they died; so their birth did not much signify. My cat has kittened, too; she has had three kittens, which again you may observe is too much of a good thing; and so it would be, if it were not for the next item of intelligence I shall lay before you. Captain and Mrs James have taken the old house next Pearson's; and the house is overrun with mice, which is just as fortunate for me as the King of Egypt's rat-ridden kingdom was to Dick Whittington. For my cat's kittening decided me to go and call on the bride, in hopes she wanted a cat; which she did, like a sensible woman, as I do believe she is, in spite of Baptism, Bakers, Bread, and Birmingham, and something worse than all, which you shall hear about, if you'll only be patient. As I had got my best bonnet on – the one I bought when poor Lord Ludlow was last at Hanbury in '99 – I thought it a great condescension in myself (always remembering the date of the Galindo Baronetcy) to go and call on the bride; though I don't think so much of myself in my every-day clothes, as you know. But who should I find there but my Lady Ludlow! She looks as frail and delicate as ever, but is, I think, in better heart ever since that old city merchant of a Hanbury took it into his head that he was a cadet of the Hanburys of Hanbury, and left her that handsome legacy. I'll warrant you the mortgage was paid off pretty fast; and Mr Horner's money – or my lady's money, or Harry Gregson's money, call it which you will – is invested in his name, all right and tight, and they do talk of his being captain of his school, or Grecian, or something, and going to college, after all! Harry Gregson the poacher's son! Well! to be sure, we are living in strange times!

'But I have not done with the marriages yet. Captain James's is all very well, but no one cares for it now, we are all so full of Mr Gray's. Yes, indeed, Mr Gray is going to be married, and to nobody else but my little Bessy! I tell her she will have to nurse him half the days of her life, he is such a frail little body. But she says she does not care for that; so that his body holds his soul, it is enough for her. She has a good spirit, and a brave heart, has my Bessy! It is a great advantage that she won't have to mark her clothes over again; for when she had knitted herself her last set of stockings, I told her to put G for Galindo, if she did not choose to put it for Gibson, for she should be my child if she was no one else's. And now, you see, it stands for Gray. So there are two marriages, and what more would you have? And she promises to take another of my kittens.

'Now, as to deaths, old Farmer Hale is dead – poor old man, I should think his wife thought it a good riddance, for he beat her every day that he was drunk, and he never was sober, in spite of Mr Gray. I don't think (as I tell him) that Mr Gray would ever have found courage to speak to Bessy as long as Farmer Hale lived, he took the old gentleman's sins so much to heart, and seemed to think it was all his fault for not being able to make a sinner into a saint. The parish bull is dead too. I never was so glad in my life. But they say we are to have a new one in his place. In the meantime I cross the common in peace, which is convenient just now, when I have so often to go to Mr Gray's to see about furnishing.

'Now you think I have told you all the Hanbury news, don't you? Not so. The very greatest thing of all is to come. I won't tantalize you, but just out with it, for you would never guess it. My Lady Ludlow has given a party, just like any plebeian amongst us. We had tea and toast in the blue drawing-room, old John Footman waiting, with Tom Diggles, the lad that used to frighten away crows in Farmer Hale's fields, following in my lady's livery, hair powdered and everything. Mrs Medlicott made tea in my lady's own room. My lady looked like a splendid fairy queen of mature age, in black velvet, and the old lace, which I have never seen her wear before since my lord's death. But the company? you'll say. Why we had the parson of Clover, and the parson of Headleigh, and the parson of Merribank, and the three parsonesses; and Farmer Donkin and two Miss Donkins; and Mr Gray (of course), and myself and Bessy; and Captain and Mrs James; yes, and Mr and Mrs Brooke: think of that! I am not so sure the parsons liked it; but he was there. For he has been helping Captain James to get my lady's land into order; and then his daughter married the agent; and Mr Gray (who ought to know) says, after all, Baptists are not such bad people; and he was right against them at one time, as you may remember. Mrs Brooke is a rough diamond, to be sure. People have said that of me, I know. But, being a Galindo, I learnt manners in my youth, and can take them up when I choose. But Mrs Brooke never learnt manners, I'll be bound. When John Footman handed her the tray with the tea-cups, she looked up at him as if she were sorely puzzled by that way of going on. I was sitting next to her, so I pretended not to see her perplexity, and put her cream and sugar in for her, and was all ready to pop it into her hands – when who should come up, but that impudent lad Tom Diggles (I call him lad, for all his hair is powdered, for you know that it is not natural gray hair), with his tray full of cakes and what not, all as good as Mrs Medlicott could make them. By this time, I should tell you, all the parsonesses were looking at Mrs Brooke, for she had shown her want of breeding before; and the parsonesses, who were just a step above her in manners, were very much inclined to smile at her doings and sayings. Well! what does she do but pull out a clean Bandanna pocket-handkerchief, all red and yellow silk, spread it over her best silk gown; it was, like enough, a new one, for I had it from Sally, who had it from her cousin Molly, who is dairy-woman at the Brookes', that the Brookes were mighty set-up with an invitation to drink tea at the Hall. There we were, Tom Diggles even on the grin (I wonder how long it is since he was own brother to a scarecrow, only not so decently dressed) and Mrs Parsoness of Headleigh – I forget her name, and it's no matter, for she's an ill-bred creature, I hope Bessy will behave herself better – was right-down bursting with laughter, and as near a hee-haw as ever a donkey was, when what does my lady do? Ay! there's my own dear Lady Ludlow, God bless her! She takes out her own pocket-handkerchief, all snowy cambric, and lays it softly down on her velvet lap, for all the world as if she did it every day of her life, just like Mrs Brooke, the baker's wife; and when the one got up to shake the crumbs into the fireplace, the other did just the same. But with such a grace! and such a look at us all! Tom Diggles went red all over; and Mrs Parsoness of Headleigh scarce spoke for the rest of the evening; and the tears came into my old silly eyes; and Mr Gray, who was before silent and awkward, in a way which I tell Bessy she must cure him of, was made so happy by this pretty action of my lady's, that he talked away all the rest of the evening, and was the life of the company.

'Oh! Margaret Dawson, I sometimes wonder if you're the better off for leaving us. To be sure, you're with your brother, and blood is blood. But when I look at my lady and Mr Gray, for all they're so different, I would not change places with any in England.'

Alas! alas! I never saw my dear lady again. She died in eighteen hundred and fourteen, and Mr Gray did not long survive her. As I dare say you know, the Reverend Henry Gregson is now vicar of Hanbury, and his wife is the daughter of Mr Gray and Miss Bessy.

THE HISTORY OF VINTAGE

The famous American publisher Alfred A. Knopf (1892–1984) founded Vintage Books in the United States in 1954 as a paperback home for the authors published by his company. Vintage was launched in the United Kingdom in 1990 and works independently from the American imprint although both are part of the international publishing group, Random House.

Vintage in the United Kingdom was initially created to publish paperback editions of books acquired by the prestigious hardback imprints in the Random House Group such as Jonathan Cape, Chatto & Windus, Hutchinson and later William Heinemann, Secker & Warburg and The Harvill Press. There are many Booker and Nobel Prize-winning authors on the Vintage list and the imprint publishes a huge variety of fiction and non-fiction. Over the years Vintage has expanded and the list now includes both great authors of the past – who are published under the Vintage Classics imprint – as well as many of the most influential authors of the present.

For a full list of the books Vintage publishes, please visit our website
www.vintage-books.co.uk

For book details and other information about the classic authors we publish, please visit the Vintage Classics website
www.vintage-classics.info

www.vintage-classics.info